# A Wash of Moonlight Fell Across Her

Her eyes opened slowly, looking up into his. "It's all right, Charlotte," he said soothingly. "You were just having a bad dream."

"Ben," she murmured, clutching at his hands, drawing him down to her. Her parted lips were close to his, her breath was warm on his cheek. Swept by a desire so powerful that it drove everything else from his mind, he put his mouth to hers, gently, prepared to draw back instantly if she resisted. But there was no resistance. Soon his kiss grew steadily more demanding and she was returning the kiss with an ardor that matched his.

**PATRICIA MATTHEWS**

This is a story only America's First Lady of Love could write. With over 16 milli[illegible] her books in print, she has stirred the heart[illegible] the world with her enthrallin[illegible] set in the romantic past. He[illegible] consecutive bestselling roman[illegible]

Bantam Books by Patricia Matthews
Ask your bookseller for the books you have missed

EMBERS OF DAWN

MIDNIGHT WHISPERS (with Clayton Matthews)

TIDES OF LOVE

# Embers of Dawn

by Patricia Matthews

BANTAM BOOKS
Toronto / New York / London / Sydney

EMBERS OF DAWN
*A Bantam Book / May 1982*

*Doubleday Book Club edition March 1982*



*Book designed by Cathy Marinaccio*



**Library of Congress Cataloging in Publication Data**

Matthews, Patricia, 1927-
Embers of dawn.

I. Title.
PS3563.A853E4 813'.54 81-17549
ISBN 0-553-01368-8 (pbk.) AACR2

*Published simultaneously in the United States and Canada*

*Bantam Books are published by Bantam Books, Inc. Its trademark, consisting of the words "Bantam Books" and the portrayal of a rooster, is Registered in U.S. Patent and Trademark Office and in other countries. Marca Registrada. Bantam Books, Inc., 666 Fifth Avenue, New York, New York 10103.*

PRINTED IN THE UNITED STATES OF AMERICA

0 9 8 7 6 5 4 3 2 1

*This book is dedicated*
*to the ladies*
*who serve behind the scene,*
*with much appreciation,*
*to Jean, Eunice, and Ruth*
*of the Jay Garon Agency*

*Lovefire*

The fire of love starts with the barest flame,
A glance, a touch,
Such simple things can start,
Without a word, a kindling of the heart,
A glowing warmth, we almost fear to name.

A love may smoulder, banked beneath the days,
And pride, like leaves,
May cover it from sight,
But then the flame must catch, and all alight,
The heart is liberated in the blaze.

And if the fuel is good, the fire bright,
If care is taken
To protect the flame,
The fire can last, and grow, and will remain,
A warmth to keep you through the darkest night.

# Chapter One

CHARLOTTE King rose from the red soil of the depleted garden patch where she had been attempting to wrest the last reluctant tubers from the dying sweet potato vines.

As she rose, she reached up to push back a strand of the thick, wiry, red hair that had fallen free from the cord with which she had bound it back. Her hair, along with the reddish freckles that lightly speckled her face and body, was an inheritance from her grandmother, one Charlotte felt she would have been happier without.

As she pushed back the unruly curl, her fingers left a smear of the red soil across one cheek, but she did not know it, and could not see how the mark heightened the color of her eyes, which were an unusual, almost electric, blue.

Charlotte was a tall girl, fine-boned, and thin now from the shortage of food, and her gingham dress—too large on her thinned-down body—did nothing to show her to an advantage. Yet she had a striking figure, and her movements showed a grace and control that was pleasant to see.

It was a sweet, hot, South Carolina morning, the sky clear and piercingly blue; but the morning breeze had already died, and the day showed promise of the stifling afternoon heat to come.

Charlotte wiped her hands on her apron and reached around to massage her lower back. She felt exhausted already, and the day was hardly under way. So far she had fixed a meager breakfast for herself and her bed-ridden mother, done the breakfast dishes, slopped the one scrawny pig the Yankees had not found, fed the few chickens that were all that remained of the once flourishing flock, and now was attempting to find something to eke out the rice and greens that were destined to be their noon meal.

Sighing, she looked down at the potatoes—thin and scrawny, but enough to fill them up for this afternoon. Tomorrow . . . well, she would worry about that when it came, she had enough to do just trying to cope with today.

Stooping, she picked up the sweet potatoes and placed them in her apron.

As she turned toward the house behind her, she had a clear view of the dusty road which ran by the house, not more than fifty yards away. There was a figure coming down the road: a man, she could see now, a soldier in the faded gray of a Confederate uniform.

She gathered her apron with one hand, and shielded her eyes with the other. The man limped along with the aid of a crude crutch under one arm. The thick dust of the road rose about him as he dragged one foot, his left. The dust shimmered in the still air, making it difficult to see.

Charlotte stood tense, one hand shading her eyes, as he made his tortuous way toward her. Her heart went out to him, the returning warrior, lamed and defeated, returning to a ruined world.

Step by halting step, he drew closer, until her heart recognized what her eyes had already seen. "Jefferson!"

The soldier's head lifted at the sound of the name.

"Dear God, it's Jefferson!"

Quickly, Charlotte began to run, still clutching the half-filled apron with one hand, holding her long skirts up with the other. Across the garden and into the road, running awkwardly because of her burden, but never considering dropping it. Tears had come to her eyes, and she could barely see.

The man had stopped, and was standing now, leaning on his crutch in the middle of the road. He was thin, oh,

God, so thin! And older, much older than his years could have made him.

She flung herself upon him, grasping his shoulders under the rotting gray cloth, and noticing the lack of bulk there. His shoulders had been so broad when he went away, the Kings were always heavy-shouldered men.

"Oh, Jefferson!" she cried. "We thought you were dead!"

Her brother attempted a smile, but fatigue and pain turned the expression into a grimace. She wanted to comment, to express concern for his condition, but was afraid it would hurt his pride.

"Come, Jefferson," she urged, helping him with her one free arm. "Let me help you into the house."

He said nothing, only leaned against her, letting her take most of his weight, seemingly so weak and worn that even a single word would have been too much.

With considerable effort, Charlotte managed to get him up the steps to the porch, where he dropped into the old oak rocker that had belonged to Gardner King, their father. Jefferson's face was paper white, with an unhealthy green cast, and she felt her heart thudding with sympathy and empathic pain.

"I'll get you something to drink," she said, hurrying into the house, wondering what she could give him. She thought of the bottle of whiskey that she had been keeping aside in case her mother had a really bad spell. Well, Jefferson needed it more.

Dropping the sweet potatoes into a wash basin, she turned to the cupboard. There was fresh mint, and a little sugar left, and with trembling hands she crushed some into the bottom of a tall tumbler, automatically preparing the drink that both Jefferson and his father loved. She had prepared it too quickly, she realized, yet haste seemed necessary. Carrying the mint julep in her hand, she returned to the porch and her brother.

His eyes were closed, and his chest seemed barely to be moving. Tentatively, she touched his arm. His eyes opened, and for a moment he did not appear to be aware of his surroundings.

"Here," she said, holding the glass to his lips, "drink. It will make you feel better."

He nodded, and greedily began to suck at the liquid, as she tilted the tumbler. As the first drops went down his throat, Jefferson opened his eyes fully and shot her a glance, his eyes suddenly alive, but he continued to drink until the glass was empty. He had been parched, that much was clear.

Charlotte's mind was already busy with what she would do next. He must be starving. She would kill one of the few remaining hens, and make a soup. While the soup was cooking, she would fix him some of the sweet potatoes. They would be hot and filling.

Gazing down at him, she saw that he was asleep, his face showing tension and fatigue even in slumber. Feeling again something of the pain he must feel, she went into the house and returned with a worn comforter, which she spread over him, for despite the growing heat of the day, he looked chilled through, as if his blood did not have enough warmth to keep him alive.

After placing the comforter around him, Charlotte sank down on the porch by his side, leaning against the rocker, remembering the times she had sat in this same place, by the side of her father.

But Jefferson was home! Things would be better now. He would heal, get his strength back, and take over what was left of the farm. She would help him, and together they would get the place back into operation. No longer would she have to bear alone the burden of the farm and her mother. Jefferson would take care of things as soon as he was well.

She reached over to touch his trailing hand. It was pitifully thin and covered with barely healed scars. Smiling, she gave way to the luxury of relaxation. She closed her eyes, and allowed herself to think of a future where the King land once again flourished, and no one was hungry.

The reunion between her mother and brother was not quite all that Charlotte had hoped for.

Jefferson had been home for two days before he said he felt strong enough to make the trip up the stairs to his mother's bedroom; and even then, it seemed to Charlotte, he showed a strange lack of feeling in his greeting. Oh, he kissed their mother's sunken cheek, and even smiled and told her that he felt better than he looked in an effort to ease her worry over his appearance; yet there was no real emotion in his voice, or upon his face, after the first expression of dismay upon seeing Alice King's condition.

Charlotte had grown accustomed to her mother's appearance, but there had been a vast change in the rosy-cheeked, amply curved woman who had presided over the King household with a steady and generous hand before Jefferson went away to war. Her pale hair, once the color of ripe wheat, was faded and growing gray, and the soft, high-colored skin of her face was now sagging and yellowed. As for the once ample figure, Alice King was now thinner than Jefferson, a mere sack of skin containing bones and organs. She was failing day by day.

Charlotte held her mother's hand firmly, angry and embarrassed at Jefferson's lack of feeling. He was ill and tired himself, she knew, but this was their mother!

When they left the sickroom, and were back downstairs in the parlor, he demanded, "What is it? Has the doctor told you?"

"A growth in her chest. It keeps spreading."

"I saw the same thing in prison camp. She's dying." It was a flat statement, spoken without visible emotion, and Charlotte squirmed in anger. Why was he talking like this, acting like this? His responses were not what she had expected of him, based on the person he was—or had been. He seemed as alien to her as a stranger, and Charlotte did not know how to react to this new person who seemed to inhabit her brother's skin.

She rose from her chair. "I'll see to our supper. It won't be the kind of meal we used to have."

He said dourly, "Nothing will ever be like what we used to have."

Charlotte went into the kitchen with a heavy heart,

uneasy and concerned, all the earlier joy at his return gone. He'll get over this, whatever it is, she thought; it will take a little time, that's all.

When the meager meal was prepared, Charlotte served it in the dining room, at the long table which seemed much too large for just the two of them.

Jeff picked at the food on his plate, taking a sip of bourbon between bites. The first bottle was long since gone, and he had gotten another from somewhere. His narrow face seemed to wear a permanent shadow, and Charlotte had to use all her willpower to keep from wincing whenever his gaze met hers. Those brown eyes, once so alive and sparkling, struck her as empty of all life.

"It's all gone, Charlotte, everything," he said suddenly. "Not only everything that Daddy worked so hard to build for us, but the whole South. It's dead. It'll never live again, the damned Yankees have seen to that." His short laugh burned with the bitterness of abject defeat. "It'll never be the same, *I* will never be the same again." He drank the remaining bourbon in his glass with a toss of his head.

Her heart ached for him, this emaciated, defeated hulk of the man. At the same time she felt a prick of annoyance. The war had been pure hell, she knew that as well as anyone, yet there was the King pride to consider. They had to pick themselves up out of the dirt and rebuild. Somehow, she had to ignite a spark of that pride in Jefferson.

She said brightly, "It's not all gone, Jefferson. Not quite all."

His gaze was uncomprehending. "Of course it is. What are you saying?"

She jumped to her feet. "Come along, I'll show you!" She took his hand and tugged at it. "Come with me, Jefferson!"

He scowled. "Sis, I've just come back from hell. Can't it wait, whatever it is?"

She set herself against any pity for him. The last thing

he needed right now was pity. "What I've got to show you will raise your spirits."

He shook his head again. "I'm afraid nothing will do that."

"This will, I promise you. Come on!"

He sighed and climbed to his feet, going with her without further resistance. Charlotte took a lamp from the wall and carried it out into the warm darkness. The lamp cast a pallid glow before them. She led him to the tobacco shed between the house and the barn.

Her hand on the door latch, she paused to look at him. "I had some warning before the Yankees came. The Hollisters sent Jimmie over to tell me that the soldiers were coming, looting and burning. So, with Jimmie helping, we moved it all to the cellar underneath the barn floor. Then we covered the trapdoor with dirt, straw, and horse dung. The soldiers didn't notice the trapdoor. I was fearful they might put the torch to the barn, but they didn't!" Charlotte knew she was chattering, yet she couldn't seem to help herself. "They didn't burn it! Fortune was with us!"

"What didn't burn, Charlotte?" he demanded with rising impatience. "What on earth are you babbling about?"

"This!"

She threw open the door, and they were immediately assailed by the pungent aroma of cured tobacco. Charlotte held the lamp high, and they could see the racks of golden-leafed tobacco.

"It's all bright leaf. It came from Daddy's last crop, the first time he used the new curing process."

Jeff gaped around. "Daddy grew this? When?"

"The year he died, while you were away at war. If the Yankees had found this, they would really have stripped our cupboard bare. Thank God I had enough warning to hide it away."

Jeff's momentary interest had waned. He said dully, "Charlotte, I fail to see what all this has to do with me. So, you were clever enough to squirrel away a store of tobacco. What does that have to do with anything?"

"But don't you see, Jefferson? This tobacco is worth a lot of money. Very little tobacco has been grown here during the war, and now that it is over, it will be in demand. It will take some time for the growers to get back into production."

"But why is this supposed to cheer me up?"

"With the money from the sale of this tobacco, we can get back on our feet, and have money to get our land back into production."

"You mean you're thinking of farming the land? You expect *me* to become a farmer?" He stared at her in disbelief. "Charlotte, I've just gone through four years of misery and pain, I am not about to return home and become a farmer!"

"But the Kings have always been close to the land. How many times did Daddy tell us about his granddaddy coming to this country and settling on the land?"

"My dear sister, there is something you don't seem to realize yet," he said with a weary sigh. "The days of the fine plantations are gone forever. No more can a gentleman planter sit on the veranda, sipping bourbon, while his slaves grub in the fields . . ."

"Daddy never kept slaves, you well know that!"

"It doesn't matter." He gestured. "So he paid the workers. Even if we could find reliable people to hire, we couldn't pay them. If we start working this place, *we* will have to work the land. Like slaves, we'll have to work. Or rather, *I* will."

She said determinedly, "I will work right alongside you."

"You, a woman working the fields? No Southern lady labors in the fields. What would our neighbors think?"

"I'm not concerned about our neighbors. I'm concerned about . . ." She paused, looking at him closely. "But you will have to do *something,* Jefferson. What are you going to do with your life, if you don't work the land?"

"The way I feel right now, I don't intend to do anything for a spell. Certainly I'm not going to grub away at raising a tobacco crop."

"How are you going to support yourself? Or do you hope that I will support you, Jefferson?"

He straightened, and for a moment a touch of the old, fierce pride struck his eyes. "No, I don't expect that. I am no longer a child, Charlotte. And you needn't worry about me, I'll manage just fine."

He turned on his heel, left the shed, and limped toward the house. Charlotte, delighted that she had aroused a show of spirit in him, hurried after him. She caught up with him just as he entered the house.

He ignored her, limping painfully on toward the dining room.

"Jefferson, are you going to finish your supper? It's cold now, I can warm it up if you like."

"Don't bother. It's not food I'm going after. I want another drink." He tossed the words back over his shoulder like hurting pebbles.

Charlotte felt a pang of dismay. "Aren't you going to say good night to Momma?"

He stopped in the doorway to the dining room, and turned a cold face to her. "I have nothing more to say to her. What can we talk about? How we've both suffered the cruelties of this world? No, thank you, dear sister. You tell her good night for me. Tell her"—his face turned savage—"that I'm busy drowning my sorrows in bourbon. Perhaps she should do the same."

He pushed open the dining room door and went inside, closing it after him with a slam of finality.

Charlotte stood without moving, torn between anger and compassion. He had had a hard time of it, she did not doubt that for an instant, but then so had many other Confederate soldiers. They had been returning since the end of hostilities, and most of them she knew were busy resuming their lives where they had left off.

Jefferson had to make a fresh start, he had to put his life back together, and the longer he waited the more difficult it would be for him. Yet, underneath the hurt and the defeat, she had glimpsed one brief flash of the King pride; and she was astute enough to realize that if she pushed him too hard now, she would risk alienating him forever.

She would have to force patience on herself, and allow time to work a healing miracle. However, the angry part of her mind spoke to her—liquor was not the answer. Thank God there was not another bottle in the house! Since Jefferson had no money, he would be unable to purchase more. On that she would stand firm—he would get no money for liquor from her! What little money she had was desperately needed. If he would not do anything about improving their lot, she would have to do it on her own.

And if Jefferson had not pulled himself together by the time she had sold the tobacco, she would not give him a penny of that money, either!

She turned and started up the stairs to the second floor and her mother's bedroom. On the landing she paused for a few moments to get a grip on herself. It would not do for Momma to suspect that she had quarreled with Jefferson; it would never do for their mother to learn that he preferred drinking to coming up to say good night.

Features composed, she smoothed her skirt, opened the door, and went in. As she had suspected, Alice King was asleep. Propped up in bed, her head had drooped to one side. In the yellow light from the bedside lamp, her drawn face looked even more pale and wasted.

Charlotte went around to the side of the bed and touched the woman gently on the shoulder. "Momma, slide down in bed. You'll get a crick in your neck, lying like that."

Alice King woke up with a small cry, her faded blue eyes unfocused for a few seconds. Then she smiled with an effort. "Charlotte! I reckon I must have dropped off." She craned her neck, and said eagerly, "Where's Jefferson? Where's my boy?"

Charlotte experienced a small irritation. Jefferson had always been their mother's favorite. Then she chided herself, ashamed of such thoughts. She forced a smile. "He is still exhausted, Momma. I scolded him into going to bed early."

"I'm just happy my baby boy came back to me," her mother murmured, already dozing again.

Charlotte smoothed the damp hair from her mother's forehead, and stood musing down at her as she drifted into sleep. Dr. Burns was old, well past his prime, and Charlotte had the feeling that he was well out of touch with any recent medical advances, yet he was the only doctor available to her, at least the only one willing to treat Alice King without being paid in cash—he took his fee in tobacco.

*Soon, Momma,* Charlotte promised silently, *soon we'll have the money from the tobacco, and then I'll get a doctor from Charleston.*

It did not take Charlotte long to discover that selling her tobacco was not going to be as easy as she had believed. The buyers in Durham badly needed tobacco, true, but none of them had the cash to pay for it. They offered to take it on consignment, and then pay Charlotte when their money came in; but they could not promise how soon that would be, and she needed the money now.

They all told her that the only man in Durham who had available cash was Sload Lutcher. Charlotte had never met Lutcher, who was a relative newcomer to the area, but she had heard a great deal about him. His origins were obscure; Lutcher had arrived in Durham during the war, and started a money-lending operation. Rumor had it that he had grown rich operating brothels in New Orleans, and had left the city when the war began; but one fact everyone agreed on—he had unlimited funds.

There had been a need for his services in and around Durham. Money was scarce during the war; even a banker had no funds to loan. Now, of course, it was even worse, and Lutcher found plenty of clients. His rates were exorbitant, and Charlotte had heard that he had foreclosed on several farms near Durham.

She finally concluded that she would lose nothing by paying Lutcher a visit. She had exhausted all the possibilities in Durham, and to go to another town would mean that she would have to haul her tobacco to market, and she wanted to avoid that. Anyway, she was not going to borrow money, but to sell the man something.

Sload Lutcher had an office in a warehouse building on Jackson Street, three blocks up from the railroad station. She ventured into the building timidly, and was immediately struck by the rich aroma of tobacco. The warehouse was half-full of the dried leaves, and a crew of men, mostly black, was busy stacking it. At the rear of the warehouse another crew was chopping tobacco leaves into the finished product. The inside of the vast structure was hot, and a fine tobacco dust filled the air, like a dry fog. She sneezed twice in succession.

"Good Heavens," said a merry voice behind her, "such a big sneeze for such a delicate young lady!"

Charlotte whirled around. Facing her was a small, plump man, with a round face, dancing brown eyes, and a smiling mouth. She stared at him, dumfounded, dazzled by his attire. He wore a high-crowned hat, white as snow, but beneath the hat he was a riot of colors—a coat of rich, cherry velvet, plum-colored breeches, boots an ox-blood red and polished to a high gloss. His shirt was ruffled, a vivid yellow in color, and he wore a flowing cravat of kelly green. A stickpin held the cravat in place, and in the center glowed a ruby as red as his boots.

As though aware of what she was thinking, the little man preened. "Awed by my wardrobe, are you, young lady?" He half-turned, and a ray of light struck fire from the ruby. "I'm taken with it, myself."

Charlotte had to laugh. Evidently, he was vain as a peacock, and yet there was something so clownish about him that it was difficult to take offense. "Awed is probably as good a word as any, sir. Certainly I have never seen anything to match it!"

He beamed a smile at her. "Good, good! That's the effect I strive for. When I am working, I want to be certain that I am the center of all eyes."

"And what exactly is your profession?"

He drew himself up to his full height of five-feet-four.

"I, my dear young lady, am a tobacco auctioneer by trade. My name is Clyde Watson. Called Dandy by some." His brown eyes twinkled. "I cannot imagine why."

"I am Charlotte King," she said. "I've heard of tobacco auctioneers, but we've seen little of them around Durham. I have never observed one at work, myself."

"That is why I am here, to expose the uninitiated to the fine art." He waxed enthusiastic. "The tobacco industry is on the verge of a great explosion, mark my words, and the men of my profession will play an important part."

"Do you work for Mr. Lutcher?"

"I have just been closeted with the person in question." He made a face. "I doubt that Mr. Lutcher will ever engage my services. He lacks the foresight. But tell me, Miss King, why are you here? Are you engaged in the tobacco business?"

Charlotte gave a start. Intrigued by this man, she had momentarily forgotten her purpose here. "In a small way. I came to see Mr. Lutcher."

"I hope you will be more successful than I. You will find his office back there, up those stairs."

Charlotte followed his pointing finger. In the dim recesses of the warehouse was a flight of wooden steps going up to a narrow balcony, and she could see doors opening off the balcony.

"Then I had better get on with it."

"I wish you good fortune, dear lady. And may I present you with my card, should you ever have need of my services."

He handed her an embossed card, and dipped his hat with a flourish. "I bid you good day, Miss King."

Charlotte went on toward the rear, threading her way through the racks of pungent tobacco, and up the steps. The office she sought was at the very end of the balcony, with the name, Sload Lutcher, on the door, which stood open. Peering in, she saw a man behind a broad desk, head bent over some papers. She knocked on the door.

The man glanced up. "Yes?"

"Mr. Lutcher?"

"That's me." He had a deep, growly voice. "What can I do for you, madam?"

"Miss. Miss Charlotte King." She ventured into the office.

He stood up, and she was struck by his great height, and his thinness. He stood well over six feet, but he was so thin that she fancied she could see his bones through the skin. He appeared as emaciated as Jefferson, and she had to wonder if he had been ill. He had abnormally long hands, covered with a profusion of black hair, like the hairs on a spider's leg; but it was his face that held most of her attention. It was long, and bony, with cheekbones so prominent that they threw shadows on his lower face. He was smiling, his lips drawn back too far, showing teeth like yellowed fangs, and she thought of a grinning skull, and shivered.

But it was not until she met his eyes that she felt a chill. They were small and black, set deeply into shadowed sockets, and as expressionless as buttons.

"King?" he said musingly. "Any relation to Gardner King, who owned the tobacco acreage north of town?"

"Yes, he was my father."

"I heard he died shortly after I came to Durham. My condolences, Miss King. Now, how can I be of service to you?" His gaze grew intent. "If you've come to borrow on your land, I must tell you that I am not lending money on land at this time. I am land poor, as they say." His thin lips stretched in what struck Charlotte as a predatory smile. "I have been regrettably forced to foreclose on several farms, and it does not pay me to farm them."

"Yes, I have heard about that," she said, a little more tartly than she had intended. She hurried on, "I didn't come to you to borrow money."

"Why did you come then?" His manner was more distant now.

"I understand that you are buying tobacco?"

"That is my primary business these days, tobacco. But I must have been misinformed. I didn't know you had raised a tobacco crop since your father died."

"I haven't, but I still have in my possession Daddy's last crop."

"Sherman's soldiers did not get it?"

"No, I kept it hidden away from them. Would you be interested, Mr. Lutcher?"

"I would, Miss King. Of course I would have to inspect the tobacco. I can't very well buy it sight unseen."

"Of course not. I anticipated that you would wish to inspect it."

Lutcher looked down at his desk, and leafed through a small notebook. "Would tomorrow afternoon be convenient? At, say, three o'clock?"

Lutcher came early the next afternoon. Charlotte was cleaning the kitchen after serving dinner to herself and Jefferson—he had eaten only a few bites—when she heard voices on the porch. Hastily, she dried her hands, whipped off her apron, and hastened toward the porch. She knew that her brother was there. He had demanded a fresh bottle of bourbon, and when she had told him there was none, he had limped out to the porch.

Jefferson was in conversation with Sload Lutcher when Charlotte came out. A spanking new buggy and a black horse stood before the house. Lutcher wore an expensive black broadcloth suit, and his boots were polished to a high gloss. In fact, he had one booted foot propped upon the porch railing, and was fastidiously scrubbing the yard dust from it with a handkerchief.

He straightened up, doffing his hat to Charlotte. He said gravely, "Your brother was just relating some of his unfortunate experiences in the prison camp, Miss King. The manner in which the Yankees treated some of our poor soldier boys is a disgrace. Indeed it is!"

And where were *you*, Mr. Lutcher, she thought, when those poor soldiers were fighting and dying? She did not voice the thought, of course. Instead, she said, "I'll show you the tobacco now, Mr. Lutcher."

"Certainly, Miss King."

Jeff said, "I'll go along, Sis."

Charlotte felt a stab of hope. Was he finally taking an interest in business? Then the realization came to her—his mind was set on the money she hoped to get for the tobacco! For a moment she thought of asking him not to come, yet she knew that that would cause a scene, so she said nothing.

In the tobacco shed Lutcher strode slowly up and down between the racks, his hands behind his back, head back, sniffing.

From behind him, Charlotte said, "As you can see, it's prime bright leaf. Daddy was a fine tobacco grower."

"I've seen better grade tobacco, but it's not bad," Lutcher said judiciously. He came to a halt, facing her. "The thing is, I've bought a lot of tobacco of late, and the market being as uncertain as it is, I must be a little more cautious . . ."

"Uncertain!" Charlotte exclaimed. "Sir, it is my understanding that there is a scarcity of tobacco, since very little was grown during the war."

"In most places that may be true, but I feel that I have over-bought. No . . ." He pursed his lips. "The most I can offer you, Miss King, is ten cents the pound."

"That is ridiculous! I would be practically giving the tobacco to you. I can't let it go at that price!"

"You have my sympathy, Miss King. It is obvious to me that you are in dire need of money, but I am a business man, not a philanthropist." His spare smile was supercilious. "But to show you that I am not unfeeling, I will go to fifteen cents a pound. That is my absolute limit."

"I would burn it first!" Charlotte was trembling with anger. "You, sir, are a scoundrel! I have heard the stories about you, and now I see that they are all true. You know that the other tobacco buyers have no ready cash, and you're taking advantage of that fact. The South is beaten to its knees, and we could expect such treatment from the Yankees, but not from one of our own. What you are proposing is legal theft, sir! Why don't you just hold a gun to my head, and send your lackeys in here to *take* our tobacco?"

Lutcher had gone quite pale, and for the first time those expressionless eyes showed emotion—a rage as hot as the fires of hell.

"No man would dare talk so to me, and I will not countenance such epithets even from a woman."

Her head went back. "Then you are free to leave, sir."

"Charlotte . . ." Jeff plucked at her elbow. "You shouldn't talk so to Mr. Lutcher. He made us what he must consider a fair offer. Perhaps we should accept it."

"No!" She flung his hand off. "I will not be taken advantage of, by a Southerner even more despicable than a Yankee carpetbagger! This is still King property, sir. I must ask you to leave."

"It may not be King property for long, if you persist in this attitude," Lutcher said between gritted teeth.

"But so long as it is, you are not welcome here."

"Very well, I shall go. But you will regret this day, you have my promise on that."

Jeff said, "Please, Charlotte, I think we should consider Mr. Lutcher's offer . . ."

Charlotte ignored him, glaring at Lutcher. She felt a shiver go through her at the venom in those black eyes, and she knew that she had made an enemy for life. But she remained steadfast, refusing to look away.

Lutcher strode past her, the wind of his passing as chill as a winter blast.

Jeff limped after him. "Mr. Lutcher, I'm sure that my sister will change her mind when she calms down . . ."

Charlotte could still hear the sound of her brother's pleading voice after they were out of the tobacco shed. She stood unmoving, wondering if she had committed an act of folly. What would she now do with the tobacco?

She felt the burn of tears behind her eyes, but she refused to give way to them.

# Chapter Two

THE small farm of Bradley Hollister was situated only a half mile from the King place, on the road to Durham. It was about half the size of the King farm; even before the war, Hollister had been hard put to scratch a decent living for his family of six.

Despite his family ties, Hollister and his elder son, Joshua, volunteered early in the war. A scant six months later Bradley Hollister returned to his family, minus his right arm, lost in battle. Joshua did not return at all; the cannonball which struck his gun emplacement did not even leave enough to bury.

The Yankees stripped the Hollister farm, as they did many others; since his return, Bradley Hollister and his family had eked out a spare existence, surviving on the produce from their skimpy kitchen garden, and on what small game sixteen-year-old Jimmie, the remaining son, could find.

It was a miracle, Charlotte thought, how Bradley Hollister retained such a hopeful spirit; for despite the cruel blows which fate and the war had dealt him, he maintained a pleasant face, and none of his friends or neighbors had ever heard him complain.

Now Charlotte stood, looking at this good man, seeing his thinness and the deep lines of his face, wishing there was something she could do for him and his family, wishing there was some way to get back at the Yankees for what they had done to them all!

"Mr. Hollister, I can't pay Jimmie at the moment," she explained. "But I need someone to help prepare the tobacco so I can sell it. When the tobacco is sold, he will be the first one paid."

"Charlotte, Jimmie will be happy to help you, won't you, son?"

Jimmie Hollister, thin, rawboned, constantly hungry, had inherited his good nature from his father. He nodded shyly. "Yes'um, I'd be right tickled to help out, Miss Charlotte."

"My brother, you see, would like to help, but he's not in good health." Charlotte felt the explanation was necessary, but she hated to lie to this man, who had suffered as much if not more than Jeff, and still had come through with his spirit intact.

Hollister nodded, his face grave. "Yup, I reckon Jeff went through hell. But he'll be fine, just give him time, Charlotte. Too bad you couldn't sell your tobacco as is in Durham."

Charlotte frowned. "The only man with the money to buy is Sload Lutcher, and he only offered me fifteen cents a pound."

Hollister made a face. "That man! He came around here once, offering to loan me money on my land. I reckon he didn't think I had sense enough to know what he was up to. He keeps on the way he is, he'll soon own all the land around Durham." He spat a stream of snuff and rubbed at the shoulder from which his arm had once hung.

Charlotte winced inwardly to see the awkward asymmetry of his body. "Yes, I feel the same way." She smiled at Jimmie. "Then I can expect you in the morning?"

The youth nodded rapidly, Adam's apple bobbing. "Yes'um, I'll be there bright and early."

"Thank you, Mr. Hollister," she said. "And you as well, Jimmie."

Hollister shrugged. "That's what neighbors are for, to help friends in time of trouble or need."

Charlotte mounted her horse, an ancient mare but the only riding animal left to her, and rode toward home. She had not told Hollister what she intended to do with the tobacco once it was ready for market; she had been afraid that he would laugh at her, or think she was out of her mind.

She had not told Jeff of her plan, either. In fact, she had not spoken to him since Sload Lutcher's visit the afternoon before. As Charlotte rode into the yard, she saw her brother waiting for her on the porch. She ignored him, and rode on to the barn in the back. He limped after her, arriving in time to help her remove the saddle. Charlotte led the mare to the barn door, and gave her a slap on the rump, sending her out to the pasture, to join the two workhorses she had managed to hide from the Yankees.

Jeff ranged alongside her. "Charlotte, I want to talk to you about Sload Lutcher..."

Suddenly angry, she whipped around at him. "No! I don't wish to discuss that man, not ever!"

"Charlotte, listen to me! I know you've stayed here and kept things together, saving the tobacco, and taking care of Momma. That gives you the right to take charge of things, but don't I have some rights, too? I am a King, and this place is as much mine as yours."

She stared at him, keeping a tight rein on her temper. "I concede that you should have a say, I just thought that you weren't interested. What do you suggest?"

"I say that we should take Lutcher's offer."

"No, I will not agree to that! Tobacco is selling in some places for up to fifty cents a pound. He's offering us less than a third of that. There are over two hundred pounds of tobacco. At his price we wouldn't get more than three hundred dollars for the whole lot."

"Something is better than nothing," he said doggedly. "What are you going to do, let it rot?"

"No. I have a plan..." She took a deep breath. "I know there are stores out there desperately in need of tobacco. So I'm going to bypass the wholesalers and go direct to the retailers."

He looked confused. "I don't understand..."

"I'm going to get the tobacco ready for direct sale.

Jimmie Hollister is coming over in the morning to help me. Then I will load it into that old wagon, and peddle it store to store, or door to door if necessary!"

"You must be crazy!" he cried. "A woman, going across the country in a wagon?"

"I'll manage," she said stoutly.

"I won't allow it. My sister peddling tobacco from store to store! What will people think?"

"I care very little for what people think," she said stiffly. "If you think I shouldn't go, then *you* can go out with the tobacco. I'm willing to agree to that."

He stepped away from her, shaking his head from side to side. "No, Charlotte, no. I won't have people laughing at me."

Her voice was tight with annoyance. "Then you leave me no choice, because I intend to sell the tobacco at the best price I can get."

Charlotte and Jimmie Hollister started work on the tobacco the next morning. It was dusty, hard work. The tobacco leaves had to be beaten with wooden flails, the resulting tobacco sifted with a flour sifter, and then put into one-pound burlap bags. This prepared the tobacco to be used as snuff, or rolled into hand-made cigarettes, and this was where the local market lay. Cigar makers could have used the whole leaf, but there were no local cigar factories.

Within a few minutes the air in the tobacco shed was filled with tobacco dust, which got into Charlotte's hair and clothing, causing her to sneeze constantly. She had hoped that Jeff would volunteer to help them, but he had taken off early that morning, riding toward Durham.

Jimmie Hollister was a cheerful, uncomplaining worker, and they labored side by side, stopping only for a cold lunch of fried chicken. Charlotte had sacrificed one of their hens to the skillet; Jimmie was working only in the hope of getting paid, so the least she could do was feed him.

As they ate, Charlotte told him of her plan, steeling herself for his derision.

Instead, he lit up like a candle. "I think that's a grand idea, Miss Charlotte! A great adventure!" He added wistfully, "I sure would like to go along."

Surprised yet pleased at his reaction, she said, "I would be happy to have you go with me, Jimmie. But aren't you needed at home?"

"Naw, not right now. There ain't much to do around the farm this time of the year." His expression turned glum. "It'd probably be better at home, one less mouth to feed. You sure you'd like to have me?"

"It would make things a lot easier for me, with someone like you along to help out. I couldn't pay you very much, though, and even that will have to wait until after we sell the tobacco."

"That don't matter, Miss Charlotte. Shucks, I wouldn't expect much, aside from my eats. And I can take my old squirrel rifle along, get us a little game to eat." His enthusiasm mounted.

"Not so fast," she said, laughing. "It's not all that settled yet, my going. First, I have to see if that wagon in the barn can be repaired enough to travel. It hasn't been used since Daddy died."

"I can fix the wagon, I'm good at that." He jumped up. "Let's go look at your wagon, see how much fixing up it needs!"

Shaking her head in amusement, Charlotte went along with him to the barn. The wagon in question was several years old, setting off in one corner, covered with dust and cobwebs. It had a deserted, dilapidated look about it, and Charlotte hoped that it was not beyond repair.

Jimmie Hollister bustled around it, then squatted to peer underneath, even getting down on his hands and knees and crawling about. When he finally stood up, he assumed a judicious pose, chin resting on one hand. It was an attitude meant to convey maturity of judgment, so obvious that Charlotte had to hide a smile behind her hand.

"Yup, she can be fixed up," he announced. "It needs a lot of work. Some new floorboards, but I reckon we can scare up enough scrap lumber for that. The wheels need new rims, but I can make 'em. The spokes are loose and rattly, and need to be soaked in water for a day or so. And canvas, we'll need a new top for her, to protect the tobacco from the weather. That's the only thing you'll have to buy, Miss Charlotte. Can you-all manage that?"

"I still have some credit left in Durham. I'm sure Mr. Burns at the dry goods store will sell me enough canvas for a cover, until I can come back with some cash."

"Then I can do 'er!" Jimmie bobbed his head decisively. "Soon as we get the tobacco done, I'll start. Naw, I'll get started tonight. I can work out here by lamp light, if need be."

"Oh, Jimmie, I hate to see you do that."

"I don't mind," he said cheerfully. "I like to keep busy. Besides, you want to get this tobacco to market as soon as possible."

They returned to the tobacco shed and another half-day of hard labor. As she worked, an idea came to Charlotte, having to do with a dream she had had for some time, a dream she had hoped to share with Jeff, but now she knew that was never to be.

If she was successful with the plan for peddling her own tobacco, what was wrong with going out again, several times? She knew there were many small tobacco growers in the vicinity of Durham who were unhappy about having to sell their tobacco crops to men like Sload Lutcher, for a pittance. If they were willing to let her take their tobacco on consignment, she could turn a good profit, and that would further her dream—to open a tobacco factory in Durham. With financial conditions the way they were, many suitable buildings stood empty, available at very low rents.

But if she was to realize this dream, she needed a name for the product she was selling, a personal identification, starting with this first wagonload. The rest of the afternoon she mulled over the problem, thinking of and discarding several possibilities, always returning to her first thought—"The King of Tobaccos."

She mentioned it to Jimmie when they had finished for the day. "I'm trying to think of a name for my tobacco. The King of Tobaccos, what do you think of that?"

"I think it's grand, Miss Charlotte, I really do!"

She nodded, satisfied. "That's it, then."

Jimmie said, "I'll hike home for supper and tell Pa about everything. I'll be back later to start on the wagon."

Charlotte had never taken to needle and thread like most women of her time and place, but she had learned how to sew out of necessity. After supper that evening, a lonely meal, since Jeff was not back from wherever he had gone, and after she had taken food up to her mother, Charlotte closeted herself in a room off the downstairs hall, with the burlap sacks they were to use for the tobacco, and a spool of red thread. She began the tedious task of stitching the letters onto the sacks—The King of Tobaccos.

She lost track of time, and sat up with a start when she heard Jeff calling her name. She went to the door. "Yes, Jefferson? I'm in here."

He limped down the hall toward her. His face was flushed, his hair rumpled. It was obvious that he had been drinking.

He glowered at her. "What's that Hollister boy doing in our barn?"

"He's fixing up the wagon."

"Then you're going ahead with this insane business?"

"Yes, I told you that. And Jimmie, he doesn't think it's so insane."

He scowled. "He's what . . . ? Seventeen? What does he know about it?"

"He's even going with me, so I won't be alone. Look, Jefferson, come see what I'm doing."

She led him into the room and displayed one of the sacks, the legend showing bright against the burlap. She hoped that the family name would ignite some enthusiasm in him.

He stared at it dourly. "Well, dear sister, I can see you're bound and determined to go ahead. If anything happens, it's on your head. I wash my hands of the whole thing!"

It took Charlotte and Jimmie almost a full week to finish flailing the tobacco, sacking it, and getting the wagon ready to roll. Charlotte bought canvas on credit in Durham, and together she and Jimmie made a top for the wagon.

Then, finally, everything was done. That evening, they loaded the tobacco into the wagon and prepared to get an early start in the morning.

Charlotte stood back and surveyed the vehicle with a feeling of great satisfaction. "I'm grateful to you, Jimmie. I would never have managed without you. I realize that now."

"I'm just happy to have something to do, Miss Charlotte. I reckon she's all ready now. What time shall I be here in the morning?"

"How about six o'clock? I want to get as early a start as possible."

"That's fine with me. Good night, Miss Charlotte."

"Good night, Jimmie."

She watched the lad until he disappeared into the night, then went into the house. She had already packed what few clothes she intended to take with her. She found her brother on the front porch. From somewhere he had managed to obtain a supply of liquor, and he had a glass in his hand now, his feet propped upon the railing. She had not asked him where he had gotten the money for the whiskey, and she did not now.

"I'll probably be gone in the morning before you get up, Jefferson. So I'll say goodbye now."

"I wish you a good journey, dear sister." He toasted her with the glass. "I'll see to things here."

"And Momma, you promised to take good care of her."

"Of course I will! She's my mother, too. And I do wish you well, Charlotte," he said with apparent sincerity. "I know I haven't been acting the way a brother should, but I need more time, that's all. Maybe by the time you return, I'll be more like . . ."

"Like the Jefferson I used to know?" Touched, she reached out a hand to push his hair back. "I pray that you will be, Jefferson. With the money I hope to earn from this trip, everything will be better for all of us, you'll see."

"I wish I could believe that."

"It will, believe me. You rest and watch your health, and we'll talk when I get back."

Considerably cheered by his change of attitude, Charlotte went upstairs to bed.

Thus it was that she set out on her fateful journey in high spirits early the next morning. Both Jefferson and her mother were still asleep, and Charlotte did not disturb them.

She had debated for some time over her route of travel, and had finally decided to go generally south and toward the coastal towns. The countryside of West Virginia to the north, or Tennessee to the west, had suffered less destruction during the war, but in both directions she would encounter mountainous terrain, making travel difficult and slow. Also, she knew that the towns nearer the coast were showing a few signs of returning prosperity, since the ports were open again and sea trade was reviving. She intended to go as far south as Savannah if she had to.

As they traveled slowly along the road, she was heartsick at the desolation left by the war. The fields were depressingly empty, many of the fine plantation homes were gone, burned to the ground, and nowhere was there any sign of new construction. The smaller farms they passed, too small for the Yankee soldiers to bother with, were occupied, but the farm families idled about in the yards, staring at Charlotte with sullen, hostile faces.

At times the road was clogged with traffic of every kind—horses, mules, broken-down wagons and buggies, and a great many men on foot. A defeated people going nowhere. Most of the men were soldiers still in their gray uniforms—how apt a color, she thought, the color of defeat. The men eyed the restored wagon with envy, and many looked at her with open lust in their eyes.

Charlotte shivered. She was just as glad that Jimmie was along. She was confident that she could handle herself well in most situations, yet it was comforting to have a man along, even if he was not quite grown. He had a man's size, and the squirrel rifle he carried across his shoulder as he walked alongside the wagon was reassuring.

She intended to travel south for several days before she started peddling the tobacco, so she clucked to the horses, and they plodded on.

Peddlers of every description thronged to the South in the years immediately following the war. Stores had scant supplies to sell, and it probably would be years before their shelves were laden again, since little was being manufactured in the South. Almost everything had to be ordered from the northern industrial states, and not only were relations still strained, transportation was unreliable.

However, peddlers could load their wagons and carts at the southern port cities and travel inland from small town to small town, country store to country store, and even from house to house. Even before the war the itinerant peddler had been prevalent throughout the South. He was not only a source of goods for the isolated hamlets, but also a prime source of news. He was welcomed as a messenger, passing along to both blacks and whites tales of runaway slaves, stories of national and international import, and news of the gathering clouds of war—to many, the peddler brought the first news of the declaration of war. Since he was of great value in this regard, he was accorded equal status by the blacks, poor whites, and plantation owners.

The peddler was even more welcome in the years immediately after the war, not only for badly needed goods, but also for news, since lines of communication were even scarcer than before.

A great many of the peddlers were Jews.

One such was Benjamin Ascher.

German Jews, the Aschers came to the South in 1830, emigrating from the ghettos of Germany. Ben's father, Levi Ascher, settled in Charleston, South Carolina, and became a shopkeeper. Ben, the last of his six children, was born in 1840.

When he was old enough, Ben worked in his father's store when not in school, as did his brothers and sisters. When war was declared, the two older Ascher boys joined the Confederate Army; Peter, the second eldest, was killed at Bull Run.

Ben, although a Southerner born and bred, was adamantly opposed to the institution of slavery; although of an age to do so, he refused to fight for it. When this became known, he was ostracized in Charleston, not only by the citizens of the city, but by his own family as well, for they were fiercely loyal to the South.

During a violent discussion, Levi Ascher, then in his sixties, an imposing figure of a man, with a full black beard, lost his temper. "You shame me, my son! This country has been good to us. It has provided us with a good living. Your grandparents were scorned and abused in Europe, and were always on the edge of starvation. Here, we are considered equals by our neighbors, and my store is well patronized by them. Now, when sons are needed to fight for the South's very existence, you refuse."

"If by equals, you mean being accepted into the fine households here, wined and dined while being waited on by men and women in bondage . . . Yes, to that extent we are equals. I do not believe in making men slaves, Poppa, and I will not fight for it."

"I do not agree with slave-holding, either, Benjamin, but it is the way of life in the South, and we live here. I do not believe in war, either, in my sons fighting and perhaps dying, but it is also the way of things."

"But it is not my way, Poppa."

"What can you know?" Levi Ascher said scornfully. "You have yet to attain your majority. Why must the young always be so arrogant in their beliefs?"

"I am sorry if you think me arrogant," Ben said doggedly. "But it is what I believe. I will not let expediency change the way I believe."

"You are stubborn, as well as arrogant, Benjamin." His father sighed. "You will be thought a coward if you do not fight."

"If I must, I will accept that. Don't worry, Poppa, I won't stay in Charleston to shame you."

True to his word, Ben left Charleston the very next day. He left on foot, with a bulging canvas pack on his back, crammed with calico, trinkets, and numerous other items for sale. All during the war years, he tramped the dusty roads of the South, managing to avoid the areas where battle raged. He traveled the back roads, braving yapping dogs in the yards before the shacks, to be met with men with rifles across their chests, with a wife and children behind them, peering out at him.

Most of the families he visited were isolated from the conflict and cared very little for it. Money was scarce, of course, and Ben swapped his goods for whatever was available—chickens, home-made quilts and comforters; in turn, he traded these items in the cities for more trade goods.

He had an uncanny instinct for business, and through shrewd bargaining, always trading up, he prospered. As the tide of war began to turn against the Confederacy, Ben experienced some pangs of guilt about profiting from the bloody conflict, yet he had never considered it his fight, and he *was* providing a much needed service—for many of the families he dealt with, he was their only source of goods. So why should he feel guilty?

There were occasions, especially when it became clear that defeat was imminent, that he encountered questions about why a fellow of his age and obvious good health was not soldiering.

But Ben was a strapping, broad-shouldered young man by this time, with thick black hair, snapping dark eyes, and even features, and he presented an imposing presence. He never backed away from a challenge, and there were only a few times when he had to use his fists. He did not like to fight, but he developed a skill for it, and that, together with his great strength and agility, usually left him the winner, unless the odds were prohibitive.

He had the acumen to recognize the end long before it came, and had the foresight to convert all his currency into gold, realizing that Confederate currency would be worthless if the South went down in defeat.

A month after hostilities ceased, he returned to Charleston to find the town in shambles, its economy virtually destroyed, and his father deep in disillusionment. Levi Ascher still had the store, but he had little cash to purchase goods, and his customers had no money with which to buy what he could stock.

"You were right, my son," he said to Ben. "The war was a grave mistake, a disaster. I have lost a son, and I may lose my business any day now."

"I prospered, Poppa. It's sad that I had to prosper while the South was dying around me, but as you once said to me"—his spare smile was grim—"that is the way of things. But I do have money. Gold, not worthless Confederate currency. I am willing to use some of that gold to replenish your stock . . ."

Levi Ascher brightened. "Then you are going into the business with me?"

Ben shook his head, and said gently, "No, Poppa. I aim to continue what I've been doing, until something better comes along. I find that I enjoy it."

His father grimaced. "A peddler! What kind of a life is that? Come in with me, and we can build something that will be a monument to the Ascher name. I will make you a full partner."

"It is a good life, Poppa. I have freedom that I would never have with you. I love you, Poppa, but I well know what would happen if I came in with you. Even as a full partner, things would always be done *your* way. You know that is the truth of it."

"What do you plan to do then, Benjamin?" The older man stiffened, drawing himself up. "This gold you mention... I will not be the object of charity!"

"Poppa, Poppa," Ben said in a chiding voice. "I worked hard for that gold, I have no intention of simply giving it away. What I have in mind is this... We will use it to restock your store, and from that stock, from time to time, I will take goods to sell on my journeys. In that way, we both benefit. Is it agreed?"

It was agreed, and soon Ben was out peddling again. But he was not on foot with a pack on his back this time. He bought a horse and buckboard, loading the buckboard down with goods to sell or barter.

During the ensuing months, Ben traveled many long miles, visiting small farmers and homes of the emancipated slaves. He became a familiar sight to all, and the freed blacks began calling him the "rolling store man." Both whites and blacks gathered around eagerly as he spread his goods on wooden and earthen floors alike. He opened the spices, filling the rooms with marvelous odors. He arranged bright ribbons and colorful cloth—pretty things that the womenfolk had not seen since the war began. Since cash was still scarce, he usually bartered his goods for whatever they had to offer.

A new phenomenon was springing up all through the South—the country store. Young men returning from the war had no money, but foresighted wholesalers devised a plan whereby the farmers could purchase supplies on credit. In exchange for a mortgage on his crop, the farmer could buy seed, food, clothing, and even farm implements for the coming year. Country stores grew across the countryside, popping up overnight like mushrooms. The storekeeper served as postmaster, mortician, arbiter of local disputes, and in some instances, even held political office.

This system worked to the peddler's advantage as well. The stuff he received in barter for his goods, much of the time, he could in turn sell to the country stores for cash.

Thus it was that Ben was in a small, wayside store late one fall afternoon just outside of Florence, South Carolina. As he drove his buckboard up before the store, he noticed a covered wagon parked nearby, with a gangly youth lounging against one wheel.

He climbed down, stretched, nodded politely to the youth, and went into the store. It was dim inside, and empty except for the owner, an ex-Confederate soldier who had just opened the store a few months back, and a woman in a gingham dress. The storekeeper, Len Thompson, was engaged in an argument with the woman. She was tall, with long, thick, red hair, and Ben could see freckles on the curve of the cheek turned his way. She was arguing heatedly, motioning with slender, long-fingered hands. There was a burlap sack of tobacco on the counter before her.

As Ben came closer, he saw letters stitched on the sack: The King of Tobaccos.

The woman said vehemently, "I can't sell my tobacco on consignment. I could have done that back in Durham. I need the cash."

Len Thompson spread his hands. "I am sorry, Miss King. I just don't have the cash on hand. Now, if you'd care to look around the store. Maybe we could work out a swap, your tobacco for some of my goods."

The woman's shoulders slumped in discouragement. "That's what others say. Everybody needs tobacco, but not enough of them are willing to pay."

"It ain't that I'm not willing, I don't have the cash. Maybe your next trip?"

"That is of little help to me now," she said in a tired voice. "Well, I do thank you for your time, Mr. Thompson."

As she turned about, her glance met Ben's, and he felt something like a shock. She had eyes of the most startling bright blue, like a gas flame, eyes that shone with intelligence, and at this moment, despair. She was beautiful, with a strong, almost too-vivid beauty, and she was young, much younger than he had supposed. As she left the store, she moved with a consummate grace.

Len Thompson said, "Howdy, Ben. I feel sorry for the girl, but what can I do?"

Ben nodded. "I'll be right back, Len."

He hurried outside. The woman was striding determinedly toward the wagon. He called, "Miss King!"

She turned a cold face toward him. "Yes?"

"Could I have a few words with you? I'm Ben Ascher."

She hesitated, and he could see that she had to make an effort to be courteous, for she was still deep in her own thoughts. "I am Charlotte King. And this is Jimmie Hollister."

She indicated the youth who had straightened up with a wary look at Ben's approach, and now reached into the wagon bed and produced an ancient rifle.

Ben had to smile. "You have no need of the rifle, son. I mean you no harm. It's just that I overheard that exchange inside, Miss King, and I have a word of advice for you. Forgive me if I'm being too forward."

"Advice? What advice is that, sir?"

"Well, from what I overheard you have a wagonload of tobacco you're selling?"

"Yes, I do. It is my late father's last tobacco crop, and it is fine bright leaf."

"I'm sure that it is." He pointed to the buckboard. "I am a peddler by profession, also."

Charlotte said eagerly, "You wish to buy my tobacco?"

"I'm afraid not, Miss King."

Her face fell. "Nobody seems interested in buying it."

"Oh, I might take a sack or two off your hands, but that is all I have room for. The thing is, you're making a mistake, if you continue the way you handled Len Thompson. Cash is very scarce, you must know that. So, instead of cash, you must start taking goods in trade . . ."

"But then I'll be no better off!" she said in dismay. "I could have done something like that back in Durham. I am desperately in need of cash, Mr. Ascher."

"Aren't we all?" he said dryly. "But that is the way of things, at this time, in the South. You must learn to make it work to your advantage. And it can be to your advantage. Take Len in there, for instance. You can trade your tobacco to him, I'm confident, for a value exceeding what you would get in cash, since he does need tobacco for his customers."

"But then what would I do with what I receive in trade?"

"Take it to those storekeepers who *do* have cash on hand. Certainly, it is a more involved procedure, but also more profitable in the long run. Otherwise, I am afraid that you will return with most of your tobacco unsold."

She pushed her fingers into her hair in a distracted gesture. "I know nothing of trading goods!"

"Then you must learn," he said gently. "I have made several trips through this region, and I know the storekeepers with available cash." Quickly, he gave her the names and locations of several in the immediate vicinity. "How much tobacco do you have?"

"I started with just under two hundred pounds. I have managed to sell a dozen sacks, but still have most of it left."

"With the names I gave you as a start, I'm sure you can unload most, if not all of it."

Her shoulders went back in determination, and her eyes flashed. "I will do as you advise, starting with Mr. Thompson!" She took two steps toward the store, then paused to look at him appraisingly. "I do thank you, Mr. Ascher, but I must admit to some curiosity. Why are you doing this?"

He shrugged negligently. "Just call it a helping hand from one peddler to another."

Watching Charlotte King stride on toward the store, Ben thought, Why indeed? Poppa would have thought him touched by the sun, giving away trade secrets to a competitor.

Yet, there was something about this woman, this girl, that vastly appealed to him. Ben had had his share of women during his travels, but all had been casual encounters, and he had never once felt the current of powerful attraction that he had experienced the instant their eyes had met inside the store.

Since Charlotte King was working much the same territory that he was, it was certainly possible that he would come across her again.

# Chapter Three

CLINT Devlin threw in one card. "I'll take one."

Across the table Remson dealt him a card. Clint picked it up and took a quick peek. A four. It gave him two pair, fours and eights. He felt Marcy's warm exhalation of breath on his head, but the only outward sign of excitement she gave was the tightening of her fingers where her hand rested lightly on his shoulder.

With a steady hand Clint picked up the thin cigar resting in the saucer and drew on it. He had been playing the four Northern cotton buyers for three hours, and this was the first halfway decent hand he had drawn. Although he had been betting conservatively, he was down over a hundred dollars, money he could ill-afford to lose. If Lady Luck favored him, he just might get well on this hand.

When the last card was dealt and the opening bets went around the table, everyone dropped out but Clint and Harvey Remson, the dealer for this hand, a beefy, loud-talking individual in clothes so rumpled it looked as if he had slept in them.

"Well, Reb, looks like it's come down to you'n me. I bet it all..." He thumbed through the bills before him, and then shoved all his money into the pot. "Seventy-five big ones."

Clint kept his face inscrutable, but he experienced a quiver of doubt. Had Remson drawn a better hand? Mentally, Clint totaled up the money he had left. To match Remson's bet would just about wipe him out. Yet if he backed down he would be turning away from the best hand he'd had all afternoon. He had learned during the progress of the game that Remson was a reckless bluffer.

With a shrug Clint dug into his pocket, and counted out seventy-five dollars under the edge of the table, then plumped the money down. "I'll call your bluff, Remson."

"Bluff, is it?" Remson cackled triumphant laughter. "You have to go some to beat me, Devlin! I've got . . ." Without waiting to see Clint's cards, Remson spread his hand on the table top. "Four aces! Let's see you beat them apples!"

Clint leaned forward, blinking at the four aces. Marcy's fingers dug painfully into his shoulder. He said slowly, "I reckon I can't. I only have a measly little two pair." Unobtrusively as possible, he let both hands drop below the level of the table, and one hand groped for the handle of the Colt in his belt.

"This will teach you to play with the big fellows, Reb," Remson crowed, as he reached out with both hands to scoop in the pot.

"Perhaps you're right, friend, but suppose we wait before you rake the money in." Clint brought the Colt up, cocking it with a sound shockingly loud in the suddenly quiet hotel room. The muzzle was pointed at Remson's heart. Clint said softly, "You cheated, friend. Not only that, but you were stupid about it, dealing yourself four aces, while I had one myself." He turned over his cards, and tapped his fifth card with his left forefinger. "Marcy, collect my winnings, and let's depart the premises."

As Marcy Reynolds quickly gathered in the pot, stuffing the bills and coins into her reticule, Clint carefully got to his feet, ever watchful, the Colt bearing on Remson, whose face was red with rage.

"Go out ahead of me, Marcy," Clint said, "and I'll be right behind you."

Remson bellowed, "You won't get away with this, Reb!"

"Oh, I think I will, Yank."

He backed slowly out of the room, the pistol moving back and forth between the players at the table. In the corridor outside he jammed the Colt into his belt, and said urgently, "Let's make haste, my dear. To the stables. Fortunately, I anticipated a hasty departure, and have already packed our saddlebags. All we have to do is saddle up and ride out."

Marcy gave him a puzzled look. "But what's the hurry, Clint? You caught that man cheating, so you won fair and square."

"Fair and square doesn't count for much with those fellows." Hand under her elbow, he was urging her down the stairs. Marcy was beautiful and a great bed companion, but she was not the brightest woman Clint had ever known. "When they have a few minutes to recover their wits, those fellows, at Remson's urging, will come haring after us. I would deem it wise to put this town behind us."

Outside the small hotel, he turned right, heading for the stables two blocks away. He and Marcy had been in Fayetteville, North Carolina, for three days. Clint had come into town with almost a thousand dollars in his pocket, hoping to buy cotton, which was selling cheaply in the South. Bought here for twenty cents a pound, it could be sold at over forty cents the pound in the North. Unfortunately for Clint, most of the cotton had already been bought by Northern speculators, like the four men in the poker game; they were waiting around for a train to ship their cotton north.

Failing to buy his cotton, Clint had lingered, getting into another poker game two days ago, in which he had lost all but two hundred of his thousand dollars. Today, he had been lucky enough to recoup some of it—if he could get out of town all in one piece.

He ducked into the stable with Marcy, and went about saddling the two horses. Marcy tried to help, but only succeeded in getting in the way.

Exasperated, he slapped her well-rounded haunch. "Why don't you just step back out of the way, sugar, and let me get on with it? With you helping, we'll be here until Christmas."

Pouting, Marcy stepped aside. In her late twenties,

with long black hair, hot brown eyes, and a complexion as smooth as cream, Marcy had been working in a tavern in Savannah when Clint encountered her. He had taken her to bed and found her not only willing but extremely skillful in the erotic arts, and he had proposed that she accompany him for a spell.

Not only did Marcy provide divertissement for Clint, but she was also a big help during the frequent poker games such as the one he had just quitted, diverting the players' attention from the game.

I've fallen onto sorry times, he thought bitterly; to haul a woman along with me to distract poker players!

He wasn't much better than a professional gambler. Sure, there were ex-Confederates around in more dire straits, but Clint refused to equate himself with them. He had brains, had unflagging energy, and he possessed a burning ambition—he was determined to become a wealthy, powerful man. He had come through the war without a scratch, he had fought with dash and courage—for what he knew was a losing cause from the beginning. Going in as a private, he had ended the war as a major, and had been awarded the Confederate Cross of Honor for valor under fire following the Battle of Spottsylvania Court House.

At the end he had emerged covered with glory, and with a fistful of Confederate dollars as worthless as ashes. Since Clint had been raised in an orphanage in Atlanta, he had no family to go home to. Even the orphanage had been destroyed when Atlanta burned. Yet he did not go forth burdened with the bitterness of defeat, as did so many others. *He* would make something of himself.

So here he was, a few paltry dollars in his pocket, and about to flee the wrath of four irate poker players.

Tightening the girth of the roan horse Marcy was to ride, Clint faced around. "All right, love, mount up."

When he had helped her into the saddle, Marcy pouted down at him. "It seems to me we never stay in one place more than a few hours."

He was getting sick and tired of that blasted pout!

Suppressing his irritation, he said lightly, "I told you I was a traveling man, sugar."

"Where are we going now?"

Considering the question, Clint did not answer until he was in his own saddle, the reins in his hand. "South, I reckon, into South Carolina, maybe even on into Georgia. I should be able to find *some* place where all those damned Yankee cotton buyers haven't been."

It was close to dark when they rode south out of Fayetteville. Clint rode looking back over his shoulder for the poker players to come raging after him, but there seemed to be no signs of pursuit. Nonetheless, he was not easy in mind until the town was well behind them.

They did not make camp until close to midnight, not until Clint calculated he had put enough distance between them and Fayetteville. They made camp in a grove of trees alongside a meandering brook. He gathered wood for a small fire, filled the coffee pot with water from the stream, and set it on the fire. Marcy had already unrolled her blankets and was sound asleep between them.

Squatting on his heels by the fire, Clint lit a cigar and waited for the coffee to perk. In the firelight his strong features stood out in sharp relief, his high cheekbones and strong nose outlined by the coppery glow cast by the flames. His face looked as though there could be a trace of Indian blood in his heritage, but since he knew nothing of his parentage, Clint had no way of knowing. He had been found in a basket on the doorstep of the orphanage in Atlanta, a slip of paper pinned to the blanket in which he had been wrapped, with two words, Clint Devlin, written on it.

With his thick, light brown hair, merry hazel eyes, and smiling mouth under a trim moustache, Clint was considered uncommonly handsome by women. In addition, at twenty-eight, he was an even six feet, with square shoulders, and a trim body that moved with an economical grace. He was good with his fists, handy with weapons, and possessed a temper too volatile for his own good.

He was in a temper now as he brooded into the flames,

but he was angry at himself. By nature, Clint was an optimist; he tended to look on the bright side of things, yet the fact remained that the war had been over for close to a year, and he had not achieved any of the goals he had set for himself.

He knew there was a fortune to be made in cotton at this particular time. The textile factories in the North badly needed cotton, so they could get back into full production. All he had to do was find a place where the rapacious speculators had not been, invest what money he had, sell what cotton he could buy for a good profit, and then reinvest that. It could pyramid into a tidy sum by the time the cotton boom had peaked out.

The pot boiled over, the coffee sizzling in the flames, and Clint snapped out of his reverie. Using his kerchief on the pot handle, he poured a tin cup of coffee. Wrapping his hands around the cup, he sipped, drinking two cups of coffee before the cigar was smoked down.

He felt the pangs of hunger, and remembered that they had skipped supper. He glanced over at Marcy, wondering if he should roust her out of the blankets. But she was always grumpy when wakened out of a sound sleep. It did not seem worth the effort, and he was weary. He could make it through the night. He always woke with the sun anyway, and he wanted to get an early start.

He set the half-empty coffee pot to one side for reheating in the morning, kicked dirt over the fire to put it out, and unrolled his blankets.

He removed his boots, then his breeches and shirt. The night was a little chilly, but being a fastidious man, Clint disliked sleeping in his clothes. He spread his blankets next to Marcy's, and settled down. If past experience was a reliable guide, Marcy would snuggle next to him before the night was over, and their combined body heat would keep them warm.

As Clint had anticipated, he woke some time during the night to find her snuggled close, her body fitting against his back spoon-fashion. Smiling, he went back to sleep.

He awoke a second time to Marcy's hands on his body, and her lips in his hair. Opening his eyes, he saw that the sun was turning the eastern sky pink. He lay very still, so she would not realize that he was yet awake. But soon her skilled caresses brought him to such a stage of arousal that he could no longer hide it.

"Damn you, Clint Devlin," she growled in his ear. "Stop your pretending. You haven't been asleep for some time!"

"Now how did you know that?" he said innocently.

"Well, it's certainly not because I'm a mind reader, that's for sure . . ."

He turned on his side, cupping her breast, effectively shutting her up. Eyes closing, she shivered. Although she had gotten into the blankets fully clothed except for her boots, she was now naked. He fondled her glowing body with urgent hands.

She groaned, and eyes still closed, she raised her face, blindly seeking his mouth. Locked together in the fierce kiss, they rolled back and forth. In their gyrations, the blankets were thrown back. The morning air was cold on Clint's exposed flesh, but the heat of Marcy's body was such that he did not feel the cold.

No matter what her other flaws—and they were many—Marcy was rollicking good fun, robust and uninhibited in her love-making. Now, as he touched her intimately, the laughter left her face, and she lay back with half-closed eyes, guiding him to her, and then into her.

Her face went out of focus, and she sighed softly, lying lax and open to him for a moment. And then she moved frantically, arching up to meet him, as they synchronized their movements into the heated rhythm of love.

As her rapture broke, Marcy murmured throatily, "Ah, Clint! You're good, so good for me. Ah, ah!"

After the rage of their passion had subsided, they lay tangled together, breathing heavily. Clint cradled his face against her neck, and she stroked his tousled hair. The blankets had been completely thrown off by their furious activity, and Clint felt the perspiration drying cold on his back.

He was thinking of moving and covering them up, when he heard footsteps on the dry leaves behind them, and then a gasp of shock. Quickly, Clint rolled off Marcy, trying to remember where he had left the Colt, positive that Remson had found them, not only at an indelicate moment, but also at a most vulnerable one.

Then he froze as he saw the young woman in a long, gingham dress, a wooden bucket in her hand, standing at the edge of the trees a few yards away. Clint had a glimpse of long, red hair, bright blue eyes, and a strongly sculptured face, and he relaxed, grinning lazily.

"Good morning, ma'am. I'm sorry that I'm not wearing a hat to doff, but as you can plainly see . . ." He gestured to his nakedness.

"Oh!" The woman's hand flew to her mouth, and her face blazed a bright red.

Gathering up her skirts with her free hand, she whirled and ran, disappearing into the trees.

Charlotte did not consider herself a prude, but what she had just seen was disgusting! A man and a woman naked on blankets, and she would have to have been blind not to realize that she had stumbled upon them making love. Shameless, like two woods animals rutting! And it had not seemed to bother them that she had come upon them at such an inopportune time. Certainly not the man; he had not seemed in the least disturbed.

Yet, as she hurried back to where they had made camp last night, she found herself recalling certain features of the man—a handsome face under a shock of unruly light hair, a mobile mouth curving in a mocking smile, wide shoulders and chest, with very little body hair, tapering down to narrow hips, and at his groin . . .

With an effort she wrenched her thoughts away from that particular area. The only time she had ever seen a naked male body was once when she had spied on Jeff and two other boys swimming without clothing one summer, but Jeff had been only eleven at the time.

She was slightly out of breath when she reached the wagon. They had made camp just off the road at dusk last night, being unable to get closer to the stream because of the trees. After eating a quick breakfast, Charlotte had discovered they were low on water. While Jimmie hitched up the team, she had taken the bucket down to the creek for water.

Now, Jimmie was just finishing as she approached. She hastened to the water barrel lashed to the side of the wagon, and pretended to dump a bucket of water into it. It was still a quarter full, they could fill it somewhere else. She was not about to tell Jimmie what she had just seen!

"All ready, Miss Charlotte," he called.

She climbed up onto the wagon seat, picked up the reins, and clucked to the horses. The wagon creaked out onto the dusty road, headed north. They were going home! The wagon was empty of tobacco; she had sold it all, and for a good profit.

The thought of her success erased all other concerns from her mind, and she forgot about the pair on the blankets.

She was fully determined to make other trips, now that she had learned how to do it properly. But if that nice man, Ben Ascher, had not been so generous with his advice, the trip would have been a disaster. Charlotte hoped that she would encounter him again on her travels, so she could express her gratitude more fully.

She had followed his good advice, bartering her tobacco at the country stores for goods, which she then in turn sold for cash to those store owners who had money. Once she got past the initial stages, Charlotte found that she had a knack for shrewd bargaining, and, true to Ben Ascher's promise, she made a larger profit in the end than if she had sold strictly for cash. It had averaged out to close to fifty cents a pound for the tobacco. She was going home with almost a thousand dollars!

She could get a reliable doctor for her mother. If she

could not find one near home, she could now afford to take her mother to a larger city, where good doctors were available. And there would be money left over for things for herself and Jefferson. If she managed carefully, there would even be money to purchase more tobacco, and go out peddling again.

Charlotte could not remember when she had been so happy, certainly not since the war began, destroying the happiness she had known when her father was alive, and the Kings had been a close-knit family.

She began to sing softly to herself, in a clear, alto voice.

Without realizing it, her voice had risen, and Jimmie, beside her on the wagon seat, smiled at her. Charlotte broke off, somewhat embarrassed.

"You sound happy, Miss Charlotte."

"I am, Jimmie, I am! Everything has worked out so well for me, for us! Now I can pay you back what I owe you. Aside from helping me with the tobacco and getting the wagon in shape, I don't think I would have managed the trip without you along."

"Aw, it's nothing, Miss Charlotte," he said, abashed. "You would have managed just fine. You are a grand person."

Admiration shone in his eyes, and something else . . . It took Charlotte a moment to realize what it was. Lowering her eyes, she gazed at him from the thicket of her lashes, seeing how tall he had become, seeing the width of his shoulders, despite the boyish thinness, seeing the growing thickness of his young neck. Yes, he was a boy, but he was quickly becoming a man; and she had not seen it, for she had known him so long as a child.

Dismay filled her. However was she going to cope with this?

For the first time, she felt uncomfortable in his presence, and the feeling angered her. Why, when things were going well, did they always have to change? Fate never seemed to allow good things, happy times, to remain the way they were. She could feel Jimmie's worshipful eyes still on her face, and she clucked crossly to the horses. She was being a fool! A boy must grow up, must become a man. She could not expect him to stay a child forever. And it was natural enough, she supposed. She was the only woman under fifty that the boy saw regularly. He would forget his infatuation quickly enough when he met some girls his own age.

Her thoughts turned again toward home. She was eager to get there, wondering how she was going to bear up for the time it would take to get home. What grand news she had for Jeff and her mother!

It was mid-afternoon when Charlotte pulled the wagon up before the house. As she pulled on the reins, stopping the horses, Jeff opened the front door, and stepped out onto the porch. She cried, "Jefferson, I'm back and everything went splendidly!"

He did not move from the porch, and she felt a pang of disappointment. He could at least show enough enthusiasm to come forward to greet her. She jumped down from the wagon seat, and said to Jimmie, "I would appreciate your taking the wagon to the barn and unhitching the team, Jimmie. I want to speak to Jefferson, and run up to see Momma."

Jimmie nodded. "Yes, Miss Charlotte."

He gathered up the reins and started the wagon around the house.

She hurried up the steps to Jeff. His face was grave and intent, but Charlotte scarcely noticed, so delighted was she to be returning home triumphant. "Jefferson, it went very well. I sold every sack of the tobacco, and got nearly fifty cents a pound for it! Now I can see to it that Momma gets proper medical attention."

"Charlotte . . ."

Her voice overrode his, "I'm going up and tell her now."

As she started past him, Jeff seized her arm in a restraining grip. "Charlotte, it's too late for that."

She stared at him without comprehension. "Too late? Of course it's not too late! All Momma needs is a decent doctor."

"Charlotte, it's too late for doctors, it's too late for anything. Momma died, some time yesterday afternoon."

Charlotte went numb with disbelief. She grasped at the last thing he said. "Some time? Don't you *know?*"

"I . . ." He swallowed, his glance sliding away. "I wasn't here. I was out . . ."

Her hand fastened on his arm, and she said angrily, "You promised to look after her. You promised!"

"Charlotte," he said miserably, "there was nothing I could have done. She just . . . died."

Tears stung her eyes. "After all I went through, after getting the money for a doctor, it's all for nothing. If I had stayed here to look after her, she would still be alive!"

"Charlotte, there was nothing you could have done, nothing *anybody* could have done."

Crying openly now, she turned away. In a choked voice, she said, "Of what use is the money now? I might as well burn it for all the good I'll get out of it."

"About the money . . ." He cleared his throat.

She stared at him through a film of tears. "What about the money?"

"While you were gone . . ." He refused to look at her. "I needed money desperately, so I went to Sload Lutcher. He was kind enough to loan me seven hundred dollars on the farm, but only until you got back. It's all gone, Charlotte, all spent. He has to be paid, or the farm will belong to him."

# Chapter Four

ALICE King was buried the next afternoon, in a grove of trees behind the house, alongside the grave of Gardner King, her husband.

It was a clear, sunny day, with a slight autumn bite in the air; and Charlotte shivered as a light wind penetrated her thin, cloth jacket, and rattled leaves of the big cottonwood, in whose shade her mother now rested. She felt empty, drained of all feeling; she had cried for a long time last night, but now there were no tears. She stood with dry eyes, listening dully as Bradley Hollister spoke a few words over the plain pine coffin.

The funeral was sparsely attended. The Hollister family was there, along with two other neighbors, and Jeff stood alongside Charlotte. As Hollister finished with a prayer, Jeff stirred, and Charlotte felt his gaze. She refused to look at him. Any feeling she once had for him was frozen inside, and she knew that it would remain so forever. She would never be completely convinced that their mother might not still be alive if Jeff had been in attendance.

Bradley Hollister approached her. He said gently, "Charlotte, why don't you and Jeff go on up to the house? Jimmie and me, and the other fellows, we'll take care of the rest of it."

"All right, Mr. Hollister," she said listlessly. "I thank you for your kindness."

With a last lingering look at the pine box, she turned

away and trudged toward the house. In her mind she said, "Goodbye, Momma; I'm sorry . . . for everything."

She heard footsteps behind her, and Jeff's voice, "Charlotte, wait up. I want to talk."

She would not look at him. "I have nothing to say to you."

He caught up to her. "You'll have to talk to me some time. You can't just ignore me forever!"

She walked on, unheeding.

"Charlotte, I *am* sorry," he said in an agonized voice. "I'll try to do better, I swear I will. I don't know what has gotten into me since I came home."

Goaded, she snapped, "It's too late to be sorry, Jefferson. Momma is gone, and now I'm going to have to see Sload Lutcher, or our home will be gone as well!"

She strode on toward the house, Jeff falling back. She dreaded the next hour or so. The neighbors had all brought food, and one neighbor's wife was in the house now, preparing everything. It was an ordeal Charlotte dreaded, being a hostess, when all she wanted to do was hide in her room. But that would be ungracious of her, so she steeled herself to face it, hoping that it would not go on too long, so she could ride into Durham and confront Sload Lutcher with his villainy.

She got through the afternoon all right, accepting condolences as graciously as possible. These people were her friends, and friends were hard to come by in these difficult times. She avoided Jeff, and soon he was slipping out and returning looking rumpled and flushed, and she knew that he had a bottle secreted somewhere. Paid for with Sload Lutcher's money, she thought with a twinge of disgust.

Unfortunately, for her plans, the last mourner did not leave until well after dark, and it was too late to ride into Durham. Worn out from her grief, Charlotte went to bed the minute the last guest was gone, and slept well, considering her state of mind.

She left early the next morning for Durham, after a skimpy breakfast, letting herself out of the house without waking her brother.

She rode up to Lutcher's tobacco factory shortly before noon, and marched straightway up to his office. When she appeared in his doorway, Lutcher leaned back with a smile.

"Well, Miss King, congratulations! I understand that your peddling tour was successful."

"It was," she said tartly. "But I feel that your congratulations are spurious, sir. I doubt very much that you wished me success. For your information, I received an average of just under fifty cents a pound for my tobacco."

He shrugged. "Was it worth your trouble, Miss King? I should think that it would bother you, a woman alone, being a common peddler."

"I wasn't alone. Bradley Hollister's son, Jimmie, accompanied me." She allowed malice to show in her voice. "Not everyone is intimidated by you, Mr. Lutcher. Now, I believe that my brother owes you the sum of seven hundred dollars. I have the money to pay, and I would like the note he signed as security."

He shrugged again. "Very well." From his desk drawer he took the note, and Charlotte removed seven hundred dollars from her purse, and exchanged the money for the note.

"You are more of a cad than I thought, sir, taking advantage of my brother's weakness, and bringing about my mother's death."

He looked at her coldly. "I had nothing to do with your mother's death. My condolences, Miss King. As for your brother, he is of age. I didn't go to him, he came to me. And you will note that I didn't charge him interest, as other money-lenders would have done."

"That was not out of the goodness of your heart, sir. You hoped that my selling trip would be a failure, and I wouldn't be able to repay the loan. Then you would have taken over our farm for a mere pittance." Anger now boiled in her, and her fingers clenched around the edges of her purse. "I forbid you to transact business with Jefferson again. If you do, sir, I will see that you regret it."

His calm demeanor was not shaken. "I would suggest

that you discuss that with your brother, Miss King. I am a businessman, and nobody tells me with whom I may or may not do business." Now his smile was dangerous. "And I would advise you to watch your tongue, miss. Threats do not become you, and certainly have no effect upon me."

Charlotte's fury grew. In a shaking voice, she said, "You are a vile man, Sload Lutcher. You're a vulture feeding off our ill fortune. My brother's spirit was broken by his war experiences, and you're taking advantage of that! I know of no man more despicable, sir!"

Lutcher had gone bone white. He rose, terrifying in his great height. His deep-socketed eyes blazed. "You grand plantation people consider yourselves too good for people like me who have to labor hard for our money . . ."

"Our farm could hardly be called a grand plantation, Mr. Lutcher, and from what I hear you labored little for your wealth. Being a fancy man in New Orleans could scarcely be called labor!"

"Enough!" Lutcher slammed his hand down on the desk. "I will not listen to more of this! You are on *my* property now, Miss King, and I demand that you leave!"

"Gladly, sir."

In an elaborate gesture she gathered up her skirts, high off the floor, as if to avoid contamination, and swept out of the office. Head high, she marched along the balcony, and out of the building.

Her anger had drained away by the time she mounted her horse and headed out of Durham, and she was weak from reaction.

The realization came to her that she had made an enemy for life of Sload Lutcher. He was a dangerous man, arrogant in his ruthlessness and vicious greed.

However, she did not for one minute regret anything she had said, for it had all been true, every word! Men like Sload Lutcher had to be shown that not everyone cowered in fear before them.

After all, what could he do? No matter how angry she had made him, he would not dare do bodily harm to her.

She kicked her heels against the horse's flanks and rode on toward home.

Sload Lutcher strode back and forth in his office with long, angry strides. It had taken all his will power to keep his hands away from the throat of that damned King woman. Her condescending arrogance had been maddening!

All his life he had been plagued by the scorn and contempt of people of her class. In New Orleans the upstanding, genteel plantation gentlemen and the high-and-mighty gents from the Garden District had patronized his establishments, rutting with his strumpets, and ignored him as though he did not exist.

Lutcher had taken their money with gritted teeth, growing rich in the process. But the bottom had fallen out of his business when the Yankees had blockaded New Orleans. Even without the blockade, he had known that the war would destroy his brothels. In time, Confederate currency would be worthless, so he had rid himself of the brothels, converted his money into gold, and left New Orleans for good.

He had traveled back and forth across the South, looking for a place with the best opportunities. For a while he had considered heading north, but he knew that his best chance lay in the South. North, he would have to compete, while the South would be in ruins for years to come, prey to a man with money and ambition, and the willingness to ride roughshod over any competition.

His final choice had been Durham. Lutcher had sensed that he would be able to gobble up acreage from the impoverished farmers and plantation owners for only a fraction of the land's worth. But by the time the war came to an end, he saw an even better opportunity for quick wealth and power—tobacco.

Lutcher was still eager for land, especially the fertile tobacco land around Durham, but to make land investments pay dividends took time. The production of snuff and cigarettes offered the best opportunity for quick wealth, and he gradually turned his efforts in that direction. With his available money and the need for that money by those with tobacco to sell, he was able to accumulate a large quantity of the leaf, and was just now getting his factory into full production.

He had encountered little resistance in his efforts to buy tobacco—until Charlotte King. At first she had been a small irritant; after all, she only had two hundred pounds, with slight possibilities for growing more. Lutcher had been able to laugh away her resistance, sure that she would, in the end, come begging him to buy her tobacco at any price.

Now it was a different story. She had managed to profit by resisting him. That was bad enough, but what if she became an example for the other tobacco growers? If they followed her lead, Lutcher would soon find himself in short supply for his factory.

He had to do something to discredit her, and quickly. Not only for his economic welfare, but to pay her back for her defiance. She was from the same cut of cloth as those who had spurned him in New Orleans. He would not suffer that again!

He stepped to the door, and bellowed, "Jenks! Cob Jenks, get in here!"

In a moment a burly man in rough clothing came hurrying along the balcony. Jenks was a man of brutal nature, with little brains, but he had found a perfect spot for his talents working for Sload Lutcher. Lutcher paid him well, and thus bought the man's blind loyalty. Jenks had long arms, almost to his knees, and the bony structure of his face and the thick growth of hair on his hands and forearms gave him a simian appearance. He had a reputation for being "rough as a cob," and his real first name had long since been forgotten.

"There is a job you must do, Jenks," Lutcher said without preamble. "I want you to get on it at once. Forget everything else for the time being."

"Right you are, Mr. Lutcher! You tell me, I'll do it," Jenks said in his raspy voice.

"The woman who just left here, did you see her?"

"Yes, sir, I saw her." Jenks smacked his lips. "A purty thing, ain't she?"

"That's Charlotte King. She's giving me trouble, and I want it to stop."

Jenks' pale gray eyes took on a shine. "What do you have in mind for me to do?"

"First, her brother, Jefferson. He's the one you've been supplying with liquor and steering to a doxie from time to time."

Jenks bobbed his head. "Yup, I know that fellow. For a gent beat up by the war, he's sure got him an appetite for drink and the girls."

"I also think he might be interested in cards from time to time. Steer him into a few games, but make damned sure that he loses."

"That'll be no trouble. I know just the game. They'll strip him clean as a plucked goose."

"Now to the woman. She refused to sell her tobacco to me, and went out peddling it. She's probably going to try it again. I want you to have a word with those farmers with tobacco to sell. Tell them that if they sell to her, they can expect my factory to boycott them in the future." Lutcher smiled unpleasantly. "Make it even stronger than that, but be sure there are no witnesses when you give them the word. Hint that they may find their tobacco barns burned to the ground if they deal with her."

"I'll see to it, Mr. Lutcher."

"And if all else fails and she does collect another load of tobacco to peddle, I want you to take a couple of men with you and follow her. Fire her wagon and tobacco, if naught else works. Perhaps . . ." Lutcher grinned coldly. "Perhaps you might have a bit of sport with her. That should discourage her."

"That would be a pleasure, a purty like that. How about the lad with her?"

"Who is that?"

"The Hollister squirt. He went along with her the last time, so I hear."

"Oh, yes, she did mention him. He shouldn't cause three men any trouble." Lutcher fell silent for a moment, thinking. "I have an even better idea. Miss King has the misconception that she stands high above the rest of us. A little gossip spread around in the right places should take care of that. Here is what I want you to do, Jenks . . ."

The morning after her confrontation with Sload Lutcher, Charlotte hitched the team to the wagon and drove over to the Hollister place.

The Hollisters, father and son, came out to meet her. Bradley Hollister said, "I thank you kindly, Charlotte, for the money you paid Jimmie. It comes in handy, indeed it does."

"I was only too happy to be able to pay him what I owed him. He was worth much more. Without him, I don't think I would have made it through."

She smiled warmly at Jimmie, and he colored, his gaze sliding away. She cautioned herself to be careful what she said to the youth; one wrong word and his emotions would rocket out of control.

Charlotte returned her attention to the elder Hollister. "I need Jimmie, if you can spare him. I'm going peddling again, but since my own tobacco is all sold, I have to go among the farmers, and try to talk them into letting me take theirs on consignment."

Bradley Hollister was frowning. "I heard something that could mean trouble for you, Charlotte. The word is that a man named Cob Jenks, Lutcher's toady, is going from farm to farm, warning everybody not to let you have their tobacco. If they do, Lutcher will not do business with them again."

Charlotte experienced a twinge of alarm. "I never thought he'd go that far! Do you suppose the farmers will heed his threat?"

Hollister shrugged. "Maybe, maybe not. Lutcher ain't very well liked, but he's about the only buyer for their tobacco in these parts, even if he does pay bottom prices. I know"—he brightened—"suppose I go along with you,

Charlotte, instead of Jimmie? I'm better acquainted than you are. Most of the farmers know me, and maybe I can convince them they'd be better off going along with you, than knuckling under to Sload Lutcher."

"I would appreciate that, Mr. Hollister. I will gladly pay you for your time..."

"No, no." Hollister held up his hand. "Just call it a helping hand to a neighbor."

It was soon evident that Bradley Hollister's presence was indeed a great help. Threats from Lutcher's minion aside, Charlotte was greeted with skepticism by most of the tobacco farmers, but Hollister was able to overcome their resistance, in most instances.

Many of the tobacco growers had already sold their crop, yet a number had held back, hoping that they would be able to get a better price than that offered by Sload Lutcher. As soon as they got over their initial wariness of a woman, and when Hollister had told them how successful Charlotte had been with her first trip, the majority agreed to let her take their tobacco on consignment.

Very few paid heed to Lutcher's threat of a boycott. One farmer told her, "I lived with enough fear during the damned war. I was afraid of being killed every minute I was awake, so why should I cave in to this kind of pressure? And from a southerner, to boot! You can take my tobacco to peddle, Miss King. If it don't work out, Lutcher ain't the only market for my tobacco in North Carolina."

Within the week Charlotte had her wagon loaded with tobacco, and she prepared to depart early on a Thursday morning. Jimmie had readily agreed to accompany her again. On the eve of her departure she was alone in the house. Jeff was off somewhere; she had not seen him since their mother's death.

She was packing her trunk when she heard a knock on the front door. She opened it to Bradley Hollister. He seemed uneasy about facing her when he stepped into the entryway.

"Charlotte," he began, "I don't know just how to say this..." He broke off with an embarrassed look.

"What is it, Mr. Hollister?"

"It's Jimmie."

"What's wrong? Has something happened to him?" she said in alarm.

"No, no, he's fine. It's just that he can't go along with you."

"He can't? But he said he loved peddling trips."

"He does, he does, and he's real upset that I won't let him go. But something has happened, you see."

She looked at him closely. His face was pink with embarrassment. In a gentle voice she said. "Tell me, Mr. Hollister."

"There's talk going around, dirty talk, I'm sorry to say. Talk about a lad of seventeen going off with an unmarried young woman. People are saying it's a disgrace."

Charlotte gasped. "But that's terrible! Who would tell such lies?" She touched his arm. "Surely you don't believe something like that? Nothing has happened, I swear!"

"Oh, I know that, Charlotte," he hastened to assure her. "You don't have to swear to me. But it's not my believing or disbelieving, but what my neighbors believe. If it was only me, I wouldn't be concerned but . . ."

"I understand, Mr. Hollister." Charlotte patted his arm. "You're worried about Jimmie."

"More about you, Charlotte. A young woman has to be careful her good name ain't besmirched. Jimmie now, he could live it down."

"If I'm your concern, you needn't worry. I care little what people think. If they have dirty minds, that's their problem, not mine."

Hollister was shaking his head from side to side. "But I do care. If me or mine should be the cause of you getting a bad name, I would never forgive myself. The thing is, the way Jimmie's feeling, he just might sneak off to join you anyway. Should he do that, I want your promise you'll send him packing back home."

"You have it, Mr. Hollister." Charlotte worried her lower lip, her mind racing. "I wonder who started such a rumor, especially now that I'm about to go out again. It's been nearly two weeks, and nothing's been said."

Hollister's lips thinned in anger. "It's Lutcher's man, Jenks. After he failed to discourage the farmers from dealing with you, he went around telling people what a shame it was, a young woman such as yourself and a lad of Jimmie's age traveling together. I thought of loading that old rifle of Jimmie's and go looking for him, but I ain't so good with a rifle anymore, what with this and all . . ." He nodded to indicate his missing arm. "I'm only half a man nowadays."

"You're more of a man than most I know," she said quickly. She reached out to touch his one arm. "But it's better this way, Mr. Hollister. To look for Jenks with a rifle would only make it worse. I *am* sorry that I've gotten your family involved in this. Tell Jimmie that for me, will you?"

"I will, Charlotte. And don't you be fretting about me and mine, we'll survive. Are you . . ." He hesitated. "Are you still going ahead with your trip?"

"I most certainly am," she said strongly. "Nothing that Sload Lutcher can do will stop me."

And yet, after Hollister was gone, Charlotte was not so confident. She remembered the many war derelicts she had seen on the roads; a lone woman with a wagon loaded with tobacco and trade goods would be easy prey for them. For a moment she toyed with the idea of asking Jeff to accompany her, but she discarded the notion. She had set the future in motion, and she was determined to plow ahead.

She remembered an ancient pistol Gardner King had kept around the house, and went looking for it. She finally came across it in a trunk in the attic. It was a Collier's flintlock five-shooter, made in 1810. Charlotte knew little of guns; she had always been afraid of them. But when the war broke out, her father had taught her how to load and fire the flintlock pistol, as a protection in the event she ever had need of it. At least she had learned how to handle it, in a rudimentary fashion.

She gripped the pistol in both hands, aiming it at the wall. Rage welled up in her, as she closed her eyes and Lutcher's sneering face swam across her vision. She had always doubted that she could fire the pistol at anyone, but now she knew that she would gladly kill Lutcher. What a despicable thing he had done, spreading a filthy rumor like that!

Poor Jimmie! He would probably never speak to her again.

She lowered the pistol and went downstairs to finish packing.

When she left early the next morning, the pistol was on the seat beside her, ready to fire. She carefully arranged a fold of her skirt to conceal it.

It was just dawn as she pulled the wagon out onto the road. The morning was quite chilly, and she rode with a shawl pulled tightly around her shoulders.

A mile from home, she heard running footsteps behind the wagon. Tensing, she groped for the pistol, and then relaxed, chiding herself. It was not going to be a pleasant trip if she started jumping at every unusual sound, and the wagon hardly out of sight of the house.

In a moment Jimmie Hollister was trotting alongside her seat. She pulled at the reins, halting the team.

Jimmie had his rifle in his hands. He must have been running all the way from home, since he was breathing hard.

He held the rifle out to her. "Since I can't come along, Miss Charlotte, I thought maybe you'd like to take this along with you, for protection."

"That's sweet of you, Jimmie." She smiled softly. "But you'll need it, to keep the squirrel hordes under control while I'm gone. Besides, I'm taking along an old pistol of Daddy's."

"Miss Charlotte . . ." He gulped, looking away.

"Yes, Jimmie?"

"I'm right sorry about the gossip going around. You know I'd never do . . . do anything to . . ." He stumbled to a halt, his face bright red.

"I know, Jimmie, I know. But it's a hard fact you have to learn, many people in this world have filthy minds. They're willing to believe anything horrid about other people."

Without thinking, she reached down to touch his cheek in a caress. He jumped, and she drew her hand back.

He mumbled, "I wanted to call Jenks out for the lies he's been telling, but Pa wouldn't let me."

"It'll be all right, Jimmie. The best way to handle a thing like this is just to ignore it. If you try to do anything, that would only make people believe it the more."

"But you're going to be all alone, Miss Charlotte!" he said in agony. "It ain't right."

"I'll be fine, Jimmie. Now you go on along home, and don't worry. I'll be back before you know it."

She flicked the reins, and the horses moved out. Jimmie quickened his step to keep pace with the wagon for a few steps, then dropped back with a wave.

An hour later down the road, Charlotte had cause to doubt the confidence she had expressed to Jimmie Hollister. Hearing the hoofbeats of a galloping horse behind the wagon, she paid scant heed, since there was quite a bit of traffic on the road.

But when the overtaking horse loomed alongside, slowing to match the pace of the wagon, she glanced over, startled.

A squat man with a brutish face grinned over at her. "Well now, what's a purty like you doing driving a wagon out here all alone? You should be home, purty, taking care of the needs of some lucky gent!"

His visage had the look of an ape, and the backs of his hands were matted with black hairs. Recalling a vague description she had heard, Charlotte knew who the man was.

"You're Cob Jenks, aren't you? Sload Lutcher's hired thug?"

He looked startled, then scowled darkly. "I work for Mr. Lutcher, sure, but I ain't no thug!"

"That's *exactly* what you are, from what I've been told. And you're the man who has been spreading filthy lies about me and Jimmie Hollister."

His grin was ugly. "Well now, I wouldn't be calling them lies. What else would a purty like you be doing riding around the country with a strapping lad?" He leered. "The lad good between the blankets, is he?"

"You, sir, are a foul-mouthed scoundrel!" she said in a furious whisper.

"Just telling the truth as I see it. The thing is, I don't know why you bother with a lad when there's a man around such as myself." He nudged his horse closer. "So why don't you step down from this here wagon, and I'll show you what it's like to be with a real man?"

Charlotte's hand closed around the pistol on the seat beside her. As Jenks leaned closer, she brought the ancient pistol up and around, cocking it.

"Stand away, sir!" She thrust the pistol at him, the muzzle inches from his nose.

Jenks went pale, staring wide-eyed at the pistol. He said nervously, "Careful with that thing, lady! It looks old enough to blow apart and send us both to Kingdom Come!"

"I would gladly take that risk, before I'd let you lay a hand on me. And don't delude yourself, Mr. Jenks, I know how to use it and will do so." She thrust the pistol closer. "Now turn your horse and ride off at once. If I see you anywhere near my wagon again, I will not hesitate to kill you."

Jenks held up his hands. "All right, purty, all right!" He sneered. "But you won't always be having that cannon handy. I'll catch you without it, and then we shall see what we shall see!"

He reined his horse around, and Charlotte waited tensely until she heard the sound of galloping hoofbeats fade into the distance. Then she went weak with relief, voicing a prayer of thanksgiving that she had had enough foresight to bring the pistol along.

She drew the horses to a complete halt and sat huddled up for a moment, shivering. Cob Jenks was an evil man, a perfect cohort of Lutcher's, capable of anything. For a little she contemplated abandoning the trip. If she was going to have to be on guard every minute, how could she hope to accomplish anything?

Then she sat up, gathering herself in determination. His purpose had probably been to discourage her, but he would not succeed! She had driven him off this time, she could do it again, if necessary.

She flicked the reins, and drove on.

Charlotte gradually relaxed over the next several days, for she was not bothered again. She concluded that Jenks, like most bullies, was a craven coward underneath all the bluster; he would leave her alone now, after she had convinced him that she would stand up to him.

One thing that buoyed her spirits was the success of her trip. All the storekeepers she dropped in on were eagerly awaiting her arrival, anxious for her tobacco. They were unable to get tobacco from other sources, and all were looking for her to provide them with the needed product. The first trip had paved the way for her, and she soon realized that she could have disposed of twice as much tobacco. Another thing that was going to speed up her trip was the fact that most of the storekeepers had cash on hand this time, hoarding it in anticipation of her appearance, and she would not have to barter as much as she had before.

It was soon apparent that she would be able to dispose of all the tobacco within a week, which was to the good. The sooner she could return and get another load together, the better.

Consequently, she remained on the road longer hours than she ordinarily would have, peddling each day until after sundown. The one drawback to this was that she was not always able to find a decent place to camp before darkness fell.

One day she found herself on the road long after dark, searching vainly for a place to camp. She was somewhere in South Carolina, and she seemed to recall, from her first trip down this same road, that a stream was somewhere just up ahead. But after it became full dark, nothing looked at all familiar, and she finally decided to spend the night by the side of the road as soon as she spotted a place to pull off.

She sat up at the sound of hoofbeats behind the wagon. Since nothing had happened after the encounter with Jenks, she had ceased carrying the pistol on the seat beside her. She turned about and searched frantically on the floor of the wagon behind the seat.

Just as her fingers closed around the weapon, she felt the wagon shift, and realized that someone had jumped onto the seat. She twisted about quickly, swinging the pistol around. She had time to glimpse a familiar face looming over her—Cob Jenks!

Charlotte cocked the pistol and aimed it at his face. Before she could fire her arm was seized from behind and twisted up. The pistol discharged harmlessly into the air. It was only when her arm was bent cruelly back, causing her to cry out, that she realized that a second man was on the seat. The pain forced her to let go of the pistol, and it fell to the ground.

Jenks laughed. "Well, purty! Not so feisty now, are you? Let's haul her off the damned wagon, Jess." He raised his voice, "Barney! Give us a hand here with the bitch."

There were three men, at least three! Before Charlotte could collect her wits enough to struggle, three pairs of hands were laid on her, and she was jerked off the wagon seat and thrown brutally to the ground. The breath was knocked from her. Immediately she was picked up, and they began dragging her off the road.

"What are you doing?" she managed to gasp out.

Jenks laughed again, a high, screeching sound that caused her nerves to crawl. "You'll soon know, purty. By the time we're finished with you, you'll only want a hole to crawl into and hide, forgetting all about your tobacco!"

She began to struggle then, but it was no use. She did not have a chance against three men. One on each side had her arms in a strong grip, and Jenks was behind her. She felt him hoist her skirts, his hands crawling hungrily over her body.

She opened her mouth, and screamed shrilly. A clout alongside the head dulled her senses, and a callused hand was clamped over her mouth.

# Chapter Five

BEN Ascher had heard that Charlotte King was back in the area again, with a new wagonload of tobacco, and he had been trying to catch up to her for three days.

On this particular day, from the information given him by the last storekeeper, he should be only about an hour behind her. Since he was in a buckboard, Ben calculated that he should be catching up to her at any time; yet when full night came on, he still had not seen her wagon.

He kept on going, bent on overtaking her, keeping his horse down to a walk. There was a moon, but the night was cloudy, and it was difficult to see very far ahead.

It had been a long day, and he was drowsing in the seat when he was jolted into awareness, as his horse snorted and reared in the traces. Instantly alert, Ben pulled back on the reins, drawing the buckboard to a halt.

He could see a covered wagon directly in front of him, stopped in the middle of the road. A sense of danger set his nerves to humming. Now he saw three saddled horses tied to the wagon, yet there was no sign of the riders. The wagon looked like Charlotte's, but where was she? And who, and where, were the riders belonging to the horses?

Ben tied the reins off, and prepared to get down, then froze as a scream came from a stand of trees off to the right. Quickly, he reached for the Colt he kept holstered in the boot, and scrambled down to the ground.

As he paused for a moment to get his bearings, the scream came again, muffled this time. Colt in his hand,

Ben started in the direction of the sound. He wanted to rush headlong, but he held back, knowing there were three men. He would be of no help to Charlotte if he blundered foolishly into an ambush.

He stepped off the road and into the trees. He could hear scuffling sounds now. Then a voice roared, "God-damnit, Jess, can't the pair of you hold the bitch still whilst I get my breeches down?"

Ben crept up behind a tree. He peered around it, just as the moon broke through the clouds. His breath caught at what he saw. Charlotte was spread-eagled on the ground, a man on each side of her, trying to hold her still. Another kneeled between her spread thighs. Charlotte's dress was up around her waist, and her legs gleamed white against the dark ground.

Anger raged through Ben. Disregarding further caution, he stepped out from behind the tree, the pistol held in both hands.

"Hold it right there! I'll blow the head off the first man who moves a muscle!"

The three men froze in position, gaping around at him. Ben moved closer, making sure they saw the Colt.

One man holding Charlotte let her go, and bolted to his feet, one hand diving under his coat. Ben fired, the bullet kicking up dirt between the man's feet.

He said harshly, "The next one will be fatal. That is the only warning shot I'll fire. Now . . . All of you on your feet."

The pair still on the ground got slowly to their feet. Ben noted that the one who had been kneeling before Charlotte was an ugly fellow, with hirsute hands and face. Ben surmised that he was their leader.

"You there!" Ben pointed the pistol at him. "Take your gun out of your belt and drop it onto the ground."

"Look, stranger, this is no affair of yours," the man said in a raspy voice. "What are you doing butting in?"

"I'm making it my affair. Now do what I tell you, or I'll lodge a bullet in your leg, and you'll have to crawl away."

Hastily, the man fumbled at his belt and dropped his weapon into the dirt.

Ben motioned with the Colt. "You two, do the same, and hurry it up. My patience is running out."

When all three pistols had hit the ground, Ben motioned again with the Colt. "I saw three horses tied out there. All of you just back away toward the road. Then mount up and ride off. If I don't hear the hoofbeats of three horses by the time I count to one hundred, I have five bullets left, and you can believe me when I tell you that I am a good shot!"

Two of the men backed away at once, but the hairy man lingered. "Listen, mister . . ." He motioned. "How about our guns? It's not safe to ride about unarmed these days."

Ben grinned unpleasantly. "The weapons stay with me. Call it the spoils of war. Now move!"

The man departed reluctantly. Ben risked a glance over at Charlotte; she lay without moving, and he supposed that she had fainted. He longed to comfort her, but he did not dare until he was sure the three hardcases had left. He did stoop to pull her dress down, then moved quickly into the trees near the road. He waited tensely. In a minute he heard saddle leather creak, and the sound of hoofbeats heading north. He made himself wait until he could no longer hear them before he hurried back to Charlotte.

As he knelt beside her, Charlotte stirred, moaning. Ben put a hand under her head and raised it. "Miss King, are you all right?"

She opened her eyes, but stared at him without recognition, and he said quickly, "They're gone, Miss King. I'm Ben Ascher, remember me?"

"Mr. Ascher?" She paused, closing her eyes for a moment, then opening them again. "Yes, I remember you. You say they're gone? Thank God! And thank God you arrived when you did!"

"You *are* all right?" he asked anxiously. "They didn't . . ."

"No, you arrived in time," she said faintly. "Only my dignity and pride are injured."

"The lad I saw with you before . . . Did they do something to him?"

"He didn't come with me, I'm alone."

"That wasn't wise, Miss King," he said severely. "There are many rough and desperate men roaming these roads at night. Like those three."

"I had no choice in the matter, and it was not by chance that those three attacked me. I know the man who is their leader, a man by the name of Cob Jenks. He's from Durham."

"You know him?" Ben said in astonishment. "You mean he followed you on purpose?"

"Yes . . . Mr. Ascher, it's a long story, and I'd be happy to tell it to you, but could it wait until we set up camp? You are . . ." In a sudden burst of panic, she clutched at his hand. "You will share my camp for the night? I don't know what I'd do if they came back." She shuddered.

"I wouldn't dream of leaving you alone tonight," he said reassuringly. "I am quite familiar with this road. About a mile along is a stream and a small glade, a fine place to camp for the night. I'll lead the way in my buckboard, Miss King."

After helping Charlotte to her wagon, Ben returned to the buckboard, then pulled around her and led the way to the spot he remembered. When Charlotte had halted her wagon behind him, he unhitched her team and his own horse, while Charlotte unloaded food and cooking utensils from the wagon. Ben filled three buckets with oats from his own supply, and tied the horses off, leaving them happily munching. Then he gathered wood and quickly made a fire.

He said, "Do you feel up to making supper, or should I? I've learned to be a pretty good cook during all my travels."

In the firelight her smile was wan. "No, I'll do it, Mr. Ascher. It'll give me something to do to keep my mind off what just happened."

As Charlotte made coffee, a pan of cornbread, and heated up a kettle of leftover stew from the night before, Ben, sensing that she was not yet ready to talk of the night's events, made idle conversation. "From what I hear, you've been quite successful with your tobacco peddling."

This time, her smile was more robust. "Yes, thanks to you."

"Now what did I have to do with it?" he inquired.

"That little bit of advice you gave me on my first trip was a great help. It made that trip a success, and this one promises to be even better. Save for your advice, I would have failed miserably, I'm sure."

Ben was a touch embarrassed. "What I did was nothing more than anyone would do."

"That's not true, Mr. Ascher. I represent competition for you, and many people would go out of their way to keep from helping competition. Here, let me have your plate." Ben held out his tin plate, and Charlotte dished out the stew. "I hope you don't mind reheated stew."

"I don't mind in the least." He took a few bites. "This is excellent, and the cornbread as well."

They were silent for a little as they ate hungrily. Ben noted that Charlotte's spirits had revived somewhat. She was a strong woman, he realized; it would take more than an assault from three thugs to discourage her.

"I must admit to some curiosity, Miss King. How is it that a woman like you is out here peddling tobacco?"

"A woman like me?" She looked at him intently.

He flushed. "What I meant was, why would *any* woman do such a thing? Also, you are obviously a young woman of some refinement, and I thought..." Flustered, he laughed. "I'm getting in deeper, aren't I? But it is unusual, in these times, for a woman to go peddling from store to store."

"In a way, it was forced on me, Mr. Ascher..."

"Please." He held up a hand. "Can't we make it Ben?"

"All right, Ben. If you will call me Charlotte. I would think that the favors you've done for me entitle you to that."

Ben smiled. "I accept the bargain. Now, please forgive the interruption, and continue your story."

Beginning with the death of her father and the hidden cache of tobacco, Charlotte told him everything that had happened to her. It was the first time she had told the story to anyone, and the telling was a sort of catharsis. She felt relieved of a great burden when she was finished.

Ben said thoughtfully, "This Lutcher sounds like a proper scoundrel. You really believe that he sent his man Jenks and the others after you?"

"I'm convinced of it. There would be no other reason for Jenks to follow me. There is certainly no doubt that he spread those filthy rumors about Jimmie Hollister and myself."

"Lutcher must be a man obsessed to go to such lengths."

Charlotte's smile was rueful. "I suppose I made a mistake, in saying the things I did to him. But I don't regret them. Every word I said was true! But aside from that, Sload Lutcher is fearful that if I succeed in my plan, other tobacco growers will sell to me, and leave him without tobacco for his factory. I can only hope . . ." She shivered suddenly. "I hope that you discouraged those men tonight, and they won't come back."

He leaned across to take her hand. "You're not going on alone, Charlotte, I've made up my mind to that. Until you've sold all your tobacco, I intend to tag along."

Charlotte stared at his hand holding hers. It set up a tumult of feeling inside her, and she thought of removing his hand, then concluded that it might be making too much of a friendly gesture.

"I can't allow you to do that, you'll likely lose money traveling with me." She added hastily, "Not that I don't appreciate the offer, it's very kind of you."

"I have no set route. Most of the storekeepers you'll be seeing are my customers as well. This way, I'll combine business with pleasure, and it *will* be my pleasure, I assure you, Charlotte." His smile was touched by tenderness, and his eyes glowed warmly.

Thrown even more into confusion, Charlotte jumped to

her feet. "Well, it's been a long, hard day, and one I'd just as soon forget. I'll clean up the dishes, and get to bed."

Ben also got up, and began helping her. When they were done, and Ben had kicked dirt over the fire to put it out, Charlotte went to her wagon to make her bed.

Ben said, "I'll put my blankets under the wagon, Charlotte. I'll be close at hand, my gun by my side. I'm a light sleeper. I've learned to do that during the past few years on the road. It's saved my life a number of times."

Charlotte climbed up onto the wagon bed. "Good night, Ben, and thank you again." Her face was luminous in a splash of moonlight.

"Good night, Charlotte," he said softly.

Charlotte undressed quickly and slipped between the blankets. It was indeed comforting to know that a man slept beneath the wagon, within easy calling distance. It gave her a feeling of security she had not known since the death of her father. He was a very capable man, Ben Ascher, in full command of himself. She thought warmly of the way he had handled the three toughs . . .

She forced her thoughts away from that episode, determined not to think of Jenks and his companions.

Yet, when she went to sleep, her slumber was troubled, broken by nightmares.

Ben was indeed a light sleeper, but he was also usually able to go to sleep immediately when he bedded down. Tonight, he was having trouble. He was uncomfortably and acutely aware of the presence of Charlotte King only a few feet above his head, and his thoughts lingered on that moment by the fire when he had captured her hand. When they had touched, a current of heat had passed from her hand to his, like a small flame leaping at the addition of fuel.

Charlotte was a lovely woman, warm and outgoing, and Ben knew that his first feeling had been true—he was in love with her. Love at first sight was a concept he had often heard about, but never truly believed in. Now he knew that it could indeed happen.

At last he drifted into sleep, only to be awakened abruptly by a scream from the wagon. Instantly he threw the blankets back, his hand groping for the Colt. He came out from under the wagon in a ready crouch, all his senses alert for danger; yet he saw nothing untoward as his glance raked the area. There were no men, no horses in sight.

Quickly, he climbed up onto the wagon seat, parted the canvas, and peered inside. A wash of moonlight fell across Charlotte on her blankets. As he watched, she moaned and struck out with one arm. It was obvious she was dreaming.

After a moment's hesitation, Ben got into the wagon bed, leaving his gun on the seat. He took her hands between his, and softly called her name.

Her eyes opened slowly, looking up into his face. "It's all right, Charlotte," he said soothingly. "You were just having a bad dream."

"Ben," she murmured, clutching at his hands, as if seeking comfort from him; and she drew him down to her. After a moment's resistance, he lifted the blanket and stretched out beside her.

Halfway between sleep and wakefulness, Charlotte snuggled against him, pillowing her head on his shoulder. She was warm from sleep, her body incredibly soft in his arms, and Ben wanted her with an ache that was beyond pain.

I would be the worst kind of a cad, he thought, to take advantage of her now.

Yet, in a short while, she moved again, her head rolling along his shoulder, and her hair fell like a soft, scented veil across his face. Her parted lips were close to his, her breath warm on his cheek. Swept by a desire so powerful that it drove everything else from his mind, he put his mouth to hers, gently at first, prepared to draw back instantly if she resisted. There was no resistance, and his kiss grew steadily more demanding. Charlotte was passive at first, but soon she was returning the kiss with an ardor that matched his.

Unable to stop himself, his hands moved over her body, molding the soft curves of her figure through the flimsiness of her night garment.

When she first felt Ben's lips on hers, Charlotte was still half asleep; and thought she was dreaming again, a nice dream this time, for there was nothing frightening or threatening about it. On the contrary, it was pleasant, extremely so. As her blood warmed to the gentle caresses, a wanting began in her, a wanting she had often experienced during the years since adolescence that had never been gratified.

Feeling Ben's arms gently holding her, feeling his tender touch, was such a marked contrast to the brutal treatment at the hands of Jenks and his cohorts that Charlotte welcomed it. Somewhere in the back of her mind, she knew that what would happen soon would offer surcease from the frequent and tormented urgings of her body. There was no thought of right or wrong, it seemed the most natural thing in the world.

She moaned in Ben's arms, tossing and turning, her body aflame with a fierce need. Her nightgown was up now, and his hands were on her flesh. She muttered, "Nice, oh so nice!"

As his knuckles lightly brushed her inner thigh, she arched against him. Instinctively, she reached down with exploring fingers, and found the throbbing rigidity of his manhood through his breeches.

Ben groaned, and moved back far enough to unbutton his breeches. Then he was back. Charlotte welcomed him with a muted cry. As he went into her, she felt a sharp stab of pain, quickly gone in a rush of pleasure. She put her arms around him, her hands stroking his back, feeling the movement of powerful muscles there.

The sensations aroused by his continued thrustings were new to her, and she shivered under the assault on her senses, finally managing to adjust to his quickening rhythm.

Bright lights danced behind her eyelids as they sped

together toward the final moment of rapture. A spasm seized her, and at the same instant Ben moaned, shuddering.

As the fury of feeling slowly subsided, for a time out of time, Charlotte drifted in a pleasurable daze, holding Ben close to her.

Then slowly awareness returned, and sanity, and she fully realized what she had done. According to all that she had been taught, what she had done—what *they* had done—was very wrong.

Yet, if what they had done was so bad, why did she feel so good? Her mind still full of the events that had just transpired, reliving again the riot of feelings that had just turned her world upside down, Charlotte wanted to laugh aloud and stretch like a contented cat, but something warned her not to reveal what she felt to Ben.

She moved slightly, murmuring, and Ben, accepting this for the hint that it was, slipped away to lie beside her. His mind, as well, was a battleground of conflicting emotions. He felt that he should apologize for something, yet he was not sure what, and also he had the feeling that to do so would cheapen what had happened. He knew now, with a sureness that had only been strengthened by their love-making, that he was hopelessly in love with her. He wanted to tell her of his feelings, but his fear that it was too soon inhibited him.

In the end, he said nothing. He adjusted his clothing, and leaned over to kiss her lightly—a kiss remarkably chaste after what had transpired, yet tender for all that.

He murmured, "Good night, Charlotte. Hopefully, you can sleep without dreaming now."

Charlotte, drowsy now, only spoke his name, softly. And after he was gone, she did sleep. The nightmares did not return.

The next morning, as though by mutual, unspoken consent, both behaved as if the events of the night had not happened.

After a quick breakfast, Ben harnessed Charlotte's wagon, and then his buckboard. "Charlotte, I'll follow behind you in my buckboard. That way you can set the pace, and Jenks won't be able to sneak up on your wagon from behind."

"Mr. Ascher . . . Ben, you sure I'm not inconveniencing you? I feel fairly certain that you frightened Jenks off for good. He's probably halfway back to Durham by now."

"I'm not as sure about that as you." His gaze grew intent. "Are you trying to get rid of me? Last night, you seemed happy to have my company for the rest of your journey."

"No, no, I'm not trying to get rid of you." Charlotte felt her color rise. "If you're sure I won't be holding you back, I'm happy for your company."

"You won't be holding me back," he said gravely.

As her wagon moved out, Charlotte's thoughts were on the man behind her. Despite her admitted enjoyment of last night—and she *had* enjoyed it, even now the thought of it made her cheeks flame and her body kindle—she was determined that it would not happen again.

It was not that she felt particularly guilty, nor did she feel like a scarlet woman, as older women of her acquaintance had always whispered was the way a woman should feel from such sinful activity. It was simply that an emotional entanglement with Ben Ascher at this time represented a threat to her independence, to her determination to pull herself up from the poverty left by the war and make something of herself.

Her experience with men was limited, yet she sensed that Ben was not the kind of man to take what had happened between them lightly; he might ask for, or at least expect, a commitment; and she was not ready for that.

From now on, she would be careful to keep a distance between them.

Shortly after the noon hour, they pulled up before a country store, the first stop of the day.

As the wagon stopped, Charlotte noticed a man lounging against the store, smoking a thin cheroot. A planter's hat shadowed his face, but now he straightened up, tipping his hat back. There was something hauntingly familiar about him, but she could not quite put her finger on it.

By now Ben had drawn his buckboard up beside her wagon. He jumped down to give her a hand, and they started into the store.

He halted as they drew abreast of the man with the cigar. "Clint! This is an unexpected pleasure!" There was a friendly warmth in Ben's voice.

"Hello, Ben," the man drawled. "How's the traveling store man?"

"I'd like you to meet a friend of mine," Ben said. "Charlotte King, this is Clint Devlin. Clint is a cotton buyer."

"How do, Miss King." Clint Devlin grinned lazily, and then Charlotte remembered him.

"I didn't recognize you, Mr. Devlin, with all your clothes on," she said icily. The words just slipped out, and she was suddenly horribly embarrassed. Whatever would Ben think?

She stole a glance at him, and saw his baffled look.

He said slowly, "I don't understand . . ."

"Oh, Miss King and I have met. In a manner of speaking," Clint said gravely. "But we were not what you might call formally introduced."

He was an infuriating man, Charlotte thought. Again, she spoke without thinking. "Where is your lady friend, Mr. Devlin?"

His eyes mocked her. "She was more of a traveling companion than a lady friend, Miss King. At the moment, I'm traveling alone."

At the mention of a lady friend, Ben seemed to relax a trifle. "That, Charlotte, is a rather unusual situation, you must realize. I am hard put to recall a time when Clint was without an . . . uh, 'traveling companion.' "

Clint laughed, still staring into Charlotte's eyes. "We all fall onto hard times, Benbo. Even me. But tell me, how come you are in the company of a lady?" His glance took in the buckboard and wagon. "You seem to be traveling together."

"Miss King is on the road peddling tobacco," Ben said coolly. "She was set upon by some ruffians last night, and I was lucky enough to happen along in time to come to her aid."

Clint's gaze moved back to Charlotte. "Lucky indeed."

The implication of his remark mortified Charlotte, and she said angrily, "I am very grateful to Mr. Ascher. He was gallant enough to rescue me from a nasty situation, and has consented to accompany me for the remainder of my trip."

Clint said dryly, "If you happen to ever be in need of another gallant, I am always available."

Charlotte, annoyed by Devlin's arrogant manner, gave him a cold stare, and swept past him, and into the store.

Ben did not mention Clint Devlin again until they made camp that evening. Charlotte had been uncommunicative all day, angry with Clint Devlin, even angrier with herself. If Devlin had such thoughts about Ben traveling along with her, how many others might think the same? And, her face grew hot at the thought, with some reason! She must part company with Ben, yet hesitated for two reasons. First, it would be rude, after what he had done for her; second, although she did not wish to admit it, even to herself, there was still a lingering dread that Jenks and his two toughs might yet be lurking about, waiting to find her alone again.

As they ate their meal, Ben said, "I wouldn't take Clint Devlin's remarks too much to heart, Charlotte. Clint loves to josh people. Also, he's a confirmed cynic, and tends to attribute his own often roguish motives to everyone else. How did you happen to meet him, anyway?"

"Oh, we camped close together one night," she said in an offhand manner. "We met inadvertently, without ever being introduced." She took a sip of coffee. "If Devlin believes the worst, what will other people think?"

He said dryly, "What has happened to the Charlotte King who defied the gossips of Durham?"

She flushed, uncomfortable under his probing gaze. "*That* gossip was about a young lad. Only people with dirty minds believed that."

"Charlotte, the people you contact out here aren't your neighbors. They're only interested in doing business with you, and have no interest whatsoever in your private life."

She began refilling his plate. "Well, at least one more day will see me done, all my tobacco sold," she said with satisfaction. "Then I can turn toward home, and you can go your own way, Ben."

"Trying to get rid of me again?"

She answered too quickly, "No, of course not. But I feel guilty about interfering with your business."

"You're not going to get rid of me that easily. You seem to have forgotten Jenks. He could still be out there. No, my dear Charlotte, I'm remaining with you until I see you home safely to Durham."

"I can't have you doing that, Ben!" she said in dismay. "You have your own business to tend."

"Are you worried about that, or worried about what your neighbors might think if you come back home with a man in attendance?" he said shrewdly. "As for interfering with my business, I've been thinking about expanding my territory, and Durham would be a good place to start." His eyes twinkled at her across the fire. "Especially now that I know someone there."

Charlotte was silent, devoting herself to eating. Ben Ascher was persistent, that was for sure. In truth, she was just as glad that he would be accompanying her all the way home, especially since she would be carrying about a thousand dollars, and much of that money belonged to the tobacco farmers. If Jenks were to waylay her on the way home and rob her, there was no way she could face the farmers who had trusted her.

At the same time, she dreaded the moment when it came time to go to bed tonight. What if he insisted on . . .? She felt her face grow hot again. Was she worried about him, or about herself? Would she have the strength to say no, with the memory of last night still in her mind?

How can I expect to fend him off, she thought with a twist of amusement, since he is a man, and much stronger than I am?

Somewhat to her consternation, there was no need to fend him off. When it came time to retire to the wagon, Ben said merely, "Good night, dear Charlotte. Sleep well."

He helped her into the wagon, turned his back on her, and returned to the fire and a final cup of coffee. Charlotte peered from the wagon as he squatted by the fire. Hadn't he enjoyed last night? She realized that she was hurt by his off-hand manner. It was a woman's place to spurn the man, not the other way around!

She had to laugh at her pique, yet she was still nettled when she got into her blankets.

Ben, in his blankets under the wagon, lay awake for a long time, acutely aware of Charlotte's nearness. He knew that it would be a mistake to push himself on her tonight, especially without some indication that he would be welcomed, and he had received no such indication from Charlotte.

By nature Ben was a patient man. He had found the old axiom, "Everything comes to him who waits," to be applicable in most situations. True, he had never had occasion to apply it in a romantic relationship; but since he wanted any relationship with Charlotte King to be long-lasting, he deemed it wise to exercise patience.

Unfortunately for his peace of mind on this night, logic did not appease his physical urges, and he waited in wakefulness for Charlotte to cry out again in her sleep, so that he might have an excuse to go to her.

The cry never came.

The last of Charlotte's tobacco was disposed of the next day, and she turned the wagon toward Durham. She did not again try to dissuade Ben from accompanying her, for she did feel more secure with him along.

Their days went by pleasantly enough, but they were wary of each other in the evenings before bedtime, each careful not to say the wrong word. They did not again share the same blankets.

There had been no further sign of Cob Jenks and his men, and Charlotte had almost forgotten about him as she drove the wagon up before the King house.

Then, as she reined the team in, Jenks stepped out onto the porch. Charlotte went cold with dread. Then anger surged in her. How dare he have the effrontery to be on her property, in *her* house!

Ben came hurrying up to give her a hand down. In a low voice he said, "It's all right, Charlotte. I'll handle it." He closed his hand around the Colt in his belt. "You stay back while I talk to him . . ."

"No. He has no right here!"

She thrust his staying hand away and stepped toward the porch. "What are you doing on my property, sir? I demand that you leave at once!"

Jenks leaned against the porch pillar, grinning insolently.

Ben stepped up beside her. "I suggest you do as she asks, Jenks. This is her property, and you are trespassing."

Jenks straightened up. "It ain't your property any longer, purty."

"What are you talking about?" Charlotte said in confusion. "Where is my brother?"

Jenks shrugged. "Last I heard, he was in Durham. As for what I'm talking about, your brother sold this place, lock, stock, and barrel, to Mr. Lutcher. Here"—he took a piece from his pocket and waved it—"is the bill of sale. All legal and proper."

"I don't believe you!" Charlotte said angrily.

"Well now, purty, the name scrawled across the bottom is . . ." Jenks made an elaborate show of unfolding and reading the paper. "The name here is Jefferson King. That's your brother, now ain't it?"

Charlotte said tightly, "If his name is on there, he must have been forced to sign!"

Jenks laughed coarsely. "The only thing forcing him to

sign was all that money he owed for liquor, doxies, and gambling. Mr. Lutcher had to pay his debts..." He glanced at the bill of sale again. "Plus a thousand dollars in cash, it says here." His swarthy features took on a mean look. "So it's you two who's trespassing. This here property now belongs to Mr. Lutcher, and that includes everything in the house. Count yourself lucky I don't take that wagon and team as well."

Charlotte's head came up in defiance. "This is my home, you'll have to throw me off!"

Jenks growled, "I can do that, if need be." He raised his voice. "Fellers, come on out here!"

Two men came from the house to stand alongside him. They carried rifles cradled across their arms.

Ben touched her shoulder. "Charlotte, we can do nothing here. Let's go into town and consult an attorney as to your rights in the matter."

Charlotte allowed herself to be led away. On the wagon seat, as she drove away from her home of twenty-two years, she was blinded by tears of despair.

# Chapter Six

JEFF King, barefoot and wearing only a pair of breeches, sat in the frayed chair in the shabby hotel room, a glass of bourbon in his hand. He stared unseeingly at the wall, trying not to think.

He started as a bold knock sounded on the door, and his hand jerked, setting the liquor to sloshing in his glass. Placing the glass on the floor, he got up and limped unsteadily to the door.

A buxom, heavily painted woman stood in the doorway. "You Jefferson King?" At his nod, she said, "I'm May. Cob Jenks sent me."

His glance lingered on the snowy swell of bosom showing above her low-cut gown. "Come in, May."

She swished past him as he stepped aside. Her scent was heavy, cloying. Jeff closed the door and threw the bolt.

As he turned toward her, May was already at the narrow bed, shucking her dress. She wore very little beneath the dress, and she was bare within seconds. She gave him a seductive, up-and-under look, and lay back on the bed. She beckoned. "I'm ready, love."

Jeff removed his breeches and got onto the bed with her, hoping for a time of forgetfulness. He was not even sure that he could function—he had been drinking all afternoon. But May had the erotic skill to arouse him sufficiently, and soon he was between her raised thighs and inside her.

As he thrust into her, May crooned, "That's it, love! Ah, you're a real man, not like too many I know. Quickly now, quickly! That's it!"

Jeff attained his brief spasm of pleasure, all too soon, and she briskly disengaged herself and began getting into her clothes.

He lay sprawled on the bed, watching her. That's the trouble with a professional, he thought; it's over and done so quickly. With another woman he might have been able to lose himself for a long time; but what woman would have him, a cripple, without being paid?

He thought of asking May to spend the night, but now that his weak lust had been appeased, he was filled with disgust, not only with her—caked with flaking powder and rouge, awash with that heavy perfume—but with himself as well.

As she wriggled into her dress and turned to go, Jeff sat up. "The money, it's on the dresser against the wall."

"You don't have to pay me, love." She turned a false smile on him. "Cob Jenks, he's paid me already. He said you could think of it as a bonus, whatever that means."

Jeff choked back a bitter laugh. A bonus! Thirty pieces of silver paid to Judas! He had betrayed his own sister, and now a Judas payment—a gift of a harlot—made it complete.

When the door had closed behind May, Jeff got up, put on his trousers, poured himself a glass of bourbon, and pulled the room's one chair up before the window.

He sat, sipping bourbon, staring down as darkness spread across the streets of Durham.

Jeff knew that the things he had done since returning home were wrong, but he could not seem to help himself. He blamed it on the war. If the South had been victorious, he may have emerged intact, but as it was, his very soul was scarred beyond redemption.

He had fought against it, fought against the seduction of Lutcher's money, but the only time he felt a whole man again was when he was full of liquor and with a woman; or when he sat across a poker table with cards in his hand.

The money before him, Lutcher's money, gave him an equal status with the other men in the game. But Jeff had never been a good poker player, and the liquor in him made him even less a one, and he lost steadily. However, there was always the hope that the next game would start a run of luck, and he would win big, thus able to go to Charlotte with all his pockets stuffed with money, and she would be proud of him.

It was his due! He pounded on the arm of the chair in frustration and drank. He had been through almost four years of hell; it was not fitting that he should come home to grub in the dirt like a common field hand. He deserved more than that.

While Charlotte was away the first time, he had borrowed the seven hundred dollars from Sload Lutcher for liquor and pleasure with women. He had been sure that he could win enough at poker to repay the loan; but his luck had been bad, and he had lost what money he had left.

He had felt terrible about Charlotte having to pay the money back out of her own earnings. He had tried to tell her so, but she would not listen.

Realizing that she had been upset about their mother's death, he had forgiven her for that. The day after she left on the second trip, Jeff had gone to Lutcher and borrowed money again, sure that his poker luck would turn. He had lost the thousand he borrowed in one night. When he returned to the money-lender for more, Lutcher had told him that the only way he, Jeff, could get more money was by the sale of the King farm. Lutcher would consider the debt canceled, and would add another thousand dollars, in exchange for Jeff's signature on a bill of sale for the property.

Jeff had finally agreed, rationalizing that the farm was worthless anyway. With another thousand dollars he could recoup his losses and set Charlotte up in style in Durham; a farm was no place for a woman of Charlotte's breeding. If it was left up to her, she would waste away her life on that farm. He was doing her a favor!

But his fine plans had failed, again. The question was, what was he to do now? He had about fifty dollars left, hardly enough to buy meals and pay his hotel bill for a week.

A thought edged into his mind. Charlotte would be returning any day now. If this trip had been as successful as the first one, she would have money. After she had a few days to absorb the shock about the sale of the farm, and get over her initial anger, perhaps he could approach her . . .

No! He thumped his thigh with a fist. A man's pride could only bend so much. Besides, this had been the last straw; she would never forgive him for this last betrayal.

Lutcher had hinted that he might find some use for him. Jeff hated to go to the man again, but if he was desperate enough . . .

He drained the last of the bottle, stumbled to the bed, and fell into a drunken slumber.

When Charlotte went to an attorney in Durham, Ben accompanied her. Ralph Chambers was in his sixties, and had practiced law in Durham for most of his life. He was respected, fully competent, and Charlotte's father had used his services on those few occasions when he needed legal advice.

A plump man, with a fleshy face, jowls hanging like dewlaps on a hound dog, Chambers always wore a gloomy expression, and it got even more morose after Charlotte had related her tale of woe. With a sigh he said, "Miss King, there isn't much to be done, as I see it. Certainly you can take both your brother and this Sload Lutcher into court, but in my opinion, it would cost you a great deal of money, and in the end you would emerge with nothing."

Charlotte cried, "But I must have some rights!"

"I fear not, Miss King. Historically, the eldest son is considered the proper heir. Your brother was perfectly within his rights in selling the King farm. Do not misunderstand, I think both he and Lutcher are contemptible, not considering your wishes in the matter. Unfortunately, morality has no bearing on a legal matter of this nature."

"What you are saying is, women have no legal rights at all," she said bitterly.

"That is all too true, especially as relating to property rights," the attorney said sadly. "Perhaps some day that will change, but in this instance you have little legal recourse. That is only my opinion, of course, and you may wish to consult another attorney on the matter."

"That would be a waste of time, Mr. Chambers, I'm sure. I suppose I realized all this, but I'm so angry that I felt I had to do something." She stirred, getting to her feet. She felt old and weary; even her body felt heavy and unwieldy. "How much do I owe you, sir?"

"Nothing, my dear. I would feel like the worst kind of a cad, charging you for such disheartening advice." He also got to his feet. "If I can ever be of service again, please do not hesitate to call upon me. I was an admirer of your father. Gardner King was a fine man, so different from . . ." He broke off, embarrassed.

". . . so different from his son," Charlotte said dourly. "Thank you again, Mr. Chambers."

Ben took her arm, and they left the attorney's office. It was mid-afternoon, and the winter sun was unusually warm. Charlotte looked about dazedly, and stopped, her face turned up to the sun.

"I just realized," she said slowly, "it'll soon be Christmas. It's going to be a great Christmas, isn't it, Ben? Momma dead and gone, my own brother turned against me, and my home sold out from under me!"

"Charlotte . . ." Ben touched her arm. "Feeling sorry for yourself? That doesn't sound much like the Charlotte I've come to know."

"Oh, no! I'm not feeling sorry for myself. I'm furious!" she said fiercely. "I've never been so angry in my life. I have to find a way to get even with Sload Lutcher!"

"You're not thinking of something foolish, I hope. I despise this man, whom I've never even met, as much as you do, Charlotte, but so far everything he's done seems legal to me. Except for Jenks' attack on you, and that would be difficult to lay at Lutcher's door."

"I'm not thinking of anything illegal, Ben. I want to defeat him at his own game. I don't think I ever told you, but I've had a dream, since the war ended, and even before. I want to start up a tobacco factory in Durham, manufacture my own product like Lutcher is doing. I'm convinced that the tobacco industry is about to grow into something big."

Ben looked at her in speculation, scrubbing his knuckles across his chin. "You can still do that."

"How? I had in the back of my mind to either mortgage the farm, or sell it, for enough to lease a building here in Durham, and for enough to at least begin production. Now I no longer have the farm. It would take forever to save up enough money peddling tobacco. By that time, it would probably be too late."

"There still might be a way." He looked both ways along the street. "I'm hungry, let's have a bite to eat and talk about it."

He escorted her to a small restaurant in the next block. Charlotte had missed breakfast in her anxiety to talk to the attorney; and in her agitation over his negative news, she was still not hungry.

But in the small, clean cafe, good cooking odors aroused her appetite. Ben ordered for them: fried chicken, cornbread, and hoppin' John—blackeyed peas and rice—and sweet potato pie.

When the food came, Charlotte ate hungrily, only half-listening to Ben. He talked animatedly, telling her for the first time of his life in Charleston, and the reason he had taken to peddling. She wondered why he was telling her all this, finally concluding that he was merely talking to take her mind off her troubles.

But then she suddenly realized that there was a point to his seemingly rambling dialogue, as he finished, "And so I've been looking for an opportunity to get into a sound business, with a good growth potential. I like peddling, but I don't intend to do it for the rest of my life."

She looked at him with interest. "What do you have in mind?"

"Well . . ." He hesitated, uncharacteristically fumbling for words. "I agree with what you said, that the tobacco business is headed for boom times. But to make it pay, it must be done on a large scale, with a good-sized factory, a crew of skilled workers, and several salesmen out in the field."

"That all sounds great, Ben, but . . ." She spread her hands in a hopeless gesture. "I simply do not have the money for all that."

"I well know that, Charlotte," he said soberly, "but what I have in mind is a partnership. I've made quite a bit of money over the past few years. I would be willing to invest in a plant and whatever else we need."

She was shaking her head. "But why do you need me? What can I offer any partnership to equal your investment?" She peered at him in sudden suspicion. "This wouldn't be because you feel sorry for me, would it?"

"No, Charlotte." He laughed. "I like you a lot, a hell of a lot, in fact, but I'm not all that altruistic. I'm unknown here in Durham, and I think Durham is the logical location for such an operation. On the other hand, you're well-known, and you've already gained the respect of the tobacco growers. One valuable contribution you'd be making would be what businessmen call goodwill. Don't worry, Charlotte, you will definitely be an asset to any partnership. I know you well enough to realize your dedication to hard work, your ambition, and drive."

Charlotte stared at him, worrying her low lip. "Somehow, that doesn't seem enough, Ben. It's possible I could earn my way in a partnership. I would most certainly try like the devil. But I have a feeling you're not telling me everything."

"All right, I'll be frank. There is another reason I would need you, if I did this." He looked at her squarely.

"And what is that, Ben?"

"I'm Jewish, and there are a great many people who do not like, or even refuse, to do business with a Jew. With you dealing directly with any business contacts, that problem would not arise."

"I've never heard of anything like that around Durham," she said in astonishment. "There are a number of Jews living here, and I've never heard of any problems."

"They are probably shopkeepers and such like. But everywhere we go, we Jews carry a reputation for being sharp in our business dealings. Undeservedly so, but there it is. Shrewd, my people are, true. Southerners are still wary of dealing with us. On a small scale, there is no problem, such as dealing with shopkeepers. There is also another aspect, having to do with the war. It is said of us that the Jews did not fight, but instead made fortunes from the war. This, again, is untrue. There were some ten thousand Jews who fought for the South in the war, and I don't know of any who made a fortune from it. My own father, for instance, lost everything, including a son. But unfortunately"—his smile had a twist—"I chose not to fight, so if people we were to do business with learned of this . . ." He shrugged.

Recovering from her initial surprise at his proposal, Charlotte found the concept exciting. Her mind was busily considering all aspects of it, but she was cautious enough not to display any strong interest.

"The way you put it, Ben, a partnership sounds fine, but I can see many obstacles, many problems, before we could ever get started."

He smiled slightly. "And I'm sure many more, unforeseen problems will crop up, but if we keep looking toward what *can* be if we're successful, it will be worthwhile."

She laughed. "You're an optimist, Ben Ascher. For instance, you mention cigarette making. Now I fully realize that cigarettes are the coming thing. But cigarettes are new, and so far no company, in or around Durham, has produced hand-made cigarettes. They've stuck to snuff, chewing tobacco, and tobacco for pipe and roll-your-own cigarettes. I understand that hand-rolling cigarettes is something of an art, requiring experienced people. We can find people, men and women both, around Durham for the other jobs, but where would we find workers capable of producing tailor-mades?"

"From New York," Ben said instantly. "Cigarette production is getting into full swing up there. They managed to get the jump on the South because of the war. But again, the South is the logical place for cigarette production, since the tobacco is here."

"But how can we be sure these skilled people would be willing to come down here?"

"They will be quite happy to come," he said emphatically. "They immigrated to this country to escape the ghettos of Europe, and in New York they're living in even worse conditions, living in slums and working long hours for slave wages. Pay them a decent wage, and they'll come in droves, eager to bring their families into decent homes, with plenty of fresh air and open spaces."

"You seem to know an awful lot about them, Ben."

"They're my own people, Charlotte. They're immigrant Jews, coming to America in search of a better life, and so far not finding it."

"You've given this a lot of thought, that's obvious. I thought you'd just begun to think about this whole plan a few days ago."

"About the tobacco business, yes." He nodded, his face grave. "But I've been aware of their plight for some time, and a dream of mine has been to start up some industry that would make use of their talents."

Charlotte smiled, and reached across the table to touch his hand lightly. "Who said you're not altruistic?"

"I'm not, not really. These people are skilled cigarette makers, Charlotte, and their talents will benefit us, as much as it will them." He leaned forward eagerly. "What do you think? Are you willing to give it a try?"

She drew back, wary again. "It's so sudden, so new, I have to think about it. What are your immediate plans, Ben?"

"Well... I have to return to Charleston for more trade

goods. I sold all that I had. Then I will probably come back through here. This is new territory for me, so I think I'll expand my route to cover it."

"By that time I will have made a decision. I'll think about it meanwhile. Is that all right with you?"

"That's fine with me. In fact"—he smiled—"I wouldn't want it any other way. I wouldn't trust a partner who made such an important decision without some thought. What are you going to do meanwhile?"

"First, I have to find a place to stay. There's a rooming house here in town, operated by Widow Carstairs. I'm sure I can rent a room there. Then I have to make the rounds of the tobacco growers, and pay them their money."

"You're not thinking of going out peddling again, are you? Alone?" he said in alarm.

"I may. But if I go, it won't be alone. If Bradley Hollister won't let Jimmie accompany me, maybe I can talk him into going himself. He needs the money."

Ben was frowning. "A one-armed man? He'll be of little help if Jenks comes after you again. I wish you wouldn't go, Charlotte. Or at least wait for me."

"I can't cower in fear of Cob Jenks for the rest of my life. There is one thing we should understand about each other, Ben Ascher," she said heatedly. "Especially if we are to become partners . . . You do not give me orders. If I decide to go peddling again, I will. Nothing you can say will stop me!"

"I am only concerned about your welfare, Charlotte," he said gently. "I care for you, after all. And we did share a few minutes of . . . uh, intimacy."

She stiffened. "I've been wondering when you would bring that up."

"What am I to do, forget it ever happened?"

"I would prefer that, yes."

"I'm sorry, I can't oblige you there. I shall never forget that night."

"It will never happen again."

"Never? Never is a long time, dear Charlotte."

"There is something else you must understand. I am not going into partnership with a lover. It will be strictly business between us."

His dark eyes regarded her sorrowfully. "If that is the way you wish it. I do love you, Charlotte, I want you to know that..."

"You see? That's just the sort of talk I'm afraid of, putting things on a personal level."

"Afraid? What are you afraid of? There have been instances of a man and wife being partners in business. Give yourself a chance, you might come to love me in time." He smiled slightly. "I'm told that I sort of grow on people. You do intend to get married some day, I'm sure."

"Not for a long, long time."

Charlotte had already made up her mind about Ben's proposition, but she did not tell him of her decision. She saw him off the next day for Charleston, promising to have an answer for him when she saw him next. It had occurred to her that if she kept him in suspense it might strengthen her bargaining power when the time came to form the partnership.

When she had settled in at Widow Carstairs' boarding house, Charlotte saddled one of the wagon horses and made her rounds of the tobacco farmers. It was possible that if she went to Lutcher, he would at least allow her to return to the house for her riding horse and some personal items, but her pride would not allow her to go begging to him. She wanted no favors, large or small, from Lutcher; she would survive. In this way she would be starting out new, without any reminders of the past. Her resolve to best Sload Lutcher at his own game was the prime factor in deciding to form a partnership with Ben.

It was with this thought foremost in her mind that she approached all the farmers who had given her their tobacco on consignment. After cautioning them to keep it a secret, she asked each one the same question: If she, and Ben Ascher, opened a tobacco factory in Durham, would they supply her their tobacco on the same terms? Happy with Charlotte's turning a tidy profit for them, all the farmers were eager to cooperate with her. With the money they were making now through her efforts, they would be able to seed in a large crop for the coming year, a crop that would be ready for harvesting and curing by the time her plant was ready to open.

Buoyed by their support, Charlotte rode toward Durham in high spirits. She had promised all of them that she would return with the wagon during the week and pick up another load for peddling. With this in mind, she stopped off to see Bradley Hollister on the way.

"I'm going out on another trip," she said forthrightly. "It will probably be my last, since this load will just about take care of all the available tobacco in the area. If you still don't want Jimmie to accompany me, Mr. Hollister, I would like for you to come along."

Hollister studied her intently, scrubbing at the empty arm socket. "Won't that cause even more talk, Charlotte? Traveling around the country with a grown man?"

"I don't mind, if you don't." She laughed suddenly. "Maybe we'd better consult your wife about it. If anyone should be concerned, it should be her."

"My wife trusts me, Charlotte, there will be no problem there," he said gravely. "Did you have any trouble on your last trip?"

"I did. That's why I need someone with me." Succinctly, she told him what had happened, telling him as little about Ben as possible. "Mr. Ascher had to return to Charleston for more trade goods, and I'll be leaving before he gets back."

"I'll be happy to go along with you, Charlotte." He added grimly, "I would love a chance to gun this Jenks down like the cur dog that he is, should he try to bother you again."

Clint Devlin's luck had finally turned, and he was a happy man as he took payment from a cotton buyer for forty bales of cotton. They were at the railroad station in a small town not far from Florence, South Carolina.

As Clint folded the bills and put them into his pocket, Hampstead, the buyer, said, "I can use all the cotton you can scrounge up, Devlin. Will you have any more soon?"

"I doubt it, Hampstead. I've scoured the countryside for the past month, and it's just about all gone. I was damned lucky to find this batch. It's been stored in a barn from even before the war. The farmer was killed in battle, and his wife didn't even know about the cotton until a few days ago."

What Clint did not tell the buyer was that the wife had sold the farm and was moving north for good. She had been delighted to unload the cotton for a minimal price. Clint had made a good profit on the transaction.

Hampstead said, "Well, if you come across any, wire me and I'll buy it. You know where to locate me."

Clint nodded, and Hampstead turned away to supervise the loading of the bales into a boxcar. Clint fired a small cigar and leaned against the station house, idly watching the loading.

This was the third cotton deal he had made in the past two weeks, and he was flush. He had more money on his person than at any time in his life. It presented him with a problem—what was he going to do with the money? He had stayed away from poker games since parting company with Marcy, and he had no intention of seriously gambling again. Clint could not be considered a prudent man by any means, yet gambling was not all that important to him. Before, it had been a means, hopefully, of improving his financial condition, a hope that had failed miserably.

His problem now was, how to invest his money and make it multiply. What he had told Hampstead was true. Cotton was in short supply throughout the South now; the country had been scraped as clean as a scavenged skeleton, and few farmers were growing crops this year. Clint might be able to find a few stray bales, but it would take much time and effort, and would hardly be worthwhile. No, he had to find something new to get into, and he could not afford to wait too long. He liked to live well, and living well could erode his pile quickly.

He straightened up from the wall, flipped the cigar away, and started across the dusty street. He was almost across when he heard hoofbeats coming down the street. He did not look around until a voice hailed him, "Clint! Clint Devlin!"

He halted, facing around as a buckboard drew up alongside him. Ben Ascher smiled at him from the driver's seat.

"How are you, Benbo?" Clint said. He liked Ben Ascher, and he did not make friends easily. He was open to most people, but basically it was a salesman's facade, and he was very careful to whom he gave his friendship. But Ben was not only a decent man, in Clint's estimation, he was also very intelligent and could fend for himself with the wily fierceness of a cat defending its territory.

Clint said, "Are you staying in town, Ben, or on your way through?"

"Passing through, Clint. You remember Charlotte King, the lady who was with me the last time we met?"

"I sure as hell do. She was a lady I'm not likely to forget soon."

"Have you seen her?"

"Nope. Lost her, have you?"

"In a manner of speaking. I hoped she would wait for me back in Durham, and not come out here alone again. But she is a strong-minded lady and disregarded my wishes. But I do know that she's in the area, and I'm trying to catch up with her."

"Even if she's been this way, Ben, I could easily have missed her. I just got into town this morning with a load of cotton."

"Well, she can't be far ahead of me. I'll keep going until I catch up."

"Mind if I ride along with you for a spell? I have no more business here."

"I'd be glad for the company, Clint. But I am rather in a hurry."

"It'll only take me a couple of minutes to get my horse saddled. My saddlebags aren't even unpacked."

"Don't bother to saddle up. Throw your saddle in back, tie your horse off on the buckboard, and ride up here with me. We can talk more easily."

A few minutes later they were heading out of town at a fast clip. Clint leaned back with a sigh, lighting a cigar. After a little he slanted a sly look over at Ben. "What's with Charlotte King, Benbo? Are congratulations in order?"

"Not according to Charlotte. I know that she's the woman I've been looking for, but I mentioned marriage, and she's not having any." Ben smiled slightly. "At least not now. She has a mind of her own, does Charlotte, and she's bound and determined to become somebody before she even considers marriage." He paused for a moment. "But we are thinking of becoming business partners."

Clint's interest perked up. "Business partners? What kind of business?"

"The tobacco business, what else? We've talked of starting a company in Durham." He looked at Clint with shining eyes. "We both agree that tobacco is the coming thing. We'll buy the tobacco from the farmers around Durham, package it as snuff, chewing tobacco, and ready-made cigarettes."

"Cigarettes?" Clint made a droll face. "I've always thought they are fit only for sissies. For a man, there's nothing like a good cigar."

"And I happen to think that the use of tobacco in any form is a filthy habit, maybe even injurious to the smoker's health."

Clint glanced at him with arched eyebrows. "But you're still going into the production and sale of it?"

Ben shrugged. "It's a business, and one, I happen to think, that offers a great future. So long as it's not illegal and it's what people want, why should I stand back?"

"I'm still not sure about hand-made cigarettes."

"Then that's where you're wrong, Clint. Traveling with Charlotte for just those few days opened my eyes. These country stores can sell all the tobacco they can get their hands on. Look at John Ruffin Green and his Bull

Durham. He's making a fortune with that. An attractively packaged box of cigarettes already made will sell, believe me. Think how much easier it will be for the smoker to just shake out one already made and light up, without going through all that business of rolling your own. I know that ready-made cigarettes are already a big business up north, and they have to buy their tobacco from the South. We're already here, where the tobacco is, and whoever gets in on the ground floor will have the jump on future competition. With an effective sales force in all the big cities, the possibilities are limitless."

Clint's mind was working furiously. He was excited by the vista opened up by Ben's words. Shielding his building interest, he said, "You may be right. For some time now, I've been thinking of how producers of any product are missing a bet in not spending heavily on advertising. I'm thinking big, not just a few lines in a newspaper.

"I'm thinking of painted posters, in bright, eye-catching colors, along the roads. Signs to go on fences, barns, and empty houses. Maybe"—he grinned—"even a little sex, seductive dollies on the posters, trumpeting the product: 'I like a man who likes Such-and-Such Cigarettes!' That sure as hell should catch the men's attention. Maybe even some kind of a traveling show, collect crowds, give them a free show, and plug a product at the same time. There are other schemes fermenting in my mind, as well. I think the future of any product lies in advertising and promotion, letting people know you have something they need, and telling them why your product is better than the competition."

Clint, realizing he had gotten a little carried away, shut up abruptly. He looked sidelong at Ben, and found him grinning widely.

"It sounds great, Clint. Just what product did you have in mind? Or maybe you're plugging for a job with us, selling tobacco?"

"Not just a job. A partnership," Clint blurted, astonished at his audacity. "A third interest in your company."

Ben whistled through his teeth, involuntarily drawing

the horse to a halt. "Are you serious? Just like that, you want a third interest? Just so you can try out your advertising schemes?"

"I'd bring more to a company than that. I have made a tidy sum buying and selling cotton the last three weeks. I'm willing to invest in your company, invest every dime. I'm fairly sure that neither of you has any great fortune to invest. Ben, you know how good a salesman I am. I'd pull my weight, you can be damned sure of that!"

"Yes, I know how good you are." Ben nodded thoughtfully, flicked the reins, and the horse started the buckboard moving again. "You might be a welcome addition to the company."

"Then you'll consider making me a third partner?"

"Whoa, Clint, whoa! We don't even have a company yet. Charlotte hasn't given me a firm answer. And as for you becoming a partner... I'm not the one to convince, Charlotte is. Without her vote, you're out, Clint."

# Chapter Seven

"SURELY you're not serious!" Charlotte stared across the fire at Ben Ascher, her eyes wide with astonishment. "You're not only proposing that we take in a third partner, but a man that I've seen for about five minutes, all told."

Ben said defensively, "I know Clint, Charlotte, quite well, and I happen to think that he would be an asset to our company."

"*Our* company!" she said derisively. "Our company isn't even formed yet."

Hunkered down alongside Ben, Clint Devlin drew on his cigar and smiled crookedly at her. The two men had caught up with Charlotte and Bradley Hollister that afternoon, and they had all made their camp together. And now Ben had come up with this insane proposal!

Ben was looking at her with a frown. "You mean, you haven't decided yet about the company?"

"Oh, I've decided. I decided that before I left Durham. Not only that, but I've already paid a deposit for a year's lease on an empty building," she said smugly.

"A little premature, don't you think?" Ben said.

"No, I don't. If Sload Lutcher gets wind of what we're planning, I wouldn't put it beyond him to tie up all the available buildings in Durham."

"How would he find out? Surely you haven't told him?"

"Of course not. But in gathering this last load of tobacco, I did query all the farmers if they would be willing to sell their tobacco to us, when and if we get our plant going."

"You have been busy," Ben said somewhat grumpily.

Clint said, "Who is this Sload Lutcher? You didn't mention him, Benbo."

"Lutcher is a scoundrel," Charlotte said vehemently.

Clint grinned lazily. "There are a lot of those around. That word has even been applied to me."

"I don't know you well enough to know if it fits, Mr. Devlin. But if you are anything like Lutcher, I know for sure I don't want you for a partner."

Ben said, "He's a money-lender, Clint, among other things. He's Charlotte's sworn enemy." Quickly, he sketched in Charlotte's troubles with Lutcher.

"So you see, Mr. Devlin," Charlotte said, "becoming my partner will not be all sweetness and light. You will have to contend with Lutcher."

Clint waved his cigar airily. "Oh, that wouldn't bother me. Without people like him in the world, to fight with, life would lose a lot of its spice."

Charlotte said, "The kind of spice Lutcher adds to my life I could just as soon do without."

"Did Jenks and his men bother you on this trip?" Ben asked.

"I've seen no sign of them."

"It was still a risk, coming out here alone."

"I wasn't alone. Mr. Hollister has been with me every mile of the way." She nodded her head across the fire at Bradley Hollister, who had so far remained silent, sipping coffee.

Hollister said dryly, "Maybe you consider her the same as being alone, eh, Mr. Ascher, being with a man with one arm?" He rubbed the stub of his arm.

Ben flushed, and said embarrassedly, "My apologies, Mr. Hollister. I meant no offense."

"None taken, sir," Hollister said amiably. "It's something I've grown accustomed to."

"It's just that I think it's an unnecessary risk, Charlotte taking tobacco out again," Ben said. "I asked her to wait until I could accompany her, but she's a strong-minded woman."

Hollister nodded, smiling slightly. "Yup, you might say that."

"I came peddling again for a very good reason, Ben Ascher," Charlotte said. "I need the money. Even if we get our factory into operation, it will be a long time, a year at the very least, before we realize any profits from it. How am I supposed to live meanwhile?"

"That's another good reason," Clint said, "for you to accept me as a partner. I have made a killing in cotton recently, and have cash to invest."

Charlotte was silent, considering him across the fire. He had a surface charm, and was definitely personable, yet how trustworthy was he? Again, she recalled quite vividly that morning when she had come across him with the woman. How could she trust a man as wicked as that? Yet a small part of her mind questioned her reasoning. She was attracted to him, she knew that deep in her heart. Could it be that she was afraid of her own feelings? She had enough of a problem with Ben in that area, another man in her life she did not need.

"Money would come in handy," she said, "but that is hardly enough reason to take in a third partner. I'm sure we could find investment money if we looked hard enough. You have to have more to offer than that, Mr. Devlin, before I will even consider it."

Ben said, "Tell her, Clint. Tell her some of the ideas you outlined to me."

Clint lit a fresh cigar, and told Charlotte about his promotional ideas, speaking with conviction of his belief that advertising heavily, and imaginatively, would be of great value to the high sales of any product.

Listening to him, Charlotte was impressed despite her reservations. It was obvious that he had a keen intelligence, and he made his points with succinct logic. His winning personality emerged as he talked, and she could readily see why he was an excellent salesman. There was also a touch of the showman about him, an actor's flair for using wit and dramatic emphasis to make a point. But then, she reflected, acting ability was probably an asset to a good salesman.

She recalled Ben's earlier comment that Clint Devlin was a bit of a rogue. She could see that in him as well; he could have been a gambler, a soldier-of-fortune—any profession that required dash and derring-do.

When he was finished, she said, "It would seem that you've given this more thought than Ben and I have."

"Not really," he said with a disarming grin. "Not about the tobacco business per se. It really hadn't entered my mind until Benbo here brought it up earlier today."

"Then how do you know so much about it?"

"That's my whole point, don't you see?" He spread his hands. "I wasn't really talking about the tobacco business. Think back over what I said. The points I made could apply to *any* business with a product to sell. Now that the war is over, competition is going to get stiffer and stiffer. No longer can a business run on the theory that a product need only be turned out, and a buyer will be out there somewhere waiting for it. A buyer in the future, in my opinion, will need to be lured into thinking he needs a product, whether he does or not, by advertising and promotion, as I've just told you."

"It sounds shady to me," she said dubiously.

"What's shady about it?" He wagged his head. "It's just good, sound business practice."

Charlotte sighed. "I never realized that it would be so complicated."

"It hasn't been, up until now, but the day is coming when a seller will have to be aggressive and take his product to the buyer. Personally, I like it that way. It'll be far more exciting, more of a challenge."

"While you talked a minute ago," she said amusedly, "I was mentally figuring out what profession would suit you best, Mr. Devlin. It just occurred to me that I left one out... You have all the makings of a confidence man."

"I've considered it," he said with his lazy grin.

"And?"

"I'm basically too honest for that."

She gave a snort of mirth.

"Tell me, Charlotte, what are the other lines of work you figured I might fit into? Who knows, I might consider them."

She felt herself flushing. "Never mind, Mr. Devlin."

"You know, there is one factor you have going for you in the tobacco business."

"And what is that?" she asked, grateful for the change of subject.

"It's a vice business," he said. "Like liquor and . . . uh, ladies of easy virtue, the demand will always be there."

"You have a rather strong view of the world, Mr. Devlin," she said coldly.

"I prefer to think of it as the realistic view."

Clint was looking directly into her eyes, and Charlotte was the first to look away.

Ben said impatiently, "Well, Charlotte? What do you think?"

"About Mr. Devlin?"

"Yes. Shall we take him in as a partner?"

"It would be foolish of me to spurn a man of so many talents."

Clint inclined his head with an ironic smile. He murmured, "It's always nice to be appreciated."

"Well!" Ben rubbed his hands together briskly. "Then we have plans to make."

Bradley Hollister said good night, and retired to his blankets under Charlotte's wagon. Charlotte, Ben, and Clint sat on, feeding the fire and drinking coffee. Clint rummaged in his saddlebags for a bottle of brandy and laced the coffee with it. When they finally retired long after midnight, a rough agreement as to their various duties had been reached.

Charlotte and Ben would share the actual operation of the plant, with Ben overseeing the employees and the physical operation of the factory, while Charlotte supervised what office staff would be necessary, dealt with the tobacco growers, and handled other business contacts. Clint was to begin setting up a sales and promotion force and start an advertising campaign. Each one was to have authority in his or her area, but any important, over-all decision was to be made together. It was decided that Charlotte would return to Durham at the finish of her trip, and start looking into what equipment they would need; she would also consult with Ralph Chambers about drawing up contracts for the farmers to sign, binding them to sell their crops exclusively to the partners. Ben was to leave soon for New York to recruit cigarette rollers.

Clint yawned, stretching. He threw his cigar stub into the fire. "That seems just about all we can decide tonight... except one thing. What name are we going to give our company?"

Charlotte said, "Why, our three names, of course. Isn't that the way it's usually done?"

"I'd rather not have my name openly associated with the company," Ben said quickly. "It could cause problems. Naturally, all our names will be on whatever documents are necessary to form the partnership..."

"Come on, Benbo," Clint said. "I know what you're thinking, but I believe you're just borrowing trouble. What the hell, if this thing works, I'd be proud to have my name right out there, in bold letters, so everybody will know about Clint Devlin!"

"That's an ego thing, Clint. I'm not concerned with that, with my name being known. My main concern is to see that the company does well, and becomes profitable."

"A man's ego is important, Benbo. Man does not live by money alone." Clint was grinning. "What do you say, Charlotte? This is our first test vote."

"I vote for your name being on the company, Ben. I vote for *all* our names."

Clint said, "You're outvoted, Benbo."

"All right." Ben sighed. "I guess I'll have to go along."

Charlotte said, "And in alphabetical order, so there'll be no argument about that. The Ascher, Devlin, and King Tobacco Company."

Clint sent her an admiring glance. "You're not only a

pretty lady, but a diplomat as well. No ego with you, putting King last."

"Ego isn't all that important to a woman," Charlotte retorted.

"But there is one thing I think we should do," Ben said. "Our product should be called the King of Tobaccos. King Cigarettes, King Snuff, et cetera. You've already established the name, Charlotte. Besides, it's a good name."

"I'll vote for that," Clint said cheerfully. "Queen of Tobaccos, now there I might have balked!"

Ten days later, Charlotte and Clint were in Durham, after seeing Ben off on the train to New York. It was Christmas week, which was no problem for Ben, since his people did not observe Christmas as such.

Clint had no family, and as far as she was concerned, neither did Charlotte. She was tempted to look up Jeff—she had learned that he was still in Durham—and attempt a reconciliation, at least for the Christmas season; but each time she thought of it, her resolve hardened. What he had done was unforgivable. He was no longer any kin of hers.

The following day, she and Clint inspected the building she had leased for their factory. The building was two stories; and the lower floor was all one vast room, formerly used as a cotton warehouse. Dust and debris littered the wooden floor, which rang hollowly to their footsteps.

Charlotte said, "Right now, with Christmas at hand, my life feels as empty as this big room."

"I'm used to it. In fact, I prefer it to the Christmases I spent in the Atlanta orphanage. You don't know how lonely Christmas can be until you've spent one in an orphanage." His usual brilliant smile was shadowed by melancholy.

"I might as well be an orphan, even with my brother living in Durham. But to the devil with that." She shook her head sharply. "It's time I got over feeling sorry for myself." She swept a hand around the room. "What do you think, Clint?"

"Since I know damn-all about the tobacco business, what can I answer to that?"

"It doesn't look like much now, I agree. But I can visualize..." She half-closed her eyes. "I can see table after table piled high with tobacco, and the cigarette makers busy as can be, and over all the marvelous aroma of cured bright leaf."

He cocked an eyebrow in amusement. "You're really excited about this whole thing, aren't you?"

"Yes! Aren't you?" she said challengingly. "You seemed so that night you talked of your plans."

"I am about that, yes." He shrugged. "I think advertising is the thing of the future, and I'm itching to get into the thick of it."

"But it could be any product, couldn't it?"

"Yeah, that's true, I suppose." He lit a cigar and strolled about the room, idly kicking at puff balls of dirt.

"Be careful of that cigar, Clint," she warned. "This place could go up like a tinder box. That's one thing about which we must warn everybody working here, to be careful of fire. With this building full of cured tobacco, fire will always be a threat."

"I'll be careful, don't worry," he said absently. "I am as excited as you about this whole project, Charlotte, but you won't see any real enthusiasm from me until we get a product ready to sell, and I can hit the road with it." He paused, looking at her with a strange expression. "I just realized something. I think the fact that you are involved is what drew me in. I told myself that it was a chance to try out my ideas, but that, I know now, is only a part of it."

Charlotte was thrown into confusion, by the intimacy of his manner. She was struck by the irony of the remark—she had agreed to accept him as a partner for much the same reason. Clint was an attractive man, and she sensed that he had the power to sway her emotions.

During the war, while Charlotte was growing through her late teens and into maturity, there had been a paucity of men around Durham, since most of them had been away at war. In that sense, she had been deprived. In the normal course of events, she would have been besieged by suitors, and would have gradually learned how to deal with affairs of the heart, but there had been none. Now, in the course of a little over two months, she had met two attractive men, and she realized that she was woefully unprepared to handle them. Most girls in her situation would have been secretly crowing with delight, but she had other plans, plans that would be thwarted if her emotions were torn.

Clint was speaking, "Since we're both orphans this Christmas, in a manner of speaking, I think we should celebrate the season together, Charlotte; at least to the extent of having dinner together on Christmas Day. What do you say?"

Suddenly Charlotte felt a sense of gratitude and expectation. Christmas season had always been a time of closeness and sharing with the King family, and the prospect of a lonely Christmas depressed her.

She heard herself saying, "I think that would be nice, Clint."

His smile was warm. "Then I shall call for you on Christmas Day, and we will see what Durham has to offer."

As it happened, there was a change in plans.

When Charlotte returned to the boarding house on December 23rd, there was a note from Clint: "Dear Lotte: There has been a slight change. I am in receipt of an invitation to a Christmas Eve ball, given by the mayor of Durham. I am allowed to bring a friend. May I consider you that friend? I shall be by for you at six on Christmas Eve. Yrs., Clint Devlin."

A ball? Charlotte stared at the note in dismay. She had no dress for such an event; most of her clothes were still at the farm. And even there, she had nothing remotely suitable for a ball at the mayor's home. There had been fancy balls regularly in the years before the war, but she had not been old enough then to attend; the only balls she had witnessed were those given by her parents, and she had not been a participant, but merely an observer, always sent to bed before the evening had progressed very far.

How on earth had Clint received such an invitation? He had been in Durham less than a week. How could he have become friendly enough with the mayor to have been invited to a ball?

But the really important question was, what could she wear? Finally, not knowing who else to turn to, she went to Lucille Carstairs with her problem.

"Land's sake, sugar, what's to be upset about?" Widow Carstairs was a buxom woman of fifty, with a booming laugh, and an unfailing sense of humor. "When my man died, I made a living as a seamstress, making dresses for the gentry of Durham. When the war came, of course, I couldn't get material, but then they no longer had the need for fancy gowns, nor the money to pay for them."

"I don't have any money, either," Charlotte said despondently. "I don't know why Clint accepted the invitation, anyway!"

"Honey, I've seen that man only the one time, but he's a handsome devil. He ask me to a ball at the North Pole, I'd be happy to go. As for money, don't fret. I think I've still got enough material left to make something suitable. You can pay me when you can."

Charlotte said dubiously, "But there's only tomorrow. Can you make it in that time?"

"Tonight, don't forget tonight," Lucille Carstairs said briskly. "We'll work late tonight and tomorrow. Sugar, if I was in your shoes, I'd stay up all night for a chance like this. The mayor's shindigs, I've heard of them. They're something, so I've been told. Now"—she rubbed her hands together—"let's get busy."

Charlotte accompanied the older woman to the attic, which was crowded with boxes and trunks. Several trunks yielded remnants of fabric, ranging in type from fine lawn to heavy brocade. In one trunk, carefully folded in muslin, Charlotte found a partially completed dress of pale green, shot silk. She unfolded it with care, and held it up to the light. Although wrinkled from the folding, it looked, to Charlotte's eyes, entirely splendid. She uttered a soft sound of appreciation, which caused Lucille to look up.

"Why, for heaven's sake," she exclaimed. "I had forgotten all about that being there. I started that dress for poor Mrs. Hunter, Thaddeus Hunter's young wife, her that died of pneumonia just a few months after the war started. When she went, I just packed it away, unfinished, and then forgot about it."

"It's beautiful!" Charlotte said. "Just beautiful! I've almost forgotten what a real ball gown looks like. It reminds me of . . ." Feeling tears coming to her eyes, she blinked them back. "It reminds me of so much that's gone."

Lucille rose from her knees where she had been rummaging in a large, metal-bound trunk, a look of purpose upon her face. "You know, as I remember, Mrs. Hunter was pretty near your size, Charlotte. Let's try this on you, and see how it fits. As I recall, it's almost finished, and if you can wear it, I'm sure that I could get it done in time for the ball. It would sure beat anything that I could whip up from scratch in the short time we have."

Feeling a rush of excitement, Charlotte stripped down to her petticoats and corset, then raised her arms so that Lucille could slip the full-skirted gown over her shoulders. The smooth silk caressed Charlotte's skin, making her feel instantly beautiful and poised. The rustle of the silk sounded exciting and elegant; and Charlotte drew in her breath, as Lucille fastened the dress around her waist.

"It fits almost perfectly." Lucille's voice was almost a crow. "And that color looks wonderful on you. Here, look in the glass."

Charlotte turned and gazed at her reflected elegance in the long pier glass, feeling a pleasant shock at the sight of the image which stared back at her. Lucille was right, the color was wonderful, soft and green as the sea; it made her shoulders look white as marble, and her hair look like flame. Cut deep over her breasts, in a low decolletage, the bodice had a softly gathered fichu which just covered her upper arms. Tightly fitted at the waist, with a point in front, the skirt flared away in tier after tier of ruffles, falling to the floor, and pooling around her feet.

"Just wait until you see it with a crinoline," said Lucille, adjusting the skirt outward. "It will be something grand! A short overskirt of lace in the same color is meant to go over the first tier of the skirt, and upon the fichu. I'm certain that the material for them is somewhere in the trunk. I'll have this finished in no time at all, and you'll be the belle of the ball, sugar. Just wait and see. You won't even be out of fashion. Most of the women will be appearing in old dresses that they had before the war."

Charlotte gazed down at the glowing fabric, and stroked it with her fingers. "My only crinoline is at home. I guess Sload Lutcher owns it now. It was falling apart, anyway, and was too awkward to wear in the wagon. He's welcome to it."

Lucille smiled. "Don't worry, sugar. I'll lend you one of mine. You can keep it. Besides, I hear from my friend, Josephine up there in Boston, that hoop skirts are soon going to become unfashionable. She said that she heard it from a friend of hers in England, across the waters. Surprising, isn't it, that somewhere in the world they have still been able to think of such things? At any rate, we have solved your problem, sugar. You will be a great success at the mayor's ball. I give you my word on that!"

When Charlotte was awakened by Lucille early in the morning, the room was frigid. Shivering, she stepped to the window and pushed the curtains aside. It had snowed during the night, a light snow that dazzled in the sunshine, lying over everything like a dusting of powdered sugar.

For the first time she began to feel like it was Christmas. She hurried through her ablutions, got dressed, and just had time for a quick breakfast before Lucille hustled her into the sewing room again.

By late afternoon, the dress was completed and pressed, and Charlotte, bathed, scented, and curled, slipped off her wrapper so that Lucille could help her on with the garment.

When it was fitted, and fastened, only then did Charlotte look at her mirrored image. Her hair, washed, set, and arranged by Lucille's niece, who had a talent for such things, was arranged in a waterfall of curls behind, and allowed to curl softly in front on either side of the center part. Pale green bows held back the curls at the sides. The arrangement, Charlotte had to admit, set off her face to great advantage, as the dress did her figure. With lace and roses in place now, buoyed up by the full crinoline, she looked not unlike some giant flower. She had never seen herself look so lovely, and tears of gratitude moistened her eyes.

"It's beautiful," she whispered. "You surely are a genius with a needle, Lucille."

Lucille smiled proudly, and touched Charlotte's shoulder, her own eyes misted with tears. "It's been a long time since we've had anything to celebrate in this house. A long time since I've dressed a lovely young woman to attend a ball. Perhaps it's a sign of better times to come." She shook her head ruefully. "I'm becoming foolish. There now, you're ready to go. I do wish I could be there to see you. But you must tell me about it, afterward."

"I shall, oh, I shall!" Charlotte turned, and in a burst of gratitude and affection, kissed the older woman upon the cheek. Lucille colored, smiled, then shook her head again, as if to shake off their sentimentality.

She said, "Let's see . . ." She stood back and surveyed her handiwork critically. "It needs a touch of something . . . You have any jewelry, dear?"

"Only a few cheap pieces. I had to sell everything else during the war. What I have is out at the house, and Sload Lutcher now has the house."

"That man!" Lucille clucked. "I swear, somebody should horsewhip him. But cheap pieces would never do, anyway. It needs something with a look about it. Wait here a minute, sugar."

Lucille went into the other room, and Charlotte examined herself again in the mirror. She had never been vain about her looks, but she had to admit that she looked amazingly attractive. Clint should be proud to show her off. . .

She felt heat rise to her face. Why should she care how Clint Devlin would feel? Yet, deep in her heart, she knew that she did care, very much.

Lucille bustled back in, carrying a small jewel box. "I have something in here, something John gave me shortly after we were married." From the box she took a gold heart on a black velvet ribbon; an emerald glittered in the exact center of the heart.

Involuntarily, Charlotte took it into her hand. The stone felt warm to her fingers. "It's lovely, Lucille! But I couldn't accept this, it must be worth a great deal."

"Nonsense, sugar!" the woman said briskly. "It is valuable, as a remembrance of John, if nothing else. But I rarely have occasion to wear it. I'm not giving it to you, dear, only loaning it for the evening."

She tied the ribbon snugly around Charlotte's neck, and let Charlotte admire herself in the mirror. The emerald glowed brilliantly, catching and reflecting points of light.

Lucille nodded in satisfaction. "You'll do, sugar, you surely will."

Charlotte was waiting in the parlor downstairs, sitting demurely, trying to hide the tremor inside, when Lucille ushered Clint Devlin in and discreetly retired.

Clint was resplendent in evening clothes, complete with top hat. Charlotte's breath caught at the sight of him. Dear God, he was handsome! Her pulse speeded up, and she felt her heart begin to pound.

Clint halted, staring at her appraisingly, and for a moment she experienced the pain of acute anxiety. What if he did not like the way she looked? All of a sudden, his opinion was terribly important to her.

"Well now!" His slow grin came. "Is this the Charlotte King I saw in gingham, driving a covered wagon and a team of horses?"

She stood up, feeling suddenly coquettish. "Do you like the gown?"

"Oh, yes, my dear, I like it very much," he drawled. "In fact, I like everything I see. You are dazzling, Lotte. I don't remember ever seeing a woman more lovely."

Inordinately pleased, she crossed the room to him. "You look quite grand yourself, Mr. Devlin."

"Do you think so?" he said with a smug air. "I found a place to rent this outfit. This is an important party tonight, Lotte. If we're going into business in Durham, we need to meet and get to know the important people in town."

"I'm curious as to how you managed an invitation. Do you know the mayor?"

"Not yet, but I sure intend to," he said cheerfully. He extended his arm. "Shall we go?"

A curtained carriage was parked outside the door. Charlotte stared at it in amazement. "How did you find the money for that? I thought you invested all your money in our company?"

"Most of it, true. But I rented this, along with the clothes, just for tonight. A first rule in business, my dear, is to put up a front. You can never be prosperous if you don't *look* prosperous."

With great ceremony he helped her into the carriage, then went around to get in the other side. He picked up the reins and started the horses moving.

"You still didn't tell me how you got us invited tonight, Clint."

"Simple. I let word leak, in a manner of speaking, being sure that it would reach the mayor's ears, that we're opening a tobacco company here in Durham."

"You didn't!" she exclaimed. "Why in heaven's name did you do that? I wanted to keep it a secret from Lutcher for as long as possible."

"My dear Lotte, you don't keep something like this a secret," he said chidingly. "You want as much advance publicity as possible. We want people to *know* what we're up to. If they start to believe what we want them to believe, that we're going to bring more prosperity to their fair city, they'll fall all over themselves to boost us along, especially the city power structure."

"You're talking away over my head, Clint. You may well be right in what you say, but Lutcher is going to be absolutely livid when he hears. There's no telling what he will do!"

"Lutcher, Lutcher! You've built this fellow up in your mind as some kind of an ogre, somebody who can get away with anything. I know"—he patted her hand—"I know you have reason to be afraid of him, after what he did to you. But things will be different now. Before you were a lone woman, now you're one-third of a partnership. Ben and I will see that nothing happens to you. Besides, what the hell can the man do? Corrupting your brother and using him to get at you, sending a tough to try and rape you... None of that will do him any good now. With a going concern, we'll be on equal terms with him. True, he may try some underhanded business tactics, but just let him try." His face was grim. "I can get just as dirty as he, if it comes down to that!"

Charlotte was silent, but she was still far from convinced. All she could think of was the pure evil that had glittered in Lutcher's eyes during her last meeting with him. Nobody who had not seen that display could even begin to understand what he was capable of.

Now the carriage was moving slowly down a street of fine homes. The street was lined with buggies, carriages, and horses. Clint pulled up before a Colonial-style house, its soaring white columns brilliantly illuminated by strategically placed lanterns and torches. Splendidly dressed men and women were moving up the walk to the house, which was well-lighted on both floors. As their carriage drew to a halt, Charlotte could hear strains of lively music coming from inside.

Excitement stirred in her, and she endeavored to push all thoughts of Lutcher into the back of her mind. She had come here to have a good time, to get some joy from the Christmas season, and she was determined to do just that!

But one of the first people she saw inside the house, after they had gone through the receiving line and had been greeted by the mayor and his wife, was Sload Lutcher! Dressed in funereal black, he stood just inside the entrance, a champagne glass in his hand.

Charlotte came to a stop, just as Lutcher's malevolent gaze fastened on her, those deep-set eyes cold as shoe buttons, as he recognized her. There was another man standing beside him. Lutcher touched the man's arm, and as the other man faced around, Lutcher motioned toward the entrance, and Charlotte.

The second man was her brother.

# Chapter Eight

WHEN Sload Lutcher first received the news that Charlotte King had started a tobacco company, his anger had flared white-hot and violent; but now he had the fire banked and under control. He had been rash in the past, letting his rage lead him into rough maneuvers such as setting Cob Jenks after the girl to terrorize her; but such tactics were no longer practical, since there were her partners to consider.

Since her company—Lutcher knew that he would always think of it as *her* company—was already well-started, he must bide his time. A threat directed at her person would likely draw retribution from her partners. Any measure aimed at defeating her would have to be indirect, and subtle. His determination to defeat her, to see her humiliated and beaten, had not lessened in the slightest.

But first, he would wait and see if her company succeeded. Other tobacco companies had tried and failed, through lack of business acumen, failure to find tobacco to keep the plant in production, or other, related reasons. Since none of the three partners, to the best of Lutcher's knowledge, had any experience in the tobacco business, the possibility of their failure was very strong; but if the King woman did succeed, if her business flourished, he would direct all his efforts toward driving her, and her partners, to the wall.

Lutcher considered himself a far-sighted man, and with

the thought that it might benefit him in the future, he believed it wise to cultivate Jeff King, although he detested the man. He despised weakness in any man, yet he recognized the fact that such weakness could be used to the advantage of a strong man such as himself; and he was certain that Jeff King would be of value to him eventually.

He had given him a position with the Lutcher Tobacco Company, at a nominal salary. He remembered that conversation: "You will work mostly in the public relations area, since you are well-known in Durham," he told Jeff, "and you are a war veteran. People allow the poor veterans a lot of leeway. Now, I don't care what you do in your private life, King. Drink and roister all you like, but I expect you to be sober and reasonably respectable while on the job."

"I can't be very respectable on what you're paying me," Jeff said sullenly.

Lutcher leaned forward, rapping his knuckles on his desk. "I believe in paying a man what he is worth. Prove to me that you're worth more, and I'll pay you more. But consider this, King... Who else in Durham would hire you? A cripple, a toper, and a gambler. And if you make the wrong move, I'll fire you in a second and see that you have to leave Durham for good. Is that clearly understood?"

Jeff nodded uneasily. "Understood."

"Good!" Lutcher studied him closely. "There's one other thing I want you to do, learn all that you can about the tobacco business."

"Why? I'm not the least interested in the tobacco business."

"You'll do what I tell you, King! Tobacco is the coming thing, and I want everyone working for me to learn it from the ground up. Now, you follow my instructions, or you'll get nothing more from me. You have that choice, do as I say, or starve. What is it to be?"

"All right, Mr. Lutcher, all right," Jeff said in resignation. "I'll do whatever you say."

* * *

What Lutcher had not foreseen was that his relationship with Jeff King would come to be of use so soon. When he was invited to the mayor's Christmas Eve ball, and learned, in a roundabout way, that Charlotte King and one of her new partners would be guests, Lutcher saw this as an opportunity to embarrass Charlotte. Without telling Jeff King that his sister would be at the ball, Lutcher brought him along as a guest, since the invitation had included bearer and guest, and since Lutcher did not know any suitable women, and would not have invited one if he had.

In Lutcher's opinion, all women were strumpets—had he not seen that evidenced during the period of time he operated his brothels? So-called ladies were no better than the public tarts under the surface. Their loose morals aside, they only served to distract a man from his main purpose—becoming a man of substance and influence. He had little use or need for sex, and that, as far as he could see, was all they were suited for.

Lutcher and Jeff arrived at the ball early, and Lutcher was careful to stand where he could easily see the front door. He did not demur when Jeff took glass after glass of champagne from the waiter's tray; he wanted Jeff to be intoxicated by the time Charlotte arrived.

Finally, his vigil was rewarded. He saw the King woman come in with a handsome man in evening clothes; Lutcher assumed that the man was one of her new partners. He straightened alertly, waiting until she passed through the receiving line. He felt an inward quiver of satisfaction as her gaze encountered his and she stopped short. He touched Jeff's arm, turning him around so that his sister would recognize him.

Jeff sucked in his breath. "Oh, my God! It's Charlotte! I have to get out of here!"

He had taken one lunging step before Lutcher seized his arm in an iron grip. Lutcher said in a harsh voice, "You're staying right here, King. Right by my side."

"You *knew* she was coming here. You did this purposely, damn you!"

"I don't know what you mean," Lutcher said innocently. "I should think you would be happy to see your loving sister, especially on Christmas Eve."

His gaze had never left Charlotte. He saw her half-turn away, as if to leave, bumping into the man who had come with her. They talked together in whispers. The man's glance was directed toward Lutcher, who smiled calmly, and dipped his head in acknowledgment. The man with Charlotte nodded back, took Charlotte's elbow, and steered her directly toward where Lutcher stood.

They stopped before Lutcher. The man still had Charlotte's arm in his grip, and Lutcher had the feeling that she would bolt but for that. She resolutely refused to look at him or her brother.

Her companion took the cigar from his mouth, and said amiably, "I'm Clint Devlin, and I understand that you are Sload Lutcher. I suppose we're going to be competitors, in a manner of speaking."

"Yes, I'm Sload Lutcher and this is Jefferson King." Lutcher grinned savagely. "But then you know him, don't you, Miss King? He's working for me now."

Charlotte finally looked at Jeff. Her eyes icy, she said, "I've heard that trash always manages to find its own level, and I see that you've finally found yours."

"Charlotte, won't you give me a chance to explain?" Jeff said miserably.

"Explain? There is nothing to explain. I understand everything perfectly. Clint, may we go now?"

"Not just yet, Lotte. I'd like a few words with Mr. Lutcher first. Since it is no state secret, I'm sure that you know all about Ascher, Devlin, and King Tobacco?"

"Oh, yes, I've heard about King Tobacco." Lutcher sneered. "The tobacco business is a rough game, Mr. Devlin. Certainly it is no business for children, or neophytes."

"The way you play it, I am sure it is a rough game." Clint was smiling lazily. "We may be neophytes to the tobacco business, Mr. Lutcher, but I can assure you that Ben Ascher and myself are not children. What we don't know we will soon learn. We aren't afraid of competition, be assured of that. I, for one, like it. Competition brings out the best in me. So, do your damnedest, Mr. Lutcher."

"I will do just that, Mr. Devlin, you may be sure. I am not a wagering man, but if I were, I would wager almost any amount that King Tobacco will not last out its first year."

Clint said cheerfully, "I'm sure we can depend on you to do whatever you can to bring that about."

"You may, sir. And despite your bravado, Mr. Devlin, I have to question the judgment of men who would enter into a business partnership with a woman." Lutcher was looking directly at Charlotte, and he had the satisfaction of seeing her stiffen, flushing with anger.

"Oh, I don't know, I think it will be interesting, in a manner of speaking. There is one other matter I would touch on, Mr. Lutcher." Devlin pointed his glowing cigar at Lutcher. He was still smiling, but his voice now was steely. "Charlotte is no longer alone and defenseless. She has Ben and I to look after her welfare. Should anything happen to her again, we will look you up and deal with you . . . Shall we say, harshly?"

Lutcher kept his face expressionless. "I have no knowledge of this alleged attack on Miss King. If Cob Jenks did that, it was on his own initiative, not by my orders."

"I won't call you a liar, sir, because it really doesn't matter. From this moment forward, when any employee of yours offers harm to Charlotte, we will hold you responsible and act accordingly." He tucked Charlotte's arm in his. "Shall we dance, my dear? I believe my business with Mr. Lutcher is concluded."

Lutcher stood without moving, his gaze following the couple as they moved into a waltz in the ballroom. He had gone beyond anger now, and was filled with a deadly purpose—he fully intended to see to the destruction of this cocky Clint Devlin, as well as Charlotte King.

By his side Jeff King muttered, "I need a drink stronger than champagne."

He plunged into the crowd, and Lutcher let him go. He

could get as drunk as he liked, Lutcher had no further use of him tonight.

Only once before in his life had Lutcher been this incensed, and that was when the slut in New Orleans had crept up on him while he was asleep. With one slice of a butcher knife, she had destroyed his manhood forever...

He forcibly walled his thoughts away from that terrible episode in his life, and concentrated on the dancing couple. No matter how long it took, or what measures were necessary, he would see them both destroyed, financially and in every other way!

In the carriage with Clint, Charlotte rode in grim silence, paying no heed to where they were going. She was thinking of Jefferson and Sload Lutcher. How could Jefferson possibly work for that man? It seemed impossible that her own brother could sink to such depths of degradation!

She had insisted that they leave the party after the one dance. Although reluctant, Clint had acceded to her wishes. "I understand, Lotte. I'm sorry. If I had known your brother would be there, I wouldn't have insisted we come. Sload Lutcher is a proper bastard. He certainly knows how to hurt you."

Now, as the carriage came to a stop, Charlotte sat up with a start, peering about. They were halted before a small, white house, in an area totally unfamiliar to her.

She glanced at Clint. "Where are we? This isn't the boarding house."

"No, it isn't. I figured you wouldn't want to go back there now, and spend Christmas Eve alone. It's early yet. If you went back now, the widow would pester you with questions."

"But whose house is this?"

"It's mine, Lotte. Rented, that is." He was smiling. "You know, for years, except during the war years of course, I have lived in hotels and rooming houses. I've always wanted a house all my own. When I found this one for rent, cheap, I took it. It has a fireplace. We can build a fire, I'll make us some eggnog, and we'll celebrate the yuletide. Sorry, I don't have a tree. I didn't have time to get one. There wouldn't be any presents to put under it, anyway."

"But Clint, it's hardly proper for me to be alone with a man in his home," she said dubiously.

"Who's to know? It's relatively isolated." He gestured around. "That's one reason I took it."

"You mean, you rented it just for that reason, so you could sneak women in here?"

"Not sneak, Lotte. Whatever I do, I do out in the open."

"That's fine for you," she retorted, "but a woman has to consider her reputation."

"Charlotte, you are an adult, a business woman, not some empty-headed belle panting after a husband, who has to worry about going to him spotless as snow."

"How do you know I'm not looking for a husband?"

He gave her a challenging look. "Well, are you?"

"No, of course I'm not," she said hastily. "But that doesn't mean that I'm a loose woman, either."

"Nobody said you were. Come on, Lotte. What are you afraid of?"

"I'm not afraid. Certainly not of you, Mr. Devlin!"

"Well then?" he said gravely. "I don't wish to spend Christmas Eve alone, and I know you don't either."

All at once, it struck Charlotte that she would appear ridiculous if she demanded that he take her back to the boarding house; and the prospect of spending some time alone with him was attractive. She refused to think beyond that. She said, "All right, Clint."

The interior of the house was furnished sparingly, but what furniture there was, was good.

"I know, it looks a great deal like a hotel room," Clint said apologetically. "I haven't had time to do much to it yet, but then you're the first person I've invited in."

She said dryly, "Should I feel flattered?"

Without answering he escorted her into the small parlor, and lit a lamp. It was cold in the house; Charlotte hugged herself, shivering.

"I'll get a fire going." Clint motioned to a sofa before the fireplace, and she sat down. There was a stack of firewood beside the hearth, and a thick buffalo hide spread on the wooden floor.

Clint quickly started a fire, and as the dry wood caught, the flames leaping high, Charlotte stretched her hands out to the welcome warmth. Clint got up from his haunches, dusting his hands together. "That should warm the room up shortly. Now I'll fetch some eggnog for us."

He left the room, and Charlotte could hear the clatter of iron in the rear as he evidently started a fire in a cook-stove. The heat from the fireplace began to take the chill off, and she mused into the flames, wondering what she was doing here. But somehow, the concern she supposed she should feel did not materialize, and she decided to let matters take their natural course. She was warm now, and comfortable, she was with an attractive man, and it was Christmas Eve. This was no time to be concerned about tomorrow.

Her eyelids grew heavy, and she was nearly asleep when Clint came back carrying a pair of mugs. He had removed his frock coat and cravat, and his shirt was unbuttoned halfway down. As he leaned down to give her one of the mugs, Charlotte could see thick, golden chest hairs in the firelight. The aroma of the eggnog was spicy, inviting.

She took a sip from the mug, as Clint sat down on the other end of the divan from her, and busied himself lighting a cigar. Charlotte said, "You make a very good eggnog, Clint."

"Another one of my many talents," he said with a flashing smile. "A warning, Lotte. It's rather potent, made with Jamaica rum, but then what the hell, it's Christmas, right?"

"Right," she said recklessly, and took another sip, setting up an explosion of warmth in her stomach.

"One thing concerns me, Clint . . ."

"And what is that, my dear Lotte?"

"All this"—she waved a hand vaguely—"the carriage and everything else."

"I like to live well, I think I told you that. And it *is* my money."

"Oh, it's not my business, your personal life," she assured him hastily. "But as I've mentioned, several times, it will be many months before we start earning a profit. What will happen when you run out of funds? I'm worried for myself, how I'm going to manage until we start making money, and God knows I'm not living well."

"You should," he said airily. "As I said earlier, a front is important. If you look successful, people tend to think that you are."

"That's fine for you to say," she said in exasperation. "But how do we finance this front, pray tell?"

"Simple. We float a loan for enough money to carry the three of us in style until we're a flourishing concern. That's the way it's done, Lotte."

"No, no," she was shaking her head, "I've seen enough of people drowning in debt during the war, and after."

"The war's over, Lotte. Things are different now, in a manner of speaking."

She stirred in agitation. "But the risk, Clint! What if we have difficulty in the beginning, and it takes far longer than we anticipate to turn a profit. We could lose everything!"

"Nothing risked, nothing gained," he said blithely. He moved closer to take her hand. "Charlotte, the risk is small, believe me. All you and Ben have to do is provide the product, I'll sell it. I'll sell tobacco like it's never been sold before."

She thought of taking her hand away, but in the end she let it remain nestled in his. "You talk of getting a loan as though it's the easiest thing in the world. Nobody has money to lend, except vultures like Sload Lutcher, and I will not consent to go into debt to him. The South is destitute, Clint. There is no money. I couldn't even get a loan on the farm before Lutcher took it, except from someone like him. Even he said he wouldn't loan me money on the place."

"There is money, there is always money around," Clint said decisively. "Perhaps not around Durham, but in Atlanta, or other large southern cities. Or, if not in the South, we can go to northern investors. Most industrialists in the North got rich during the war, and have money they'd be happy to invest down here. That's another fact of business you must learn, Lotte . . . Many wealthy men today made their fortunes by borrowing money to start. All you have to do is find the right source, and I'm sure that Ben and I, when the time comes, can find money when we need it.

"Here, let me have your mug. I'll get us more eggnog." He got to his feet, taking her mug, heading toward the kitchen again.

Charlotte realized that the first one had made her slightly tipsy—she was unaccustomed to drinking—and she should tell him she did not need another. But why bother? The fire was going well now, she was warm and cozy, and there was a sensuality about the setting, the man, and the drinks, that stirred her senses.

When Clint returned, he detoured to blow out the lamp, leaving only the firelight. She accepted the mug and drank.

He said, "Harking back to something you said a bit ago . . . About my personal life, Lotte. I wouldn't mind if you made it your business."

She looked at him narrowly. "What does that mean?"

"It simply means that I find you an attractive woman, a *very* attractive woman, and I like attractive women."

"And casual women, too, I gather."

He shook his head, his face intent. "Not so, not in this instance. There is nothing casual about the way I feel about you, Lotte. But I do want you to know this . . . I am not the marrying kind. Maybe some day I might consider marriage, but now, no matter how much I might care for you, do not expect a proposal."

"At least you're honest." Even to her own ears, Charlotte's voice sounded breathless, and she realized that she was breathing hard, and her heart was beating wildly.

"I try to be," Clint said gravely.

Setting his mug down, he leaned close, and cupped her face gently between his hands, the thumb of each hand pressing on the corners of her mouth. His face loomed over hers, so close that Charlotte could see her own image swimming in the pupils of his eyes. Then his lips were on hers, in a kiss so incredibly sweet and tender that her breath left her in a rush.

For just an instant she considered her situation, and thought of resisting. She sensed that he would not try to force her, if she slipped out of his arms and demanded to be driven home. But the after-image of that time in her wagon when Ben Ascher came to her, accompanied by the memory of how pleasant, how rapturous it had been, and every fiber of her being yearned toward that ecstasy again.

Then the instant of thought was gone, and she gave herself up to sensation.

Whereas Ben had been a more hesitant, if skillful lover, Clint was forceful, searching out the touchbuds of her passion with no hesitancy whatsoever. Yet for all that, he was tender and considerate, setting a measured pace of love-making that steadily built.

His knowing fingers unsnapped and unbuttoned, and Charlotte's clothes were removed item by item; and always his lips came back to hers, and between the kisses, his finger stroked and explored, invading new territory with the removal of each garment. His caresses set up a powerful need in her, and she moved restlessly under his touch, and waited breathlessly for the feel of his mouth on hers again.

Then she was completely nude, and as his fingers caressed her inner thighs, her wanting vaulted beyond containment. She reached up to pull him down to her, and was amazed to discover that he was also unclothed. His leanly muscled body had the feel of leashed power under her touch.

Clint picked her up, his lips never leaving hers, and turned to place her on the buffalo rug. The fur felt warm and luxurious under her back.

She gasped aloud with shock and beginning pleasure as he entered her with a powerful thrust. In passion he was demanding, driving at her with controlled violence, yet, without knowing how she knew, she sensed that he was still considerate of her own needs.

Her passion grew into a maelstrom of feeling, and when the final sunburst of rapture seized her, she cried out softly and clung to him until he shuddered, muttering scrambled endearments against her throat.

Finally they were still, and Charlotte's shattered senses gradually regrouped and coalesced into some semblance of sanity.

Clint raised his head, kissed her lightly, and moved away to lie beside her on the buffalo robe. Propping himself up on one elbow, his gaze swept the length of her body, his eyes still glowing with desire.

He touched her upthrust breast almost reverently. "You are a beautiful woman, Lotte, and a wholly feminine one. To judge by your no-nonsense, everyday manner, a man could easily mistake your true nature."

She laughed throatily. "But you, Mr. Devlin, did not make that mistake, it seems."

"I pride myself that I am a good judge of character, especially in women."

He sat up to reach for his unfinished mug of eggnog and a fresh cigar. Watching him through half-closed eyes, Charlotte supposed she should resent his smugness, but in that moment she was too content to be contentious. Besides, if he was conceited, perhaps he had reason to be. If she were to judge him solely by what had just taken place, she would have to conclude that Clint Devlin spent all his waking hours making love to women. How else could he be so skilled at it? Yet, she knew this to be an untrue picture of him. He devoted just as much time, energy, and dedication to pursuits outside the bedroom.

Her thoughts veered in a different direction, probing for feelings of guilt over what had transpired. She knew that she could make excuses—it was Christmas, and she was alone in the world. She had been seeking warmth and companionship. She had consumed too much rum. All those things were true.

Yet it all came down to one fact—she had wanted this man. And she felt no regrets, none at all. She had enjoyed making love with him, and knew intuitively that she would do it again. It did make her feel wicked, but the wickedness was a delight.

She laughed softly.

Clint looked over at her inquiringly. "Something humorous, my dear?"

"Yes, me! I'm a fallen woman, Clint. At least that's how most people would view it."

"I would say that you have just become a woman of the world, Lotte. And a sophisticated woman cares little for what people think. Do you?"

"Not really. At least not in this moment." She stretched her arms up over her head, pulling her breasts up taut and high. "At this moment I'm happy."

His gaze caressed her nakedness. "I'd say that's the most important thing. Most people in this world never know any moments of happiness, no matter how fleeting."

She smiled slightly. "I think there is a word for you, Clint Devlin. Hedonist."

"Sticks and stones," he said with an insouciant grin. He reached over to balance his cigar in a saucer and turned to her.

She stretched a hand up to touch his cheek. "Merry Christmas, Clint," she said softly.

"Merry Christmas to you, too, Lotte."

He touched her nipple, just the merest touch, and she shivered. "I must go soon."

"But not too soon, I hope." He touched the other nipple.

Charlotte clamped her hand over his, pressing it tightly against her. "I promised to tell Lucille Carstairs about tonight."

"Oh?" His head dipped, and he kissed the hollow of her throat. "About this, you're going to tell her about this?"

"No... Oh!"

His hand had touched her intimately. He murmured, "And about this?"

"Clint... Oh, God! What are you doing?"

His mouth descended on hers, silencing her protests.

# Chapter Nine

BEN Ascher was not by nature a devious man, and so it went against the grain for him to practice duplicity as he toured several cigarette factories in New York. However, he knew that he did not dare tell people that his primary purpose was to recruit their workers for his factory in Durham. He told all who asked that he was going into the tobacco business and was in New York to learn how it was done. A few times he was greeted with suspicion, but he found most plant managers willing to show him their operation.

Ben had never been to New York, and he found the raucous city intimidating, being accustomed to the more leisurely pace of southern cities like Charleston and Savannah. The streets of New York's industrial district teemed with people, all hurrying to or from some mysterious destination, and all seemingly driven by a similarly mysterious purpose.

The streets reverberated with voices pitched loud enough to cause an unknowing visitor to attribute anger to the hundreds of people pushing and shoving their way along. The cobblestones rang to the clatter of horses' hooves and the clank of iron-rimmed wheels, as carts, carriages, and delivery wagons fought their way through the throng. Ben saw every manner of dress and heard languages from all over the world.

The city had color and fascination, yet Ben knew that

he could never become accustomed to the noise and unseemly bustle.

He visited five factories altogether and was surprised, and a little encouraged, by the fact that cigarette making still took third place in importance to the production of chewing tobacco and snuff. Cigars, he learned, were produced in the main by small businesses throughout the city and sold wholesale to the larger companies, which in turn then sold them to the public.

"Cigar making sprang up before and during the war, and it is a special art. Most of the cigar making lads are Cubans." This information was given him by the superintendent of one of the larger plants, the last one Ben toured. The superintendent was an affable individual by the name of Red Bryans, who seemed delighted to show Ben the workings of his plant. "What the hell, bucko, you being from the South, your proposed factory can't be after offering us much competition, now can it?" he said after Ben introduced himself and explained his purpose. "And from what I hear you Southerners ain't all that energetic, anyways. No offense meant."

"None taken." Ben smiled tightly, remembering Bradley Hollister. "But that is a canard, to a certain extent. A few Southerners can move pretty fast, when it's called for. But actually what we have in mind is cigarette production, and your company seems to be primarily interested in turning out pipe and chewing tobacco."

"Oh, we turn out a goodly amount of cigs, but the owner thinks cigarette smoking is a fad, saying it won't last. Can't say as I entirely agree with him, but he's the boss." The Irishman shrugged, and spat a stream of brown tobacco juice onto the ground. "Maybe if he learns you fellows down there are going into cigarette production, that will get him moving more in that direction. One problem you're going to have is finding people to make the damned things. Everybody we find who knows how are foreigners, Russians, Poles, and the like. Mostly Jews."

So close was he to stumbling onto Ben's purpose here that Ben winced inside.

Bryans was saying, "Come along with me, and I'll let you see all there is to see."

Ben followed him into a large room redolent with the scent of ripe tobacco. The room was crowded with small, marble-topped tables piled high with tobacco. A cigarette roller sat at each table. Ben was surprised, and a little dismayed, to discover that more than half of the rollers were women, young girls mostly.

He commented on this to Bryans.

"Yup, that's true. Two reasons for that, I guess. We don't pay wages good enough to interest the lads, and the lasses make better cigarette rollers, anyways. Their fingers are smaller, faster, used to handling needle and thread they are, you see."

Ben's gaze swept the big room. His curiosity was aroused by a contraption in the rear, tended by three men. It consisted of a flywheel and pulley, and a great, long, wooden cylinder open at the end opposite the flywheel. As the cylinder turned, shredded tobacco poured in a brown waterfall from the open end. The tobacco was dumped onto a canvas cloth spread on the floor. As Ben watched, the cylinder stopped turning, and one of the men gathered up the cloth of tobacco by its four ends, and carried it down the room, distributing tobacco at the marble tables.

Noting the direction of Ben's gaze, Bryans said, "We call that the 'ordering' cylinder. It reconditions the tobacco coming in, for cigarette making. Now, I have me other duties to attend to. I'll have the foreman here fill you in on what you want to know." He raised his voice. "Jacob, come here, will you?"

A short man with a round face, shaggy gray hair, and twinkling brown eyes bustled over. He took a cigar stub from his mouth. "Yes, Mr. Bryans?"

"This here fellow is from North Carolina, Jacob, Ben Ascher by name. He's interested in cigarette making. Since you're in charge here, I thought you could show him around. This here is Jacob Lefkowitz, bucko." Bryans got a sly look. "You two should get along fine, speaking the same language, you might say."

As the superintendent walked away, Ben held out his hand. "I'm pleased to meet you, Mr. Lefkowitz."

"A landsman, from south United States?" The man spoke good English, but with a thick accent.

Ben grinned easily. "There are a few of us down there, Mr. Lefkowitz. You're from Europe, I gather?" At Lefkowitz's nod, Ben said, "How long?"

"Five years now."

"You speak the language well."

Jacob Lefkowitz beamed proudly. "I go to school, every night. Study hard." He waved a short-fingered hand around. "What would you like to see?"

"Everything. I am in a partnership to start a tobacco factory in North Carolina. I need to know everything."

Jacob ushered him down the room to where a pretty, dark girl who could not have been twenty-one sat rolling cigarettes. Ben watched in fascination as she spread tobacco evenly onto a rectangle of white paper. Then she rolled the shredded tobacco leaf and paper into a compact cylinder, her fingers quick and supple. Next, she sealed the seam by dipping her finger into a bowl of moist, white substance, and rubbing it along the paper.

Ben indicated the bowl. "What's the paste made from?"

"Flour and water," Jacob replied. He placed a fatherly hand on the girl's shoulder. She glanced up. Even in its weariness her thin face was lovely, and her brown eyes became animated as they observed Ben.

Jacob said, "This is Rachel. She is our best and quickest cigarette maker, and my daughter. Rachel, this is Mr. Ben Ascher, from North Carolina."

"How do you do, Mr. Ascher." Her voice was warm and vibrant, and she did not have her father's accent. Her face really came alive when she smiled, a dimple appearing and disappearing in her left cheek.

It was clear to Ben that she had inherited her father's good humor. He said, "I am pleased to meet you, Rachel. How many of those can you make in a day?"

"I can roll four a minute," she said.

Jacob beamed with pride. "Rachel is the best roller in

the shop. The others do good to average two or three a minute."

"Let's see, you roll approximately two hundred and forty an hour," Ben mused. "At ten hours a day, that amounts to twenty-four hundred a day." He whistled softly. "That's pretty good. Of course, that's not taking into consideration your luncheon time off, or other breaks during the day."

"Twelve hours a day, Mr. Ascher," Rachel said. "And we get only a half hour for lunch, and no other time off during the day."

Ben was appalled. "Twelve hours a day! That's slave labor! How do you endure it?"

"Many do not, Mr. Ascher," her father said. "You have to be . . . How would you say, hardy? Rachel is stronger than she looks. Not only does she work hard but"—he gestured around the big room—"no windows, see? Tobacco dust is bad for lungs. Rollers cough all the time. Many get sick and die. Bad, very bad."

Looking around the barn-like room, Ben saw that it was true. The room had no ventilation whatsoever, and now he noticed the workers coughing, an ugly sound in the otherwise quiet room. He also noticed that none stopped working as they coughed, and the floor was littered with filth, and even the rolling tables were none too clean. It could not be considered a healthy atmosphere by any means.

He asked, "And what do they pay you for all this?"

"Fifty cents a thousand cigarettes, Mr. Ascher," Rachel said.

He calculated in his head. "That's less than two dollars a day! Even for rollers as good as you are. God knows what the others earn."

Jacob said glumly, "They make little more than food for their table. That is the reason most rollers are women. Man with a family cannot afford to work here. How many times I tell Rachel, she should not work here."

"We need the money, Poppa. You well know that," Rachel said.

Ben filed the figures away in his mind for future reference, and switched to a less unpleasant subject. "Mr. Lefkowitz, how are the cigarettes packaged?"

Jacob stepped to a nearby table, and picked up a paper-hinged, foil-lined box. "In this. It holds twenty smokes."

Ben examined the package. The retail price marked on it was ten cents. He calculated swiftly. A thousand cigarettes would bring two dollars, which would include fifty cents Federal tax, twenty to thirty cents for the tobacco at the current price, leaving a dollar-twenty for labor, packaging, selling, and profit. If King Tobacco sent a package to market at a cost of fifteen cents—he knew that some brands were marketing for that price—it would allow them to pay higher labor costs, and use a better grade of tobacco. He understood that the best grades were used for snuff and chewing tobacco, leaving the inferior product for cigarettes. Also, the package itself was not very attractive; he was confident that Clint, with his fertile imagination, could put together a better package. Closing his eyes, he could visualize the logo, King Cigarettes, on the pack.

"Mr. Lefkowitz, could I have this?"

Jacob shrugged. "It is all right with me. What else you care to see?" He swept a hand around.

"I think I've seen enough for the moment." Ben glanced around and lowered his voice. "Mr. Lefkowitz, I would like very much to talk to you, but this is hardly the place, not for the proposition I wish to put to you. Where do you eat your lunch?"

Jacob's heavy eyebrows elevated. "We bring our lunches in pail, Rachel and me."

"Then could I buy you lunch?" Ben looked quickly at Rachel and saw her lively eyes on him. "The invitation includes your lovely daughter, naturally."

Rachel dimpled at him. "I don't know about Poppa, Mr. Ascher, but I would be most happy to accept your invitation."

Jacob was frowning. "Why do you do this? This proposition you speak of. . . What is that?"

"It is a business proposition, Mr. Lefkowitz, one that will be to your benefit. But I would prefer that you not mention it to anyone else, not at this time. Will you come?"

Jacob stared at him out of eyes dark with distrust. He finally nodded, slowly.

They had their lunch in a Jewish delicatessen several blocks away from the tobacco factory; Ben wanted to make sure there were no other workers from the plant who might see them together. The delicatessen was noisy and crowded, redolent with the smells of rich, spicy food.

After they had picked up their food and found an empty table in one corner, Jacob shook his head, an expression near awe on his broad features as he studied the spread of food. Ben had insisted that they order whatever they liked. Jacob had only done so at Rachel's urgings: "Poppa, if Mr. Ascher is purchasing our time, we should take advantage."

As they began to eat, Ben said, "Since you have very little time for lunch, I hope you don't mind if we talk while we eat."

Jacob shrugged. "I do not mind, Mr. Ascher."

"It is true that I am interested in cigarette making, but that is not the real reason I am here. I am starting a tobacco factory in Durham, North Carolina, along with two partners. We plan to go heavily into cigarette production, and for that we need skilled cigarette rollers. There are none in our area."

"This Carolina," Jacob said, "where is it?"

Ben tried to explain the geography of the South to him, but Jacob shook his head in bewilderment. "It is like a foreign country to me."

Rachel laughed gently. "The only thing Poppa knows of this country is New York. He has never been outside the city since he came to America. Of course, neither have I."

"I can assure both of you that it is a nice place to live. There is fresh air a-plenty, and a more leisurely life. Up here, you have to be careful every second on the street that a wagon doesn't run you over, or that some hurrying stranger doesn't knock you down. In Durham, there is none of that."

Jacob said, "Why do you say all this to us?"

"I say it because I want to hire you, Mr. Lefkowitz, you and your daughter. I want you to work for King Tobacco. Not only that, but I want you to recruit other rollers for us. At least fifty for when we go into production next fall. I don't think we'll be able to begin full production before this year's tobacco crop is ready. You may tell them that we will pay a rate of seventy cents per thousand cigarettes. And on top of that, we will pay the train fares to Durham."

Jacob was shaking his head. "The rollers will not like to leave their families behind."

"Oh, I should explain. They will bring their families along, of course. We will also pay their train fares." Ben looked from Jacob to his daughter. "I don't know what kind of quarters you have at present, but from what I've seen of New York, I'd wager you live in a tenement."

"That is all too true, Mr. Ascher." Rachel made a sour face. "Poppa and I are alone, but most workers have large families, and many live in just one room. The buildings are infested with rats and cockroaches and are filthy. They are too hot in summer and too cold in winter. The landlords charge high rents and refuse to spend any money on paint or repairs."

"That is the beauty of my proposition, you see," Ben argued persuasively. "In Durham, each family will be able to have their own houses, with yard space for children to play, and we have few rats or cockroaches. If you agree, Mr. Lefkowitz, to recruit the workers for us, I will start finding houses for them immediately on my return to Durham. Many houses stand empty now, because of the war, or for other reasons."

"Heavenly, it sounds heavenly," Rachel said wistfully. She placed her small hand on her father's heavily muscled forearm. "Poppa?"

Jacob was frowning, worrying his lower lip. "It is a

frightening thing, my Rachel. When I left my homeland across the water, I was a young man, and I was by myself. I did not have a daughter to worry about."

Rachel said dryly, "I am almost twenty-one, Poppa. That's hardly a tender age, so you don't have to worry about me."

"But I have roots in the city now. This is my home."

"Home!" Rachel hooted. "Anything would be better than this city. Just think of fresh, clean air, no soot and smoke. Sunshine and openness." She directed a look at Ben. "I think it sounds marvelous, Mr. Ascher."

Jacob pushed his empty plate back, and lit a cigar. He said suddenly, "Jews, are there any Jews in your Durham, Mr. Ascher?"

Ben was taken slightly aback. "Not too many, I'm afraid, Mr. Lefkowitz."

"How many young men of Jewish faith, unmarried men?"

"I'm afraid there aren't all that many," Ben answered honestly.

"There, you see! We cannot go!" Jacob threw his hands up.

"Why not, Poppa? What does that have to do with our going?"

"Young men for you, my daughter. It is time you were married."

"Poppa!" Rachel flushed, looking away in embarrassment. "This is not the time to talk about that."

"Why not time?" her father said belligerently. "I have talked and talked. You never listen to Poppa."

"I mean"—she gestured to Ben without looking at him—"before Mr. Ascher, a total stranger."

Ben said, "But surely, among all the rollers and their families, there must be eligible men."

Jacob snorted. "You think I want my Rachel to marry a cigarette maker?"

"Poppa! Now that's enough!" Rachel struck the table with the flat of her hand. "When I find a man I want to marry, I will marry, and not before!"

"In the old country..."

"This is not the old country, Poppa. Besides, Mr. Ascher..." Now she looked at Ben, her eyes suddenly dancing with mischief. "He is from Durham, and he is certainly eligible. Unless he is already married?"

Ben said without thinking, "No, I am not married."

Now it was Jacob's turn to be outraged. "Rachel! It is not proper for a young woman to be so bold!"

"Bold?" Rachel widened her eyes in innocence. "I was merely pointing out that since Mr. Ascher is an eligible man, Durham must have others. Mr. Ascher..." She looked intently at Ben, serious now. "We accept your proposition. It is a wonderful opportunity for us."

"Girl, you do not decide for me!" Jacob thundered, causing heads to swivel their way.

Rachel said, "Don't pay any attention to Poppa. He likes to grumble like a bear, but the idea appeals to him, I can tell. You shall have your cigarette rollers, Mr. Ascher."

It was "burning time."

Charlotte had asked Bradley Hollister to send word when he intended to burn the first plant bed for the new season's tobacco crop. When Jimmie rode in to inform her, Charlotte went in search of Clint.

"I just received word, Clint. Mr. Hollister is burning his new plant beds tonight. I want to watch it. It's a festive occasion,,with the neighbors coming from all around."

Clint motioned with his cigar. "I don't know why I have to tag along, Lotte. I don't need to know all that to sell tobacco."

"I think you should be familiar with every phase of tobacco, from the first seeds into the ground to the finished product. You'll find it fascinating, I'm sure. Besides, there's nothing else important to occupy your time right now." She motioned scornfully around the bank where she had found him, deep in conversation with the bank's president.

Clint sighed. "I'm making friends. That's always important in any business. And we may need Tarbuck's bank, when it comes time to swing into full production. But what the hell," he grinned lazily, "I'm sure I'll find your company more interesting than any banker's."

The tobacco season for the growers usually began in January. They waited for a few days of sunny weather. Even if snow still lay along the fences and spread like white skirts around the shaded tree trunks, a few days of warm sun were sufficient to thaw the earth.

Bradley Hollister had already selected a spot of new ground for burning, with rich, loamy soil. The land was slanted, for good drainage, and well-exposed to the sun. Hollister and Jimmie had spent the early winter months clearing the land of timber, stacking the green wood nearby, and hauling in dead branches and logs to mix with the green wood. Lastly the wood was spread evenly over the ground. It was the custom to wait until night to apply the torches; a fire was more satisfying at night.

It was just dark when Charlotte and Clint rode up to the Hollister farm in a buggy. They had brought blankets along, with ample food, and Clint had a bottle of brandy.

By the time they reached the proposed burning bed, men, boys, and a few women from neighboring farms had gathered.

Bradley Hollister came out to greet them. "Glad you could come out, Charlotte. You, too, Mr. Devlin." He grinned happily, absent-mindedly rubbing the arm stub. "It's going to be a good year, I can feel it in my bones. But for you, Charlotte, none of us would have the money for seeds and such."

Charlotte said, "There was some self-interest involved, Mr. Hollister. Without your product, we could never manage to get our factory into operation."

Just then Jimmie came charging up. "Pa, is it time?" he asked eagerly. "The boys are ready."

"Fire her up, son." Hollister laughed as the youth scampered off. To Clint, he said, "We let the young-uns do the setting and tending the fires. They make a great sport out of it. The rest, us old codgers, squat around the fires, tell tall tales, and drink a little corn squeezings. You and Charlotte find a spot for yourselves and settle down."

Already Jimmie and the other boys were running about the perimeter of the burning bed, applying torches to the stacks of wood. Flames began to lick inward from the edges of the burn.

Charlotte and Clint spread their blankets on the windward side of the fire, and settled down. From the picnic basket, Charlotte took two cups, and Clint splashed brandy into them. He picked up a burning brand, lit a cigar, and they drank from the cups.

Charlotte noticed in the crowd several farmers with whom she had done business on her two peddling trips. She spoke to them, but most of them seemed reserved, far from friendly. This worried her, since many of them had signed contracts with King Tobacco, binding them to sell this year's tobacco crop to the partners, at whatever prices prevailed at the time.

When Bradley Hollister, who had been working his way around the burn, came their way again, she beckoned him over.

"Mr. Hollister, I've noticed a certain reserve among most of the farmers here. They seem to avoid talking to me. What's the matter, do you know?"

"I'm afraid I do, Charlotte." Pulling a long face, Hollister squatted down beside them. "I was going to talk to you about it before the night was over. Through Cob Jenks, Lutcher has been issuing threats to the men, telling what he will do to them if they follow through on their contracts to sell their tobacco to you."

Charlotte tightened up. "What sort of threats?"

"Oh, nothing right out in the open. Lutcher's too shrewd a fellow for that. Hints that tobacco barns might catch fire, things like that. Or that, if they sell to you, he will never buy from them again."

"He'll be cutting his throat, if he does that," Clint said with a chuckle. He poured brandy into a cup and handed it to Hollister. "If he refuses to buy from them, where will he get his tobacco to keep his factory going?"

Hollister hoisted the tin cup in a silent toast, and drank.

"Good brandy, Clint. About Lutcher, he also sent word around that he'll top whatever price you pay."

Charlotte said indignantly, "Can't anything be done about his threats of fire? By making threats like that, he's breaking the law, isn't he?"

"Reckon so," Hollister said laconically. "But how to pin it on him? Cob Jenks is speaking for him, and I'm sure that Lutcher would claim that Jenks is doing it on his own."

"Just like he denied giving Jenks orders to attack you, Lotte," Clint said. "Remember what he said at the mayor's ball?" He drank from the cup, his face settling into grim lines. "Perhaps I should have a few words with this Jenks. I've seen him around Durham. He's a scroungy looking gent, mean-looking as an aroused porcupine. But it's been my experience that that kind of a fellow backs down when somebody calls him out."

"No, Clint, that might make matters worse." Charlotte placed a hand on his arm. "Besides, he might back down, as you say, but he's the kind of man who would just as soon kill you when your back's turned. There has to be another way." She directed her glance at Hollister. "What do the farmers say? Are they being frightened off by Lutcher's threats?"

"Some, maybe. It's hard to say for sure." Hollister shrugged. "I guess you can only wait until their crop's ready for market, to know for dead certain."

Charlotte said glumly, "By that time, it'll be too late for us to find other tobacco."

"But they all have contracts with King Tobacco, don't they?" Clint asked.

"Most of them, yes."

"Then if they sell to Lutcher instead, take them into court on it."

She shook her head. "No, I'd never do that. I'm not going to force them to do something they don't want to do."

Clint sighed in exasperation. "Lotte, I don't know about you and business. Sometimes you *have* to be ruthless.

What the hell, it would only be forcing them to live up to their legal agreements."

"I don't care," she said obstinately. "I've seen too much of forcing people around Durham to live up to their legal agreements, causing hardship and tragedy. People have lost their farms, their homes, through just such agreements."

"It's hardly the same thing, Lotte. They won't be *losing* anything, they'll still get paid for their product."

"Charlotte's right, Clint," Hollister said unexpectedly. "What she'd be doing, if she forces them, will make enemies. Now I don't know much about business, but making enemies of the very people you need don't strike me as good business."

"All right, all right, I know when I'm outvoted." Clint threw up his hands, grinning amiably.

"And if you're thinking of getting Ben to vote with you, you're wrong," Charlotte said. "I know him better than that."

"Oh, you do, do you?" He stared at her, his grin still intact. "You care to explain that?"

She flushed, her head going back. "I don't have to explain anything to you, Clint Devlin."

Hollister finished his brandy with a toss of his head, and got to his feet. "Well, I'm sure it'll all work out." He wandered off.

Clint reached over for her hand. "My apologies, Lotte. I'm a cynic, never denied it, and I tend to take the harsh view of things. Forgiven?"

Charlotte flashed him an absent-minded smile. "Forgiven."

She was busy thinking ahead, for a contingency plan in the event the farmers did renege on their contracts. Something tickled her memory. That gaudily dressed little man she had met in Lutcher's factory—the tobacco auctioneer. What *was* his name? Watson, that was it, Clyde Watson. "Called Dandy by some."

She lay back on the blankets, while Clint sipped brandy and smoked his cigar. She tried to recall everything Clyde

Watson had said, and what she knew about tobacco auctioneering. Gradually, a plan took vague shape in her mind.

She turned her head and looked over at Clint. "Clint, you said you could float a loan on our company. You really think you could manage it?"

He glanced at her with his lazy smile. "Sure thing, dear heart." His glance sharpened. "What's cooking in that devious mind of yours now?"

"I'd rather not discuss it just yet. It needs some more thinking."

She turned her face the other way to discourage further conversation. It was growing late now. The fire had died down somewhat, but the youngsters kept feeding it fresh wood, so it blazed up every so often. On both sides of Charlotte, men squatted by the line of fire, drinking and talking in drawling voices. The combination of the fire's warmth and the drone of voices made her drowsy. She drifted off to sleep. She came partly awake some time later as Clint covered her with another blanket, tucking it closely around her.

It was full daylight when she woke again. The main fire had died, except for a few smouldering logs here and there. Several small fires had sprung up around the bed, and men huddled around them against the morning chill. Clint also had a small fire going, a blackened coffee pot burbling on a bed of coals.

As she sat up, Clint looked over at her. The rising sun's rays struck his face, and Charlotte saw a faint stubble of beard along his jaw. His eyes danced. "You know, my dear, this is the first time I've ever spent the night outdoors with a lady, without sharing her blankets."

Charlotte felt a blush heat her cheeks. She looked around quickly, fearful someone had overheard his teasing remark. But everyone's attention was focused on the newly burned plant bed, where Hollister and his son, along with several neighboring men, were trodding gingerly across the still smoking earth, clearing the smouldering logs out of the way. Next, they attacked the ground with rakes and hoes, turning it. As the earth was turned, it emitted wisps of steam.

Clint moved to her side, with two cups of steaming coffee. She took one gratefully, and sipped at it. The hot coffee was laced with brandy. The pungent steam cleared her head, and sent warmth coursing through her.

"You know something," Clint said musingly, "this whole business has a ritual flavor to it, like some ancient sorcerer's rites."

Charlotte smiled faintly. "I suppose you're right, but then hasn't that always been true of planting, harvesting, and all things connected with the earth? People who till the soil, depend on it tor their livelihood, they tend to think that all things, good or bad, come from it. And if you think what's gone before was like a religious rite, watch this."

She indicated Bradley Hollister, who was now following behind the men and boys as they raked the soil carefully to remove the last clods and roots. He carried a large, wooden bowl, suspended from a harness around his neck. As he walked, he dipped into the bowl for the tiny tobacco seeds, then mixed them with ashes, and sowed them with meticulous care. All around the burn bed, men, women, and children stood silently, watching, their faces almost reverent. The men had removed their hats, and not a word was spoken until Hollister had sown all the seeds.

Then a faint cheer went up from all sides, and slowly the people began to disperse, most of them heading for their horses or wagons for the trek home.

But Hollister and those helping him were not yet done. Now they tromped evenly across the seeded earth, moving in a straight line, their booted feet marching in a precisioned rhythm, making sure that all the seeds were buried. Lastly, they picked up brush limbs that had earlier been selected for this purpose and placed them over the bed.

"It reminds me of shingling a roof," Clint remarked. He shook his head. "My God, all that work!"

"This is only the beginning. There will be other plant

beds made." Charlotte got to her feet, and as if by unspoken agreement, they began gathering up their belongings. All the while she was explaining what the farmers would do next.

"Some time in May the tobacco season really begins. The land for planting the seedlings will already have been plowed and harrowed, and rows of hills made with hoes. Then they wait for the first May rains.

"Shortly after sunrise on that day in May, Mr. Hollister and Jimmie will carefully remove the tobacco plants from these beds, and place them into baskets, handling them as tenderly as they would a newly born babe. They bruise easily. The task requires two people, a dropper and a setter. In this case I'm sure Jimmie will be the dropper. Moving along the row, he will drop a plant at each hill. Following behind, Mr. Hollister will drive a setting peg into the loose dirt, press the roots of the new plant around the peg, and then carefully fill the peg hole with dirt. By the time the long day is done, Mr. Hollister will not be able to straighten up, moving bent over all day. It's grueling labor."

Clint grunted. "I can see that." They were in the buggy now, and Clint flicked the reins, clucking softly to the horse.

Charlotte said, "How well I remember when my father was alive, before the war, and the men would come in from the fields at dusk. They would lie face down on the porch, while their wives walked back and forth across their backs with their bare feet.

"But the work is only beginning with the planting of the seedlings. As summer comes, the growers work day after day, plowing, hoeing, then priming and topping and suckering. Then the worms and the tobacco flies come to plague them. The farmers crawl up and down the rows of plants all day, turning each leaf searching for tobacco worms or the eggs of the tobacco fly. The juice from the plants gets on their hands, and if they touch their eyes, they will burn for days. I recall when one of our hands missed a tobacco worm. Daddy made him bite it in two with his teeth. That may sound cruel, but Daddy was not an unkind man, just protective of his crop. It was a lesson the hand never forgot.

"When the plants are full-grown, there is a fearful wait until August, and cutting time. There is always the danger of hail, which can destroy a whole year's work within minutes. Yet the tobacco cannot be cut until it is fully ripe.

"Finally, the cutting begins. The cutters go into the fields with their tobacco knives. With one sure stroke, they split each stalk clear to the roots. Then another stroke slices it off close to the ground, and the stalk is hung upside down on the tobacco stick to dry before being taken into the curing barn.

"In the curing barn are usually two tiers of poles, spaced about four feet apart. The top tier pole is loaded first with the heavy sticks of green tobacco. If the tobacco is not hung properly, 'house burn,' which is a kind of rot, can occur, spoiling the whole crop. And if too much heat is applied too quickly, before most of the sap is gone from the leaf, the tobacco could be scalded. Later, when the sap is sweated out, just one cured leaf touching a flame can erupt into an explosion of fire, and all the tobacco, as well as the curing barn, can burn down . . ."

Charlotte broke off. "But the curing you must see for yourself, Clint. That is another festive occasion, much like last night and this morning. When the time comes, in August, I'll let you know."

Clint shook his head, laughing. "Did anyone ever tell you, Lotte, that too much is enough? You've told me more than I need, or want to know, about tobacco."

"You can never know too much," Charlotte said firmly. "When you're out there selling, many buyers will want to know what grade of tobacco you're peddling, if it was cured right, and so forth. A buyer *should* be able to tell just by inspecting, but many of them can't."

"And that's just the reason I can't spend my time watching this curing you're talking about, Lotte. By August, we'll be on the verge of full production, and I'll be out there, selling my tail off. I'll be on the road night and day. Especially our first year. I can't trust others to do it right."

"My understanding is that a good business executive knows when and where to delegate duties," she commented.

"That's true, when you have trained men under you that you can trust. Until that time comes, I'll have to do most of it myself." Clint threw his smoked cigar into the road, and said ruefully, "Fact is, I don't know how I'll take to being behind a desk all day. I'm used to being out among people, wheeling and dealing. It's in my blood, I reckon."

"One thing you're going to have to do is give up those things." She made a face, gesturing to the road.

"What things?"

"Those cigars."

"Now just whoa up, Lotte. We're not married, you have no right to approve or disapprove of my personal habits."

"It's not your personal habits I'm concerned about. But how do you think it will look, you trying to sell cigarettes while smoking a cigar?"

He pondered for a moment, frowning. "I never thought of it in that light. You could be right. I'll tell you what, my dear. I'll compromise. When I'm with a customer, I'll be noble and forgo the cigars. Agree?"

She snorted softly. "Clint Devlin, being noble. That will indeed be the day!"

It was nearing noon when they entered the outskirts of Durham. Clint said, "I don't know about you, Lotte, but I feel grimy, and saturated with wood smoke. I need a bath and a change of clothes. As I recall, you have a change in my house. We could stop by, share a bath, and," he leered broadly, "maybe a spell in bed."

"You put it so elegantly, Mr. Devlin," she said dryly.

Since that first time on Christmas Eve, Charlotte had spent a great deal of time in Clint's little house; she had grown quite shameless about it. She enjoyed their stolen moments together, she no longer tried to deny that.

During the day she worked long hours getting as much as she could done toward preparing King Tobacco to go into full production, and she had come to look forward to the physical comfort this man offered. She supposed she was the subject of much speculation and gossip among Durhamites, but she closed her eyes and ears to it. After all, she now was, in Clint's words, "a sophisticated woman."

Now she said, "Your offer is tempting, and I will consider it, Clint. But first, let's go by the factory, and see if everything is all right."

"You are a slave driver, Lotte," he said in a grumbling voice, but he detoured by the factory building.

They had a skeleton staff now—three women to do secretarial work, a male bookkeeper, and another man to oversee the changes necessary to make the plant operative. A crew of carpenters and painters had been at work for some time. As they approached the building on Railroad Street, Charlotte viewed with pride the large letters above the entrance: The Ascher, Devlin, and King Tobacco Company. The sign had been painted two days ago. Charlotte was secretly pleased over something that developed since their company had been formed; in referring to it, everyone always said, "King Tobacco." She was a little apprehensive over how Clint would react to this; Ben did not care a whit, she well knew, but Clint was a different matter. So far, he had made no comment.

There was a surprise waiting in her office—a telegram from Ben stating that he would be arriving on the noon train from New York.

She charged out of the office waving the telegram. "Ben's coming in today! He's on the noon train, and we have to hurry if we're going to be there to meet him!"

Peering out the parlor car window as the train entered the station, Ben saw Charlotte and Clint waiting on the platform. His heart gave a leap at the sight of Charlotte. Each time he saw her he realized anew how beautiful she was. The sun struck coppery glints off her long hair, and her lissome figure was evident even in the long, crinoline-stiffened skirt and her high-necked blouse. Well aware of Clint's reputation as a womanizer, Ben had been uneasy about going off and leaving them together. Now, seeing them stand close together, his fears were renewed, for it seemed to him that there was an air of intimacy about them. He shrugged away his doubts as a flight of fancy. He could not be by her side every minute of every day.

He was down the train steps before it had come to a complete stop, and striding toward them, his bag swinging from one hand.

Charlotte's face lit up at the sight of him, and she waved. As Ben approached closer, he took note of the fact that they both looked rumpled and somewhat grimy, and Clint was unshaven. It was one of the few times Ben had seen him anything but immaculate, and he had to wonder uneasily what they had been doing together.

"Ben, how nice you're back!" Charlotte stepped up to kiss him on the cheek, and it took a conscious effort on Ben's part to keep from embracing her. Only Clint's presence prevented him from doing so.

"Benbo." Clint held out his hand. "Did you have a good trip?"

"A productive one, I hope. And how did things go here while I've been gone?"

"Moving right along," Clint replied. "About all we need now is the tobacco, and we'll be ready to conquer the world."

"Same old Clint, full of optimism."

"It seems like you've been gone forever, Ben," Charlotte said.

"It seems so to me, too, and I'm certainly glad to be back." He made a face. "If I never have to go to the big city again, I'll be just as happy."

"Come along, Ben, and we'll show you what we've accomplished." She linked arms with him. "We have a buggy."

Clint fell in on the other side of Ben, and they made their way to where the buggy waited.

When Ben had tossed his bag in, Charlotte said with an embarrassed laugh, "You'll have to excuse the way I look, Ben. We've been out to Bradley Hollister's farm all night. I wanted Clint to see how they burned new tobacco beds. We stayed there until after sunup, watching them seed the tobacco in, and we just arrived back at the plant to find your telegram. We came straight here."

Ben experienced a sense of relief, and he glanced at Clint with a slight smile.

"She's bound and determined that I watch the tobacco all the way," Clint said with a grin. "She's a determined lady, Benbo."

"But tell us, Ben," Charlotte said urgently, "did you find the cigarette rollers?"

"I did," Ben said with a broad smile. "There'll be fifty or more coming down in late August."

"Well now. It looks like we're in business, eh, Lotte?" Clint said, taking Charlotte's arm possessively.

Charlotte flushed and took her arm away. Her glance crossed Ben's, and she quickly looked off.

Ben knew then, even without the affectionate "Lotte," what had taken place in his absence. His first impulse was to smash his fist into Clint's face, but he willed control on himself, and stood back with an expressionless face, as Clint gave Charlotte a hand up into the buggy seat.

# Chapter Ten

WITH Ben's return to Durham, there began a subtle change in the relationship of the three partners. Charlotte realized this almost at once, and she was sure that Ben did, but Clint seemed blithely unaware of the undercurrents now set in motion.

Fortunately the change affected only their personal relationship; their business life went on pretty much as before. By now they had learned each other's strengths and weaknesses, and they functioned well as a team. Their days were very busy.

Charlotte was occupied with putting together a smoothly functioning office staff, and in sending out her mailings. By dint of much effort she had put together an impressive list of all tobacco buyers throughout the South, small stores and large, and she was presently engaged in sending letters to all prospective buyers mentioning the fact that King Cigarettes, as well as a secondary line of chewing tobacco and snuff, would be available in the autumn. Since the latter items represented a strong market, they had agreed that they would provide a profitable operating base until their cigarette business was flourishing.

Ben, during his sojourn in New York, had learned what machinery was going to be required for their factory. It had been ordered, and he was supervising the installation as it came in.

Clint was busy mapping out his advertising campaign, and was planning a design for the cigarette pack. He had also arranged a loan, after a rather lengthy discussion among the partners. Always the conservative, Ben had been opposed. Charlotte had swung the other way, not necessarily because of Clint's persuasive arguments, but because she had come to see that they needed capital to assure the success of their operation. The monies they had individually invested in the company would be gone long before they earned their first penny. Ben had reluctantly gone along. To Charlotte's astonishment, Clint managed to swing the loan without too much difficulty. Through John Tarbuck and his Durham bank, using Tarbuck's banking connections, Clint had put together a consortium of money men, mostly southerners but including a few northern investors; and now they had enough operating capital to see them through, barring any unforeseen disaster.

With a sly grin, Clint had told her, "Now Lotte, you see what I meant about making friends? Without John Tarbuck, I might never have been able to swing it."

She did not give him the satisfaction of openly agreeing with him, yet she knew that he was right. But she also knew that the loan would be a burden on her mind until they were free of it. However, it had been necessary; she had some plans of her own that would require financing, plans she had yet to broach to her partners.

Their first real clash of wills came about when Clint presented a sketch of the package he had designed for King Cigarettes. He had employed an artist, Josh Rowan, and the pair had worked in seclusion for several weeks. Finally, Clint was ready, and he summoned Charlotte and Ben to his office.

In one corner of the room was a covered easel. Beaming, Clint announced, "We've designed a pack that is eye-catching, to say the least!"

With a flourish he whipped the cloth off the easel. Charlotte gasped as her glance swept over the sketch. Drawn in bold strokes was a female figure perched on an ornate throne. Dressed in high fashion, the woman was posed with her skirts hiked almost to the knee, her legs perched on a velvet-covered stool. Black silk stockings sheathed shapely legs, painted a glossy, titillating sheen. The neckline of the woman's dress was uncommonly low, exposing a plunge of snowy bosom, and her lips were curved in a provocative smile. Held delicately in the woman's left hand, between two fingers, was a smoking cigarette. In bold, black letters across the top was the logo: KING CIGARETTES.

"Well?" Clint demanded impatiently. "What do you think?"

Ben was shaking his head. "It will never do, Clint."

Clint took on a look of astonishment. "And why not?"

"It just won't. It's too daring, too bold by far."

"And what's wrong with that?" Clint said challengingly. "It will catch attention, you can't argue with that. What better way to catch a man's eye than a little female pulchritude?"

"Oh, it'll catch a man's eye, all right," Ben admitted with a slight smile.

Clint glanced at Charlotte. "How about you, Lotte? You haven't said anything yet."

"I think it's terrible."

"Oh, for God's sake!" Clint threw up his hands and walked away to the window to stare out. "I never knew that I was partnered with a couple of Puritans!"

"That has nothing to do with it. I'm not objecting on personal grounds. I'm thinking of how it will shock other people, the buyers out there."

Clint turned away from the window. "The chief principle of advertising, in my opinion, is to snag the buyer's attention at once. And both of you have to admit that this will do it."

"Clint," she said in a reasonable voice, "you once said that we're in the vice business. What you're trying to do here is combine two vices, sex and tobacco. While it may be true that men will be attracted to this and buy it once for that reason, why should they buy it again for the same reason? There has to be something more. And their wives, do you think they're going to be pleased when their man comes home with this? Aside from the blatant appeal to a man's lust, having the woman on the pack smoking, of all things! Women don't smoke cigarettes, at least not in public. That will have everybody up in arms!"

"You know what's wrong with you two?" Clint demanded. "No imagination, no scope. How can a man be innovative when faced with that? This whole business needs a new and daring approach."

"True, Clint," Ben responded. "But not *too* daring, at least not in the beginning. Take it a little slow. You know, if a man can't swim, the first time he goes into the water, he doesn't dive in head first. He wades in a bit at a time."

"Spare me the homilies, Benbo." Clint waved a hand at him.

"You have to admit that you're a little, shall we say, flamboyant, Clint?" Charlotte said dryly. "That's a fine quality in a salesman, I guess, but you need us unimaginative people to keep a rein on you."

"I take it then," he peered at them narrowly, "that I'm outvoted here?"

"You might say that."

Ben nodded. "I'm afraid so, Clint."

Clint threw up his hands again, a look of suffering on his face, and it crossed Charlotte's mind that he was being unduly dramatic.

He said, "Well, you can't say that I wasn't prepared for this."

With one swoop of his hand, he ripped the sheet from the easel, crumpled it up, and tossed it onto the floor, exposing a second sketch under the first. He motioned. "How about this one then?"

There were two figures in this sketch—a man and a woman. The King Cigarettes logo was across the bottom of this one.

The woman was dressed more decorously, yet Josh's bold strokes had managed to make her figure and pose provocative, but not offensively so. She was gazing adoringly up into the man's face. He was dressed somewhat flamboyantly, and there was a cigarette in his upraised hand, smoke drifting up.

Charlotte looked more closely at his face. Amused, she hid a smile behind her hand. The man's face bore a resemblance to Clint, not markedly, but just enough to make it noticeable. She had to wonder if that had been Josh's idea, or Clint's. She resisted an impulse to ask.

Ben was not so reluctant. "Fellow looks quite a bit like you, doesn't he, Clint?"

Clint took on an innocent look, and peered closely at the face. "You know, I really hadn't noticed that. I reckon I'll have to speak to Josh about it. Must have been his idea. If you two object to the resemblance, that is."

"Why should we object if you don't?" Charlotte said with a straight face. "After all, you once said that you wanted to be visible. You can't be much more visible than that."

"Does that mean that you like this one, Lotte?" he asked eagerly.

She took her time about answering, studying the sketch from all angles. In truth, she was quite excited about it. It had the right touch of male appeal, yet it was in good taste, so that it should not offend anyone. Finally, she said slowly, "I think it will do nicely. Ben?"

"It should work," he said judiciously, smiling slightly. "At least it's not blatant. Yes, I think it should sell King Cigarettes."

"And that's what it's all about, isn't it?" Clint said with a slight edge of sarcasm. "Well, if you two approve, we can get to work. I'll tell Josh to do the final design, and we'll send in our first order. Now"—he rubbed his hands together briskly—"I think a celebration toast is called for." From his desk he took a bottle of brandy and three glasses.

Ben accepted his with a dubious look. "It isn't even noon yet, but all right, seeing as it's an occasion."

They toasted each other. Charlotte took only a small sip, studying Clint furtively. He wore an air of jubilation, and seemed not at all downcast about their spurning his first design. Charlotte had the feeling that they had been somehow manipulated, that he had known in advance that they would turn down the first one, and in face of that disapproval, would be more receptive to the second presentation. She suspected that they had just been an audience for a consummate Clint Devlin performance.

That evening she went to Clint's house. Their trysts had been fewer since Ben's return from New York, much to Clint's displeasure. Following the meeting about the sketch, Charlotte had found a sealed note on her desk: "I will expect you this evening. Clint."

Charlotte had changed her mind several times during the afternoon, but in the end she had gone. The physical attraction Clint had for her had not diminished; on the contrary, it had grown stronger with each passing day.

Clint was frowning when he opened the door. "I was beginning to think you weren't coming."

"I just about didn't."

"I would have been unhappy if you hadn't." He let her in and closed the door.

"Why this night more than any other?"

"Because this day, to me, marks the true beginning. With our cigarette package designed and in production, I can start selling. I should think you, of all people, would understand that."

"I understand, Clint, I do, but . . ." She stood on tiptoe and kissed him.

He cupped her face between his hands, and stared down into her eyes. "But what, for hell's sake? What I would have liked to have done was dine out tonight, make a real evening of it. I'm getting sick of this sneaking around, my dear. It's simply not my style."

She retorted, "I'm sorry about your 'style,' but I have no intention of hurting Ben."

"Ben Ascher is full grown, and he will survive."

"And you, Clint Devlin, are a selfish man, totally concerned with your own pleasure."

"That's the way the world is, Lotte. There are losers, and there are winners. The winner gets the spoils."

"I know you admit to being a cynic, but sometimes your philosophy of life sickens me."

"Sickens you, does it?" he said sardonically.

Before she could protest, he had his arms around her, and his mouth captured hers. Her passion flared into life at the touch of his lips, and the familiar weakness seized her, spreading to all her extremities like a debilitating fever. His artful hands caressed her, and almost before she knew it, Charlotte was on the buffalo rug, her clothing disheveled and pushed up to expose her body to his stroking fingers. The weather had grown warm, but he still had a small fire laid in the hearth.

In the light from the flames, Charlotte could see his face over hers. As usual, when he made love to her, Clint was smiling.

As always, when she came to him, the thought of resisting his advances crossed her mind, but she knew that she would not. This was the reason she came—the arousing touch of his kiss; the stroke of his hands on her bared flesh; the ache of want in the center of her being; the yearning toward the strong yet tender entry into her body.

Charlotte sighed, and reached up to pull his head down to hers. She kissed him ardently, and her hands moved fluidly down the length of his body, urging him to her.

He moved to take her. At the moment of entry, he laughed softly, and said, "Does this sicken you, my love?"

Anger caused her to start to draw away, but then he thrust into her. She relaxed, her anger gone in an instant, and she surged against him, as her pleasure began.

The ecstasy Clint always brought to her took Charlotte out of herself. For these few breathless minutes she was all feeling and passion, no thought of before or after in her mind. Her entire being was concentrated on that final shuddering spasm of rapture.

As always, it happened with unexpected suddenness. Too soon, too soon! As she gave voice to a muted cry, she clutched him, holding him captive in her fierce embrace, until their passion had subsided; and they lay still locked together, hearts thundering in unison, mingled breaths rasping harshly.

When Clint finally moved away, reaching for the inevitable cigar, Charlotte watched him for a few moments through half-lowered eyelids. He was a handsome man, a virile and skilled lover to fulfill any woman's dreams; and she knew that she would never forget the soaring pleasure he gave her.

Yet, it had to end.

If she allowed their liaison to continue, and Ben learned about it, it could result in friction between the two men, and in the end could rip their partnership asunder. The company came first with her; she had the feeling that King Tobacco would always come first. She had given up Ben—in the romantic sense—for it. She could, and would, do the same with Clint.

Clint said idly, "What's all the deep thought about, Lotte?"

"Just... things, things in general." She looked at him gravely. "You're right about sneaking around, Clint. It must stop."

He smiled broadly. "Now that I'm pleased to hear."

"No, I don't think you understand, Clint. I mean it all has to stop, all of this, our... being together, secretly or otherwise."

He began to frown. "What are you talking about, Lotte? We like each other, we're great together. I don't recall ever enjoying being with a woman so much."

"It's Ben," she said simply.

"Ben! Goddamnit, Lotte, I told you, Ben is a grown man, he has the good sense to accept the truth about us."

"And what if he doesn't?" She sat up. "This may sound like vanity, but Ben is in love with me. He told me so, he even talked of marriage."

"And what did you say to that?"

"I told him that I wasn't interested in marriage, not for a long time to come. The thing is, if he learns about us, it could cause a rift that could easily destroy King Tobacco, and I will not risk that."

"You're worrying needlessly. Ben is too sensible to allow

his personal life to interfere with business." He tried to take her hand, but she evaded him.

"Clint Devlin might not let it interfere with business. But Ben might. Anyway, I'm not taking the risk."

"Just like that, you're going to call it quits?" He shook his head with disbelief, and his eyes glinted with anger. "I can't believe this!"

"You had better believe it, Clint, because tonight is the last time. Besides, from what I've learned about you, you'll find another woman soon enough."

"Damnit, I don't want another woman, I want you, Lotte!"

Charlotte was surprised by his show of anger; she had not anticipated that he would be this upset. "Why so angry, Clint? You don't love me."

"I never said that."

"You never said you did, either." She got up and began putting her clothes in order.

"You're a cold woman, Charlotte," he said bitterly. "To you, King Tobacco is more important than anything else."

"At this time in my life, that happens to be true," she said crisply. "I will think about my personal life, after the company is a going concern."

He said sourly, "By that time, you may be a crotchety old maid."

"You know what I think?" She peered at him closely. "I think you're angry because I'm the one who is stopping it. Your male pride is wounded. Is this the first time a woman has ever done this to you? It's fine for *you* to do it, but different for a woman. Am I right?"

"Think what you like."

Her clothing arranged to her satisfaction, Charlotte started for the door. "Lotte?"

She paused. "Yes?"

"Has Ben Ascher made love to you?"

"Now that is none of your business, Clint, and I do not intend to answer you!"

"He did, didn't he? You weren't a virgin, I well know that. Is that the reason you're doing this?"

"Why, you're jealous!" For some strange reason, this knowledge gladdened her heart. "Clint Devlin, jealous! I find that hard to believe."

Laughing, she went out of the house. Her laughter died as she climbed into the buggy. Was Clint's accusation right? *Was* she a cold woman?

As she drove away, Charlotte knew that she was not. If she was cold, she would not feel this sudden sadness, an empty void inside, at ending the affair with him. She had not expected to feel this way. For a moment she was tempted to return and tell Clint that it was not over, that it would never be over.

Instead, she flicked the reins, and drove on.

# Chapter Eleven

BY late August, Clint was on the road, engaged in a task he loved, traveling from town to town, in the blistering heat and smothering dust, selling King Cigarettes.

Both Ben and Charlotte had argued that he should wait until they were in full production, but he would not agree. "I have to get started now, get the jump on the competition. By the time our plant is turning out cigarettes, others will be also. Now, most of the salesmen are biding their time until they have the cigarettes. Sure, the packs I have are dummies, holding no cigarettes, but I can still write orders; and I have the samples we made up, so that the buyers can try them."

He had a large supply of the dummy packs in the buggy with him, and he went from town to town, from country store to country store, turning on the charm, and making extravagant promises that he was not sure he could keep—always remembering to refrain from smoking a cigar while selling cigarettes.

Not only was he selling, but he was also busy with his advertising campaign. In almost every place he went he hired local painters to paint signs advertising King Cigarettes. He persuaded farmers, for a few dollars, to allow his painters to plaster huge signs on the sides of their barns. In the buggy he had a supply of posters, which he tacked on trees and fence posts alongside the roads.

The posters and barn signs were an enlargement of the pack cover Clint had designed, with a few changes and one addition. The woman looked more provocative, and was dressed a little more daringly. The addition was the words: "My Man Smokes Kings!" Clint would have liked to put the legend on the cigarette pack, but there was not enough room.

There was resistance from many of the storekeepers Clint called on, but Clint did not let that faze him. A typical scene:

"I never heard of King Tobacco," the storekeeper said dubiously.

"That may be true, friend," Clint said cheerfully. "But that is going to change. By this time next year, everyone will have heard of King Tobacco, and King Cigarettes. Everybody will be clamoring to buy them."

"I don't much cater to them handmade cigarettes. Most of my customers use Bull Durham, and roll their own."

"That's going to change, too. Mark my word. Handmades are the coming thing."

From his bag Clint took the sample pack and exhibited it proudly. "Now ain't that an attractive package? Much more so than a sack of Bull Durham. A smoker will be proud to haul that out of his pocket. And here, sir, have a sample cigarette. Made from the best bright leaf, and the very best grade available."

"I never smoke them things, myself," the storekeeper said disdainfully. "I prefer my old pipe."

"To tell the truth . . ." Clint leaned closer, speaking in a confidential whisper. "When it comes to a good smoke, I like a cigar myself." He winked.

"Do you now?" The storekeeper smiled conspiratorily.

Clint straightened up. "But then fellows in business like we are, we have to sell the customers what *they* want, not what we like. Ain't that the way of it?"

"That's about the way of it."

"Now then, if you'll give me an order for King Cigarettes, you'll be entitled to a healthy discount, being a favored customer, in a manner of speaking."

"Well now, I don't know. I'm handling a few other

brands of handmades, and those fellows might not take too kindly to my adding another line."

"Competition, that's the thing. This country was built on competition, am I right? It's healthy for everybody. If these other companies put out a good product, there's no reason they should be afraid of competition." Clint leaned forward again. "Perhaps you've heard about the signs I've been putting up, on barns, fence posts, and the like, advertising King Cigarettes?"

The storekeeper smiled. "Yep, I've heard. So you're the fellow doing that?"

"I am indeed. Now you don't see other companies doing that, do you? Man sees one of those signs, and he's going to be almighty curious about this new cigarette on the market. He'll come to your store, and you don't have 'em, what's he going to think?"

The storekeeper was nodding. "Yep, I can see where you might be right there, but still . . . Mr. Devlin, I'll tell you the truth. I just don't have the cash money to go into a new line of cigarettes right now. Times are still hard."

"Oh, I didn't get a chance to tell you yet." Clint waved a hand airily. "You won't need cash right off. We'll let you have your first order on consignment. If they don't sell, what can you lose?"

"Now that's mighty generous of you, Mr. Devlin."

The storekeeper was moving in the right direction, but not fast enough to suit Clint. He leaned over the counter, took something from his pocket, and held it cupped in his hand—his clincher. Looking around furtively, he said, "I have a little something for my first good customers, a sort of a bonus, in a manner of speaking. You carry a pocket watch, sir?"

"You bet." The storekeeper hauled a big, gold watch from his pocket, beaming with pride. "My old daddy gave me this, on my eighteenth birthday."

"Now, like most pocket watches, I'm sure it has a place in the back for a picture. Your wife perhaps?"

"Sure thing." The storekeeper pressed his thumb, and

the back of the watch sprang open. "That there's my old woman." A woman's forbidding face scowled up at Clint.

"Now just take a look at this." Clint held out his cupped hand.

The storekeeper leaned down, squinting. His face flamed bright red, and he gulped. "Woo-ee! That's some picture. I ain't never seen nothing like that."

"I had these pictures shipped all the way from Paris, France."

This part was true enough, and they had not come cheap. The picture was of a seductive, voluptuous woman, naked as Eve, posed with a full frontal view.

Clint said, "This picture is yours, sir, for free, if you place a good order with us for King Cigarettes. What you could do, you see, is slip it in behind that picture of your wife, so she would never know. Maybe you could take a peek at it before you go to bed at night . . ." Clint let his voice die away, confident that his insinuation had been understood.

The storekeeper slapped his hand down on the counter. "By cracky, I'll take that order of your cigarettes, yes, sir, I will!" He reached eagerly for the picture.

This same scene, or variations thereof, was repeated in store after store. A few buyers resisted, some even threw Clint out, flaming with righteous indignation, but by and large, the French picture was the clincher.

Neither Ben nor Charlotte knew about this little bonus to the buyers, and Clint well realized that Charlotte, at least, would be outraged. He was not particularly concerned. By the time she found out, they would be so inundated by orders for King Cigarettes that her outrage would not last long.

Before the beginning of September, Clint had about reached the end of this particular trip; he had to return to Durham soon for a fresh supply of dummy packs and sample cigarettes.

He was quite pleased with himself as he checked into a small hotel in a town north of Atlanta, Georgia. As he signed the register with a flourish and accepted the room key from the desk clerk, a voice said behind him, "Clint? Clint Devlin?"

He turned about. "Marcy! How great to see you," he said with a broad smile.

Marcy Reynolds' answering smile was tremulous, uncertain. It had been almost a year since they had parted company, after Marcy had become a little too possessive for Clint's liking. She was still ripe, still an exciting woman, but the year had not been kind to her; that much Clint could tell at his first sweeping glance. Her hair was mussed, badly in need of a trim, and her oval-shaped face was pale and wan. But the most telling of all was the frayed cuffs on her shirtwaist, a mended tear in her skirt, and the scuffed toe of one slipper sticking out from under her skirt.

He took both her hands in his. "This is a nice surprise, Marcy."

"How are you, Clint?"

"I'm fine, I couldn't be better," he said expansively. "And how are you faring?"

"Not too well," she said bitterly, "as I'm sure must be evident. I've fallen on hard times, Clint."

"Well, we all have our ups and downs," he said. "It's almost supper time, would you care to have a bite with me?"

"I'd be happy to, Clint. I'll tell you the truth, I haven't eaten yet today." She looked at him without flinching.

"Well then, you must be hungry," he said cheerfully. He turned to the desk clerk. "Will you send my bags up to the room, please?" Dropping a coin onto the counter, he took Marcy's arm and escorted her to the dining room off the lobby.

When they were seated, he ordered two glasses of wine, and then gave his attention to Marcy. "So tell me, what have you been doing since I saw you last?"

"A little of everything, nothing very successfully. I've been a barmaid, I've waited tables, and... Well, you name it, Clint, I've done it."

Including a little whoring, he knew intuitively. "Are you staying in the hotel?"

"No, I don't have the money for a room."

He did not ask why she was there; he knew the answer—she had been looking for a customer. Their wine was brought to the table, and as their glasses were filled, Clint studied her critically. Even a little frayed around the edges, Marcy was still a good-looking woman, and that slightly depraved sensuality that had attracted him to her initially still clung to her. An idea came to him, but he did not broach it at once—it needed a little more thought.

He said, "This hotel has nice rooms, with large beds. I've stayed here before. I'd be pleased if you shared mine with me, Marcy. After all," he smiled lazily, "it wouldn't be the first time."

"Oh, Clint!" She blinked back tears. "You don't know what this means to me. I will always be willing to share your bed. You *are* a nice man." She reached over to seize his hand.

He said dryly, "Let's don't get carried away. This may be only a one-night arrangement." He added cryptically, "We'll have to see."

Their food came, simple country fare, but good, hearty food, and Marcy ate everything served to her. After they had topped it off with a glass of liqueur, Clint rose. "Shall we go up then?"

He helped Marcy to her feet, and tucked her arm in his.

On the way into the hotel lobby, Marcy said in a low voice, "Clint, could I have a bath first? I'm filthy." At his quick glance, she said, "I don't have the pox, don't worry."

"I'm glad to hear it." He stopped at the desk, and said firmly, "Miss Reynolds will be sharing my room. She wishes a bath. Will you see to it?" He slid another coin across the desk.

The clerk's sly glance jumped to Marcy, then quickly back to Clint. "Right away, Mr. Devlin. The bathroom is at the end of the hall, down at the west end."

Upstairs, Clint pointed out his room and went in, while

Marcy went on down the hall to the communal bathroom. Inside his room, Clint stripped off his clothing and stretched out on the bed with a glowing cigar. He had time now to think ahead, examine his idea for flaws. He could find none; the more he thought about it, the more attractive it seemed.

The cigar was smoked down by the time Marcy entered the room. Rosy from her bath, a huge towel wrapped around her, she carried her clothes draped over one arm, as she approached the bed with an almost shy smile. She dropped the clothes onto the room's one chair, and stood over him. As her gaze moved down the length of his naked body, her eyes became smoky, and she shed the shyness like a cloak.

Apparently the unmistakable indication of his desire for her had restored her shaky confidence in herself.

"Pretty sure of yourself, aren't you, Mr. Devlin?"

"Always have been, haven't I?" he said with his lazy smile. "If I recall correctly, you once told me that was one of the reasons you liked me."

"I don't think I ever said that I liked you. I may have said that I liked what you do to me."

"Same difference," he said laconically.

"No, it's not. A woman would be foolish to like you, she would likely end up getting hurt."

Strangely, in that moment Charlotte intruded into his thoughts. She had said something to the same effect . . .

Then Marcy dropped the towel, and he ceased thinking about anything.

As she came down on her knees on the bed, Clint opened his arms and pulled her against him, rolling with her until they lay side by side, skin to skin. Her flesh was cool from the bath, yet there was an underlayer of warmth, like heat felt through a lamp globe; and as his hands roamed possessively over her silken skin, the heat grew, feeding his desire for her.

"It's been a long time, Clint," she said huskily. "It's been a long time since I held you like this, too long! Now, now!"

With ungentle hands she urged him to her, demanding that he take her. He complied, entering her. A soft sigh escaped Marcy, and they meshed together like two precision-made parts of the same machine, as if many months had not passed since last they made love together.

Marcy was as greedy as a child too long deprived of sweets and made demands on him, by voice and by the touch of her hands. Clint met her every demand, and more.

When their passion had finally run its course, they collapsed side by side on the bed. Clint fired another cigar and lay smoking contentedly.

Marcy was the first to speak. "Clint?"

"Yes, love?"

"You haven't told me what you're doing now. You still buying cotton, and playing poker?"

"No gambling, no cotton. I'm into the tobacco business."

"How?" She raised up on one elbow. "What do you mean?"

"Right now, I'm on a selling trip throughout the South."

"Selling?" She hooted laughter. "Clint Devlin a common peddler?"

He did not take offense. "Hardly a common peddler, my dear. I will have you know that I am now a third partner in a tobacco company located in Durham. My end of it is sales and advertising."

"A partner in a company? My, we have come up in the world." She whistled softly. "How did that come about?"

"Oh, through hard work, my great business sense, and my personal charm," he said, smiling.

She struck him lightly on the shoulder. "You haven't changed, I see. Can't you ever be serious?"

"Oh, but I am serious. It's an opportunity I've been looking for. Give me time, and I'll be a business tycoon. Maybe it's a side of me you've never seen, Marcy, but it's always been there."

Marcy was silent for a moment. Her voice was wistful when she finally did speak. "I suppose I always did know, in the back of my mind, that you had it in you." She hesitated, then said cautiously, "Why did you go off and leave me like that, Clint?"

He rolled his head toward her. "You're not stupid, my dear. You know very well why. You started to think that you owned me. Nobody owns me, Marcy. I go my own way. I do as I damned well please!"

"I didn't realize, truly I didn't." She placed her hand on his chest, and traced patterns with her forefinger. She said hesitantly, "Can I stay with you for a little while, Clint? Please?"

"That all depends." He caught her hand and held it against him. "I've been giving some thought to that. Something might be worked out, if you keep in mind what I just said."

"I will, Clint, I promise," she said desperately. "I promise to behave."

"I had in mind hiring you."

She reared up in astonishment. "Hiring me? Whatever for? You're not thinking of being my fancy man, are you? Because if you are . . ."

"Now why would you think that? I'm no fancy man," he said roughly, "not yours, not any woman's. What I have in mind is a job for you, helping me sell King Cigarettes."

"But I'm no peddler!"

He grinned. "I'll do the peddling, my sweet. All you have to be is your alluring, lovely self."

"But what am I expected to *do*?"

"If what I have in mind comes about, you'll be performing. I don't want to go into it any more at this time. But I'll provide you with money to live on and to buy some new clothes, until it's time. And speaking of performing . . ." He grinned. "Come here."

She came into his arms willingly, but even as he made love to her, the image of Charlotte filled Clint's mind, and this time it was Charlotte in his arms, not Marcy.

Now it was "curing time."

Since Clint was out of town—Charlotte was convinced

that he had scheduled his absence purposely—she asked Ben to accompany her to the Hollister farm for the fire-curing of Bradley Hollister's tobacco crop.

Ben was willing enough. "Sure, I'd be glad to come along, Charlotte. It sounds interesting."

Curing always started at night, and the neighbors, as they had on the night of the burning of the plant bed, had collected by the time Charlotte and Ben arrived. Small fires burned in the yard before the curing barn, an old building situated a goodly distance from the main house; and small children ran about in play, dogs yipping at their heels.

"Glad you could come, Charlotte," Hollister said. "And you too, Ben. Where's Clint?"

"He's out somewhere, selling King Cigarettes." She laughed. "He says he learned more about tobacco than he wanted to know the last time he was out here."

"Well, I'm glad you two could come out. There's ample drinking liquor around, Ben, if you care to indulge. And since we had our first frost night before last, one of the neighbors killed a hog, and brought the meat over. There's enough for everybody. Find a fire and squat yourselves down." He gestured broadly. "I'm about to fire up the drying shed. Later, I'll let Jimmie tend it."

Charlotte and Ben found a nearby fire tended by the wife of one of Hollister's neighbors. There was an iron pot suspended over the low flame, filled with fresh hog backbone cooking slowly.

Charlotte exchanged greetings with Hollister's neighbor, and then she and Ben sat on the ground across from the fire. The night was chilly, and the fire's warmth was welcome. Charlotte sat with her knees drawn up, her skirts gathered around her feet, and a blanket around her shoulders. The cooking odors from their fire, and the others clustered around, were marvelous.

Ben said, "Isn't there danger of the shed and the tobacco catching fire, Charlotte? The tobacco is pretty well dried out by now, isn't it?"

Charlotte nodded. "That's the reason somebody has to

watch it, to see that it doesn't. It'll be Jimmie's task to see that the fire is kept hot, but does not burst into flames. If a flame reaches just one tobacco leaf, the whole thing will go up."

"It's a risky business, tobacco growing," he said thoughtfully. "I have to admire these farmers. It takes courage to risk a whole year's labor, with all the things that can go wrong. Insects can ruin a crop, a hailstorm can destroy it, and then even when it's in the curing barn, like now, a fire can wipe it out."

Charlotte nodded. "It's especially bad this year, when the farmers have raised their first crop since the war. Consider Mr. Hollister. If his crop is destroyed before he can get it to market, he and his family could starve, and there would be no way he could start a crop next season. He would probably lose his farm. That's the reason all the farmers are so frightened about Lutcher's veiled threats."

"Is he still threatening the farmers?"

Charlotte shrugged. "I don't know. I haven't heard anything recently, but the threats he has already made still haven't been forgotten."

"He must be lying quiet of late." He looked at her intently. "Have you seen him, or heard anything from him?"

"No, not since the night of the mayor's Christmas Eve ball. But Lutcher hasn't given up, you can be sure. Sload Lutcher doesn't forget a grudge that easily."

"How about . . . ?" He cleared his throat. "How about your brother? Have you seen him?"

"No, and I'm just as happy. I understand he's still working for that man, and so long as he does, I do not want to see him."

"That almost sounds as if you're ready to forgive him." He was smiling slightly.

Charlotte made a helpless gesture. "I don't know, I suppose I might if he quit working for Lutcher. After all, he *is* my brother, no matter what he's done."

The woman across the fire had loaded two tin plates with hog backbone, and now came around to offer them to

Charlotte and Ben with a shy smile, along with a pan of freshly baked cornbread.

They accepted with thanks and began to eat. The meat was tender and succulent, so tender that it fell away from the section of backbone at the merest touch. Backbone from a freshly slaughtered hog had always been one of Charlotte's favorites, but this was the first time she had tasted any since the last hog-killing on the King farm, which had taken place the autumn before her father's death.

Ben said, "You look sad, Charlotte. What's bothering you?"

She shrugged. "Nostalgia, I suppose. I was remembering the last time I ate backbone. Daddy was alive then."

"Oh." He hesitated. "I thought perhaps you were unhappy because Clint wasn't here."

She stiffened, and said coolly, "Why should I miss Clint?"

"Oh, come on, Charlotte. You think I'm blind? You think that I don't know about you and Clint?"

"If there is anything between Clint and myself, it's none of your affair, Ben." And then she added, somewhat sharply, "Anyway, it's over."

He looked at her solemnly. "Then there's hope for me?"

"Ben . . ." She touched his hand, smiling softly. "I like you *very* much. I consider you my friend, as well as business partner. But let's leave it at that, shall we? Anything else would only complicate matters."

His jaw tightened, and his eyes were serious. "It won't be easy. I've told you how I feel . . ."

He was interrupted by a shout from the drying shed. Charlotte jumped to her feet, looking toward the shed. She thought she caught a glimpse of a shadowy figure running into the night, but her attention was immediately drawn back to the shed, as it suddenly flared up.

"Oh, my God, the drying shed's on fire!"

Others were already running toward the shed, and Charlotte and Ben joined them. Just before they reached it, Bradley Hollister staggered backward out of the burning building. Charlotte saw that he was dragging a limp body.

Hollister was having a difficult time with just the one arm, and Ben hurried to help him. The shed was blazing higher with every second that passed. As Hollister and Ben dragged the figure out of danger, Charlotte saw that Hollister's shirt was ablaze. She still had the blanket around her shoulders. She snatched it off and threw it around Hollister, then began to beat at it, until the flames were extinguished.

"Are you all right, Mr. Hollister? Did your back get burned?"

"I'll be fine, Charlotte, except'n maybe a few blisters," he said grimly, scrubbing sweat and soot from his forehead. "But my crop is gone up the flue." He nodded toward the drying shed.

Just as Charlotte followed the direction of his gaze, the shed collapsed in a shower of sparks. "Oh, I am sorry. What happened, do you know?"

"Not yet, but hopefully I'll soon find out, as soon as the boy comes around. He must have dozed off."

Charlotte gazed down at Jimmie Hollister on the ground. Ben was kneeling by the boy's side. Someone had fetched a bucket of water, and Ben was sponging his face. Jimmie twitched, moaning, and tried to sit up.

"Easy, lad," Ben said. "Easy."

Jimmie groaned again, and his hand went to the back of his head.

His father dropped to one knee beside him. "All right, boy, what happened in there? Did you doze off?"

"No, Pa, I swear I didn't!" Jimmie looked at the smouldering ruin that had been the tobacco shed. "It's gone, ain't it?"

"It's gone," his father said. "Now, what happened?"

"I was watching closely, my back to the door, when I heard footsteps behind me. I thought it was you, Pa. I started to turn, and I was hit on the head, knocking me out."

Charlotte remembered then—the glimpse she had of a

shadowy figure running into the woods behind the shed.

She said, "I thought I saw someone running out of the shed and into the woods, at the same time that I noticed the fire."

Ben stood up. "Which way, Charlotte?"

She pointed. "That way."

He said, "It's probably too late, but we should check. Anyone with me?"

The men gathered around looked at each other uneasily, but finally three stepped up to join Ben, and the four men hurried toward the woods. Charlotte noticed that the others, avoiding her glance, began to drift away.

To Bradley Hollister, she said, "Lutcher was behind this, I'm sure of it."

Hollister looked up into her face, and said dully, "It's likely you're right. It was probably Cob Jenks, but we'll never in this world be able to prove it. It matters little to me, anyway. All that work, gone. My whole crop gone up in smoke." His face worked. "I went into debt for the crop, Charlotte. Now I'm left with nothing."

It was the first time Charlotte had seen this normally bright-natured man give way to despair. She touched his shoulder in compassion. "Mr. Hollister, you can come to work for me in Durham, you and Jimmie."

Hope flared in his eyes, and then died. He said bitterly, "What possible use could you have for a one-armed man? I won't accept charity."

"It won't be charity. You know tobacco as well as anyone of my acquaintance. I'll find a spot for you, that I promise."

"Come along, son, let's get you into the house." Hollister stood up, helping Jimmie to his feet.

The youngster was still dazed, but Charlotte was thankful that the only damage he had sustained was from the blow on the head; except for a few scorched places on his clothes, the fire had not harmed him.

Charlotte helped Hollister support his son toward the house.

"My wife could sleep through a war," Hollister commented. "All the shouting, the fire, nothing has roused her. She's going to be some upset when she learns."

"Mr. Hollister, I'm going to release the farmers from their contracts. They will be free to sell their tobacco to whomever they wish. Would you pass the word?"

He looked at her in surprise. "You sure you want to do that?"

"I couldn't live with myself if I didn't. I can't sit idly by, while their crops are burned, one after the other."

Just as they reached the house, Charlotte saw Ben and the other three men emerge from the woods. The men branched off toward their buggies, while Ben came on. Charlotte waited on the porch for him.

He stopped at the bottom of the steps. "Nothing," he said tiredly. "Whoever it was, if there was anybody, was long gone by the time we started to search for him."

"Burned clear to the ground," Cob Jenks said smugly to Sload Lutcher. "That's one farmer who won't have a tobacco crop to sell this year."

"Anybody spot you?" Lutcher asked.

"Naw. At least if they did, it was too late. I was long gone."

"That should put the fear of God into those farmers," Lutcher said in satisfaction. He grinned savagely. "Or fear of the devil. Might be even better if one of them had burned up in the fire."

"I had to knock one out to set the fire. It was that Hollister brat, I think."

"Did they get him out in time?"

"I don't know, Mr. Lutcher. I didn't wait around to see."

"Probably not, or we'd have heard by this time."

It was the morning after Jenks had set fire to the Hollister drying shed, and they were in Lutcher's office. He opened the drawer to his desk, took out a couple of gold pieces, and handed them across the desk to Jenks.

"Good work, Jenks. Here's a small bonus for you, you've earned it. And I won't need you for the rest of the day."

Jenks grinned hugely, reminding Lutcher of a capering monkey, and bounced the gold coins in his hairy hand. "My thanks, Mr. Lutcher."

As he started out, Lutcher said, "See if you can find Jeff King out there, will you, Jenks? Tell him I want to see him right away."

Lutcher felt a strong sense of satisfaction. If this fire did not discourage the tobacco farmers from selling to the King woman, he would instruct Jenks to set another, and then another. A few fires like that, and they would come around to his way of thinking.

Restless, he got up and strolled to the window to look out, and immediately wished that he had not. A few blocks up the street was the building King Tobacco had leased. Since the huge sign, King Tobacco, had been painted across the front, bile rose up to choke Lutcher every time he looked at it. In his own mind he was convinced that Charlotte King had selected that particular building just to irritate him.

At a sound behind him, Lutcher turned, glad of the distraction. He crossed to his desk as Jeff King limped toward him.

Jeff still drank, Lutcher knew, yet he appeared for work every day reasonably sober, and except for bloodshot eyes and a puffy countenance, he showed little sign, as yet, of his nightly dissipation. Lutcher also knew that he spent most of his wages on women and gambling, but that fitted in very well with his ultimate plans for the man. And he had to give Jeff credit—while at the plant he applied himself well and had gathered quite a bit of knowledge about the tobacco business.

"You wanted to see me, Mr. Lutcher?"

"Yes, I did, King." Lutcher forced heartiness into his manner. "How are you getting along here?"

"Well enough, I guess."

"Good, good." Lutcher sat down, without inviting Jeff to do the same. "I think it's about time we started on a few things."

Jeff said warily, "What things?"

"Things you were hired to do," Lutcher snapped. "I told you in the beginning that I had use for you aside from just working here." He glowered at Jeff until he figured the man was properly intimidated. "Now, do you recall that fellow we met at the mayor's Christmas Eve ball? Clint Devlin?"

Jeff's face tightened as he nodded.

"Have you by any chance run across him since?"

"No, I haven't."

Lutcher leaned forward. "Well, I want you to cultivate his acquaintance. Don't be obvious about it, try to make it seem accidental."

"But for what reason?"

"All in good time, King. I understand that he's a sporting fellow, likes women and liquor. Two of a kind, you might say." Lutcher sneered. "You two should get on well together. You get to know him, you might steer him to a ripe doxie. I've even heard that he enjoys a good poker game on occasion. You may spend whatever is necessary to, uh, ripen this acquaintance. I'll stand good the expenses."

Jeff said slowly, "Is this an order?"

"You'd damned well better consider it such!" Lutcher snarled.

"All right, Mr. Lutcher, I'll do my best." Jeff looked confused. "But I fail to see what this will accomplish."

"That's why I give the orders, King, and you take them. To succeed in this world, a man needs foresight. You have to plan ahead." Lutcher made a steeple of his fingers and propped his chin on them. "When my plans for Mr. Devlin are fully formed, I will let you know what they are. Until that time comes, you just follow my orders." He waved a dismissing hand. "You may go now, King."

Jeff turned and limped toward the door.

"King?" Lutcher waited until Jeff had turned back before saying, "There is one thing you might try and find out when you get well acquainted with Devlin. I hear that he's got a great advertising campaign going for King Cigarettes. Find out what you can about it, without being too obvious about it. Information like that could be useful.

"Yes, sir, you two should get on well together." His smile was unpleasant. "Being from the same cut of cloth, you might say."

# Chapter Twelve

CHARLOTTE and Ben were waiting at the train station for Jacob Lefkowitz and his daughter, Rachel.

"You'll like Jacob and Rachel." Ben seemed unduly nervous. "I'm sure you will."

"I'm sure I will, too," she said, laughing. "Is there any reason why I shouldn't?"

"Well, they *are* Jewish, Charlotte, and you're not too familiar with Jews. To people who are not familiar with their ways, they may seem strange. Especially Jacob, who was not born in this country, and has never been out of New York City before."

"Ben . . ." She placed a hand on his arm. "I imagine I'm going to seem strange to them, as well. But once we all get over the strangeness, we'll be fine. Besides, why is it so important that I like them? I'm sure that I will, but if I don't, I can't see that it matters, so long as they do the job they're hired to do."

"Oh, they'll do the job, there's no doubt about that," Ben assured her. "But Jacob will be in charge of the rollers, and he's a little . . . Well, thorny, I suppose you could say. So, if he gets off on the wrong foot, the workers under him may follow his lead."

"This is important to you, isn't it, Ben?"

"Yes, Charlotte, it is," he admitted. "This is the first large exodus of the immigrant Jew from the ghettos of New York, and I desperately want it to work."

"I'm certain it will." She smiled in understanding.

"How can it fail, with you behind it? You have run yourself ragged finding houses for them."

"I made them that promise, and it wasn't too difficult. There are a large number of empty houses in Durham." He frowned. "However, there is one thing that worries me."

"And what is that?"

"I wonder how the people of Durham will react to foreigners in their midst."

"I think you're worrying needlessly, Ben. After all, our own ancestors came here from the old country."

"Not as recently as ours. And there is one big difference, Charlotte. The people of Durham are of one religion, generally speaking. They've had no experience with people of the Jewish faith, and I have to wonder how they'll take to it. It is quite different. Our Sabbath is on Saturday, for one thing, and all the rites are different." He smiled suddenly. "Listen to me, will you? I've ignored religion for years, a failed Hebrew if you will, and here I sound like I've been faithfully going to synagogue for years, when the truth is I haven't been inside one since before the war . . ."

He was interrupted by a train whistle, and they turned to look down the tracks, as the train came in sight, spewing black smoke. The rails before them vibrated musically. Brakes squealed, and sparks flew up from the rails as the train ground to a halt. Heads popped out through the open windows, and curious faces peered out at them.

When the train had come to a full stop, people began to pour from the train, whole families, with children of all ages. They carried battered suitcases, and sacks bulging with belongings. Charlotte saw all manner of dress, and she noticed there was an old-fashioned look about their clothing. All their faces wore looks of apprehension, and the moment each person was on solid ground, he or she paused, seeming to draw inwards. But soon there were so many of the new arrivals that the press from behind pushed the outer limits of the crowd farther and farther toward the station.

Ben, craning his neck to see over the heads, muttered, "Where are Jacob and Rachel? If they didn't come . . ."

At that moment a short, powerful looking man, with ragged gray hair and bright brown eyes came halfway down the steps of the car. A girl appeared behind him, peering over his shoulder. The round-faced man looked out over the crowd. He spotted Ben and waved. "Mr. Ascher, we have come to your Carolina!"

He bounced down the steps and bulled his way through the mob, the girl trailing in his wake. Reaching Ben, the man put a chewed cigar stub into his mouth, and held out his hand, beaming hugely.

Ben shook hands with the man. "Welcome to Durham, Mr. Lefkowitz." His glance went to the girl. "And you too, Rachel."

Rachel smiled, her thin face coming alive. The smile gave her features animation, and Charlotte saw a dimple appear and disappear in her left cheek.

Why, she's lovely, Charlotte thought. She glanced quickly at Ben, and saw the way he looked at Rachel, and she felt a twinge of . . . something. Jealousy? Was she jealous? She scoffed at herself. She had no claim on Ben Ascher's affections; any claim she might have had she had forfeited.

Ben was saying, "I see you managed to recruit a good number of workers, Jacob."

"Fifty, just like you ask," Jacob said proudly.

"Jacob, Rachel, I want you to meet one of my two partners. The other one, Clint Devlin, is out of town at the moment." He turned to Charlotte. "This is Charlotte King. Charlotte, meet Jacob Lefkowitz and his daughter, Rachel."

"I am delighted to meet you, Mr. Lefkowitz, Rachel."

"It is our pleasure," Jacob said formally. Then a sly twinkle appeared in his eyes. "When Ben told me we would be working for a lady, I was, what you say, doubting. I never work for a lady before."

Charlotte laughed, suddenly at ease. She liked Jacob Lefkowitz. "I hope I will soon lay any doubts you may have to rest."

Ben said, "Would you like to see our factory now, or would you prefer settling in first?"

"I'm anxious to see the factory," Rachel said. "Poppa?"

"Yes, my daughter," Jacob said with a fond smile. "If we do not like the place we are to work, perhaps we will go back to New York, eh?"

"I have little fear you won't like it, Jacob," Ben said. "Our plant is large and airy, with plenty of ventilation, and we will be employing janitors to keep it clean once we start operating."

"And when will that be?" Jacob asked.

It was Charlotte who answered, "Within two weeks or less. Just as soon as we buy our tobacco."

Ben motioned to the other rollers, who had been waiting patiently. "Since many of the families have small children, I imagine they would like to proceed directly to their new homes. I have made maps with directions to the various locations. The maps and keys to the houses are in my buggy. If you will tell them to come with us, Jacob, I will distribute the maps and keys. The houses I have for you all, by the way, are pretty much in the same area, so none of you will be far apart."

When he was escorted into the lower floor of the plant, Jacob stopped just inside the front door, gazing around appraisingly. Huge windows had been installed all around the vast room, windows that could be opened and closed easily. The room had been swept clean of the debris left by the workmen who had swarmed through the building for weeks, installing the necessary machinery.

Jacob finally nodded in approval. "It will be a nice place to work."

"And it will be kept clean," Charlotte said. She indicated the only men in the room at the moment—three black men. "I have employed a cleaning crew. When we go into full production, they will keep the factory clean of tobacco dust and other leavings. Some of the plants I have visited are filthy, including one here in Durham, belonging to a man named Lutcher. Not only is all that dust and leavings bad for a worker's health, but it gets mixed into the sacked tobacco and cigarettes."

Ben said, "This entire floor will be used for cigarette production, only the snuff, pipe, and chewing tobacco will be produced on the second floor, where the offices are also located. Jacob, I want you to see this." He led them over to a machine in one corner. "This is the latest thing, a Pease rotary cutter, for shredding the tobacco. And the carpenters just finished installing the tables where your rollers will work."

Jacob nodded his approval of the cutter. "Good, good! But this . . . not good." He swept his hand around, indicating the long, marble-topped rolling tables. There were stools situated a yard apart, each before a small cubicle constructed on the tables.

"Why not?" Charlotte demanded. "Most of the other plants I've visited have something similar."

"Too close together," Jacob said. "The hand rollers must be separated by more distance between."

Ben was frowning. "I don't understand, Jacob. What's your reasoning behind that?"

"This close they talk, talk," Jacob said laconically. "Not roll cigarettes fast enough."

"What Poppa means," Rachel said, dimpling, "is that girls tend to gossip. And about half of the hand rollers are women."

"Not only that," Jacob said, "they watch each other, both men and girls. Watch to see how many cigarettes next roller is doing. Also, rollers do not always get along so well. If they too close together, many quarrel. No." He shook his head decisively. "Tables must be separated."

Ben scrubbed a hand down across his face. "I don't know, Jacob. Don't you think you might be exaggerating a bit? These tables did not come cheap. And to bring the carpenters back in to cut them up and separate them would be expensive."

Jacob's face got a stubborn set. "The tables must be separated."

Charlotte touched Ben's arm, and drew him aside. In a low voice she said, "We've gone to all this expense to get Jacob and his people down here. We can't quibble about another few dollars, Ben."

"You have to understand these people, Charlotte, my people. There comes a point where you have to be firm with them. If they figure they can talk you into something, they will take advantage."

Charlotte shook her head. "I can't believe Jacob is trying to take advantage. After all, according to him, what he wants will only help production, and that's what we're after, isn't it? You know what I think?" She smiled at him. "I think you're afraid, because they *are* your own people, that you will lean too far in their direction. No, I vote we go along with Jacob on this. If he takes that as a sign that he can take advantage of us in the future, we'll deal with that when it happens."

After a moment's hesitation, Ben shrugged, throwing his hands wide. "Perhaps you're right. Besides, since Clint isn't here and I vote no, we'll be deadlocked, won't we?"

Charlotte laughed, and walked back to where Jacob and his daughter waited. She said, "Your tables will be separated, Jacob."

He beamed at her. "That is good. I think that I am going to like working for a boss lady, after all."

Now, it was "market time."

Beginning in the dawn hours, wagons came in the streets of Durham, all heading for the warehouse district, and they were still coming at nine o'clock, when the warehouses opened their doors to the tobacco buyers.

The wagons were loaded with either hogsheads or baskets of tobacco. The shallow baskets, about five feet across, were piled four feet high with clumps of hand-tied tobacco. At the warehouses the black warehousemen took over, removing the baskets from the wagons, tagging each with the tobacco farmer's name, then dragging them over to the scales for weighing. Lastly, they were hauled into the warehouses and lined up, row after row of baskets, with aisles in between.

The color of the cured tobacco ranged from lemon to mahogany, the quality from prime to trash tobacco. The warehouses soon turned pungent with the aroma of the cured leaf.

Promptly at nine, a black man wearing a bright uniform stood at the end of the street and raised the long horn to his mouth, blowing high, musical notes that could be heard throughout most of Durham.

The tobacco market was officially open.

At this particular time, there were not a large number of warehouses, and they were located close together, so that the buyers could walk from one to the other without too much effort.

It was late September, and this early in the morning it was chilly as Charlotte made her way along the street; but since it was sunny she knew it would be warm by midday. Although it was yet a half hour short of opening time, the street was crammed with buggies and wagons, and men moved back and forth along the street restlessly. Women waited placidly in the vehicles, gossiping, many dipping snuff. They all had shopping lists, Charlotte knew, and the stores of Durham would be open and thriving until long after nightfall, as the farmers and their wives bought things they had been in need of all year. Children and dogs chased each other along the street. The air was tangy with the mingled odors of tobacco and fresh horse manure.

Charlotte was amused to see a scrawny rooster darting about fearlessly between the hooves of horses, pecking at one pile of steaming horse droppings and then scampering on to another.

She stopped before one warehouse and looked up in smiling satisfaction. Painted above the doors was a fresh sign: King Tobacco Warehouse #3. Actually it was the only one they had, but she had learned from Clint: "Think big, Lotte."

This warehouse had been the secret project that she had worked on since the fire destroyed the Hollister drying shed and the subsequent release of the tobacco farmers from their contracts with her. It was so secret that Clint did not even know about it, although Ben had given his approval to the project.

She was waiting now for Bradley Hollister. As she waited, Charlotte watched the pinhookers at work—flashy, fast-talking men. They moved in as a farmer arrived with a wagonload of tobacco, spouting lies—the warehouses were full, no more space for tobacco, the prices were suddenly falling to new lows, et cetera. They waved money in the planter's face as they talked, and all too often the planter, desperately in need of cash and terrified that he might pass up a good opportunity, sold to them. Then the pinhookers either had their buys placed on display inside the warehouses, picking up a quick, easy profit; or the more affluent of them held the tobacco for several months, until tobacco became scarce, and then sold it for an even greater profit. Many of the pinhookers, Charlotte knew, went right out to the farms before market day and tried to fast-talk the farmers into selling then and there.

She considered the pinhookers vultures, feeding off the misfortune and bad business sense of others.

The King Warehouse was different from the other warehouses in one respect—it had an auctioneer, Dandy Watson. Under his skilled direction, the buyers would have to bid against each other for the tobacco, thus assuring the farmers of a better price. In the other warehouses, the buyer made a "take it or leave it" offer, and the farmers, most of them unfamiliar with marketing, were usually intimidated into taking whatever they were offered.

Sload Lutcher had such a warehouse, and he was the worst offender of all, managing to buy his tobacco for under its true market value. Charlotte had instructed Hollister to let all the farmers who had had contracts with her know about the auction in the King Warehouse, and she was pleased to note that it seemed more crowded than the other.

"Well, Charlotte," said a voice behind her, "you're all ready, I reckon."

She smiled around at Bradley Hollister. "I'm ready, Mr. Hollister. And excited, I might add. Every time a new phase of King Tobacco begins, I think of *that* as the true beginning."

Just then the horn blew, heralding the opening of the warehouses. Bradley Hollister offered his one arm. Charlotte took it, and they went into the bustle of the warehouse. Buyers strolled up and down the aisles between the baskets of tobacco, inspecting the displays in preparation for when the auction began.

Dandy Watson came striding toward them, round face beaming. "Ah, dear lady! I have been waiting impatiently."

Dandy was splendidly attired as usual. Today, the predominant colors were yellow and brown. He wore a vest of tobacco brown, stretched over a considerable paunch, and draped across that was a solid gold watch chain. His cravat was a sunburst of vivid yellow, and the inevitable ruby winked from the stickpin. He carried a gold-headed cane.

His merry brown eyes danced as he saw her surveying his garb. "Am I properly dressed for the occasion, dear lady?"

She had to laugh. "As always, I am almost speechless."

Dandy chuckled. "That is the idea, dear lady. As soon as the auction begins, the only voice to be heard will be mine." He stared at Hollister. "And this is your buyer?"

"Yes, Bradley Hollister. Mr. Hollister, meet Clyde Watson, known as Dandy by some."

The two men shook hands, taking each other's measure, and then Dandy said briskly, "Then let's begin, shall we?"

Hollister moved down the first aisle between the baskets, Charlotte trailing in his wake. Hollister reached deep into each basket, down past the top bundles, to examine the bottom leaves. Charlotte knew that some farmers cheated a bit, putting the better quality leaves on top and stacking those of lesser grade near the bottom, a practice called "nesting." It was Hollister's chore to discover which baskets held too many leaves of lesser grade, so he would know when the bidding began. It was a task he was good at, and Charlotte knew that he would be invaluable today.

Charlotte was determined to buy only the best grades of tobacco for King Cigarettes. She was fortunate in one respect—most of the buyers present today were buying for the chewing tobacco factories, and they were interested primarily in "wrapper" leaves, those leaves used to wrap the plugs of chewing tobacco.

Another thing that was different in the King Warehouse was that Charlotte would not allow the purchase of tobacco as speculation; everything Hollister bought today would be channeled into the factory for immediate cigarette production.

Many tobacco warehouse owners, of which Sload Lutcher was one, bought and sold tobacco for their own accounts. They did this to speculate, knowing that within a few months, at almost any time before next season's crop was in, the price of tobacco would double or even triple, and they would reap a large profit.

Dandy Watson rapped his cane for attention. As quiet fell, he announced, "The auction is about to begin, gents. Now, for those of you not familiar with tobacco auctions, the action goes fast and furious. If you can't keep up, you're left sucking hind tit." He grinned amiably. "A tobacco auction differs from other auctions you all might be familiar with. Only the actual bids are mentioned, there's never any urging from me to up the bid. The reason for this is simple. Just so you'll understand, the escalations are standard, at one cent a pound, or one dollar per one hundred pounds, until the basket goes to the highest bidder.

"Also, for the information of those unfamiliar with the procedure, I pronounce one *nun*, two is *doo*, three is *ree*. The code words for quarter-cent quotations is *wah*, and a half cent is *hah*, and three-quarters of a cent is *ree* again.

This is done in the interest of speed and an auctioneer's rhythm. I forbid any interruptions for clarification, gents. You'll catch on, I'm sure. If you don't, better luck next year. An auctioneer, gents, is an artist." He grinned again. "And an artist does not brook interruptions while at his work."

There was general laughter, plus a few ribald remarks aimed at Dandy. The auctioneer scowled and rapped his cane. "Please, gents, watch your language. There is a lady present."

The crowd subsided with uneasy, apologetic looks at Charlotte, and she realized that she was the only woman in the warehouse. She heard a few muttered requests that she leave, which she ignored.

Dandy tapped his cane against a post to gain attention. "All right, gents! It's time!"

He began with the first basket in line, the one Hollister had examined first. Dandy had already discussed a starting price with Charlotte, and with the current market price hovering at around ten cents a pound, that was the bid starter.

Dandy's chant was almost incomprehensible, not only because it consisted of mostly the code words, but also because of the speed at which he chanted. Dandy Watson had told her that he had once been timed at four hundred words per minute, while the usual tempo of an ordinary conversation was well under a hundred words a minute.

Since the first basket held no wrapper leaves, there was little interest among the buyers for it, and when Hollister bid twelve cents, and there were no more bids, Dandy rapped his cane, and intoned, "Sold King!"

As Dandy moved on down to the next basket and began his chant anew, a warehouseman tagged the basket with the price bid and the name of the buyer, and followed along in Dandy's wake to do the same with each basket sold.

Despite Dandy's rapid-fire delivery, the auction moved slowly. Aside from the fact that there were a great many baskets to be auctioned off, the buyers were still uncertain as to the bidding procedure; but gradually they got into the rhythm of it, and the proceedings speeded up considerably. Almost half of the tobacco was gone by midday, and most of it had been bought by King Tobacco. When Charlotte had proposed her idea to Ben, he had been fearful that they would not be able to buy enough tobacco in this manner to fill their needs; but it was evident now that they would purchase the quantity they desired. She was also pleased to note that almost all of the tobacco farmers who had had contracts with her had brought their leaves to King Tobacco.

She was well content and was considering leaving matters in the capable hands of Bradley Hollister when she saw a woman enter the warehouse, striding boldly down the aisle, ignoring the surprised looks from the buyers.

It was Rachel Lefkowitz. Charlotte liked both Rachel and her father, and was pleased that Ben had hired them. She had heard rumors that some Durhamites were unhappy about the presence of so many "foreigners" in their midst, and she knew that Ben was worried about something more than just rumors happening. So far nothing had, but then this was only their second week in Durham.

Jacob, she knew, was at the factory now, seeing that everything was in readiness for the day they went into production; he had been there every day since his arrival. This was the first time she had seen Rachel since the day father and daughter arrived in Durham.

She raised her hand and waved. Rachel saw her, and her face broke into a smile. She came quickly down the room to her. "This is all so exciting!" she exclaimed. "I've never seen anything like it. There's certainly nothing like this in New York, all the tobacco is shipped in."

"It is exciting, I agree, probably even more so for me. It means that we can start production next week. Why didn't your father accompany you?"

"Oh, Poppa can't spare time away from the plant." Rachel's dimpled smile appeared. "Within the short time that we've been here, Poppa has come to love it."

"And you, Rachel?"

"Oh, yes! Life in Durham is so different from the city

life I've always known. It will take some getting used to, but I'm going to love it here, I know I will." Her face became grave. "I haven't had a chance to thank you, Miss King, for allowing Poppa to have his own way. He can be demanding at times, who should know better than I?"

"Someone once said that the best employee is a happy employee. And Rachel, please call me Charlotte."

"Oh, I don't know." Rachel blinked in confusion. "You are my employer, it wouldn't be right for me to be so informal."

"Nonsense," Charlotte said briskly. "I hope we become fast friends, more than just employer and employee . . ."

She stopped as a hand descended lightly on her shoulder. A familiar voice drawled, "Well, Lotte. So this is what you've been spending my money on?"

"Clint! You're back!"

She looked around into his smiling face, and a sense of gladness welled up in her that she had difficulty concealing.

"I'm back, Lotte. I hope you've bought a lot of tobacco today, you're going to need it. I took orders for one hell of a lot of cigarettes."

"That's what this is all about." She swept her hand around the warehouse. "What do you think of it?"

He shrugged negligently. "Looks fine to me. The question is, is it working?"

"It's working. Mr. Hollister will have bought more than enough tobacco for us by the end of the day. All prime grade, too."

"I'm glad to hear it, but I'm not all that pleased about you and Ben making an important decision such as this without consulting me." His expression was stern.

"You weren't here, we didn't even know where you were, Clint. You're not very good about keeping us informed as to your whereabouts."

"I travel fast, Lotte." Now he smiled slightly.

"Besides, what difference would it have made if you had been here? Ben and I would have outvoted you. And this warehouse is going to be a paying proposition. I've seen enough here today to know that."

His attention had already wandered, his gaze fastening on Rachel. "Now just who is this lovely young lady?"

"This is Rachel Lefkowitz, one of the hand rollers Ben hired in New York. Jacob, her father, will be the foreman. Rachel, meet Clint Devlin, the third partner of King Tobacco."

Clint removed his white planter's hat and made a half-bow. "What kind of a world is this when a pretty girl like you has to roll cigarettes for a livelihood? You should be in satin and lace, sitting on a throne somewhere."

Rachel blushed a rose color. "I don't mind, Mr. Devlin. I like what I do."

Charlotte said, "Don't take what Clint says too seriously, Rachel. He is a notorious flatterer."

She doubted that either heard her, for Clint was looking deep into Rachel's eyes, and he had her hand in his. Clint was well-turned out today—white planter's hat, a light brown suit, with a white, ruffled shirt and flowing cravat, and black boots so highly polished they glittered like the surface of a mirror.

Charlotte reflected, once again, how dashing and handsome Clint Devlin was, a figure to capture the heart of a woman far more sophisticated than she suspected Rachel to be.

And noticing how Rachel continued to look into Clint's ardent eyes, caught as though mesmerized, Charlotte felt a twinge of unease, recalling Ben's proprietary manner around Rachel. By ending the affair with Clint, Charlotte had thought that she had forestalled any future conflict between her two partners. Now she was not so sure. Given Clint's proclivity for lovely ladies, he and Ben could easily come to blows yet.

"By the way, Lotte . . ." Clint turned to her. "I got into town last night, and I . . ."

"You did? Why didn't you let us know, or come to the factory this morning?"

"Well, I had a late night last night. I'd been out on the road for nigh onto two months, and I thought I had a celebration due me," he said. "The thing is, I didn't get to bed until the wee hours. But I did come by the plant. That's how I knew where you were, Ben told me."

She said dryly, "You haven't changed, I see."

"Nor do I intend to, my dear. What I started to say was, I ran into your brother last night. We had a few drinks together, and played a few hands in a poker game. He's not a bad fellow, your brother."

She went rigid. "I don't want to hear about it."

"There's nothing to hear, not really. He asked about you, by the way. I like Jeff, Lotte."

"That's your problem," she said coldly.

"Aw, come on, Lotte. He is your brother, your own kin."

"Not so long as he works for Sload Lutcher, he's not."

Clint spread his hands, and shrugged. "Well, I just thought I'd mention it."

"If you carouse with him, that is your business. But if you do it again, I would appreciate it if you wouldn't report to me. It's of no interest whatsoever to me."

# Chapter Thirteen

"THE damned woman outfoxed me!" Sload Lutcher raged. "Who would have thought that she would come up with a scheme like this auction warehouse?"

Cob Jenks said hopefully, "Shall I put the match to the barns of those farmers who put their tobacco in her warehouse, Mr. Lutcher?"

Lutcher was sorely tempted, but he shook his head. "No, it would serve no purpose. They're all empty of tobacco now, anyway. All that would burn is some old lumber, and it'll cost them little to rebuild for next season. No, she outfoxed me, I have to admit it. That only adds to the score against her. I'm going to have to be a little more devious from now on."

"But they had the warning their barns would go up if they sold to her. They'll laugh at you behind your back, Mr. Lutcher."

"Nobody laughs at me for long!" Lutcher slammed his fist down on his desk. "When I drive King Tobacco out of business, the farmers will have to come to me, begging, hats in hand. Then we'll see who's laughing!"

"So what do you want me to do next, Mr. Lutcher?"

Lutcher made a steeple of his hands, scowling in thought. "These hand rollers she brought down from New York . . . I understand they're all Jews, is that right?"

"That they are. And they're a strange looking lot, Mr. Lutcher. I was down at the train station when they came in."

"Have you heard any remarks from Durham citizens about the King woman dragging a foreign element into their city?"

Jenks shrugged. "A few fellows have grumbled, around some of the drinking places, but that's about it. Of course," he grinned, "I ain't often in the company of swells."

"Well, here's what I want you to do, Jenks. Pass the word, on the sly of course, about how terrible it is that foreigners are being brought in here by the King woman, to work in her factory. Taking jobs away from the local people, things like that. Stir them up good. I'll see what I can do with the higher-ups. I'm on good terms with the mayor and other members of the city administration. Together, maybe we can get people stirred up enough to do something about these Jews in our midst."

"I'll do my best, Mr. Lutcher." Jenks saluted, grinning, and left Lutcher's office.

He almost collided with Jeff King, who was starting into the office.

Lutcher raised his voice. "You wanted to see me, King?"

Jeff came on into the office. "Yes, sir. I thought you'd be interested in knowing that I had several drinks last night with Clint Devlin, and we were in a poker game afterwards."

Lutcher leaned back, looking at Jeff intently. "And how did the pair of you get along?"

"Quite well, I'd say." Jeff smiled reminiscently, more relaxed than he usually was in Lutcher's presence. "I like the man, and he seems to like me."

"Well now, that's good to hear. Did you learn anything of importance?"

"Not a great deal. I had to be careful on first acquaintance. He was willing, though, to talk about how his sales and advertising campaign for King Cigarettes is going." Jeff was still smiling, but there was a flavor of something else behind the surface smile. "He told me that he wrote large orders for the new cigarettes everywhere he went."

Lutcher wondered if there was a touch of malice in Jeff's smile. He said tightly, "How that woman's cigarettes are selling is of no interest to me. After all, Devlin may be taking a lot of advance orders, but they still have to deliver the product. What else did you learn?"

"Clint told me that he had signs painted on barns and other places everywhere he went, all advertising King Cigarettes. And he also told me about a little bonus he gave to all buyers who placed large orders. This . . ." He took something from his pocket and handed it across the desk. "He's a sly boots, Clint is."

Lutcher looked at the object Jeff had given him, and made a face of disgust when he saw that it was a picture of a naked woman. "Pfaugh! I'm not interested in such tripe." He tossed the picture back across his desk. "What I want to hear is information about his methods of advertising and promotion."

"That is part of it, Mr. Lutcher, apparently one of his most successful." Jeff gestured to the picture, and he definitely looked smug now.

"Don't get uppity with me, King." Lutcher leaned across his desk, his eyes deathly cold. "Is that clearly understood?"

"It's understood, Mr. Lutcher," Jeff said sullenly, and for the first time in their acquaintance, naked hatred stared out of his eyes.

Lutcher was not bothered by Jeff's hatred of him; it was his experience that hatred in an employee could be useful, so long as there was fear mixed in with it.

His stare remained locked with Jeff's. Jeff was the first to look away, his gaze dropping to the floor. Lutcher leaned back, smiling faintly. He became genial again. "But you did what I asked of you, King, making friends with this Devlin. Work on ripening it. I have plans for our Mr. Devlin."

Charlotte, accompanying Ben to the house now occupied by Jacob Lefkowitz and his daughter, was apprehensive. It was Friday night, the eve before the Jewish sabbath, and Jacob had invited Charlotte and Ben to have dinner with them. The plant was to officially open on Monday morning, and the very first King Cigarette would be made by Rachel.

"I hope I won't embarrass you," Charlotte said nervously.

Ben laughed. "Relax, Charlotte. It's not all that different. How could you possibly embarrass me?"

Although Jacob had only been in Durham slightly over two weeks, Charlotte noticed that the small house had been freshly painted. Ben pulled the buggy to a halt before the house, and got out to help her down. They went up the walk arm in arm.

Jacob, apparently watching for them, opened the door before they reached it. He boomed, "Welcome to my home, my friends!"

Charlotte took note of the black skullcap perched precariously atop his bushy head of hair. She said, "It's kind of you to invite us, Jacob."

As he ushered them in, Charlotte smelled a rich assortment of cooking odors. The interior of the house held new furniture, all arranged in good taste.

Jacob noticed Charlotte looking around, and he grinned. "You like our new furniture, eh, boss lady?"

"It looks nice. I'm pleased for you."

"Ben here, he helped. Our furniture in New York went with the place we rent. Ben went with me to the bank, and, how you say, go my note? For money to buy this."

Charlotte glanced over at Ben and caught a look of embarrassment on his face. She found his hand and squeezed it, just as Rachel came hurrying into the room. She saw Charlotte holding Ben's hand and stopped short. She wore an apron, and her face was attractively flushed from the heat of the kitchen.

"Ah, my Rachel!" Jacob bounced over to drape an arm around her shoulders. "My Rachel is a good cook, you see."

"I hope you like it," Rachel said somewhat shyly.

"And now we must have a glass of wine together." Jacob gestured expansively. "Sit, eh? You will be our first guests on the new furniture."

As Jacob left to fetch the wine, Rachel said, "I am glad

you are here. Will you excuse me? I have to return to my kitchen."

Jacob came back with a wine bottle and three glasses, a fresh cigar tilted jauntily in his mouth. The wine poured, he touched his glass to each in turn. *"L'chaim!"*

The wine was sweet and heavy, and Charlotte sipped it slowly, savoring the rich flavor of grapes.

After taking a drink of the wine, Ben said, "Is everything to your satisfaction at the plant now, Jacob?"

Jacob nodded his head rapidly. "My rollers are ready to make King Cigarettes." He spread his hands wide in an expansive gesture. "We will make more and better smokes than you have ever seen before."

"That is good news," Charlotte commented. "According to Clint, we have a huge backlog of orders to fill."

"This Clint Devlin," Jacob said. "I have not met him. My Rachel tells me that she met him at the auction house. Why is he not around?"

"His job is taking orders. He's been traveling the past two months, but he'll be at the plant Monday morning to see our first cigarette made. He is in Durham now."

"It is not because we are Jews then?" Jacob said warily.

Ben raised his eyebrows. "No, of course not. Of all the people to have prejudices, Clint would be the last. In his life there is no time for such things. He has time only for two things, pursuing women and making money."

"Jacob, have there been any incidents since you came here?" Charlotte asked.

"Incidents? Eh, what is this incidents?"

Ben said quietly, "What Charlotte means, has there been any trouble with the local people?"

Jacob seemed to withdraw within himself, his expression remote. But his shrug was eloquent. "From some, what you call the cold treatment. A few young ones jeer at us. But we are used to this in New York."

Charlotte was troubled by what he had told them, but before she commented on it, Rachel came in from the kitchen. She was wearing a small, lace circlet upon her dark curls, that looked, to Charlotte, much like a doily.

She had removed her apron, showing a simple brown dress, now ornamented by the presence of a lovely lace collar and cuffs.

"Our meal is ready," she announced softly. "Come, take your places."

Jacob smiled, no, beamed, Charlotte thought, noticing the look of pride and love that he bent upon his daughter. "Now," he said, "you will see, and taste, a real Jewish Shabbat dinner, eh. You will like it, I promise. Come."

As they entered the dining alcove, Charlotte had to admit that she was impressed. A sparkling white lace tablecloth covered the large oval table, and place settings were set with good china.

Rachel caught Charlotte's glance. "The cloth and dishes belonged to my mother. She brought them from the old country."

"They are beautiful," Charlotte said sincerely.

On the oak sideboard sat two tapering white candles in simple silver holders. As Charlotte and Ben watched, Rachel went over to them, and took a lucifer from a small enameled box. "I will say the Shabbat blessing now," she said and smiled. "The blessing that means that the Shabbat is officially under way."

The candles flared, and began to turn, and as they did so, Rachel, in a voice full of emotion, but soft and clear, began to speak: "*Baruch ata adonai eloheynu, melech ha-olam, asher kid-shanu b'mitzvotav z'tsivanu, l'hadlik ner shel Shabbat*." She glanced up and smiled. "Now we can eat."

Charlotte was moved by the simple ceremony; she looked at Ben, and caught his eye. She could see his response to her feeling in his eyes and felt warmed by his understanding.

As they took their seats, Jacob said, "What Rachel just spoke means, in English: Blessed is the Lord our God, Ruler of the Universe, who hallows us with his *Mitzvot* . . . that means, how you say, good deeds, or mercy . . . and who commands us to kindle the lights of Shabbat."

"It's a lovely ceremony," said Charlotte.

"Now," Jacob said, "I will bless the Challah, the bread, and the wine." He reached for a long, yellow loaf of braided bread, which sat in front of him, recited a blessing in Hebrew, then broke the bread and put a piece into his mouth.

Charlotte watched in fascination as he lifted the glass and took a sip of wine. Smacking his lips appreciatively, he then broke off pieces of the rich-smelling bread and passed it to each of them; and Charlotte understood that they were to follow his example.

It was an interesting and delicious meal. After the bread and wine, Rachel served a mound of savory ground meat on a bed of greens; chopped liver, she said. With it she served fresh radishes, and more of the egg bread. Charlotte found the liver unusual but tasty, and Ben, she noticed, was eating it with gusto.

The liver was followed by a thick chicken soup, in which floated small pastry packets which Rachel told her were *kreplach*. They were stuffed with a meat filling, and were quite good.

Charlotte was almost full after the soup, but that in turn was followed by a roasted chicken, accompanied by potato kugel, a dish made of grated and baked potato and onions, and sweet and sour cabbage with sesame seeds.

Charlotte managed to try some of everything, and she thought she would surely burst, yet when the dessert was served—a honey cake topped with almonds—she managed to eat some, with another sip of wine.

As they were eating dessert, Ben said, "I am reminded of a joke I heard. There was this young Jewish fellow over in Charleston, or wherever, who was visited by relatives from up North. He was asked if he didn't keep kosher. He replied, 'Certainly, we serve kosher grits.'"

Rachel laughed dutifully, but Jacob looked perplexed. "Kosher grits? What is this grits?"

Ben explained, "It's a food common in the South, and nowhere else that I know of. It's made from kernels of corn bleached with lye, and if you've never eaten it, Jacob, don't concern yourself." He waved a hand. "I never could see the attraction."

Somehow the humorous anecdote seemed to have made Jacob loquacious. As they finished their meal and then moved back into the parlor, he related how he had left Europe, a lad not yet attained his majority, and journeyed to the United States alone. His parents and two sisters had died when a plague raged through the country, leaving Jacob alone in the world.

Charlotte listened, fascinated. She had to admire the man's courage and fortitude; she doubted very much that she would have been capable of enduring the hardships he had gone through to get to this country.

And even then, she learned, the hardships had not been over. He had worked on the New York docks for a number of years, heavy labor that would have killed a less hardy soul. Shortly after he married Rachel's mother, Jacob had landed a job with the tobacco company, and slowly but surely worked his way up until he had been made foreman of the rollers when the company went into cigarette production. Rachel's mother, also an immigrant, had died ten years ago, when Rachel was eleven years old, leaving Jacob to raise her alone.

Rachel said very little all evening, but several times Charlotte noticed her eyes lingering on Ben's face. Each time her expression became dreamy and tender. Ben seemed totally unaware of her scrutiny.

She's in love with him, Charlotte thought, disconcerted. Rachel might not realize it, and certainly Ben did not, but it was undeniably true.

This thought aroused a conflict of emotions in Charlotte. First, she felt a certain sadness, as if sensing an impending loss. And that made her both angry and possessive, angry at Rachel for directing her affections at Ben, and possessive toward Ben. They were sitting side by side on the divan now, and it was only by great effort of will that she was able to restrain herself from reaching out and openly taking Ben's hand, as an overt gesture of her prior claim.

I *am* jealous, she thought in wonder; I'm jealous and I've forfeited any right to that.

She stirred impatiently. "Ben, it's late. We'd better go. It's going to be a busy day tomorrow, for both of us."

They all arose, and after a brief exchange of farewells, Jacob escorted them to the front door and opened it wide.

As he stood framed in the doorway, a rock came out of the night, and struck the side of the house a few inches from his head.

And from across the street came a chorus of hooting voices:

"Jews ain't welcome in Durham!"

"Foreigners taking jobs we should have."

"Go back where you came from."

Ben said angrily, "Damn them! Do you have a gun in the house, Jacob? A few shots over their heads will scatter them like the cowards they are."

"I have no need of a gun," Jacob said. He stepped out onto the small porch, seeming to grow larger in the spill of light from inside. He shouted in that stentorian voice: "Nobody makes Jacob Lefkowitz run. This my house, here I stay. You no-goods, you scum of the earth!"

Another rock sailed out of the dark, barely missing Jacob's head. A raspy voice shouted, "Don't threaten us, Jew! We'll send the Klan around to see you. They'll tar and feather you, and ride you out of town on a rail!"

Charlotte gasped. "That's Cob Jenks, Ben! I'd know that voice anywhere."

Jacob started down the steps, and Ben hurried forward to stride beside him, Charlotte coming along behind them. In a moment she could hear running feet in the night, and by the time they reached the gate, all was quiet.

"They're running, Jacob," Ben said in disgust.

"Yes, Jacob," Charlotte said. "I hope you don't let them frighten you. Actually it's because of us that they're doing this. Jenks works for Sload Lutcher, and I'm sure he's following Lutcher's orders. He hopes to scare you all out of town, and then we'll be without cigarette rollers."

Ben said, "And I hope you don't think that everyone in Durham is like that band of roughnecks."

"I do not scare easily," Jacob said stolidly. "It was like this in the old country. That is one reason our people left, Ben."

"What Poppa means is that Jews encounter this sort of thing almost anywhere we go." Rachel had followed them out of the house. "Even in New York it happened, but not so much there since we lived in a settlement of our own people." She took Jacob's hand and smiled up into his scowling face. "Don't be concerned, Charlotte, Ben, we do not frighten easily."

Going home in the buggy, Charlotte said, "That soured the whole evening, Ben. How can people stoop so low?"

Ben shrugged. "If they were Lutcher's people, they were paid to do it. What bothers me is, it may not stop there. When something like this begins, even with paid thugs, it has a tendency to spread, even to decent people."

"Now I can understand your fears, Ben. I thought you were borrowing trouble. Isn't there something we can do?"

"Not very much. You can be sure that it can't be traced back to Lutcher. His hands will be clean, as always. So it wouldn't gain anything to confront him with it, except the personal satisfaction of smashing his face in. I'll have a talk with Clint. Part of his function is public relations, and he is in good standing with the mayor and other higher-ups. Maybe he can have a word with some of them."

Charlotte was dubious. "Shouldn't *you* do that, Ben?"

He shook his head. "No, I'm a Jew, don't forget. It's better handled by Clint. Aside from that, he's pretty good at handling sticky situations."

Charlotte knew, without asking, that he was referring to the termination of her affair with Clint. Evidently, Ben assumed that it had been Clint's doing; she had no intention of enlightening him.

They rode the rest of the way in silence. As Ben reined the horse in before Clint's boarding house, he turned to her. "Charlotte, I'm in the mood for a little relaxation. We've both been working for months, it seems, seven days a week, from sunup until sundown."

She looked at him warily. "What did you have in mind?"

"Well, I thought Sunday we would take the day off, pack a basket, and drive out of Durham a ways for a lazy afternoon. A Sunday picnic. This warm weather may not last long."

She was already shaking her head. "No, Ben, there's too much to do, with the opening Monday morning."

"Charlotte, we would both be in better shape on Monday for Sunday off. Everything is ready. Think hard now. Is there anything you could do on Sunday that you couldn't do some other time?"

She was silent for a moment. He was right—there was nothing all that urgent, nothing that could not wait. The prospect of a picnic, an afternoon free of business concerns, became more appealing the more she considered it.

Finally she smiled, nodding. "You know, Ben, I think I'd like that. And you're right, there's nothing that can't wait."

Ben squeezed her hand. "I'll see to having a basket packed. My landlady will do it. Just be ready when I come by at eleven Sunday morning."

A few days of Indian summer had enveloped Durham, and turned the weather warm and clear. When Ben picked Charlotte up, the day was beautiful. As they drove south out of town, the sky was a brilliant blue, although a few dark clouds hovered close to the horizon to the north.

Ben nodded his head that way. "The weather could change today, but we should have ample warning in time to get back home."

As the buggy clicked along, Charlotte relaxed against the seat. Ben had the top down, and the warm sun caressed her face. She felt more relaxed than she had in a long while, and she even dozed a little.

A little farther on, Ben said, "I mentioned to Clint what we talked about Friday night."

She raised her head. "And what did he say?"

"He was indignant, as I expected. The first thing he wanted to do was rush off to thrash Lutcher, but I managed to talk him out of that. We finally decided that he would have a number of quiet discussions with people of influence, and see if we can't head off the fire before it becomes a conflagration."

"Let's hope he can do something about it."

They were beyond the city limits now, and the buggy was moving along at a brisk pace, trailing a cloud of dust behind the spinning wheels.

Charlotte mused on some changes in the countryside. The signs of desolation were slowly disappearing. Some of the finer plantation homes she glimpsed in among the big trees had been painted a gleaming white, and the fields they passed were mostly in cultivation. The area around Durham still had a long way to go to complete recovery from the war's devastation, yet the signs were hopeful. Charlotte liked to think that she had, in some small measure, contributed to the stirrings of new life. She had given the tobacco farmers hope, and if King Tobacco became a thriving industry, she would be contributing even more.

After a few miles she looked over at Ben. "Where are we going? We're getting quite a distance out of Durham."

He flashed a smile at her. "There's a good spot I came across not too long ago. It's a sort of glen, with no farms or houses close by, with a creek wandering through it. It's not much farther now."

Charlotte glanced back to the north, where the clouds were thickening, boiling ever higher. The clouds held the promise of a gathering storm, if not snow and icy winds, at least a cold rain. Instead of mentioning this to Ben, she shrugged and leaned her head back. It was his picnic, and if he knew a good spot, he should have the chance to show it to her. Besides, if it did rain, they could always put the top up on the buggy and be reasonably protected.

Soon, he began to slow the buggy, and then turned off down a narrow lane. Looking around, Charlotte saw no houses near; the only signs of life she saw were a horse and rider far down the road behind them—much too distant for her to make out the rider.

Ben drove into a grove of trees, and shortly the lane ended. He pulled the horse to a halt, and said, "We have to walk from here. It's a half mile, more or less."

Getting down, he tied the horse off to a tree, reached in the back for a large picnic hamper and two blankets, then gave Charlotte a hand down. He led her along a dim path through the trees. The ground sloped gradually downward, and it was not long before the tall trees hid most of the sky. The earth wore a carpet of autumn leaves, which crackled like paper under their feet. It was very quiet; only the sounds of their footsteps and the singing of birds in the trees overhead could be heard.

After about a half-mile they reached the banks of a small, sluggishly flowing stream. Ben spread the blankets under a huge, spreading oak near the bank. As Charlotte sat down on the blankets, drawing her knees up, Ben uncovered the basket. It was mid-afternoon now, and the smell of food escaping the basket made Charlotte realize that she was hungry.

He spread the hamper cover out on the leaves and took out a bottle of wine. "I'll put this in the water to cool, and we'll have it after our lunch." While he performed this chore, Charlotte began taking the food out—a mound of golden fried chicken, potato salad, cucumbers, freshly baked bread, a jar of tomatoes, and a jar of watermelon rind preserves.

By the time Ben returned, the food was all on the cloth, and they began to eat hungrily. There was little conversation; there seemed very little need of talk. Ben was one of the few men Charlotte knew who did not seem compelled to keep up a running conversation while in the company of a woman.

Charlotte leaned back against the tree trunk with a contented sigh. "You're a good cook, Ben Ascher."

"Thank you, dear Charlotte. I try," he said with a straight face. "Shall we exchange recipes now?"

Charlotte laughed. "You'd get the worst of the bargain, I'm afraid. I'm a terrible cook, I've never been able to get involved in it. There always seemed something much more interesting to do. In fact, I'm terrible at *any* domestic chores."

"But you run a good tobacco factory."

"I have the best of partners. But thank you, Ben." She touched his hand lightly. "Dear, dear Ben." She yawned involuntarily. "Pardon me! Would you think it awful of me if I took a nap?"

Charlotte awoke to Ben shaking her, and the first thing she saw when she opened her eyes was his worried face.

"Charlotte," he said urgently, "we'd better hurry. There's a storm right on top of us." He smiled sheepishly. "I'm afraid that I dozed off myself."

Charlotte sat up, shaking her head to clear it of sleep. He was right. The afternoon had turned dark, and what little she could see of the sky was black and threatening. The temperature had dropped sharply, and a stiff, cold wind moaned through the trees overhead.

Ben was already gathering up the remains of their lunch and dumping everything into the picnic hamper. Charlotte jumped up. By the time she had picked up the blankets and folded them over her arm, Ben had the basket repacked.

He retrieved the wine, and hurried back to her. He said brusquely, "Let's go!"

The sky grew darker, and something stung Charlotte's cheek as they hurried through the trees—it was a snowflake. Ben pushed on ahead a few feet, and by the time they attained the edge of the trees, it was snowing heavily. Her head down, Charlotte bumped into Ben, who had suddenly stopped short. She could see that he was peering around in bewilderment.

As she stepped up beside him, he turned a dismayed face to her. "The buggy, it's gone!"

Charlotte looked toward where the horse had been tied off and saw that the buggy was indeed gone. Then she remembered something. "When we turned off the main road, I saw a horse and rider behind us. I didn't think anything of it at the time, but now I'm willing to wager that someone followed us from Durham, and then sneaked up here and stole the horse and buggy. No!" She shook her head. "No, not *stole*. I'll bet it was Lutcher's man, Jenks. He took it away so that we would be stranded out here."

"Whether it was Jenks or a simple thief, it amounts to the same thing," Ben said glumly. "We're left afoot out here, miles from town."

As though to punctuate his remark, the snow began coming down harder. Charlotte said, "Maybe we can find a farmhouse on the way back, and the farmer will be kind enough to lend us a wagon or a buggy to get back into Durham."

"Let's hope so. In any event, we'd better get started before this storm gets any worse. Here, let me have the blankets."

He took the blankets from her, and folded one over Charlotte's head and shoulders like a poncho, then draped the other around himself. "It'll give us at least some protection."

He took her arm, and they started walking north toward Durham, right into the teeth of the wind and driving snow.

As they plowed along, Charlotte cast her thoughts back, and she could not remember seeing any farmhouses along the road the last few miles on their way out. It was soon evident that her memory had not played her false. A mile, two miles, passed beneath their plodding feet, and there was no sign of a dwelling of any kind.

To make matters worse, she had not worn boots, since the day had been nice when they started out. Her shoes were fine for ordinary walking, but not for hiking in a snow storm. Before the first mile had passed, her feet were soaked and ice-cold, and the mixed sleet and snow began to freeze on the ground, which became as slick as greased glass. More than once she lost her footing and would have fallen if Ben had not caught her.

Almost at once, it seemed, total darkness fell, and they could see only a few feet in front of them.

"We can't continue this way much longer," Ben said. "The snow's likely to get heavier, and we could easily wander off the road without realizing it, and freeze to death . . . Wait!"

He drew Charlotte to a halt and peered off to the left. "Is that a building over there?"

Charlotte followed the direction of his pointing finger. She thought she could see some sort of structure about thirty yards off the road, but the driving snow made it difficult to make sure. "I see something, but there are no lights. There may not be anybody home, or it may be deserted. Many of the houses are empty along this road."

"That doesn't matter," Ben said. "It's at least some sort of building, offering shelter, and that we need right now more than anything."

They hurried through the falling snow toward the building. It was a small farmhouse, and it was vacant, the windows boarded up. The door was latched from the inside, but a hard kick by Ben, and it swung open. They went inside. The relief from the wind and snow was immediate. Charlotte knew that the house must be very cold, and that the illusion of warmth would not last, but she was grateful for the respite, however brief.

There was a fireplace set in one wall. Ben closed the door, and they groped their way across the room. He found a stub of a candle on the mantelpiece, and lit it. From the weak light, Charlotte could see that dust and cobwebs lay over everything; it was plain that the house had been abandoned since the war, if not before. There were several pieces of dilapidated furniture strewn across the floor.

Together, they quickly gathered up the furniture, stacking it beside the fireplace. Ben broke the dry wood across his knee, and kneeling, he soon had a fire crackling in the hearth. Charlotte huddled close, soaking up the warmth, while Ben spread the blankets as close to the heat as he could without setting them on fire.

"There," he said, dusting his hands together, then warming them before the fire. "There will be enough wood in here to last out the night, if we have to burn the house down, room by room. A storm this early in the year should blow itself out before morning. We'll spend the night here, then leave at first light."

Charlotte still shivered from time to time. As he saw her shiver again, Ben stooped to take the bottle from the picnic basket, and poured wine into two cups. He gave Charlotte one. "Here, this should help warm you up quicker."

She drank the wine, and then held the cup out for more, which she drank more slowly. The wine did help, sending warmth coursing through her blood. Ben took the voluminous tablecloth from the basket, and spread it around her shoulders.

"Sit on the floor, Charlotte, as close to the fire as you can. The blankets should dry out soon." He turned them over to expose the other side to the fire, then delved into the picnic hamper. "Luckily, we have some food left. Hungry?"

She nodded. "I believe I am."

Ben set the uncovered basket on the floor before her, and sat down beside her. They ate the rest of what was in the basket, having another cup of wine with it. From time to time Ben got up to break more furniture to fuel the flames. Cold wind whistled through the cracks in the old house, and snow blew in in a number of places, drifting across the floor, but the area immediately before the hearth was a pocket of welcome warmth.

The long walk, the battle with the elements, had left Charlotte exhausted, and now the warmth of the fire, the food and the wine—all combined to make her sleepy. Her head drooped forward onto her chest, and she dozed. Once or twice she came partly awake as Ben broke up more furniture to feed the fire, but she drifted off to sleep again.

"Charlotte..." She jumped as Ben touched her cheek gently. "The blankets are dry now. Sleeping sitting up like that will make you stiff and sore in the morning. Let's stretch out together. If you don't object," he said with an uncertain smile. "We'll both keep warmer that way."

"I'll risk it, Ben," she said with an answering smile. "Anything to keep warm."

Ben piled more wood on the fire, then spread one blanket across the front of the fireplace; and when Charlotte had stretched out, he lay beside her, letting her have the side closest to the fire, and tucked the other blanket around them. Facing the fire, on her side, head pillowed on her hands, Charlotte stared into the flames, comforted by the feel of Ben's body against her back.

As she grew warmer, Charlotte prepared to go back to sleep, but the proximity of Ben's body snuggled spoon-fashion against her was not conducive to sleep. She wondered if he felt the same, and noticed that he was shifting his position, drawing away from her. Unbidden, the memory of that night in her wagon invaded her thoughts. She became steadily more wakeful, and restless. It had been two months or more since she and Clint had made love, and thinking of that now made her acutely aware of the urgings of her body.

"Ben..." She turned onto her back. "How deeply are you involved with Rachel?"

She felt him tense. He said warily, "I'm not sure what you mean. I like her, like her very much."

"She's in love with you."

"How can you possibly know that?"

"A woman can always tell."

"Well, I think you're wrong," he said somewhat uncertainly.

"I'm not wrong, but just so long as you're not in love with her, I don't have to be concerned."

She turned again, this time onto her side facing him. She placed her hand on his cheek and kissed him on the mouth.

He moved back. "Charlotte . . . Please don't tease me. If you know how much I . . ."

"I'm not teasing, Ben," she said softly. "I'm a brazen woman, you should know that by now. I want you to make love to me."

"Have you forgotten what you told me?"

"I haven't forgotten. What I said was I didn't want to become too involved with you, or any other man."

"Did you tell Clint that, too?"

"As a matter of fact, I did. But Clint has nothing to do with this. We're alone here, we'll be alone together all night, and I see nothing wrong if we want each other. But then, maybe you don't want me?"

He groaned. "Oh, I want you! Dear God, yes, I've never stopped wanting you!"

Without another word, he took her into his arms, and neither spoke again.

That other time Ben had been somewhat tentative, unsure of himself, but there was none of that now. There was an urgency almost savage about their love-making, as if their temporary isolation from the world had torn away all reservations, all restraints.

His mouth ground on hers, as his hands found their way boldly under her clothing, exploring her body unashamedly. Charlotte responded in kind, as his touch set up a blaze of need in her body, and she gave herself to him totally.

Her pleasure was already at a fever pitch when they finally came together, and Charlotte cried out when Ben went into her.

Their passion was wild, a mutual frenzy of need. Each was equal to the demands of the other. Mouths locked in a kiss, bodies moving in rhythmic unison, they drove together toward that final moment of shuddering, ultimate pleasure; and Charlotte could not help but feel a fierce joy that she could initiate such a response in Ben. If he felt this strong a need for her, he could not be in love with Rachel. Could he?

They remained bound together until the last throbs of sensation had passed. Then Charlotte's arms loosened from around Ben. Taking this as a signal, he moved away.

In their wildness the top blanket had been tossed aside, and the fire had died. Her body cooling, Charlotte felt the chill drafts from the wall cracks buffeting her exposed body like pin-pricks of ice. She quickly adjusted her clothing, and Ben retrieved the blanket and placed it over her. He got up to break more furniture for the fire.

Charlotte watched him through heavy eyes, a pleasant lassitude stealing over her. She was almost asleep when he returned to their makeshift bed, once again snuggling against her back.

"Charlotte," he said almost shyly. "I . . ."

"Don't say anything, Ben." She stretched a hand up to touch his cheek, which lay on her shoulder. "Good night, dear Ben."

He sighed. "Good night, Charlotte."

But before she went to sleep, a disturbing thought wormed its way into her mind. It was painfully evident that they would not be able to leave this place until morning, if then. By the time they managed to find a farmer willing to lend them a vehicle to transport them back to Durham, they would not be able to get back until late, and the first King Cigarette was due to be made by Rachel at eight sharp. What would everyone think when they finally straggled in, obviously having spent the night together?

And Clint . . . Clint would be there. What would go through his mind, when he realized the truth?

# Chapter Fourteen

NOW, it was production time.

Long before eight on Monday morning, the plant was ready to start cigarette production. The rollers were there at a quarter to eight, and the cutter had shredded the first tobacco, and Rachel was ready to make the first cigarette, under the hovering supervision of her father.

At eight the rollers were all gathered in a semi-circle around Rachel's table, and Jacob paced impatiently back and forth behind her, keeping the other rollers back far enough so that she could work unimpeded.

Everything was ready—except that Ben and Charlotte were missing.

Clint was also pacing back and forth, in front of the plant, furiously smoking a cigar and glancing at his watch every few minutes. Where the hell were they? When it had become clear that both Ben and Charlotte were late, Clint had sent Jimmie Hollister to check both their rooming houses. Although he did not show it outwardly, Clint was worried. It was totally unlike Charlotte to miss this event; this was the moment her whole life had been pointing toward for a full year. It seemed to him that only a disaster of some kind would keep her away.

He paced, waiting for Jimmie. The fierce snowstorm of last night had passed, leaving the day crisp but beautifully clear, and the sky overhead was a bright blue, almost blinding in its intensity. The snow was already melting on the ground.

Clint took out his pocket watch and checked the time again. It was just eight o'clock. He turned the watch over and clicked the lid open. The French picture, the last one in his possession, nestled in the lid, the nude woman smiling seductively up at him. He had ordered another batch of pictures for his next selling trip. To his knowledge, Charlotte still did not know about the pictures. He thought of telling her about them before he left on the impending trip, and smiled to himself at the thought of the outrage she would undoubtedly register.

"Mr. Devlin..."

He faced about as Jacob Lefkowitz hustled up to him. Initially he had been dubious about Ben going all the way to New York to hire cigarette rollers, and foreigners at that; but his fears had been eased when he had observed the expertise Jacob had brought to the operation. Besides, he liked the man.

"Yes, Jacob?"

"It is eight o'clock, eh, the time we were to start. The workers are becoming impatient."

"No more impatient than I am, Jacob. I can't imagine what's delaying them. I've sent Jimmie Hollister to check their respective boarding houses. He should be back shortly. If he can't find them, we'll just have to go ahead without them."

Jacob nodded and returned inside. Clint resumed his pacing. To divert his thoughts from his concern over Charlotte's unexplained absence, he let his mind jump ahead to the upcoming trip.

Over the past few months he had visited most retail outlets within all the surrounding states, and placed good-sized orders for King Cigarettes in all of them. Through her mailings Charlotte had covered the more distant places, and according to her, she had received a good response.

Much of the time during the next month or so, Clint would devote to a different type of selling campaign. All the towns of any size in the tobacco country had marketing sections such as the one in Durham, and a few towns even had warehouses. He intended to take Marcy along on the coming trip, and hawk King Cigarettes on the streets of the market sections during market days. Marcy would put on a sort of show, singing and a little dancing, in daring costumes; he had discovered that she had a surprisingly good singing voice.

In this manner he hoped to attract an audience of buyers, and after Marcy had their attention, he would introduce them to King Cigarettes. It smacked of a carnival, he reflected wryly; and yet market days always had a carnival atmosphere—one more attraction would not be amiss.

Again, he thought of Charlotte, and Ben, in connection with the brazen showmanship he had in mind. Eventually, they were bound to find out what he was doing, and there would be an accounting. He hoped that, by that time, his tactics would be so successful that any disapproval from them would be blunted.

Some day, Clint mused, advertising of a product would be more dignified; but since he was one of the first to really embrace the concept of letting the whole world know about what he was selling, who had the right to be critical? There was one thing he was absolutely sure of—first, you had to get their attention. And if what he had in mind did not get their attention, his name was not Clint Devlin!

His reverie was broken by the sight of Jimmie Hollister hastening toward him. The youngster was out of breath when he skidded to a stop.

"Well, Jimmie, what did you find out?"

"Not too much, I'm a-feared, Mr. Devlin. First off, I went to Miss Charlotte's boarding house. Her landlady said that Mr. Ascher picked her up in a buggy at midday yesterday. Then I went to Mr. Ascher's boarding house, and *his* landlady says she had packed a picnic basket for Mr. Ascher."

"A *picnic*? Oh, Christ! Where'd they go, did she have any idea?"

Jimmie shook his head. "I reckon not."

"It has to mean that they were caught out in that storm last night and couldn't make it back."

"Maybe I should go looking for them?"

"Where? East, west, north, south? Hell, we don't even know in which direction they went," Clint said disgustedly. "No, they'll show up eventually." Yet, Clint was not all that sure. Something could have happened to them. Even as he turned and strode purposely into the factory, worry nibbled at his mind.

He made his way through the workers around Rachel, and said to Jacob, "Miss King and Ben Ascher have been delayed, Jacob. We can't wait any longer. Let's get started."

The workers stirred in anticipation, and Jacob said happily, "All right, my Rachel, now we begin!"

Clint watched intently as Rachel made the very first King Cigarette. He had never seen it done before, but Ben had explained the process to him in detail, as it was done in New York. In addition, Ben had told him that Jacob had some innovative ideas of his own, ideas that the plant owner in New York refused to adopt, no matter how much Jacob had pleaded.

Now Clint was able to observe Jacob's ideas put into practice. The most novel one was the small trench, the exact length and thickness of the cigarette, which had been grooved into each table. The second innovation was the small strip of felt which had been sewn over the palm of the glove Rachel wore on her right hand.

As she began, she fitted the cigarette paper into the small trench, then put the proper amount of shredded tobacco onto the paper. Next, she swept her gloved hand over the protruding edge of the paper and rolled it into a cylinder in one unbroken motion. At the same time her ungloved hand, the left, was dipping into the paste which was used to seal the cigarette paper.

A cheer went up as she held the rolled cigarette above her head.

Jacob clapped his hands. "Now we all go to work, eh! Proceed to your tables."

The workers scattered, going to their assigned tables.

Clint stood where he was, watching Rachel, who had turned back to her work, now to roll enough cigarettes to fill the first King pack, which was due to occupy a place of honor in a glass case in Charlotte's office.

Each marble table had a number, and a can, which was numbered to correspond with the table number. Each can held three pounds of tobacco, enough for a thousand cigarettes, and each roller was required to produce that amount of cigarettes for each can of shredded tobacco. Charlotte had instructed Jacob to be very strict about this; it was a necessary precaution to control costs, since the rollers were on piecework.

Now Rachel faced around again, and held out the first full pack of King Cigarettes. Clint took it with a feeling of something like awe, and turned it over and over in his hands.

"It looks great," he said, feeling his face break wide in a foolish grin. "It looks absolutely great!"

"Is it all right if I have a look at it?" Charlotte said from behind him.

Before he could react, she had plucked the pack of cigarettes from his hand.

Clint turned slowly. Both Charlotte and Ben looked unkempt—in fact, they looked downright disreputable. Ben sported a day's growth of beard, and Charlotte's clothing was badly wrinkled. Obviously, they had not been to their respective boarding houses, but had come directly to the plant from wherever they had spent the night.

Ben, Clint noted, had the grace to flush a dark red when their glances crossed. He mumbled something, and walked over to Jacob, halfway across the room.

"It does look great, Rachel," Charlotte said. "You did a fine job."

Rachel did not look up from her busy hands. "Thank you, Miss King."

"I'm glad you approve, Lotte," Clint said laconically. "I suppose now I'm going to catch the devil from you for giving the go-ahead, for not waiting for you and Ben?"

"Of course not." She refused to look directly at him. "You did exactly right. We agreed to produce the first King Cigarette at eight sharp this morning." She fell silent, all her attention concentrated on the cigarette pack.

After a moment she looked up, her glance roaming over the busy rollers at their tables. She moved down the row of tables, Clint trailing after her. Finally she stopped, nodding in satisfaction. "We're in operation at last. I'm glad Ben thought of bringing experienced rollers in from New York. If we'd had to train unskilled workers, it would have taken forever."

"The way in which I plan to sell King Cigarettes, they'll never be able to keep up."

She shrugged. "So? We'll hire more rollers."

"Where will you put them?" He swept his hand around. "This whole floor is taken up now."

"Then we'll lease another building." She frowned at him impatiently. "What's wrong, Clint? Are you piqued because something Ben and I planned without your advice and consent is working well?"

"No, that's not it at all. I congratulate both of you. This will do fine for the first year, but if I increase sales as much as I intend to, we'll have to look into other alternatives."

"Such as?" she said coolly.

"I've heard about a new invention, a machine to produce tailor-made cigarettes. If this machine works, its use will eliminate any need for hand rollers. One machine can do the work of three times this many hand rollers."

"Honestly, Clint!" she exclaimed in annoyance. "This is the very first day of production, and you're already jumping ahead to something brand new, something not even tested as yet."

He grinned lazily. "Another business axiom, my dear . . . If you don't think ahead, somebody may not only catch up but get ahead of you."

She snapped, "Spare me your axioms, Clint, please!

I'm not in the mood. After last night..." She fell silent, her gaze going off.

"Well?" he prompted.

"Well what?"

"About last night. Aren't you going to offer at least some sort of explanation?"

"I don't owe you any explanation, Clint Devlin."

He was amused to see color sweep her face. "Not about your personal life, no, which I take it you mean, you and Ben. But this was an important moment, this morning, in your *business* life, Lotte. And you weren't here."

"Ben and I..." She cleared her throat. "We were caught out in that storm last night. We were lucky to get back when we did. You know about the snowstorm, don't you?" She added sarcastically, "Or were you so busily engaged in *your* personal life you didn't even notice?"

"I noticed, Lotte," he said steadily. "Sarcasm doesn't become you, and going on the offensive won't help you."

"If anyone is being offensive, it's you."

"Offensive, am I?" His temper flared. "Who was it told me that it was all over between us because you didn't want to cause trouble between Ben and myself? Who was it told me that there would be no more emotional involvements with your partners? Did you say all that, Lotte, or did I just imagine it?"

Now she met his gaze defiantly. "It's true, I said that."

"Then it must be all right to be considerate of Ben's feelings, but not mine, is that it?"

Her head went back. "Just because we were caught out together all night in the storm doesn't mean anything happened between us."

"Are you about to tell me that nothing did?" he asked softly. "If you do, I won't believe you for a minute. One look at the pair of you this morning told me everything."

"What difference does it make to you? Why should you care?" she cried. "I'm sure you don't spend many lonely nights while on the road."

He stared at her for a long moment, then said tightly,

"You're right about that, my dear. In a manner of speaking."

He wheeled about and strode out of the building. Charlotte stood staring after him, hands clenched into fists at her sides.

From across the room Ben had been watching Clint and Charlotte worriedly, and had noticed that they were arguing heatedly. He had about decided to walk over and intervene, when Clint faced about abruptly, his face stormy, and stalked out.

Ben walked over to Charlotte, who stood staring after the departing Clint. He touched her arm. "Charlotte, Clint seemed upset. Did you have a quarrel?"

She looked at him with wounded eyes. "I think you could safely say that."

"What about?" Even as he voiced the question, he already knew.

"About last night, of course. I told him that it was none of his business, and he got angry . . . No, don't say anything, Ben," she said, as he started to speak. "I'm weary of the whole thing and don't wish to discuss it. Clint Devlin has no business questioning me about my private life."

She turned and walked quickly toward the stairs leading up to the second floor. Ben looked after her helplessly. As he glanced away from the stairs, he noticed Rachel Lefkowitz staring at him. Forcing a smile, he crossed to her table.

"How is it going, Rachel? I saw the first pack of King Cigarettes you made. A fine job. I'm just sorry I wasn't here to watch you make them."

"Are you, Mr. Ascher?" The brown eyes were somber.

"Of course I am. It's a moment we've all been looking forward to, but it couldn't be helped. We got caught out in that storm last night, and just couldn't make it back until it was too late."

"You *couldn't*? Or didn't want to?" she said in a small voice.

Ben peered at her in astonishment. Why should she be so upset about him being with Charlotte all night? Then he remembered Charlotte's remark about Rachel being in love with him. It was true! He discovered that he was inordinately pleased by the fact that Rachel should care this deeply. Ben was not a vain man, yet he was human enough to be flattered that a lovely woman such as Rachel Lefkowitz should be attracted to him.

However, this sudden knowledge started thoughts tumbling through his head at a bewildering rate, and he realized that he was not prepared to deal with them—at least not until he gave the situation some thought.

"I don't believe I have to account to you, Rachel," he said more curtly than he had intended.

He turned away so quickly that he did not see the wounded expression that came over Rachel's face. Blinking back tears, she turned about to concentrate determinedly on her work.

As he looked across his desk at Jeff King, Sload Lutcher was pleased. "You did good, King, very good indeed. You did exactly what I wanted, becoming such good friends with this Clint Devlin."

Jeff looked surprised, and his expression became wary, as though such unusual praise from Lutcher might be some sort of trap being laid for him.

He said cautiously, "Thank you, Mr. Lutcher."

"Yes, you did fine." Nodding, Lutcher made a steeple of his hands. "Now I think that it is time to take a step toward the future. From what you tell me, I gather there is friction between the three partners in King Tobacco."

"All I know is that Clint wasn't too happy last night. He drank a little more than is his habit, and he grumbled darkly about my . . . uh, about Charlotte."

"Did he go into particulars?"

Jeff shook his head. "Nothing specific. He did mutter something about what's sauce for the goose is sauce for the gander, but I'm not sure what he was talking about. I do happen to know that he's dissatisfied because he feels that Ben Ascher and Charlotte don't approve of some of his promotion schemes."

Lutcher's gaze sharpened. "The picture, do your sister and her Jew partner know about the naked woman?"

"I don't believe so."

"Then I want you to see to it that she does. That should get her back up."

Jeff looked unhappy. "I don't know, Mr. Lutcher. She is my sister, even if she doesn't want to own up to it."

"Do it, just do it!" Lutcher rapped the desk. "Now, it's time you left my employ."

Jeff's mouth dropped open. "What? I don't understand..."

Lutcher let him suffer for a moment, before he said, "Don't let it worry you. We're the only two who will know the real truth. You see, you'll still be working for me, but everybody else will think you've been fired." Lutcher leaned back, his thoughts jumping ahead, spinning out his web.

"I just plain don't understand, Mr. Lutcher," Jeff said in a baffled voice.

"You'll understand as much as I want you to," Lutcher snarled. "You've learned tobacco, King, I'll hand you that. Now you're going to put that knowledge to good use. You're going to become a pinhooker. The big warehouse sales are mostly over by now, but the smaller towns throughout the tobacco belt will still be having them. You're going to hit them one after another, and buy as much tobacco as you can. Don't worry." He held up his hand. "I'll be financing you. I'm not going to be tight-fisted in this. I'll spend whatever I have to to drive your sister and her partners to the wall." He peered at Jeff closely. "That should please you. You told me that it's unseemly for your sister to be in business, especially business run only by men."

Jeff was nodding. "That's true. But I don't see how this will do it."

"Damnit, King, will you listen to me? You'll be told what you need to know, as we go along. And if it works as

I plan, you'll come out of it a big man around Durham, with money in your pocket, well thought of and respected. What I intend to do is make you rich quick. Or," his grin was calculating, "make it appear that you are. Being a shrewd pinhooker is about the easiest way to get rich quick these days. I've known several who bought wisely, held onto the tobacco until the price went out of sight, then sold for a small fortune. That, King, is what you're going to do, or appear to do. The tobacco you buy, naturally, will eventually end up here, but people won't know that. Clear, so far?"

"Clear, Mr. Lutcher," Jeff said slowly.

As the impact of what Lutcher had said sank in, Jeff's entire manner changed. He stood up straighter, and he had taken on a dreamy expression. Lutcher knew what he was thinking, as clearly as if he could read his mind. Jeff King was thinking of living high, wearing fine clothes, traveling in style, throwing money around recklessly. Well, let him continue thinking just that; it suited Lutcher's purpose very well. It would be costly in the early stages, but well worth it if the plan worked. And there would come a day when he would grind Jeff King's face in the dirt. Oh, would he enjoy that! But first the sister; then the brother.

He said, "The minute you leave this office, King, you no longer work for me, as far as anybody knows. Spread the word around, and so will I."

Jeff nodded, smiling openly now.

"There is one other thing. In your travels around the tobacco belt, make sure you hit the same towns as Clint Devlin. I want you to continue to cultivate his acquaintance. By the time this year is out, by the time you supposedly have your fortune made, I want the pair of you to be thick as thieves."

He made a dismissive gesture, and did not begin to grin until Jeff had left, closing the door after him. Then Lutcher permitted himself a chuckle. "Thick as thieves."

How apt!

If the plan he had in mind worked as he hoped, Clint

Devlin and Jefferson King would stand disgraced, disgraced as badly as if they *had* been exposed as thieves!

Standing on the back of the wagon bed, Clint raised his voice, "Gather round, gents, gather close. Come one, come all! It's all for free, a free show to be enjoyed by all, guaranteed not to cost you one cent! Gather round and be entertained!"

Beside him, Marcy jittered nervously. Dressed in a low-cut dress of glittering satin, a gloss of paint and rouge on her face, she looked enticing enough for any man, and the men began to drift toward the wagon and the sound of Clint's voice. It was a small town, and the crowd on this market day was not large, but Clint passed up no opportunity, no matter how small the gathering. He well knew that word of mouth was valuable, and he intended to spread the word about King Cigarettes throughout the South.

Behind him the banjo picker he had hired plucked a few strings as he tuned up. In an aside to Marcy, Clint said, "For God's sake, Marcy, will you settle down? We've been doing this for over a month, and you're still jumpy as a cat on a hot skillet."

"Crowds always make me nervous," she whispered back.

"Crowds are what it's all about, my dear," he said, grinning. "Think about it this way, all those men out there are gathering just to see you." He gestured to the banjo player, who started playing "Dixie."

Marcy sang the first verse without moving. Then the banjo player broke into jig time, and she began to strut back and forth in the small space allowed her. As she sang, Marcy began kicking her legs high, showing a flash of red stockings sheathing her shapely limbs.

The men hooted, clapping their hands in rhythm to the music. Ribald suggestions came from the crowd. Clint could see the few women in the audience registering shock. Here and there one tugged at her man, trying to draw him away. Most of them resisted.

As the song ended, Clint said in a carrying voice, "Now don't go away, gents. Our Marcy here, straight from Paris, France, will favor us with another song and dance, one which, I promise you, will shake you right down to your toenails. So stick around. It's all free, and I'm not selling a thing, my word on that. I do, however, have free gifts for one and all." He reached down to shove a basket around in front of his feet, the same kind of basket that the tobacco farmers used to take their products to market. It was filled to the brim with packs of King Cigarettes.

"Gents, I represent King Tobacco, out of Durham, North Carolina. Some of you may have heard of us, some may not. This is our first year in production, but you'll be hearing plenty from us in the future, believe you me. King Cigarettes are the finest on the market, made from the best prime grade of bright leaf, and rolled to perfection by the best cigarette hand rollers in the whole wide world. And..."

He reached into the basket and filled both hands with the packs. He began tossing them out into the crowd one at a time. "Smoke the cigarette fit for a king, gents. Smoke a King and you'll never smoke any other brand. You may well ask how I can afford to give these fine cigarettes away for nothing. The answer is simple. I am willing to bet that once you've smoked our brand, you'll run, not walk, to the nearest store and *buy* your next pack. Our motto is, '*Our* customers are satisfied customers!'"

All the while he had been talking, Clint had continued tossing out the packs of cigarettes. Now the basket was empty. He turned to Marcy with a flourish. "I promised another song and dance from our pretty little songbird, gents. Here she is, in appreciation of your kind attention!"

Marcy struck a pose, one hand at her hair, the other holding her skirts up high enough to reveal her ankles. A rebel yell rang out loud and clear from the crowd.

Marcy smiled suddenly, her nervousness forgotten, and that look of bawdiness that Clint had seen so many times in hotel rooms took over. To the tune of "Come Dwell With Me," she began to sing:

"Come sleep with me, come snooze with me,
And our bed shall be, our bed shall be,
A pleasant place that's in King's Place,
Where I'll show you my jewel case.
I've got a treasure you've never seen,
And you've a spot that it will screen;
Twill please you when in bed we be,
And then we'll plough the deep..."

"Hold up! Stop this at once!"

The voice was an angry shout, and Clint looked down in astonishment into the face of a stout man standing at the foot of the wagon. Suddenly, a pistol appeared in his hand, and he fired a shot into the air.

The crowd started to scatter in all directions, and within seconds they were all gone. Clint felt rather than heard the banjo picker scrambling off the wagon.

Clint said angrily, "What's the meaning of this, sir? Who are you?"

"I'm the sheriff of this here town, and the pair of you are under arrest!" the stout man exclaimed.

Clint gaped down at the sheriff. "Arrest us? For what, man?"

"For putting on an obscene public performance. We're decent, God-fearing folks in these parts, and we don't cotton to anything like that hussy was doing."

"Who says it's obscene?"

"I do, and that's what's important," the sheriff said smugly. "Come along peaceful now. You wouldn't want me firing off another shot, now would you?"

Clint sighed and jumped to the ground, reaching up to give Marcy a hand down.

"Clint," she said in a small, frightened voice, "what's going to happen?"

"Nothing. Don't worry about it, my dear." She looked far from reassured, and he did not blame her, for he did not have the slightest idea of what would happen next.

As the sheriff escorted them up the street, Clint said, "Sheriff, you're not thinking of putting us in jail, are you?"

"Yup." The sheriff spat tobacco juice onto the ground. "Can't do nothing else until I can haul you two up afore a judge, and the circuit judge don't come around until next week."

"But the lady, sheriff," Clint said in dismay. "Surely you don't want to see her languish in jail that long? Surely there's something you can do about that?"

"Well now, I don't know." The sheriff got a calculating look, one finger stroking his round chin. "I reckon I could set bail."

"How much?"

"Fifty dollars apiece, I reckon that'd be about right."

Clint's dismay grew. In his pocket was fifty-four dollars and some change. As they neared the jail, he sighed, and said, "All right, sheriff. I'll post bail for Marcy. As for me, I guess you'll have me as a guest, until your judge comes around. I don't have enough money for both of us."

Inside the sheriff's office, Clint glumly counted out fifty dollars. Of course, he could send a telegram to Durham, but the thought of facing Charlotte's scorn was too much. Damned if he would send out a cry for help! He would rot in jail first.

Marcy touched his arm, and said timidly, "Thanks, Clint. I'll get a room in the hotel and wait for you. And I'll take care of the horse and wagon meanwhile."

"Sure, Marcy," he said dully. "You do that."

# Chapter Fifteen

CHARLOTTE followed the stout sheriff to the rear of the building where the jail was housed. There were four small cells, and at first Charlotte thought they were all empty.

Then the sheriff said jocularly, "You have company, Devlin. A devil of a pretty lady, I must say, for the likes of you."

The sheriff stopped at the last cell, rattling his ring of keys against the bars. In the murkiness of the jail, Charlotte could see Clint lounging on an iron cot, smoking a cigar.

The sheriff turned to her. "Sorry, Miss, I can't let you into the cell," he said apologetically. "You'll have to talk to him through the bars."

Past his shoulder, Charlotte saw Clint get to his feet leisurely and stroll over to the bars. She said acidly, "This will be fine, sir. I have no wish to be confined in a cell with a common criminal."

The sheriff nodded, grinning. "Just give me a holler when you're ready to leave, ma'am. I'll hear you in my office." He went down the short corridor and closed the heavy door to the cell block.

Clint grinned at her through the bars. "Hello, Lotte. It's nice to see you, my dear, but I don't think it was nice of you to call me a common criminal."

The insolence of him! In jail, on a criminal charge, and apparently it concerned him not at all. She tightened up inside. "If you're not a common criminal, what are you?"

He studied her through a thin veil of cigar smoke, the smile gone now. He said in a dry voice, "Like I said, it's nice to see you, Lotte. If you're referring to the charge that fat sheriff lodged against me, it's so much smoke."

"Well..." She gestured. "You *are* in jail."

"All he's after is a little graft. When he gets his bail money, he'll drop all charges, depend on it."

"There's more to it than that. Everybody will know that a representative of King Tobacco has been thrown in jail for putting on an obscene show!"

He said softly, "Have you seen this so-called obscene show?"

"Of course not!"

"Then don't jump to conclusions. There was nothing obscene about it. A touch risqué, perhaps." He was smiling again, that lazy, infuriating smile of his. "It was calculated to draw an audience, and that it has done, in every town I've been in the last month." He tapped cigar ash on the floor. "Have you seen the orders that I've written? I haven't kept an accurate count, but the business I've done for King Tobacco within the last month has to be up into many thousands of dollars. That's what it's all about, isn't it?"

"That's always your excuse!" she said harshly. "I suppose if you killed someone, you'd use the same excuse."

"It's possible, if it had helped to sell cigarettes," he said with that maddening grin.

"Well, I happen to think that this whole affair is disgusting, and it will make King Tobacco a laughingstock everywhere."

"Now there you're wrong. Oh, people who don't know any better may laugh, but those people in the business will only be envious." He tapped the bars with his cigar. "You know what will happen in the next town where I repeat this performance? The news of my being arrested will draw a larger crowd than ever. People will come out of curiosity. I couldn't ask for better advertising than being arrested this way."

She clenched her fingers around the bars until her

hands ached. "There will not be a repeat performance! Clint, I forbid it!"

"You forbid? Advertising and promotion are my department, Lotte, and so long as I am a partner in King Tobacco, I'll run my department as I see fit."

"Wait until Ben hears about this!"

"You mean you haven't told him yet? You're slipping, my dear."

"If he knows of it, it didn't come from me. I was over in the next town when I got word about this. We're running dangerously short of tobacco, so I've been on a buying trip for the past two weeks, purchasing what tobacco I can find."

"And who's responsible for your running short, pray tell?" He jabbed at his chest. "Me, and my 'obscene' advertising."

"And this . . ." With trembling fingers Charlotte delved into her purse and produced a picture. Without looking at it, she poked it through the bars at him. "You're responsible for this as well, aren't you?"

He took the picture, one eyebrow elevating in amusement. "Guilty, Lotte. Pretty, ain't she?" He handed it back to her, and she took it automatically. "Where did you get the picture, Lotte?"

"A storekeeper's wife came to me with it. She said she had found it in her husband's pocket watch. She was very indignant and upset about it. She thought it was disgraceful that you should be passing out such pictures."

"And the storekeeper, did you talk to him about it?"

"Of course not." Charlotte felt herself flush. "I wouldn't consider such a thing."

"What was his name?"

She frowned in thought. "Hill, I think. Yes, Jed Hill."

Clint was nodding. "Do you know the size of the order Jed Hill placed with me after he knew he was getting that picture as a bonus?"

"Oh! You're impossible, Clint! You always have the same answer."

She glared at him through the bars. He shrugged, then

turned away to walk over to the window to stare out.

Charlotte steeled herself, and said to his back, "This woman you're traveling with, who's flaunting herself so shamefully before all those men . . . That's the woman you were with the first time I saw you. Is she also the one in the picture?"

He grinned around at her. "You mean you couldn't tell, Lotte? Marcy didn't have any clothes on when you saw her that time, and neither does the woman in the picture. You should be able to tell them apart easily enough. Of course it isn't Marcy." He turned and came back toward her. "I sent all the way to Paris for those pictures. Class, all the way."

Charlotte tried to keep her voice steady. "You're sleeping with her, aren't you, this Marcy?"

"Now that, my dear Lotte, is none of your damned business." His face hardened. "You don't have the right to ask me that question. Maybe you did, once, but no longer." He stepped up to the bars. "Lotte, why did you come here, anyway? To scold me? To snoop into my private life? Or to bail me out of jail?"

"Not to bail you out, that's certain," she said. "I wouldn't squander company funds. You got yourself into this mess, Clint, now get yourself out."

"And you, Charlotte King," he said mockingly, "are a cold, hardhearted woman. To think that you'd let a man, your own partner at that, languish in jail."

She turned on her heel and strode away. Of course she was going to post bail for him, that was the reason she was here, but let him remain in the dark for a little longer. Maybe it would teach him a lesson, if that was at all possible. She raised her voice, "Sheriff! I'm leaving now!"

She was halfway to the door when Clint said, "Lotte?"

Against her will she halted, looking back. "Yes?"

"I can't figure how a brother and sister can be so different."

She tensed. "What do you mean?"

"Jeff was here an hour ago. He's arranging bail for me now."

A bitter rage rose in her throat, almost choking her. Blindly she plunged toward the door, calling, "Sheriff! Let me out of here!"

The instant the door had closed behind Charlotte, the smile left Clint's face. Damn the woman! She was the most exasperating female it had ever been his misfortune to know!

She could be sweet and warm, completely feminine—he had seen ample evidence of that. But at other times, like today, she was a totally different person. Clint realized that he had deliberately provoked her, yet she had it coming. How dare she march in here, all proper and pious, chastising him for things he had done, when they were all toward the benefit of King Tobacco? He had proven his case, by the cascade of orders he had sent to the office. She had no right, no goddamned right!

Abruptly, he realized that he had been methodically pounding his fist against the bars, and pain shot up his arm. He looked at the fist in surprise and saw that he had lacerated it; blood flowed freely.

He laughed aloud. Even when she was not present, she had the ability to hurt him.

Thank God, he would be out on the road selling for most of the year from now on. On the necessary trips back to Durham he would not be required to stay long. And no matter what Charlotte's opinion of his promotional tactics might be, they were working, and that *was* what it was all about. His dream had been to become rich and powerful, and he was well on his way toward that goal.

Strangely, that thought was of little consolation to him at that moment. He sighed, wrapped his bleeding hand in his handkerchief, then lit a cigar and sat down to wait for Jeff King to return.

A half hour later, Clint was in the sheriff's office, receiving his personal effects, while Jeff watched the sheriff carefully count the fifty dollars he had just given him.

Satisfied, the sheriff looked up. "All here. You're free to go, Devlin."

Jeff frowned. "Don't I get a receipt, sheriff?"

"A receipt, Mr. King?" the sheriff asked innocently.

"Never mind, Jeff." Clint touched Jeff on the arm.

The sheriff leaned back, smiling at Clint's acumen.

Clint said, "It's been a pleasure doing business with you, sheriff."

"Same here, Devlin," the sheriff said solemnly.

"I was planning on leaving your lovely town in the morning. Is that all right with you?"

"Fine with me, Devlin. I'll be happy to see the last of you." The sheriff tapped a finger on the desk. "But just don't come back here and try to put your show on again."

"Oh, you can be sure of that," Clint assured him. "I wouldn't want to shock the good citizens of your town."

Outside, Jeff said indignantly, "We should have insisted he give us a receipt. Now we have no proof that he's holding bail money for you."

"Come on, Jeff. We kissed that fifty dollars goodbye, along with the fifty I put up for Marcy. It all goes into his pocket. Don't worry, I'll see you get your money back." He clapped Jeff on the shoulder. "Thanks, Jeff. I appreciate your coming to my rescue. I was in somewhat of a pickle."

Jeff looked faintly embarrassed. "We're friends, aren't we? It was the least I could do."

"I hope we're friends, yes." As they started toward the hotel where Marcy was staying, Clint said, "I should think that working for Sload Lutcher, you'd be wise to a thief like that sheriff. I understand that Lutcher is cut from the same cloth?"

"I thought I told you." Jeff was looking off. "I'm no longer employed by Lutcher."

"Oh? No, you hadn't told me." Clint arched an eyebrow at him. "I was curious, I'll admit. We've come across each other . . . What? About four times these past few weeks? I've been wondering about that, but I figured that if you wanted me to know, you'd tell me. I did know that you're a pinhooker, but I thought you were buying for Lutcher. On your own, are you?"

"Yes, and I'm doing fine. With the tobacco I've already managed to buy and store away, I could make a killing, if I'm lucky. I could be a rich man, Clint."

There was something that rang false about Jeff's manner, but Clint did not have the time, nor the inclination, to ponder it. He had other things on his mind.

He clapped the other man on the shoulder again, and said absently, "Good, Jeff, I'm glad to hear it. Nothing gladdens my heart more than a man with ambitions, who realizes those ambitions."

Marcy's hotel was in sight now, in the next block, and Clint wanted to hurry. But he curbed his impatience, slowing his gait to accommodate Jeff's limp.

He realized that Jeff had been speaking. "I'm sorry, Jeff, my mind was on other things, and I didn't catch what you just said."

"I said that I didn't have any ambitions, not until recently anyway." Jeff still did not look at him. "I certainly didn't when I came home from the war. All I wanted to do was crawl into a bottle and let the world go by. That's why Charlotte got so angry with me, and I can't say that I blame her all that much."

"Speaking of your sister . . ." Clint chuckled. "She was at the jail to see me."

Jeff stopped. "When?"

"Between the time you came to see me earlier and when you returned a bit ago."

"What did she want? Did she come to get you out of jail?"

"Oh, no, not your dear sister." Clint laughed harshly. "She came to chastise me, what else?"

Jeff sighed. "I haven't seen her lately, of course, but from what I hear, she's changed a great deal. That's what comes of a woman being in a man's business."

Clint looked at him intently. "Perhaps you should try to reconcile with her, Jeff. Now that you're no longer working for Lutcher and you're making it on your own, she might look upon you more favorably."

Jeff turned his face away and limped on toward the

hotel. In a low voice he said, "You could be right, Clint, but I doubt it. She's washed her hands of me, and I can't say that I blame her for that, either. Anyway, I'm not ready yet to risk it. Maybe after some more time has passed."

They were at the hotel now. Jeff said, "I told your friend Marcy that you'd be getting out, Clint. She's expecting us."

Marcy was sitting on a divan in the hotel lobby, watching the door. The moment she saw Clint she jumped up with a glad smile. Clint noticed that another woman was sitting with her.

Marcy rushed to meet him. Taking his hand, she kissed him. "Am I glad to see you, Clint! I was afraid you might be in there forever!"

"The jail has never been built that could hold Clint Devlin, my dear." He winked, then gave her a brief hug, looking past her shoulder at the woman on the divan—about Marcy's own age, with long raven hair, snapping black eyes, very pale complexion, and a full figure.

As she stepped back, Marcy noted the direction of his glance. "Clint, I want you to meet my new friend. Lucinda Parks, meet Clint Devlin, my employer. And this is Jeff King, his friend."

Lucinda got to her feet, smiling, and curtsied. She murmured, "How do you do, Mr. Devlin? Marcy has told me a great deal about you."

"I'm sure," Clint said dryly. "Hello, Lucinda."

Jeff, his manner at its most charming, stepped forward to take Lucinda's hand, and bowed over it. "I am pleased to meet you, Lucinda. May I say that I find you most charming?"

Lucinda colored, looking directly at him for the first time.

Marcy babbled on, "Poor Lucinda was deserted by her husband two days ago, Clint. He just up and rode off without her, leaving her without any money, and with a hotel bill."

Clint drawled almost inaudibly, "That sounds like a familiar story."

"What I was thinking, Clint . . . Lucinda says she can sing, and dance as well. Would it be possible for you to employ her, take her along with us?"

It was on the tip of his tongue to refuse, but a thought popped into his mind, staying him. What a marvelous way to thumb his nose at Charlotte! After her tirade at the jail, she would get the message loud and clear if he continued his performances with not one but *two* women. And Marcy was right—two female performers would add to the attraction. The additional expense would not be too great, and it would only be for the rest of the year. He had no intention of continuing it beyond that; it would no longer be necessary. By that time Clint was confident that he could dream up a completely new method of promoting King Cigarettes.

"I think you have an idea there, my dear. Mrs. Parks, are you agreeable?"

"Oh, yes!" Lucinda bobbed her head. "Marcy has already discussed it with me. It would be a godsend for me, Mr. Devlin."

"It's settled then, you go along with us."

"Oh, Clint!" Marcy threw her arms around his neck. "You are a nice man. I take back everything bad I ever said about you." She disengaged herself, stepping back. "Now, I'm starved, we're both starved, Lucinda and me. I think this all calls for a celebration, perhaps some champagne and a nice supper."

"That sounds great, Marcy, but I'm afraid my purse is rather flat, until I can send a telegram back to Durham for some expense funds."

"Don't worry about it, Clint, I'll stand us all champagne and supper," Jeff said expansively. "It'll be my treat."

Clint studied Jeff thoughtfully, belatedly assessing the changes in the man since the Durham days. On the surface Jeff certainly had a more respectable look. He was well-dressed and carefully groomed, his eyes were clear and firm, and even the lines of dissipation had disappeared. In Durham, he always had a seedy, faintly furtive manner. Yet it was more now than a surface appearance—he carried a look of inner confidence. He was indeed a new person; apparently all he had needed was to be his own man.

True, there was still that underlying hint of something false about him, as if he was still not *quite* sure about himself in this new guise. Clint finally decided that Jeff just needed more time to adjust to his new role in life.

Clint said, "I don't see how we can turn down an offer like that, do you, Marcy?"

It was indeed a grand evening—champagne and a fine supper. Jeff more talkative than Clint had ever seen him, and he pressed ardent suit to Lucinda, who responded wholeheartedly. Clint enjoyed himself, but all evening Charlotte, and the bitter scene at the jail, was on his mind.

He did not regret joining the partnership, since it was the best chance he would probably ever have to realize his dream, yet it was difficult operating with the thought of Charlotte's disapproval always in the back of his mind.

Marcy interrupted his thoughts with a touch on the back of his hand. "Sweetheart, why so broody? You're way, way off somewhere."

He smiled palely. "Nothing for you to be concerned about, my dear. It's not every day a man gets arrested. It brings on dark thoughts." He looked around the table. The second champagne bottle was empty, the food was eaten, and Jeff and Lucinda were absorbed in each other. "Shall we repair to the hotel, friends? I'm weary. I never could sleep in jail."

Back in the hotel, Clint was amused at the charade played out by Jeff and Lucinda, both making an elaborate show of going to their respective rooms. In Marcy's room, Clint said, "Want to wager against Jeff slipping into your new friend's room before the night's far along?"

Marcy shrugged. "I see nothing wrong in that. Lucinda

needs a man, and Jeff strikes me as a good choice. You don't know what it does to a woman's self-esteem to be deserted by her man."

Clint turned away and began preparing for bed. For just a moment he wished that he had his own room; he had little desire for a romp with Marcy. Yet he knew it would cause bad feelings if he got another room for tonight.

He grinned ruefully to himself. Since when did Clint Devlin spurn a desirable woman in his bed?

Damn you, Lotte, he thought, it's all your fault.

In bed Marcy was ardent and demanding. Clint tried to put all thought of Charlotte out of his mind, and give his full attention to the willing woman in his arms.

But even as he made love to her, even in their shared ecstasy, a corner of his mind was otherwise engaged.

Finally, as he lay on his back, Marcy asleep and snuggled up against his side, he let his mind worry at the problem.

If he and Charlotte continued at loggerheads every time they met, there was the ever-present danger of a violent clash of wills. As strong-minded as they both were, any such clash, Clint well realized, could sunder their partnership. And that he did not want; certainly not at this time, when they were on the verge of a breathtaking prosperity. Even given the fact that he was an optimist by nature, Clint was positive in his own mind that such was the case. By this time next year King Tobacco would be a force to be reckoned with, a flourishing concern. In fact, he would not be at all surprised if they grew to be the top tobacco company in the United States.

For that reason alone, he had to do what he could to avoid any confrontations with Charlotte, any situation where the friction between them could erupt into an explosion.

He determined to stay away from Durham as much as possible in the coming year.

As for any further romantic involvement with Charlotte, that was a closed issue. He had to resign himself to that fact.

Even with everything sorted out in his mind, or so he

told himself, Clint felt a welling of sorrow, a feeling of indefinable loss, as he finally drifted off to sleep.

Earlier that same day, in the buggy heading north toward Durham, Charlotte's thoughts ran pretty much along the same lines.

She knew that she had behaved badly in the jail, but the damned man was so aggravating! He bulled his way ahead, damn the consequences; and what was even more galling, he never showed the slightest remorse.

Yet she had to admit to a grudging admiration. Even at his most outrageous, Clint Devlin had such a dashing flair that it was difficult to completely disapprove of him. Not that she would ever admit such a thing to him. Good heavens, no! A charming reprobate, that was the perfect phrase for him.

But his charm would never work on her again, she was grimly determined of that.

Yet, however reprehensible, his selling methods worked, and worked very well indeed. The first year of King Tobacco was going to be a success. Clint had written such a huge backlog of orders that it would take them until next summer, at full production, to fill all the orders. And without those orders, where would they be? They might have managed to show a small profit, but nothing on such a scale as this.

If she wanted King Tobacco to succeed, Charlotte had no choice but to let Clint have his way. Much as she might disapprove, she made up her mind not to interfere again. When the next selling season came around, perhaps such shameless promotional tactics would not be necessary. Then, she would meet with Ben and discuss the possibility of initiating some sort of rein on Clint.

It never once entered her mind that she would not receive Ben's agreement and full cooperation.

Meanwhile, she concluded, she would have to avoid any more scenes such as the one today. She fully recognized that, given their opposite natures, another such confrontation could result in an irrevocable breach, and that must be avoided.

Unbidden, the thought of that shameful picture nudged into her mind; it still resided in her purse. And with that thought came another, equally unwelcome. If Clint was out of jail, he would soon be in bed with that Marcy person; and the images this conjured up in Charlotte's mind were almost as vivid as the graphic picture.

She reached for her purse on the seat beside her, opened it, and groped for the picture. As her fingers closed around it, she grew still. Without volition she closed her purse, letting the picture remain where it was.

With an angry exclamation, she clamped both hands around the reins and flicked them violently, urging the plodding horse into a faster gait.

# Chapter Sixteen

NOW, it was celebration time, a time for rejoicing.

Exactly one year had passed since Rachel Lefkowitz had rolled the first tailor-made cigarette, and King Tobacco was a roaring success.

In point of fact, King Tobacco was something of a legend in the industry. In one short year it had outstripped most companies, including Lutcher Tobacco, and had come to rival Bull Durham and W. Duke & Sons.

And since this was true of King Tobacco, Clint Devlin had become even more of a legend. His name was on every tongue in the industry. The backcountry storekeepers, as well as the city buyers, had taken him to their hearts. He had dazzled them, wheedled and conned them, and charmed them; and if a buyer did not have one of Clint's famous Parisian nudes in his pocket watch, he was scorned by his fellows.

Everyone loved his flamboyant tactics; he entertained them, as well as provided them with a product that sold, due to his efforts, almost as fast as they could stock them. His arrival was an event to be endlessly discussed after his departure. He brought color and excitement into lives too often drab.

Clint Devlin, in the minds of many, was held almost solely responsible for the unprecedented success of King Tobacco.

This did not bother Ben Ascher unduly; however, Charlotte resented it. It was not that she begrudged Clint his proper credit, for she knew that success could not have happened without him.

"But darn it," she stormed to Ben the week before King Tobacco's anniversary date rolled around. "We deserve *some* of the credit!"

Ben was smiling. "We played our part, Charlotte, I agree. But it doesn't bother me that Clint is receiving the lion's share. He loves it, or hadn't you noticed?"

"Oh, I've noticed. How could I not notice? He struts around like a peacock." She added, tartly, "And dresses like one, as well."

"I think you're being a little harsh on him. He likes to be in the limelight, I'll admit. But then he was honest enough to admit that back in the beginning. Personally, I'm just as happy that all the attention is on him."

"You may be happy, but I'm not. And it's not just ego, either. If it was someone else, another man, I'd feel the same way. It's because I'm a woman, Ben, don't you see? Men refuse to give women any credit for business sense. They all think I shouldn't be dirtying my pretty hands with such matters. I'm sure that they think all I've contributed to our success is to look pretty, bat my eyelashes becomingly, and be decorative for the men!"

Ben sobered, taking on a look of concern. "I understand how you must feel, Charlotte, but it would seem that the business world is not yet ready to accept women on an equal footing with men. I do want you to know that I fully realize how very much you're responsible for our success, as do most of our employees. I'm sure Clint knows, too."

"Hah! Even if he does, he'll never admit it. Speaking of Clint, in his telegram he said he wanted the three of us to have a meeting while he's here for the anniversary celebration."

"I've noticed that you seem to avoid him of late."

"The man irritates me, so I stay out of his way."

Ben was smiling softly at her, and Charlotte knew what was in his mind. They had been intimate a number of times over the past year. It had been pleasant, more than pleasant, but Charlotte was searching for a way to end it, again. It was not so much for her own sake as Rachel's. She had noticed that Rachel was becoming increasingly withdrawn at the signs of their intimacy—it was impossible to keep it a complete secret. It had gotten to the point where Rachel seemed downright hostile in Charlotte's presence.

To get the conversation back on safe ground, she hastened on, "I don't know what Clint wants to discuss, but I have a feeling that it may be about his promotional campaign for the coming year. And I think it's time we laid down a few restrictions, Ben, tone down some of the schemes he's been using."

Ben was already shaking his head. "I don't think we should do that, Charlotte."

She was taken aback. "Surely you don't approve of some of the things he's doing?"

"Whether I approve or not has little to do with it. It's working, we both well know that. My father once told me, Don't tinker with something that works."

"Don't quote axioms at me!" she almost snarled. "That's what Clint always does to excuse everything. It drives me crazy! I agree, reluctantly, that his schemes have worked. I was wrong about that. But the thing is, they're no longer needed. Aside from the morality of it, it's not dignified. We can dispense with all that now."

"Can we? To do so would be a risk, and I, for one, am not prepared to take that risk. Let Clint alone, let him do what he does best. We have granted him pretty much a free rein, and I think we should continue to do so. You know, we have done some things here at the plant that did not meet with his wholehearted approval, yet he accepted our decisions with good grace. We should grant him the same privilege, Charlotte."

"Do you know some of the things he's been doing? Do you know about the..." She broke off, intending to mention the picture, and then remembered that one still reposed in her purse—for whatever reason she was not sure.

"The picture of the nude woman?" Ben was smiling.

"Oh, yes, I know about that, I've known for some time. And I also know how effective it's been. And it's harmless. I've never held with all those prudish notions that a woman, any woman, should never be seen unclothed except by her husband, and a great many people don't even approve of that."

"I'm not a prude, Ben, you know that," she said sharply. "I just happen to think that such promotion schemes are not dignified."

Ben laughed. "Clint would tell you that dignity has nothing to do with it."

"I'm sure he would. But with or without your approval, Ben, I'm going to face him about it when we have our business meeting."

Originally, Charlotte wanted to give the anniversary celebration party on Monday, to turn a working day into a holiday. The salaried workers would have welcomed such an arrangement happily, but she mentioned it first to Jacob, and he was adamantly opposed.

"The rollers work on piecework basis, and they would lose a whole day's pay."

"But that's no problem, Jacob," Charlotte said. "We're willing to pay them what they would earn on an average working day. Naturally I wouldn't expect them to celebrate that day without pay, while the people on salary would be receiving full pay."

Jacob was shaking his head, but he was also smiling broadly. "You are a nice person, boss lady, to offer to do that, eh? But the rollers are a proud people. They would look upon it as charity."

Charlotte was exasperated. "*You* say that, Jacob, but how do you know how they feel unless you talk to them about it?"

He drew himself up. "*I* speak for my people."

And so, the anniversary party took place on a Sunday. It was an affair that Durhamites would talk about for some time to come. Charlotte had planned on having the party exclusively for King employees, but Clint, who arrived in Durham earlier in the week, was appalled.

"Lotte, you must be daft! This is the first real opportunity to let Durham, and the world, know what we've accomplished here."

They were not alone, Ben was with them, and so their conversation was confined to the party.

Charlotte said, "But if we do that, the employees may feel slighted. I intended this to be just for them."

"What is more important, the employees or King Tobacco? Don't be naive, Lotte, for that's what it comes down to. Hell, we couldn't ask for a better opportunity to put the company on the map."

"He's right, Lotte," Ben said. "And I don't think you have to worry about the employees feeling slighted. I think they will be flattered, since they are very much responsible for our success."

Charlotte finally gave in, admitting to herself that their logic was unarguable. And it turned out that the employees *were* pleased, being the center of all the attention, in a way.

The hand rollers' tables were converted into buffet tables, and they groaned under every kind of food imaginable. Other tables had been set up, holding enormous bowls of liquor-laced punch, and a number of barrels of beer were resting on sawhorses.

All the dignitaries of Durham had been invited and were present, including Washington Duke and owners of other tobacco companies, both from Durham and nearby towns. Charlotte halfway expected to see Lutcher's sneering face among them, but apparently even he did not have that much gall. Reporters from various newspapers, even from cities as far away as New York, were also present.

Altogether over three hundred people were in attendance, and the party was a great success; that was evident to Charlotte early on. A temporary platform had been erected at one end of the big room, and there was a succession of speeches from Durham dignitaries, and the partners were called upon to say a few words.

Charlotte confined herself to a simple expression of gratitude to everyone for attending, and Ben did the same; but Clint talked for fifteen minutes, extolling the rapid success of King Tobacco, and promising even greater things to come. He was an eloquent speaker, witty, charming, and clearly popular with all present.

Clint was in his glory, that much was clear. Attired in a suit dove-gray in color, a flowing cravat, and with an expensive cigar going, he circulated through the throng after his speech, receiving congratulations, and was the recipient of much back-slapping.

A person would think he had done it all on his own, Charlotte thought angrily. Then her good sense prevailed, and she took a moment to assess her motives. She was clearly envious of his popularity; her ill-feeling sprang from "sour grapes." Oh, there were other reasons behind her anger at him, but it was plain to her that the main reason was that she was envious.

As the afternoon waned, she noticed that Clint was as popular with the workers as he was with the guests. And that was hard for her to fathom as well. He was acquainted with only a handful; to most of them he was nothing more than a name. She did observe that Ben's surmise was correct—the employees all enjoyed themselves, and seemed to accept the fulsome praise for King Tobacco coming from the speaker's platform as their just and rightful due.

Considering all the alcohol flowing, it was a remarkably well-behaved crowd. Charlotte had been fearful of some friction between the townspeople and the Jewish workers, but none developed.

As the celebration began to wind down and many of the people had left, she found herself alone with Clint for a few minutes. She commented, "I'm surprised by one thing, Clint. Pleased as well, of course."

"And what is that, Lotte?" he said, amused. "Surprised that everyone is enjoying himself, including you?"

"No, not that. What I feared was some sort of trouble

from the townspeople with Jacob's people. I understand that Ben told you about the incident at Jacob's house last fall?"

"He told me, and I took action immediately."

"What action?"

"I had private meetings with influential people, from the mayor on down. I told them that they'd better see to it that people stayed in line. I told them if Jacob, or any of his people, were harassed any more, King Tobacco would fold up its tents and move to a town where people were not so bigoted."

"You told them that?" Her eyes widened. "You took a lot on yourself, Mr. Devlin, appointing yourself spokesman for King Tobacco."

"Ben appointed me, I didn't. He told me to do something, and I did. Besides, it worked, didn't it? Whether I was speaking for you or not."

She had been looking off, and as his meaning penetrated, she glanced at him in distress. "I didn't mean that I don't approve of what you told them. I do, wholeheartedly..." Her voice died as she saw the mischievous twinkle in his eyes, and realized that he was goading her. She choked back a heated retort, and looked away again.

Clint lit a fresh cigar, and said, "I did something today, too, warning the powers-that-be that if there were any incidents here today, we would certainly consider relocating the plant. And that's why everything went off so well. Do you realize that King Tobacco is now on a par with Duke and Bull Durham? If we pulled out of Durham now, it would hurt the town. When you have the power, Lotte, don't hesitate to use it."

"Another Clint Devlin maxim?"

He grinned engagingly. "If you wish to interpret it that way."

"I suppose what I was really afraid of was that Sload Lutcher would send some of his thugs in here to stir up trouble."

"I took care of that, as well. I passed the word, through the mayor, that if there were any outside troublemakers here today, we would assume they were in Lutcher's pay and act accordingly."

"Well, Mr. Devlin, it seems you covered all possibilities."

He inclined his head modestly. "I try, Miss King, I try my humble best." He sobered. "Has there been any trouble from Lutcher of late?"

"Nothing that amounted to very much. Oh, he tried again this year to coerce the farmers into selling him their tobacco crop instead of to me, but there wasn't much he could do about them selling at an open auction. I hear that he had trouble buying enough tobacco for his needs this year," she said in grim satisfaction. "He refused to bid top dollar at the auction."

"Perhaps he's given up harassing you."

"I wish I could believe that, but something tells me that he will always carry a grudge against me."

"Well, at least your brother is no longer working for him. That should make you happy."

Charlotte said coldly, "You told me that already, but I'm not sure that I believe it."

"Believe it, it's true. Jeff is on his own, a pinhooker, and doing very well at it. You haven't even spoken to him?"

"No, and I have no intention of looking him up. If he wants to apologize, he can come to me."

"Now that's a childish attitude for a grown woman." He shook his head in reproof. "You should consider yourself fortunate that you have a brother. Take me, I've never had any family at all."

"I've never noticed you suffering for lack of companionship," she retorted. "Where is your friend Marcy? And the other one, whatever her name is. I understand you have two now."

His smile turned taunting. "Her name is Lucinda. Marcy and Lucinda, they make quite a pair."

She felt a need to wound. "I think that's disgusting!"

"Disgusting, is it?" His voice was suddenly harsh. "Why is it, Lotte, that we scratch at each other, when we try to talk?"

"Perhaps that's a question you should ask yourself."

He shrugged, his anger gone as suddenly as it came. "Why should I, my dear? It's not all that important to me."

He turned on his heel, striding off. She stared after him in dismay. He was partly right, she was honest enough with herself to admit that. Why did she feel such a compulsion to claw at him this way? It was a question she had asked herself innumerable times, and she had yet to find a satisfactory answer.

There was one thing she did know—this certainly was not a good omen for their meeting in the morning.

Charlotte, Ben, and Clint met together shortly before noon in Charlotte's office.

The harsh words she had exchanged yesterday with Clint still rankled in Charlotte's mind, and she went on the attack immediately.

"If you've called this meeting to get our approval for a repeat of last year's advertising tactics, you're not going to get it!"

"Now Charlotte," Ben cautioned, "don't be so hasty. I never said I'd side with you on this issue."

Clint was smiling at her. "You're one stubborn lady, you know that, Lotte? You never give up, do you? Well, I have news for you, my dear. That's not the reason I wanted this meeting."

"It's not?" she said in astonishment.

"Nope," he drawled. "As for advertising and promotion this year, I have different plans. I have already told Marcy and Lucinda that I wouldn't be needing them any longer."

Prepared to do battle on the issue, Charlotte was thrown into confusion. "Then why didn't you tell me that yesterday?"

"I thought it would do you good to fret a little longer." He paused to light a cigar, while Charlotte stood tight-lipped, holding onto her temper with an effort.

The cigar going to his satisfaction, Clint said, "The advertising schemes I have been using are no longer needed. The things I did, that you thought so awful, were to get King Cigarettes noticed, to make people familiar with them." He laughed. "You might compare it to a gunshot fired off in a crowded room, where everybody is talking at once. So, everybody shuts up and gives full attention to the shooter."

"That's an apt metaphor," Charlotte muttered. "I'm surprised to hear you admit as much."

Clint ignored her comment. "Oh, I'm still going to put up posters, signs on barns, and the like. But no more street shows, no pictures of naked ladies." He grinned at Charlotte. "That should please you, Lotte."

She was silent, not sure whether to believe him or not.

Ben said, "I confess to being a little confused, Clint. Are you dropping all promotion for our cigarettes, except for the signs and posters?"

"Not at all, Benbo. I plan to spend money advertising in newspapers, magazines, whatever. That's the future of advertising, but most businessmen don't seem to grasp that fact yet. What I intend to spend the most on are salesmen."

"Salesmen?" Ben looked puzzled. "But you use salesmen now."

"Sure, I have four men. *Four!* Last year I covered a hell of a lot of territory all on my lonesome. This coming year, I'm employing at least thirty salesmen. I might even consider hiring women, if I can find any suitable. I've already interviewed several men."

Charlotte gasped. "Thirty salesmen! That will cost a fortune."

"There you're wrong, Lotte. Not a single one will be on salary. They will work strictly on commission. I'm using an incentive program. They will receive a certain percentage on each order they write. The more orders they write, the higher their percentage. If they don't sell cigarettes, they don't cost us a penny. They won't even be on an expense account, not until they prove they can sell. What better incentive than that to write orders?"

Charlotte said dubiously, "But can you employ salesmen

on that kind of an arrangement? It seems a little heartless to me."

"Heartless? King Tobacco is not a charitable institution. And to answer your question, I've had over a hundred applicants since I put the word out. Unemployment is still quite high in the South, you both should know that. Unfortunately, most of the unemployed are useless to us."

Ben was smiling in admiration. "You do move fast, Clint, at anything you do. I have to hand you that."

"I do my best, Benbo," Clint said with false modesty, aiming a mocking glance at Charlotte.

"Is that what you called this meeting for?" she said tartly. "It seems a waste of time, since you've gone ahead on your own, without waiting for our approval. As usual, I might add."

"No, that's not the reason. I have something else to bring up, to both of you." He drew on his cigar, and exhaled a thin screen of smoke. "I spent the early part of this morning going through the books and records. And it's just as I suspected."

Charlotte said quickly, "There's nothing wrong with the books!"

"Of course not. That's not what I meant." He took a deep breath. "But we have a huge backlog of unfilled orders, and the way things are going, we'll never catch up."

"You're exaggerating, Clint," Ben said. "I won't deny there is a backlog, but don't forget that we've had a problem getting tobacco. Last year's crop was the first decent one since the war, and every tobacco company in the country has been scrambling for tobacco. Charlotte spent a great deal of time scouring the countryside for a basket here and a basket there, whatever she could find. But this has been a good crop year, production has more than doubled over last year, and Charlotte and Bradley Hollister bought enough last week at the auction house to carry us through for months, and she'll be purchasing more as we need it."

"And I doubt that this coming year's orders will equal last year's," Charlotte remarked. "Don't forget there was a dearth of the finished product for the storekeepers as well. Now, most of them have a supply on hand."

Clint was shaking his head. "Not the way I figure it. I'm confident that I can double last year's sales."

"Where's all that modesty you showed a moment ago?" Charlotte said in a dry voice. "But granted you do double sales, what's your point?"

"My point is very simple. We have to increase production."

Ben shrugged, spreading his hands. "So, we just hire more rollers. I'm sure Jacob will have no trouble recruiting all we need."

"That's a stopgap measure," Clint said, "and employing more people to make cigarettes is too expensive in the long run. We have to plan for the future *now,* and not wait around."

Ben frowned at him. "I'm afraid I don't quite follow, Clint. What are you getting at?"

Charlotte, harking back to an earlier conversation, knew what he was getting at. She could only hope that Ben would not go along with Clint's idea.

"I'm talking about cigarette machines. They make tailor-mades one hell of a lot faster, and far cheaper. We should invest in one now."

Ben said thoughtfully, "I've heard that several different models have been invented. I've never seen one in operation, but I've been told by people who have that they're giving a great deal of trouble, always breaking down and at great expense. They're too new, Clint, they haven't been fully tested yet."

"They work, I've seen them work," Clint said stubbornly. "Sure, they're far from perfected, but the inventors will solve all the problems in time. The thing is, I've been secretly meeting with the patent holder on one." He began to pace in his excitement. "Like other patent holders, he's not selling the machines outright, but leasing them on a royalty basis, so much for each cigarette made.

The going royalty is pretty steep, but this fellow is so anxious to get his machine installed and working, sort of a showcase, in a manner of speaking, that he is willing to give us a huge discount, not only for a year, but forever, if we'll install his machine now."

Pacing, Clint smacked his fist into his palm. "Hell, we'd be crazy to pass up such an opportunity! When those machines become popular, as they're bound to, the patent holders will gouge the cigarette manufacturers outrageously."

Charlotte had to restrain a smile. Clint was the consummate salesman, almost an irresistible force. When he got worked up like this, it was very difficult not to be swept along on his tide of enthusiasm.

Ben, however, was not easily swayed. "On the other hand, if this fellow's machine is a failure, if it never becomes fully operational, we'd be stuck with it forever." He added caustically, "In a manner of speaking."

Clint stopped pacing, and fixed an angry glare on him. "I expected better from you, Benbo. With that kind of an attitude, we'd still be sailing the seas with only the wind for power, and instead of riding a train to New York, we'd have to creep along in a covered wagon!"

Ben said, "Could be we'd be better off, did you ever think of that?"

Clint threw up his hands in disgust. "Now you're against progress!"

"No, not against progress as such," Ben said doggedly. "But I am against rushing headlong into something of this nature."

Charlotte said, "It seems to me you're both forgetting the hand rollers in this discussion."

"I haven't forgotten them for a minute." Ben gave her a grateful look. "But I'm glad *you* brought them up, Charlotte."

"What about the rollers?" Clint demanded.

"We've brought them all the way down here from New York, relocated them in a foreign environment, they're here hardly a year, and you're talking of doing away with them altogether."

"That isn't the issue here, Lotte."

"Oh, but it is. To my way of thinking, it's a very important issue."

Clint sighed. "Hell and damnation, when will the pair of you ever learn that a business is not a charitable institution?"

"I don't consider King Tobacco a charitable institution at all," Charlotte said. "But I think the people working for us deserve some consideration. Without them, we wouldn't be in business."

"All right, all right! Let's examine the situation of the rollers. First off, I'm not talking about replacing them today, tomorrow, or perhaps even next year. Ben is right about one thing, the machines aren't perfected yet. But the only way they *can* ever be perfected is to have them in operation for a time. By that time we'll have a big jump on the competition. As for the rollers, they'll have plenty of time to find jobs elsewhere."

Charlotte was staring at him in disbelief. "And you accuse me of being naive! What do you suppose Jacob will think if we were to install one of your machines? What do you think he would do, he and the others?"

"For God's sake, what could he do? I respect Jacob, I like him, but he doesn't *own* the factory. We can't be ruled by what he thinks, or what he might do."

"You're cruel and selfish, Clint Devlin. Of all things, I would never have thought this of you. Do you ever think of anything but yourself, of the main chance?"

He recoiled slightly, looking at her with widening eyes. "If I don't think of myself, who will?" Then he shook his head as if to clear it. "I'm not thinking only of myself, I'm thinking of you two as well. I should think you'd be able to realize that."

Charlotte said grimly, "I think this conversation is finished. This is the last I want to hear about cigarette machines!"

Clint looked first at her, then at Ben. "I come up with a scheme that won't cost the company a cent, but will almost certainly put us in a position to be way ahead of the competition, and what happens?" His eyes were cold, and his voice burned with bitterness. "Is it because it's something I've come up with? You two do things behind my back, but even if I don't approve, I go along anyway."

Ben tried a conciliatory tone. "It's not that, Clint. But you're premature. Wait a year, maybe two. Then it'll be time to consider such a radical move."

"No! I'll be goddamned if I'll wait!" In a violent gesture he threw his cigar across the room. Then he looked at them with his lips set in a thin line. "I take it then, Miss King, that you're voting against it?"

"I most certainly am."

"Ben?"

Ben heaved a sigh. "I'm afraid I must, Clint, I'm sorry."

"Then you leave me no choice."

Charlotte said, "What's that supposed to mean?"

"I can't stay with the company any longer, if I'm to be thwarted at every turn."

Ben frowned. "Now don't be hasty, Clint."

"And if you're putting on one of your famous acts, in the hope we'll change our minds, it's all wasted effort," Charlotte said.

"Oh, it's not an act," Clint said stonily. "I assure you it's not an act. I'm putting my partnership in King Tobacco up for sale this very day."

# Chapter Seventeen

JEFF King felt his tension coil tighter and tighter, as his buggy entered the outskirts of Durham. It had been months since he had been in Durham, and those months had been the happiest he had experienced since he had gone marching off to war. During this time on his own, Jeff had become almost a whole man again. Even his limp did not seem to bother him so much.

He had also noticed changes in his behavior. He was drinking less, and had stopped gambling entirely. The only indulgence he had not given up was Lucinda Parks. He smiled, momentarily forgetting where he was bound, as he recalled these past few months with Lucinda. Traveling along with Clint and the two women, Jeff had come to know Lucinda very well indeed. She was a fine, loving woman, and he fully intended to make her his wife the moment she could legally free herself from the rapscallion who had deserted her.

Lucinda had wanted to accompany him to Durham, but Jeff had regretfully left her behind, fearful of what Durhamites would think of her, given his unsavory reputation with women.

His thoughts returned to the benefits he had derived from these months spent working as a pinhooker. The thing that pleased him most was his acceptance as an equal by those in the tobacco business. Even more pleasant had been the slow-dawning knowledge that he *was* an equal—he could hold his own with the best pinhookers.

If he had the finances, Jeff was confident that he could make it on his own. During the past months, he forgot for days on end that he was working for Sload Lutcher, that it was Lutcher's money which was financing him.

That, he supposed, was the reason he was depressed by having to return to Durham. The telegram he had received from Lutcher summoning him here had been a painful reminder that he was still Lutcher's man. He refused to speculate as to the reason for the summons; he had long since given up attempting to fathom the workings of Lutcher's devious mind.

It was late afternoon when he drove the buggy around to the rear of the Lutcher plant, where there was a back door that opened to the stairs leading directly up to Lutcher's office, making the possibility of his being seen unlikely.

He found Lutcher in his office. There were times when Jeff wondered if the man ever spent any time anywhere else. The one time he had seen Lutcher away from his office was at the mayor's Christmas Eve ball two years ago.

Lutcher smiled genially at him, and motioned to a chair. Jeff was wary—he had long since learned that Lutcher was at his most dangerous when he put on that genial manner.

Lutcher leaned back, making a steeple of his fingers. "Well, King, I haven't seen you in some months. I must say you're looking fit." Lutcher's eyes turned cold as he surveyed Jeff's fine clothing. "And better dressed."

"I do have to look prosperous," Jeff said defensively. "I can't very well compete with other pinhookers looking like a tramp."

"True, true. And you *have* been doing well. The tobacco you bought has come in handy here. Your sister," Lutcher's lips pursed as though he had bitten into something sour, "has all the growers in her pocket, it seems. She managed to buy most of the tobacco coming into Durham this season." He leaned forward. "But I was referring to more than clothes, King. You look in better health, and the hangdog look is gone."

"Well, I guess you might say I've found myself." Jeff laughed uncertainly, realizing how pompous the remark sounded. And why was it that his confidence drained out of him like water from a leaky bucket when he was in this man's forbidding presence?

"Just so you don't get too cocky, King," Lutcher said unpleasantly. "Don't forget for a minute that without my money behind you, you would still look like a tramp."

"I admit that your financial backing is a great help," Jeff said, a defiant note in his voice. "But I've learned that I can compete on even terms with the others."

"Learned that, have you?" Lutcher growled. "I'm glad to hear it, because I'm going to give you the chance to move up in the world, and this new confidence you seem to have in yourself will be useful."

Instantly wary, Jeff said, "Move up? What do you mean? I'm quite content with what I'm doing, Mr. Lutcher."

Lutcher seemingly struck off on a tangent. "Being out in the country like you've been, I don't suppose you've heard the most recent news?"

More alarmed than ever by Lutcher's smug manner, Jeff said cautiously, "What news is that?"

"Your good friend, Clint Devlin, has come to the parting of the ways with your sister and the Jew."

Jeff blinked in astonishment. "What happened?"

"I don't have all the details." Lutcher shrugged. "The reason is not important, but last week, Devlin announced that his third partnership in King Tobacco is up for sale."

Jeff whistled softly. "I'll be damned! I knew that Clint was unhappy about some things, but this I didn't expect. Has he sold his partnership yet?"

"Not yet. It seems he's not getting many takers, for some reason," Lutcher smiled coldly. "And that's where you come in, King. That's why I sent the telegram ordering you back to Durham."

"I fail to see how I figure in."

"You are going to buy Devlin's third interest in King Tobacco. You will use my money, naturally, since you don't have any of your own, but nobody will be told of my interest, except my lawyer. I'll be your silent partner, so to speak."

For just a moment Jeff was elated. To be a third owner of King Tobacco, even if only *thought* to be a partner, was a dazzling prospect; it sent his spirits soaring. Then he crashed back down to earth, as he slowly grasped all that such an arrangement entailed.

He knew, in one intuitive leap, what was in Lutcher's scheming mind. He said grimly, "I'm to be your Trojan horse, is that it?"

Lutcher arched an eyebrow in surprise, then laughed aloud. "I sometimes forget that you're a member of the southern aristocracy, King, blessed with the classical education of your kind, all worthless as cow dung. Does it surprise you that I even know what you're talking about?" He leaned forward, his eyes flat and as expressionless as slate. "Yes, you've put your finger right on it, that's exactly what I have in mind for you."

Determined not to give in this time, Jeff shook his head, sitting up straight. "No, I won't do it. I won't do this to Charlotte. I know I'm a weak man, but this kind of treachery is asking too much."

"Oh? Too much to ask, is it? I'm not asking, King, I'm ordering." Lutcher's voice was soft but as lethal as a snake's warning hiss. "My, you have grown a little backbone out there all on your own, haven't you? It appears that I brought you back just in time. Now you listen to me, you drunken, wenching, worthless cripple, and listen closely. I've made you into what you are, whatever *that* is, and I can break you just like that." He snapped his fingers with a sound that made Jeff jump. "Everything you have belongs to me, including the fine clothes you have on. I can strip you down and send you out of here without even your drawers, if I've a mind to. I imagine you've become quite accustomed to the good life these past months. That is another reason I sent you out there, so you'd know what it was like. You think you can give all that up now?"

"If I have to, I can."

"I wonder." The man's smile was cruel. "All the fine

clothes, good food, and liquor. And the woman you have acquired for yourself. Oh, yes, I know about her. There's nothing about you that I don't know. Now hark back to what you were when I picked you out of the gutter. A sot, without money for the next drink, clothes a beggar wouldn't wear, and not even a decent place to sleep. You want to go back to that?"

Jeff was silent. He closed his eyes, but that did not keep out the images of the degrading existence that had been his before he entered Lutcher's employ. For the first time in a long while, he said a silent prayer, "Dear God, give me the strength to resist this man!"

Lutcher went on relentlessly, "Not only would you sink back to that level, but you would be disgraced in Durham, as well as in the tobacco business. You have no idea how much damage a few words from me can do to your reputation. For instance, I can tell people that you are a thief, that you stole from me, for money to drink, to wench, and to gamble. Given your reputation before you went to work for me, people will tend to believe the worst. You will never be able to hold your head up in Durham again."

Lutcher made the steeple with his fingers, turning genial. "On the other hand, what's so terrible about what I'm asking of you? I'm not demanding that you harm your sister physically. All I ask is that you become her partner, so that you can keep me informed as to their plans over there. And when a decision is to be made, a vote required of the partners, you will consult with me, and accept my advice on which way to vote. Now, is that so terrible? The very worst that can happen will be that she will be forced to get out of the tobacco business. And isn't that what you want?"

Jeff simply stared at him. He was wavering before the man's logic. After all, what *was* so terrible about it?

Still smiling, Lutcher continued, "Look at the good side, King. You will continue to live well, you will be thought of as a man of substance, instead of scorned. People will seek you out. They will ask your opinion. And if, in the end, my plan works, I shall take over King Tobacco, and I will retain you to run the company. Doesn't that appeal to you? Oh, yes, you may send for your woman, this Lucinda Parks. I have no objection to that." His voice hardened. "Now, those are your two choices. Which shall it be?"

Jeff took a deep breath. "Tell me what it is you want me to do, Mr. Lutcher."

Clint had about concluded that he was hoist with his own petard. What an ironic twist! Nobody wanted to buy his partnership in King Tobacco because all the potential buyers credited him with the phenomenal success of the company. As one man put it, "Why should I buy your third interest, Devlin? The way I understand it, you're the fellow largely responsible for their success. If you're gone, it may fall apart."

And so it went, with prospect after prospect. A number of tobacco company owners offered him a job, but Clint refused to even consider the offers. What guarantee did he have that history would not repeat itself? If he did not have the freedom he desired as a partner, he certainly could not expect it as a mere employee; and if he went to work for someone else, that would mean the end of his dream.

He had not been back to the factory since the parting of the ways ten days ago, and he had not seen nor spoken to Charlotte.

Ben Ascher did come to see him after the bitter scene in Charlotte's office. "Clint, I think you were too rash. Shouldn't you reconsider and come back? Charlotte's pride would never allow her to ask you, but I think that she would be happy if you came back and asked."

"How about *my* pride, Ben?" Clint said. "There is no way I could bring myself to do that." He shrugged. "Sure, Lotte's difficult, sometimes, but it's not only that. If I'm to do what I want, I have to have complete freedom, and acceptance of at least *some* of my ideas, my suggestions. As it is, I'm frustrated at every turn."

"You're exaggerating again, Clint. This is the first time we've really come down hard on you."

"Maybe the first, but not the last. And it may be the first time you've both come down hard on me, but it's not the first time for Charlotte. She's a strong woman, Benbo. I respect her for that, but I sure as hell have no intention of bowing down in apology every time she gets her dander up about something. Ben . . ." He looked Ben straight in the eye. "Say I humbled myself, went back, and soothed her ruffled feathers, would you then back me to the extent of agreeing to installing one cigarette machine on a trial basis?"

Ben was already shaking his head. "I'm sorry, Clint, I simply cannot support you on that at this time. And it has nothing to do with Charlotte. I think I'm more against the idea than she is."

"Then why the hell are we wasting each other's time this way?" Clint raised and lowered his shoulders. "Ben, what happened yesterday would have happened sooner or later, given our temperaments, Lotte and me. It was inevitable, I should have realized that long ago. So it's better it happened now. Now you two will have time to learn to work together with your new partner."

"Any idea who that might be?"

"Not the slightest. It's a little early yet."

"And nothing I can say will change your mind?"

"Nothing."

"Well . . ." Ben heaved a sigh. "It was nice while it lasted, Clint, and I want you to know that I realize how much you have contributed to our success." He held out his hand. "Thanks for that, and I wish you nothing but the best."

Clint shook the proffered hand. "Likewise, Benbo, likewise."

After ten days had passed, Clint decided he would have to go farther afield if he was to sell his partnership. He had exhausted every possibility in Durham and the surrounding towns, and there were no takers. So be it. He would try Atlanta, Charleston, Savannah; if need be, he would go as far as New York.

His bags were packed, ready to leave in the morning, when he had a surprise visitor. He had eaten a solitary supper, and was enjoying a last cigar before retiring, when the knock came at the door.

He opened it to find Jeff King on his doorstep. "Jeff, what a pleasant surprise! Come in, come in."

"Hello, Clint. I hope I'm not intruding?" Jeff edged inside tentatively.

"Nope, I'm all by my lonesome." Clint smiled broadly. "No woman here, if that's what you mean. What brings you to Durham? The last time we talked, you told me you would be coming back here only when necessary."

"It was necessary," Jeff muttered, his glance sliding away.

Clint shrugged away his puzzlement at Jeff's behavior, and said, "Well, I'm delighted to see you. Sit down, Jeff. A drink? I have some good Kentucky bourbon."

"No, thanks, Clint." Jeff shook his head and moved to the chair indicated.

Clint sat down across from him and picked up his cigar. "Maybe you've heard that I came to a parting of the ways with your sister?"

"Yes, I heard. That's the reason I'm here, Clint." Jeff cleared his throat. "This is a business call."

Clint gazed at him quizzically. Was Jeff about to offer him a job?

"Have you sold your interest in King Tobacco yet, Clint?"

"Nope. Nobody seems too interested. I'm all packed, as a matter of fact, ready to try elsewhere."

"That won't be necessary, Clint. I want to buy your third interest."

Clint reared back in his chair, swept by astonishment. "You? *You* want to buy my interest in King Tobacco?"

"I do." Jeff did not look at him. "I finally made that killing I told you I was hoping for. I've got the money now, and I want to invest in something more substantial than being a pinhooker."

"But how about Lotte, how about your sister?"

"Well, I figure that this way, I will at least be where I can keep an eye on her. Oh, I know she won't like the idea . . ."

"Now you can be damn sure of that!"

"But there's really nothing she can do about it." Jeff looked up in sudden alarm. "Is there, Clint? I mean, she has nothing to say about who you sell to, does she?"

"Nope." Clint shook his head. "That is one thing we agreed on at the start. Any time one of us wanted to sell out, he doesn't need permission from the other two." Suddenly, he began to laugh. His laughter grew until he was rocking back and forth. Finally he managed to get it under control, and swiped at his streaming eyes. "Oh, this is rich, goddamned rich! If I had wracked my brain until I was a hundred and three, I could never have dreamed up a better way to put a burr under her tail!"

Jeff had not joined in with Clint's mirth. Throughout it all, he had remained unsmiling. Now he said, "Tell me how much you want for your share, Clint."

"Just like that? No haggling, Jeff?" He eyed the man askance. "That's not the way to conduct business, telling *me* to set a price."

Jeff said steadily, "We're friends, Clint, and I want you to get what you think you deserve."

"There are no friends in business, Jeff. Another Clint Devlin axiom. But far be it from me to argue. I'll not be asking for the moon, anyway. My original investment didn't amount to a hill of beans, but the work and the thinking that I've put into King Tobacco should be worth a bit. The company had a hell of a year, I suppose you know, and it should continue to flourish." He hesitated for a moment in thought. He had intended to ask a price of seventy-five thousand dollars for his third interest, with the expectation of being haggled down somewhat. "Since you don't wish to bargain back and forth, Jeff, I'll tell you how much I have to have. I'm going to use the money to start my own company here in Durham, in competition with King Tobacco, and the others. I thought I should warn you of my intentions."

Jeff shrugged. "That's all right with me." He smiled suddenly, as if privy to some private joke. "Not only is it all right, but I wish you well, Clint."

"I've made a study of how much I'll need to start out, and I can't do it for less than fifty thousand, and that's scaling it damned close to the bone."

"That's your price?" At Clint's nod, Jeff said, "Then it's a deal."

"Just like that?" Clint shook his head sharply from side to side.

"Just like that." Jeff got to his feet. "I'll pick you up here at ten in the morning, we'll go to an attorney to draw up the necessary papers, and I'll give you a bank draft for fifty thousand the instant the papers are all signed." He held out his hand. "A deal then?"

Clint was not a man to be easily shaken by any sudden turn of events, but this had happened with such shocking suddenness that he was somewhat dazed as he accepted Jeff's handshake.

"It's a deal," he said, and began to grin.

Rachel Lefkowitz did not come to work on Wednesday morning. Ben did not discover this until the afternoon, having spent most of the day busy in his office. But her absence was one of the first things he noticed when he finally came downstairs.

He sought out Jacob immediately. "Jacob, where's Rachel? This is the first time I can remember her being absent from work. I certainly hope she isn't ill?"

"Not ill, Ben." It was clear that Jacob was a very troubled man.

"Then what is wrong, Jacob?"

Jacob busied himself lighting the stub of a cigar in his mouth. It was an indication of his agitation. They had a no smoking rule in the plant; the threat of fire was always imminent. Although Jacob and his cigars were inseparable, he chewed on one during working hours, and never lit it. Ben did not reprimand him for this oversight, but waited patiently.

"My Rachel," Jacob finally said, "told me she is returning to New York."

Ben was stunned. "Returning to New York? For God's sake, Jacob, why? I thought she was happy here."

"Women, they are not like us, eh?" Jacob spread his hands in an expressive gesture. He said, eagerly, "Ben, you will talk to her?"

"I most certainly will, my friend. I'll go right now. She's at home?"

Jacob bobbed his head. "She is. This I would appreciate, Ben."

Ben left the building at once. He saddled his horse at the stable up the block, and rode to the Lefkowitz house. Rachel took some time answering his knock, and he was beginning to fear that Jacob had been in error about her being at the house.

Then he heard her footsteps, and the door swung open part way. At the sight of him she started to close the door. Ben was quick-thinking enough to jam his foot into the narrowing crack, his boot stopping the door.

"Rachel," he said urgently, "I must talk to you."

Rachel gave a shrug and stepped back, allowing him to push the door open. She turned away, her back to him.

"Rachel, your father tells me that you're thinking of returning to New York. Is that true?" She nodded without looking at him. "But for what reason? I thought you were happy here? Rachel, will you look at me!"

He took her by the shoulders and turned her to face him. He was dismayed to see tears in her eyes. More gently, he said, "Tell me, Rachel, what's wrong? Is it something at the plant?"

"No, everything is fine at the plant. All of us, we couldn't be more content."

"Then what is it?" he said in exasperation.

"You don't know?" She looked intently into his eyes.

"Of course I don't know!"

"Then I'll tell you." She stepped back out of his grasp, and faced him proudly. But despite her defiance, her face looked vulnerable, and her eyes reminded Ben of a wounded animal.

"I know this is brazen of me, a woman isn't supposed to say such a thing to a man... I'm in love with you, Ben Ascher."

He could only stare at her, mute.

"And that is why I must leave Durham. This past year has been awful for me. I watch you with Charlotte... Miss King, and my heart breaks a little more each time. I just can't go through it any longer." She was close to tears again. "I can't, Ben! It's too much to expect of me."

"Rachel, my dear, dear Rachel, please don't leave." The words were spoken without thinking, simple words coming from his heart.

She blinked against the tears. "Why? Why shouldn't I?"

"Because I... Because I care for you too much to see you go away. I guess I've never realized, until now, how much it means to me to see your sweet face every morning. Please, Rachel. Don't go."

"Ah, Ben! My love!"

Then she was in his arms, her mouth warm and sweet on his. He tasted the salt of her tears. Then he ceased to think at all, shaken to the soul by the depths of passion in Rachel, a passion that he had never suspected in one who was usually so quiet and demure.

His own response was immediate, and he knew, dimly, that he had wanted Rachel from the very first moment he saw her.

In a gesture that was without reservation, so full of trust and love that it moved him deeply, she took her mouth from his, linked arms with him, and led him into her bedroom. She moved away only to close the door, then was back in his arms again.

They were completely lost in each other, totally forgetful of the fact that they were in her father's house, and the possibility that he might come home unexpectedly. All they could think of was their vaulting need. It blazed like a raging conflagration.

And then they were together on the bed, flesh to flesh, no clothing to inhibit them.

Ben knew without being told that Rachel was a virgin, and thus he was gentle with her.

But after he had entered her, tenderly probing, Rachel, after an instant of cringing away, a muted cry wrung from her, rose to him and clung. She became all woman in that instant, fierce and demanding, the sexual rhythm of her lithe body a goad to urge him on to greater effort.

They were swept up in that sweet swell of passion which, finally, turned into a blaze of ecstasy that neither had ever experienced before.

When they were finally apart, yet still close together, Rachel's head cradled on his chest, Ben felt a sense of great wonder, of discovery. He thought of Charlotte with only a twinge of regret. He had loved her in a way, still loved her, but the attraction, he realized now, was mostly physical. There had never been this feeling of oneness that he now shared with Rachel. Rachel was not just a woman, she was a part of him, part of his blood and sinew, and his love for her was an ache, a pain, that would never diminish but only increase with time, and could only be eased temporarily by holding her in his arms like this.

He raised her head up on a level with his, and looked into her swimming eyes. "Will you stay now?"

She bobbed her head, the dimple appearing and disappearing, and Ben realized that the dimple had not been much in evidence of late. He had hurt her, and the knowledge now hurt him in turn.

He said tenderly, "You know this means that you'll have to become my wife, Rachel Lefkowitz."

The dimple came again, and remained this time. A glow seemed to emanate from her. "I should certainly think so. Rachel Ascher. How many times have I repeated that name to myself in the dark of the night?"

Charlotte, busy with paperwork on her desk, glanced up at a cough from her open office door. "Ben! Come in." She smiled with pleasure.

Her smile died as she noted the unusual gravity of his features. "Is something wrong?"

"Well . . ." He hesitated, then squared his shoulders. "It depends on how you look at it. There's something I must tell you, Charlotte. We've always been reasonably honest with one another." He began to smile, a smile almost foolish as it spread and spread. "This afternoon, Charlotte, I asked Rachel to marry me, and she accepted."

Charlotte was not surprised, but she was stunned by the unexpectedness of the announcement. "I knew Rachel was in love with you, I told you, remember? But I never thought that . ." She got to her feet, coming around the desk to him. "Congratulations, Ben." She embraced him, hiding her face from him, afraid that she would reveal her hurt. For she was hurt—she felt as if the whole world had crumpled around her, she felt as if the earth under her had suddenly turned to shifting sand. Ben was her stalwart, her support, her ally, her lover . . .

He said huskily, "This isn't going to make any difference between us, is it, Charlotte?"

He tried to move her back to where he could see her face, but she resisted. She laughed shakily, and said in a voice that she hoped was steady, "Of course not, Ben! Why should it make any . . . ?"

Her voice died as she stared past him. Jeff stood framed in the doorway, staring at her soberly, his eyes wary.

"Jefferson! What are you doing here?" She stepped back from Ben, who turned an astonished face toward her brother.

"Hello, Charlotte. How are you, Ben?"

She said harshly, "You didn't answer my question! What are you doing here, Jefferson?"

He smiled slowly. "I thought it was time I was meeting my new partners."

She gaped at him. "What are you saying?"

"I just bought Clint Devlin's third interest in King Tobacco. Don't you think that's a good idea, Charlotte, keeping it in the family?"

# Chapter Eighteen

THE twin shocks—Ben's announcement that he was marrying Rachel, and Jeff's statement that he now owned a third interest in King Tobacco—were almost too much for Charlotte. For the first time her resolve wavered. Not only was she affected emotionally, but physically as well. The strength seemed to drain from her.

She swayed, as the room seemed to whirl around her, and she might have fallen if Ben had not caught her arm in support.

Dimly, she heard his question, "Charlotte, are you all right?"

She gathered her resources, shook his hand off, and said, "Of course I'm all right! Why shouldn't I be?"

She walked around behind her desk, and this simple action seemed to help her regain her assurance. She sat down, and looked across the room at her brother, who had limped a few steps into the room. It was the first time she had seen him in almost two years, and there was a marked change in him. He was well-dressed, well-barbered, and he was clear-eyed, and more self-assured than she had ever seen him.

She made an effort, and managed to keep her voice controlled. "Now, let me understand this. You claim you bought Clint's partnership?" At his nod she asked, "How did that come about?"

He arched an eyebrow. "What do you mean, sis? His

interest was for sale, so I bought it. It's as simple as that, Charlotte."

"Not so simple as that." She leaned forward, trying to keep her temper. "Is this whole thing a conspiracy between the pair of you? Did you conspire together to bring this about? I understand that you've become good friends."

"My dear sister." Jeff shook his head. "How could we have done something like that? *Why* should we do that? I wasn't even in Durham when I learned that Clint was selling out. When I heard, I hurried here and bought him out. No conspiracy, just a straightforward business transaction."

"He didn't consult us about selling to you."

"He didn't need to. Clint doesn't need your approval of the person he sells to."

She looked at Ben. "Is that true?"

Ben nodded slowly. "That's true, Charlotte. We agreed, don't you remember? Any time we wanted to sell our share, we were free to do so."

"At that time selling, any of us selling, was the farthest thing from my mind." She looked back at Jeff. "Where did *you* get the money to buy Clint out? I'm sure he didn't sell cheaply."

His gaze jumped away, then he looked back, meeting her eyes. "I earned it, Charlotte. I've been doing quite well this past year, and I made a tidy sum when the price of tobacco took its big jump."

"A pinhooker," she said scornfully. "They're not much better than pirates, in my estimation."

"You may not have a high opinion of pinhookers," Jeff said steadily. "But it's one way to make a lot of money quickly in the tobacco business."

Charlotte was silent for a few moments, looking steadily at him. She was still far from satisfied. Something did not strike her quite right.

As though reading her mind, Jeff said quickly, "Give me a little credit, Charlotte. I know how I was before, and I no longer blame you for being angry at me. You had the right, but I have changed, for the better, I hope."

She remained quiet, studying him. He had changed, she could not deny that. She still blamed him for the loss of the farm, and the death of their mother, yet he had suffered greatly from the war; and if he had finally straightened himself out, she should give him his chance.

She sighed, her glance going to Ben, who had been quiet during the exchange. "I suppose we should be grateful that Clint didn't sell his interest to Sload Lutcher. It would be just like him to do that to spite me. Ben, what do you think?"

"What's to think?" He looked at her with a shrug. "Jeff is now the legal owner of a third interest in King Tobacco, there's nothing we can do but accept that. I think we should accept it with good grace, and give him his chance. But he's your brother, Charlotte."

"Yes, he's my brother," she said musingly. "The next question is, Jefferson, what are we going to do with you?"

"Do with me?" He stared at her in confusion. "I'll do my share as a partner, I promise you that."

"Doing what? Clint handled the promotion and advertising end of it. Ben and I have already discussed hiring someone to replace him. Surely you don't claim to be qualified to handle that chore?"

"No, I don't make that claim. But I'll hold up my end, don't worry. During the time I worked for Lutcher, I did learn tobacco, from the ground up, as much as I know you don't like to hear his name."

"Well, I reckon we can find something for you to do. Clint had an office down the hall, even though he rarely used it. You can occupy his old office." She waved a hand in dismissal. "Just don't get in the way until we decide what to do with you."

Resentment flared in his eyes. "I suppose you know that Clint is starting his own tobacco company here in Durham?" he said with an edge of malice.

"No, I didn't know, but any competition he might offer doesn't worry me," she said with more confidence than she felt. "He might be able to sell, but he has to produce something to sell first."

Jeff said, "I wouldn't judge him short. Clint is a resourceful fellow."

"Why are you blowing his trumpet, Jefferson? If he succeeds, we might be forced out of business, and then where would you be? If you want to make yourself useful around here, go down to his old office and figure out what we can do to see that he isn't successful."

Jeff flushed, gave her a dark look, and limped out of the office.

"Weren't you a little rough on him, Charlotte?" Ben said. "There's a great distance from what he was before to what he is now. He has come a long way back, and not many people are capable of doing that. You should be proud, not scornful."

"He has yet to prove himself to me, Ben." Then her shoulders slumped, and she felt the sting of tears behind her eyes. "Don't you think I want to be proud of him? I once loved him and I want to again, but I can't help but believe that Lutcher corrupted him. Everything Sload Lutcher touches, he corrupts."

"Charlotte, give Jeff a chance. After all, he has King blood in his veins. I think he's looking for a chance to redeem himself in your eyes." Ben reached across the desk and touched her cheek with his knuckles. "I have some things to do, we'll talk more in the morning. Try not to be too hard on him."

Charlotte sat at her desk for a long time after Ben left. The shadows lengthened, she heard the factory slowly closing down, and soon she knew everyone was gone except the cleaning crew. Darkness crept into the room, and still she sat on, not bothering to light a lamp.

She had never felt so bereft, so alone. Not even during the war years had she felt so desolated; at least her mother had been alive then. Now she had no one. Clint was gone, gone for good. Ben was still here, but she could no longer lean on him for emotional strength—he had declared his love for someone else.

She thought back to the beginning of King Tobacco, and her determination to devote all her energies and emotions in a single-minded drive for success. She had done that, and success beyond her dreams was in her grasp now. But in gaining that, had she lost everything else? Was she doomed to a barren existence? More importantly, was Clint's accusation correct? In driving toward success, had she become cold, a woman without love, a woman who did not *need* love?

The last, she knew in her heart, was not true. She needed love, she needed warmth and affection and closeness as much as any woman. Yet, if she had lost the ability to give love, how could she expect to receive it in return?

And now Jefferson had reentered her life, and she had turned a stone face to him as well. For a moment she was strongly tempted to rush down the hall to his office and forgive him for everything. She was even on her feet and starting around the desk when she stumbled against a chair in the dark and almost fell. He would be long gone by now, as was everyone else.

She groped for the lamp on the table and lit it. As light spread across the room, she regained a measure of her emotional equilibrium. The moment of weakness passed, and she firmed up her resolve.

If Jefferson proved himself to her, they would become brother and sister again; but she refused to allow a moment of weakness drive her into a premature action.

And Ben, Ben had once loved her, and he was not married as yet. Perhaps there was hope still. This was sudden, this new relationship with Rachel. Perhaps if she, Charlotte, told Ben that it was not hopeless between them . . .

No! She rejected the thought as unworthy of her. Squaring her shoulders, she blew out the lamp and left the office, and the building, grimly determined to follow the route she had mapped out for herself. If love had no place in her life, so be it. She was strong enough to survive.

Over the next two weeks Jeff gradually fitted himself into the fabric of King Tobacco. He made himself useful in many ways; since they were into full production with the new crop of tobacco, another mind and pair of hands were welcome.

Charlotte kept herself aloof from him, but from the things Ben reported to her, she learned that Jeff *was* knowledgeable about tobacco. The only area where he was ignorant was in the production of tailor-made cigarettes; since Lutcher had not yet converted his plant into the production of tailor-mades, Jeff had no experience at that.

"But he's a quick learner," Ben told her. "He spends as much time as he can spare from his other duties among the rollers."

"If he gets in the way," Charlotte said, "tell Jacob to hustle him out."

"Charlotte . . ." Ben sighed patiently. "He is not in the way, and Jacob tells me that he's a help. Not only that, but he gets along well with the rollers. Isn't it about time you were softening a little? Most of the time you ignore Jeff as though he isn't here."

"I . . ." She hesitated, then nodded reluctantly. "You're right. He does seem to be carrying his share. It's time we had an executive meeting, Ben, we have a decision to make. Ask Jeff to be in my office at two tomorrow. You be there, also." She smiled suddenly. "I can't very well deny him that privilege, can I, since he's a third partner? But if he tries to make trouble about any decisions we agree on, that's the last meeting he'll attend. Tell him that for me."

"What's this meeting about? I'm pretty busy. I hope it's important."

"It is important, Ben. I've found someone to replace Clint, in charge of advertising and promotion, and I've asked her to come in tomorrow afternoon. We both should talk to her, before making the decision whether to employ her or not."

"Her?" Ben stared. "A woman?"

"A woman." She bristled. "Anything wrong with that?"

"No, not if you think she can do the job."

"I think she can do the job, yes, but you have to share the responsibility of the decision."

He looked at her appraisingly. "And if I don't approve of employing her, you'll think it's because she's a woman, is that it?"

"Of course not!" she snapped. Then she backed off, smiling ruefully. "It did sound like I was putting it on that basis, didn't it? No, Ben, I know you for a fair man. You'll judge her on her ability to do the job, and nothing else."

The woman in question was Sarah Goldman. She was not young—probably in her early forties, Charlotte judged—but she had the energy of someone half her age, and she gave off ideas like sparks. She was from New York, and had been a widow for ten years, with two children to raise. During those ten years she had supported herself and her children by doing advertising for one of the major department stores in New York.

"But the owner of the store has a low opinion of advertising," she told her audience of three. "The money allowed us was not much more than that allotted to the store's maintenance division." She shook her head. "But that was not the worst of it." Her brown eyes blazed. "The man in charge was there when I went to work ten years ago. He took all my ideas, and told everyone they were his. He died six months ago. And what did they do? They replaced him with another man, from outside the store."

Charlotte said, "That, I promise you, will not happen here, if we employ you." She laughed. "Of course we don't *have* a real department to handle advertising as such, not at this time. It will be your task to build one."

Ben leaned forward. "Charlotte hasn't told me, Mrs. Goldman. How did you learn about the position?"

Sarah Goldman looked from Ben to Charlotte uncertainly. "Your foreman, Jacob Lefkowitz, sent me a telegram. He's a distant relative. I hope this won't get him into trouble?"

"No, no." Ben was smiling. "I had a hunch that was how it came about." He glanced amusedly at Charlotte. "I don't know how we ever managed without Jacob."

Sarah told them that she knew little about the tobacco business, but she was willing to learn. "And I'm a quick learner. On the train coming to Durham, I sketched out some rough drawings of advertisements for newspapers, perhaps some magazines, and the like."

As Sarah began spreading out the sketches for their inspection, Charlotte said, "You don't by any chance know Clint Devlin, do you, Mrs. Goldman?"

Sarah paused, looking up with a frown. "I don't think so. Who is he?"

"He's the man who was doing this job before, and he expounded on newspaper advertising."

"The concept of newspaper advertising is far from new, but few businesses have yet to come around to accepting it."

Her sketches were rough, but they were bold, eye-catching, and quite exciting. Charlotte, Ben, and Jeff examined the sketches one at a time. Charlotte was a little surprised, yet pleased, at her brother's interest, also at his grasp of Sarah's purpose.

Finally Charlotte said, "Have you seen enough, Ben?"

He nodded thoughtfully, pulling at his lower lip, still absorbed in the sketches.

"Any questions for Mrs. Goldman?"

He looked up with a smile. "No, I think I know all I need to know."

"Mrs. Goldman, would you be so kind as to wait just outside for a few minutes, while we confer?" Charlotte said. "We won't take long, I assure you."

After the woman left the office, Charlotte said, "Well, Ben?"

Jeff spoke up unexpectedly, "I think we would be crazy not to employ her. I'm convinced she will do a great job for us."

Charlotte stared at him in astonishment. "Well! And you're the one who always railed against women in business."

Jeff looked down at the floor. He mumbled, "A person can change his mind, you know."

Ben laughed. "I vote with Jeff, Charlotte. We should

consider ourselves fortunate that a person of her caliber is available to us."

"I guess it's unanimous then." She was a bit dazed, having expected at least some argument.

She crossed to the door and opened it. "Sarah, you now work for King Tobacco." Smiling, she held out her hand. "And since you now work for us, I hope I may call you Sarah. We'll talk about salary later in the day. I'm sure we can come to a reasonable agreement."

"I'm sure we can." Sarah shook Charlotte's hand gratefully. "And you certainly may call me Sarah."

Charlotte detained Jeff for a moment after Ben left with Sarah to find her office space. "Jeff," she said hesitantly, "I want to . . . Oh, darn it, welcome back, brother!" She kissed him on the cheek.

Jeff shuffled his feet in embarrassment, looking away. Then as if by sheer force of will, he looked directly into her eyes. "I want you to understand one thing, sis . . . Just because I voted with you today doesn't mean that I always will. If I think you're making a wrong decision, I'll vote against you."

"I wouldn't expect anything else," she said cheerfully. "After all, you're a King, and just ask anyone, they can tell you how stubborn and wrong-headed *I* am."

What Charlotte had no way of knowing, of course, was that Jeff was voting the way Sload Lutcher had ordered him to vote; and this filled him with shame, so much shame that he had found it difficult to meet her gaze.

After Ben had told him yesterday what the meeting today was about, Jeff had sneaked into Lutcher's building last night.

Lutcher had listened closely as Jeff told him the purpose of the meeting, then rubbed his hands together in great glee. "Good, good! It couldn't be better for our purpose. Most of the time I'll be telling you to vote against your sister and the Jew, but this time I want you to vote with them. It'll put them off-guard for the next vote."

Jeff looked at him without comprehension. "You want me to vote to employ this woman?"

"Yes! Don't you see, King?" Lutcher peered at him over the steeple of his fingers. "A mere woman could never take Devlin's place. She'll never be able to handle it, no woman could. Not only is she a woman, but she's a Jew. This is perfect, perfect! With her handling advertising, watch their sales drop."

But later that afternoon, as he left the building after work, Jeff thought back to the scene in Charlotte's office, and he was not so sure that Lutcher's judgment was correct in this instance. Sarah Goldman struck him as imaginative, and certainly energetic. Perhaps she was not on a par with Clint, but with the groundwork Clint had laid, Jeff had the feeling that she would do a fine job advertising their products.

For some reason Lutcher's judgment of people, usually so astute, was warped when it came to women. At first Jeff had thought that he hated Charlotte because she had defied him, and successfully, but he had gradually realized that Lutcher hated all women.

However, Jeff's feeling that Sarah Goldman was a good choice, that Lutcher was in error as to her competence, did nothing whatsoever to ease the shame and guilt he felt. He was a traitor to Charlotte's cause, and the time would come soon when Lutcher would demand that he vote against her best interests. So long as Ben voted with her, no great harm would result, but if for some reason Ben did not, damage could be done.

Jeff did not know how long he could keep up the pretense. To make it even worse, today Charlotte had gone a long way toward accepting him back in her good graces. It had been a fine feeling, but spoiled by the fact that he had earned it under false pretenses.

Head down, he trudged toward the small hotel near the train station, where he was staying until he could find better quarters.

He longed for a drink. For the first time in months he felt a powerful urge to pour drink after drink down his throat, seeking alcoholic oblivion that would temporarily blot out his shame. He resisted and limped on, but even this small victory failed to lift his spirits.

There was no one at the small desk as he started across the cramped lobby, but fortunately he had his key. As he limped toward the stairs, a voice called his name.

He halted, turning, and saw Lucinda hurrying toward him. "Lucinda, what are you doing here?"

Without answering she threw herself into his arms and kissed him hungrily. His own hunger was immediate, and he returned the kiss, his surprise at her sudden appearance momentarily sidetracked. He gloried in this display of her love for him; it was the first time since the war that a woman had given her love to him without reservation. His hands roamed over her body, caressing the fullness of her figure through the dress. They were both becoming aroused, and this shocked Jeff back to an awareness of where they were.

He darted a glance at the desk. It was still unoccupied, but he knew that the clerk could return any minute, and the hotel had a strict rule—no women permitted.

"Quickly, darling," he said in a hoarse whisper. "Come with me."

He hustled her up the stairs to the second floor, and down the hall to his room. It was after dark, and the room was black as pitch when he let her in. He left the door open until he could grope his way across the room to the bedside table and light the lamp.

He turned around to face her, drinking in her beauty—the long raven hair in disarray after their embrace downstairs, and the black eyes glowing with love for him. He gestured lamely around the room. "I'm sorry, sweetheart. This is a terrible room, I know. I haven't had time to find a better place."

"It doesn't matter, I've seen much worse. So long as you're in it, I'm happy."

He strode past her to close and bolt the door. "Now tell me, Lucinda, why are you here?"

She looked hurt. "Aren't you glad to see me?"

"Of course I'm glad to see you, but that's not the point."

"You said you'd send for me, but you haven't. I just couldn't wait any longer."

"I would have in time, but there have been... Well, some developments that delayed me. But none of that really matters. I'm delighted that you're here." He kissed her lingeringly.

"Jeff..." She looked up at him with shining eyes. "I received some good news last week... I suppose I'm terrible for considering it good news, but I can't help feeling that way. George is dead, Jeff!"

"George?"

"My husband. He was killed in St. Louis in a card game. That means I'm free, darling. We can get married!" She hugged him, then looked up again, apprehension shadowing her fine eyes. "If you still want to, that is."

Jeff pulled her face down against his chest. "Of course I still want to marry you." He was staring blankly at the wall. He did want to marry her, but he had to wonder how many problems it would cause.

"Then we can get married soon. I reckon we should wait a decent interval," she said, voice muffled against his chest.

Jeff shoved all concerns from his mind; and putting a finger under her chin, he tipped her face up. "I love you, Lucinda."

"And I love you, darling Jeff."

It had been three weeks since they had been together, and the closeness of their bodies ignited their passion. It took only seconds for them to disrobe and fall together onto the narrow bed.

With Lucinda, warm, loving Lucinda, Jeff was a whole man again, the limp forgotten, the wretchedness of the year after his return from the war forgotten. In bed Lucinda was without inhibitions, wantonly exploring his body, doing all the things that she had learned would arouse him.

They made love with a finely tuned intensity, with concern for the other's needs. When Lucinda locked her thighs around him and signaled her release with a stuttering cry, Jeff felt an enormous pride in his ability to bring such joy and ecstasy to her.

But when it was over and they lay side by side on the small bed, his pride sloughed away. He was being as false with her as he was with Charlotte, and this increased his guilt two-fold. He had told Lucinda very little about himself, and nothing at all about his dealings with Lutcher. Lucinda had assumed that he was what he seemed, a pinhooker, and he had said nothing to disillusion her. But now he knew if she was to live with him, if she was to become his wife, she must be told the truth. It was entirely possible that she would turn away from him in horror and loathing when she did know the truth; yet it was a risk that he had to take, if he was to live with himself.

He told her everything, beginning with the loan from Lutcher, which Charlotte had to repay, and his sale of the King farm to Lutcher. He told her of his going to work for the man, and his being Lutcher's man even as a pinhooker. And then he told her of his present perfidy. "Everyone thinks that I'm now a third owner of King Tobacco," he concluded bitterly. "When in fact I'm Lutcher's shadow man, paid to do what I can to harm my sister."

Lucinda had listened without comment. Now she rolled toward him, face on his shoulder, running her hand lovingly down across his face. She murmured, "Poor darling, you have had a hard time of it."

He raised his head to stare down at her in disbelief. "That's all you have to say? Doesn't what I've told you disgust you?"

"No, I'm not disgusted. I love you, Jeff. I will always love you, no matter what you do. I've never loved a man before, and I know I'll never love another. I never loved George, I married him to get away from home. He was an awful man, Jeff. He never treated me like a real person. You do, and that's worth everything to me."

"I don't see how you can condone what I've done."

She stroked the corner of his mouth with her forefinger.

"I didn't say I condone it. I understand how it could have happened. And you've changed, you told me that."

"Not enough," he said glumly. "I'm still doing Lutcher's dirty work."

"You'll think of a way to get out from under his thumb. Together, we'll think of a way. I know something you can do now." Smiling, she raised up on one elbow. "When Lutcher tells you how to vote in these partnership meetings, how does he know how you vote?"

"How does he know?" He blinked at her, confused. "Why, because I tell him."

"Exactly." She smiled slyly. "I'm sure your sister or the other partner don't go around telling people how they've voted on company matters. So, if you feel like voting with your sister, opposite the way Lutcher wants you to vote, who'll know?"

"But that would be . . ."

"Lying?" She smiled at him again. "But if it would help your sister? And wouldn't it be getting back at Lutcher?"

"By God, it would, wouldn't it? I'll do it!" He hugged her. "Woman, you are a devious wench."

"Of course I am. Women have to be, to survive in a world run by men."

# Chapter Nineteen

DURING the next two weeks, Charlotte drove herself hard, seeking forgetfulness in work. This was their busiest time of the year, and she was at the plant before eight in the morning and remained long after dark. By burying herself in her duties, she was able to forget her personal problems. By the time she finally went to bed she was usually so exhausted that she slept like the dead.

Now and then, however, something awakened her in the hours before dawn, and she would lie sleepless in the dark, staring up at the unseen ceiling above her head, her thoughts moving to Clint, then to Ben—endlessly circling from one to the other.

At least everything was going beautifully at the plant. The rollers were working two extra hours a day, operating smoothly under Jacob's direction; and despite Clint's dire prediction, they were slowly making inroads in the backlog of orders.

Rachel was still at her table, but her efficiency was below par, in Charlotte's estimation. Every time Ben was within her range of vision, Rachel stopped working and sat staring at him with mooning eyes.

In her annoyance Charlotte spoke to Ben about it. "For heaven's sake, Ben, marry the girl, will you? Then at least maybe we'll get some work out of her!"

Ben smiled in amusement. "You're urging me to get married, Charlotte? I'm surprised."

Charlotte was somewhat surprised herself, not sure

what had prompted the question. "You said you were engaged, so why wait?"

"Several reasons. First off, this is our busy season, as you know. Neither of us can spare the time away from the plant. Secondly, and more importantly, Rachel will be quitting work when we get married, and we'd miss her if she quit making cigarettes at this time."

A small thought nudged at Charlotte's mind. Was Ben having second thoughts? She pushed the thought away, and said, "I'm not sure how much we'd miss Rachel. Every time you come around, she stops working and follows you around with her eyes."

He laughed, clearly flattered. "I'll try to keep out of her sight as much as possible, Charlotte. That's the best I can do."

Sarah Goldman was working out fine. Naturally, it was going to take some time to get her plans into full operation, but since they were not in need of new orders, that presented no problem.

And Jeff. . . Charlotte was inordinately pleased at how well Jeff was working out. He labored as long and as hard as she and Ben, and he was on good terms with all the workers, and was well-liked. He worked at increasing his knowledge of tobacco, and Charlotte discovered, to her pleased surprise, that he knew as much about buying quality tobacco as she did; and she was thinking of teaming him with Bradley Hollister as soon as the pace of work slackened off, sending them out into the countryside on a buying trip. It was an onerous chore she would be happy to be relieved of.

And one day he gave her another pleasant surprise. He came into her office in mid-morning, a comely woman on his arm. Beaming, he said, "Charlotte, I want you to meet Lucinda Parks. Lucinda, this is my sister, Charlotte."

Charlotte stood, coming around the desk, studying the woman frankly. She remembered Clint mentioning the name, and knew this was the woman who had helped Clint with his street show.

"How do you do, Lucinda?" Charlotte said. The woman

was more than comely, she was a mature beauty, with a stunning figure artfully displayed with fashionable clothes, and jet-black hair framing a piquant face. She struck Charlotte as being, if not a few years older than her brother, at least much more mature. But then, she concluded, that was probably all to the good.

"I'm pleased to meet you, Charlotte," Lucinda said in a throaty voice.

"Have you two known each other long?" Charlotte asked casually.

Jeff put his arm around Lucinda's shoulders, his love for her changing his face, giving it softer lines and dreaming shadows, turning him into an entirely different person. "Almost a year now, isn't it, Lucinda?"

Lucinda nodded. "Yes, darling."

Perhaps that helps explain the change in him, Charlotte thought; Lucinda has been a steadying influence.

Jeff said, "We're going to be married, sis."

Charlotte went to them, taking their hands in hers. She said sincerely, "I'm glad, glad for both of you. May you be very happy. When will it be, Jefferson? We'll have to plan a wedding Durham will never forget!"

Jeff looked alarmed. "No, nothing like that, Charlotte, please. It might embarrass Lucinda. You know the reputation I have in Durham."

Involuntarily, Charlotte looked to gauge Lucinda's reaction.

Lucinda said gravely, "Don't worry, Charlotte, I know. Jeff has told me everything. Personally, I don't care what people might think. Jeff would be the embarrassed one, not me. And we don't wish to get married too soon. I was married, you see, and my husband hasn't been dead long. It wouldn't be seemly to wed too soon."

Jeff tightened his arm around his intended's shoulders. "Charlotte, I thought I'd show Lucinda around the plant. Is that all right?"

"Certainly it's all right, Jefferson. I'd go along with you, but I'm pretty busy. Enjoy yourselves. It was nice meeting you, Lucinda."

After they left Charlotte returned to her desk, but she was too bemused to do much work. Ben was getting married, Jefferson was getting married—it depressed her. She felt left out, unwanted, unloved. Would she hear next that Clint was getting married?

She scoffed at herself. What nonsense! This was twice during the last two weeks that she had ended up feeling sorry for herself. It was time she put a stop to such dreary thoughts. She was the third owner of a phenomenally successful tobacco company, she was the talk of Durham, and she was only just beginning.

What reason did she have to mope?

With an iron determination she plunged back into her work.

Charlotte still resided at Lucille Carstairs' boarding house. She could afford better quarters now, and Ben kept urging her to move—it was hardly fitting for a woman of her standing in the community to be living in a boarding house.

She always promised to think about moving, yet she had never really considered it seriously. The boarding house was comfortable, and Lucille was now one of her best friends. Since Charlotte did not entertain, about the only thing she did at the boarding house was eat two meals a day there, and sleep. But its chief attraction was the closeness to the plant; she could walk back and forth to work.

When it was not raining, it was especially nice this time of the year, past the humid heat of summer, yet too early for the wintry blasts out of the north.

This particular morning was brisk but still, the autumn leaves under her feet still sodden from the night's dew. Early as it was, few people were about as yet, and the streets were empty. Charlotte strode along briskly, enjoying the morning, her mind almost empty of thought.

Slowly, almost imperceptibly, a feeling of uneasiness crept over her. Her step slowed, and she looked left, then right, completely baffled. There was no immediately discernible reason for the feeling. There was only one person in sight, a tall man coming down the block toward her.

Dear God, it was Sload Lutcher!

Although his face was partially hidden by a black, flat-topped hat canted low on his forehead, there was no mistaking that tall, skeletal figure. Even from this distance she fancied that she could see those deep-set, malevolent eyes peering at her from the shadow cast by the tilted brim of his hat.

Unreasoning panic struck at her. Why was he walking on this particular street? It had to be to intercept her. Charlotte had walked the same route twice a day for almost two years, and had never encountered him. All her instincts screamed at her to turn and run back to the boarding house. At the very least, detour out into the middle of the street to avoid him.

No! She would not be intimidated by this man! She had never shown fear of him before, why should she now?

Straightening her shoulders, head back, she picked up the interrupted rhythm of her stride and walked on. She would have walked right on past, ignoring him, but Lutcher stepped directly into her path, and she was forced to stop.

"Miss King," he said genially, removing his hat. "It is a pleasure to see you."

"Is it?" she said coldly. "I cannot say the same, Mr. Lutcher."

"Now why should there be bad feelings between us after all this time? There are none on my part, I assure you." The thin smile on his face did not reach his eyes, which were flat, staring at her without expression.

"I do not believe you, sir."

He shrugged his narrow shoulders. "Believe what you like, Miss King. I should think you would be well content with life these days. Your business is a success, for the time being, although I do suppose you feel the loss of Devlin." Now a spark of malice struck his eyes. "It is my understanding that he was largely responsible for your prosperity. I do hope that you will not fall on hard times, now that he has departed."

"We shall manage quite well, thank you. The person we hired to replace Mr. Devlin, Sarah Goldman, is working out very well."

His eyes flickered. "Surprises me that a woman could handle Devlin's job," he said in a sneering voice.

"You do tend to underestimate women, sir."

"Perhaps I do, but it is my conviction that women have no place in business." His pale skin took on a faint flush. "And your brother, I understand that he is back in the fold."

"He is, he bought Mr. Devlin's interest in the company."

"King has come up in the world from the wencher and sot he once was. He did very well working for me, and I was sorry to lose him."

She said steadily, "Your loss was our gain, it seems, Mr. Lutcher."

"Oh? He is working out well then, is he? I should think that he would be a thorn in your side, with the bad blood between you."

"That no longer exists, now that he is no longer employed by you, sir."

"Oh? Not even when he votes against your best interests?"

"I don't know what you mean, Mr. Lutcher. There have been no problems in that respect. We have held partnership meetings three times, I believe, since he came into the company, and not once has he voted against Ben and I. Just yesterday we met to decide whether or not to send to New York for more cigarette rollers, and the vote was unanimous."

Now Lutcher's face darkened dangerously, and his voice was angry as he said, "You must be making sport of me, Miss King. The way I heard it your brother has opposed you all the way, except for the vote to hire the Jew woman."

"The woman you refer to, sir, has a name, Sarah Goldman. And I'm sure I don't know where you got your information about our partnership meetings. I assure you that Jefferson has voted with me on every issue. I know that you would dearly love to cause another rift between us, but if this is your means of doing so, you have failed miserably. Good day to you, sir!"

She started past him, and he seized her arm in a strong grip. "You are lying to me, Miss King, and I do not take kindly to being lied to!"

Charlotte stood very still, an icy rage building in her, driving out any fear of this man. "You will take your hand from my arm this instant, Mr. Lutcher, or you will regret it. What would people within hearing think if I screamed rape at the top of my lungs?"

"Rape?" Lutcher dropped his hand away, wiping it on his trousers. "Woman, the thought of having physical relations with you, by force or otherwise, revolts me!"

"Likewise, Mr. Lutcher," Charlotte said with dignity.

She strode on down the street, ears painfully attuned for the pound of his footsteps behind her. She refused to look around, but now that the encounter was past, a strong reaction set in. Her heart was beating wildly, and her skin crawled where he had touched her. She shivered, and despite her determination, her step quickened as the distance widened between them. She knew that he had not moved from where she had left him; she knew as surely as if she had turned to look that he was staring balefully after her.

She shivered again, and did not feel entirely comfortable until she was about to enter her building. She was almost running as she went inside, and she barely avoided colliding with Jeff.

"Whoa, sis!" Laughing, he caught her arm. "I know you love your work, but I didn't expect to see you running to get here . . ." His voice died as he caught sight of her face. "What is it, Charlotte? What's wrong?"

Breathing heavily, she gasped out, "I just met Sload Lutcher up the street."

His hand tightened on her arm. "Did he try to harm you?"

She shook her head. "No, no, I don't think even he would dare do that, not in broad daylight."

"Then why are you so upset? I know you despise the man, but even so . . ."

"It's what he said, not what he did."

Jeff let his hand fall away. "What did he say?"

"Oh, he was nasty, as always. I think he's furious at you for making it on your own, Jefferson, and he said things to try and make me upset with you."

He said tightly, "What things, Charlotte?"

"That you have been voting against me in everything that comes up. He says you have opposed me all the way. Of course, he was lying, hoping to create trouble. But then when I told him that you had never voted against me, not once, he had the gall to call *me* a liar!"

Jeff simply stared at her, his face paling.

"Now don't get upset, Jefferson. It's not that important." She patted his cheek. "Now that we're together again, Lutcher can't really harm us. And you know something? I don't think he scares me so much now, I don't think I'll ever be quite so afraid of him again. Now, I have to rush, or I'll be late."

Jeff stood without moving, staring after Charlotte as she hurried away. He was filled with despair.

Charlotte was wrong, oh, so wrong!

They had more reason to fear Lutcher than ever before. Learning that he, Jeff, had been lying to him about the way he had been voting in the executive meetings, Lutcher would be livid with rage. There was no foretelling what lengths he would go to now.

Jeff opened his mouth to call out to Charlotte, so he could confess his perfidy; but he closed it again, and stood watching her vanish at the top of the stairs. He simply could not do it. Just thinking of the contempt that would be on her face when she learned the truth made him quail inside.

Having Lucinda with him the past two weeks had strengthened Jeff, and daily he had contemplated just how, and when, he was finally going to stand up to Sload Lutcher. Lucinda had almost convinced him that he could do it, but he had not quite been ready.

Now, it was too late.

Jeff knew that if he did not go to see Lutcher, the man would summon him; and if he did not answer the summons, Cob Jenks would be dispatched to fetch him, dead or alive.

Dear God, how he needed a drink!

Torn with indecision, he turned and slipped out of the plant. He walked the streets of Durham for most of the day, wrestling with the problem. He wanted desperately to go to Lucinda, seek her advice, but he did not. He had brought it all on himself, and any decision made should be his alone. He also fought a winning battle over his desire to forget his troubles in a bottle of whiskey.

In the end he decided to confront Lutcher and defy the man to do his damnedest. The worst he could do was kill him, and Jeff had finally reached the conclusion that he would be better off dead than living the lie he had lived for over a year.

This decision made him feel better, yet he still did not have the courage to tell Charlotte. He did feel that he owed Clint Devlin an explanation. Before he went to face Lutcher, he headed for the building Clint had rented for his factory.

Clint was in a rage. Smoking a cigar furiously, he circled the cigarette machine in frustration. Martin Forester, the machine's inventor, watched Clint worriedly, wiping his greasy hands on a wad of waste.

The machine, a weird contraption large enough to dominate the whole end of the dilapidated building Clint had leased, had been installed ten days ago. At first he had been sardonically amused at the size of this machine to be used to manufacture an object as small as a cigarette, but he was no longer amused. Forester had fussed with it for a week before he pronounced it ready to operate. Until today it had failed to produce a single, usable cigarette. Clint had lost count of the times it had broken down.

But today was the last straw. Two hours ago Forester had once again announced proudly that it was ready. It had produced three cigarettes—one that had split at the seam when Clint picked it up in his fingers; a second that had come from the machine as lumpy as badly rolled bread dough; and finally a third, which was perfect. The moment the machine produced this one cigarette, it had coughed, spat smoke, and died with a dreadful, clanking sound.

Now Forester said, "I'll have it fixed in no time, Mr. Devlin. I promise it'll be repaired by morning. I'll work all night, if necessary."

Clint said savagely, "Forester, you've been saying that since the day it was installed."

Forester looked offended. "I told you that it was far from perfect, that it would take some time to get the kinks out."

"Far from perfect? Hell, it's a disaster! I've got people here standing by on salary, with nothing to do. I've promised buyers that I would have cigarettes for them no later than this week."

"You're getting my machine for nothing, and it costs you nothing until it produces," Forester said aggrievedly. "I'm the one who is putting in unpaid time."

"Costing me nothing, you say?" Clint roared. "God-damnit, man, it's costing me a fortune, so long as it doesn't produce!"

In his rage Clint turned and delivered a vigorous kick to the metal base of the machine. Pain shot up his leg, and he limped back and forth, swearing under his breath. A childish gesture, but he felt a little better.

What he did not tell Forester, what he dared not tell him, or anyone, was that he was nearly at the end of the line. He had badly underestimated the money needed to get into operation, and he was about out of funds. If he did not fill some orders this week, he would be unable to pay the salaries of the people he had hired. Since they had only been working for him a short time, they owed him no loyalty, and it was a cinch that they would quit if they were not paid.

The enthusiasm that had kept him fired up all along was abruptly gone, and he had to face the fact that if this damned machine did not start to function his dream was over.

He recalled Ben's prophetic words: "You're premature."

Although he hated admitting it, Clint knew that Ben was right. He had moved too fast, and he was about to pay the price. He knew in his gut that Forester's machine was a failure. Even if, as promised, the man got it working again by morning, it would break down again, and again, and again!

Clint was a proud man, and to admit failure, even to himself, was galling. The last time he had failed had been in the war, and that he had never viewed as a personal failure—he had simply fought on the losing side.

So what did he do now? Did he go back to Charlotte and Ben, hat in hand, properly humble? He ground his teeth together, biting through the cigar, which fell unheeded to the floor. He could just hear Charlotte's jeering voice: "The high-riding Clint Devlin has fallen on his face!"

Of course he could not go to them. What did he have to offer? Certainly he could not buy his partnership back—he hardly had enough money to keep him in cigars for a week.

"Mr. Devlin?"

His head swiveled around. "What is it, Forester?"

Forester held out the stub of the cigar Clint had bitten through. "You dropped your cigar."

Clint took it, staring at it in wonder. Hysterical laughter seized him, threatening to engulf him. He managed to control it.

"Mr. Devlin, about the cigarette machine?"

"What about it?"

"Shall I work on it tonight, and see if I can get it operating again?"

It was on the tip of Clint's tongue to tell the man to take

his damned machine and disappear with it, when he saw Jeff King enter the building, and stop to look around uncertainly.

Clint said, "Do whatever you like, Forester. Right now, I don't think that it makes a great deal of difference. No matter which way the frog jumps, I'm in over my head without a paddle."

With a flip of his hand to Forester, he started across to Jeff. "Jeff, you wouldn't be interested in swapping your third interest in King Tobacco for a company all of your own, would you?"

Jeff looked startled. "What do you mean?"

"I was being facetious, more or less. What I mean, my friend"—Clint waved a hand around disgustedly—"is that I'm not going to make it. I backed the wrong horse." He grinned bitterly. "My own horse, too."

"You're telling me that you're failing here, Clint?" Jeff asked in disbelief.

"That is the gist of it. I'm dead, about all that's left is to bury me." He sighed. "Couldn't happen to a nicer fellow, right?"

"What I have to tell you, I'm afraid, is going to make you feel worse. I have a confession to make. Please bear with me until I've finished. Then if you never speak to me again, I'll understand."

Clint frowned at him. "You're not making a hell of a lot of sense, Jeff."

Jeff's head went back. "That third interest of yours I bought, Clint. *I* didn't buy it, I used Lutcher's money. He actually owns it, I don't even own the clothes I'm wearing," he said bitterly.

Clint was literally staggered. "Sweet Christ! You mean you're a front for Sload Lutcher?"

"That's what it amounts to," Jeff said abjectly. "And you don't have to spell it out, I know what that makes me."

Clint said, "Before I start making judgments, I'd like to know how this came about. Come over here, I don't want anyone else hearing this."

They moved across to a corner of the room, and sat on two wooden crates, facing each other. Clint lit a fresh cigar, and said, "Go ahead, I'm all ears."

Jeff told him everything, sparing himself nothing. Clint smoked furiously, but aside from that, he let no emotion show.

When Jeff was done, Clint whistled softly. "God, what a barrel of rotten apples this is! One thing I find hard to believe is that Lutcher would spend fifty thousand dollars just to have a spy inside King Tobacco."

"Well, I think he had more in mind than that. He hopes to use the information I feed him to drive Charlotte and Ben out of business, then take over the company for his own."

"Lotte knows nothing of this?"

Jeff shook his head. "No, I didn't have the guts to tell her, Clint."

"She will have to be told, she and Ben. Now that it's out in the open, perhaps we can convince Lutcher to sell the partnership back. It certainly won't do him much good now." He laughed suddenly, "'We,' I said. That's hardly appropriate now. But since I started the whole thing by walking off in a huff and selling my third, I'll do what I damned well can to make it right again."

"Clint... You haven't said what you think of me, of what I've done."

Without answering directly, Clint said, "What are you going to do now?"

"The minute I leave here, I'm going straight to Lutcher, and tell him that I'm finished with him."

Clint's gaze was intent. "I doubt he'll take too kindly to that."

"I'm sure he won't, but it's come down to that now, since he's aware that I haven't been following his orders. The only other choice I have is to run, and that I refuse to do." He smiled without humor. "But if not for Lucinda, I probably would."

"Facing Lutcher like that takes courage, Jeff."

"I don't know how much courage it'll take, but it's too late now, whatever I do. I don't want to face him, I'm scared to death."

Clint smiled suddenly, placing a friendly hand on Jeff's shoulder. "My giving you the devil, telling you how wrong you've been, will accomplish nothing. You know that already. Besides, I think you've had a rough enough time of it, and your own guilt is punishment enough. The war did strange things to many men, Jeff. You're not the only one who was affected by it. It destroyed some men for life. But you, you've come back part way. You've sure as hell changed a heap from when I first met you."

"Not changed enough, it would appear." Jeff got to his feet. "Well, I might as well get it over with."

Clint also got up. "Want me to go along with you?"

"This is something I have to do on my own, Clint, but I do appreciate your offer. Anyway, with you along, it would only make Lutcher angrier."

Clint nodded. "I think Charlotte and Ben should know at once. I'll take that chore off your shoulders." His grin was wry. "Christ, I'd almost rather face Lutcher than Lotte."

As Jeff started away, Clint detained him for a moment. "I'll round up your sister and Ben, take them to the plant, and tell them what's up. I'll wait exactly one hour from now, Jeff. If you're not back by then, I'll come looking for you."

It was after dark when Jeff entered the rear door of Lutcher's building. The downstairs area was dark, shut down for the day, but Jeff was positive that Lutcher was waiting for him, either for him to show up in person, or for Cob Jenks to bring him back forcibly.

The door to Lutcher's office stood open, light streaming out. Jeff took a deep breath, and went into the room.

Lutcher sat motionless, gazing at him with expressionless eyes. "Well, King," he said in a flat voice, "I was wrong. I was convinced that you were in the next county by now. Or perhaps your sister didn't tell you about our little conversation this morning?"

"She told me," Jeff replied.

"And you still dare to face me?" Lutcher's eyes narrowed. "Are you drunk, King?"

"I haven't had even one drink, Lutcher." It was the first time that Jeff had not affixed a "Mr." to the name, and he was proud of himself.

Lutcher seemed not to notice. He moved suddenly, slapping the desk with the palms of his hands. "You lied to me, King!" A spasm of rage worked his face. "You lied to me, at least twice, about how you voted. And for that you're going to be sorry."

"That's not all I've done, Lutcher. I've just come from a talk with Clint Devlin."

"Oh?" Lutcher became very still, only his lips moving. "And what did you and Devlin talk about?"

"About you, mostly. I told him every rotten thing I've done for you. I told him that my interest in King Tobacco really belongs to you, not me, and right now, Clint is telling my sister and Ben Ascher about it."

Lutcher's normally pale face went even paler. For a long moment, he seemed rendered speechless. Then air escaped his lips in a hiss, and his voice furled like a whip. "You did *what*?" His voice began to climb. "You worthless piece of cow dung! You've ruined everything I've planned so long for!"

"I certainly hope so."

"Oh?" Lutcher jutted his face forward. "By that remark, you've just signed your own death warrant!"

Jeff managed to keep his voice steady. "You do what you feel you have to do, Lutcher. I'm no longer afraid of you." And to his own astonishment, Jeff realized that this was true.

Without raising his voice, Lutcher said, "All right, Jenks, kill him. Now!"

Jeff heard a single footstep behind him, and he had just started to turn when he heard a gunshot, and something slammed into his back with tremendous force. He was driven forward against Lutcher's desk. He clutched at it for just a moment, and then the strength left him. He fell face down onto the floor.

Oddly enough, there was no immediate pain, and he did not completely lose consciousness, but there was a numb area in his back, which was slowly spreading.

As from a distance, he could hear Lutcher's voice: "Is he dead, Jenks?"

A boot prodded him in the side. Something told Jeff to close his eyes and feign unconsciousness.

Jenks said, "If he ain't dead, Mr. Lutcher, he soon will be. He's bleeding like a butchered hog."

"Then drag him into the vacant office next door, let him die there." Lutcher's voice changed. "Then I want you to perform a task for me. How long do you think it would take to round up about fifteen of your toughs?"

"Shouldn't take more than an hour." Jenks laughed. "Most of 'em will be drinking around town."

"All right, do it. Then give them axes and sledgehammers and take them over to King Tobacco. I want everything destroyed, machines, those marble tables, everything but the tobacco. That I want you to bring back here to me. That will be at least part compensation for the fifty thousand I invested through King here. If anyone tries to stop you, smash them as well. That damned woman has frustrated me long enough. I want her finished once and for all."

Jeff could hear the gloating satisfaction in Jenks' voice, as he replied, "Me and the fellows will do a bang-up job for you, Mr. Lutcher. It's about time that King woman got what's coming to her."

"Drag King into the next room before you do. I don't want him bleeding all over my office floor."

Jenks said hopefully, "Another bullet, in his head this time, will stop the bleeding."

"No, I want him to suffer a little, if he's not dead already. When you finish with the other chore, bring one of your men back here with you. Then take King out into the countryside and bury him."

Jeff felt Jenks take hold of his feet and start to drag him across the floor. The pain struck then, blinding pain such as he had never experienced, and he welcomed unconsciousness.

# Chapter Twenty

CHARLOTTE had worked late at the plant, and the other boarders had already eaten their suppers by the time she arrived home. As was her custom, Lucille had saved a plate for her, and warmed it up. Charlotte ate a solitary meal in the kitchen. She was just finishing when Lucille came back into the room.

"You have a gentleman caller, dear."

Charlotte glanced up from her plate. "Who is it?"

Lucille smiled broadly. "It's that handsome devil, Clint Devlin."

"I don't want to see him. Send him away."

"I think you should see him, Charlotte. From his manner, I gather it's serious."

Ben! Had something happened to him? Or to Jefferson?

With a gasp Charlotte jumped up and hurried down the short hall. Clint stood just inside the door, his hat in his hand.

"Has something happened to Ben?" she asked breathlessly.

"Ben's in my buggy outside. I picked him up first . . ."

"It's Jefferson then!"

"Your brother's fine, at the moment, as far as I know. But it's him I want to talk about."

"What is it? Tell me!"

He shook his head. "Not here. At the plant. I want both you and Ben to hear what I have to tell you, and the plant's neutral territory." He laughed. "In a manner of speaking."

"Damn you, Clint Devlin, you're as aggravating as ever!"

He shrugged. "You wouldn't want me to change, now would you, Lotte?" He took her arm. "Come along."

He escorted her outside and helped her up into the buggy beside Ben.

As Clint went around to get in on the other side, Charlotte said to Ben, "Do you have any idea what this is all about?"

"Not the slightest. He turned aside all the questions I asked."

Clint overheard Ben's remark. "All in good time, Benbo." He flicked the reins, starting the horse into motion. "But there is one thing I can tell you now. I owe you an apology, both of you. You were right about the damned cigarette machines. I banked everything on the one I got, and it's a failure. And that means that I go down along with it. The Devlin Tobacco Company is a bust before it ever got off the ground."

"Oh, Clint, I *am* sorry!" Charlotte said in distress.

He glanced at her in surprise. "Now that's a reaction I didn't expect, Lotte. I expected you to gloat."

"I would never do that, Clint, and I'm hurt that you would think that of me. We've had our disagreements, I know, but I would never gloat over your ill fortune."

"I'm sorry, too, Lotte. I beg your pardon, I shouldn't have said that." He sighed. "It's just that these past two weeks have been one disappointment after another. And what makes it worse, it's my own damned fault. I jumped before looking." He laughed. "Now that is not a Clint Devlin axiom, but it's one I should have heeded."

Ben said, "There's no way you can put it all together, Clint?"

"No way that I can see. I have no money left to hire cigarette rollers, and the damned machine is broken down, probably for good. No, I'll just call in my losses, regroup, and start over."

Charlotte said impulsively, "There's always a place for

you with King Tobacco, you know that. Unfortunately, not your old job though, that's taken."

"That's damned nice of you, Lotte," he said, pleased. "I'll give it some thought. But what we're going to talk about in a few minutes will have some bearing on that, I believe."

He had pulled the buggy up before the plant, and Ben had helped Charlotte down by the time Clint tied off the horse and came around to them. Ben opened the front door with his key, and called out, identifying them to the night watchman. They went up to the second floor, to Charlotte's office. Ben lit the lamp on her desk.

Charlotte faced Clint with her hands on her hips. "All right, Mr. Devlin, what is the great mystery?"

Clint was busy lighting a cigar. When he had it going to his satisfaction, he looked at her. "I want to preface what I have to say. Right this minute, Lotte, your brother is facing Sload Lutcher, severing all relations with him."

Charlotte was frowning. "But I thought Jefferson had already done that?"

"Not exactly. That's what I have to tell you. But I wanted you to know that Jeff is showing one hell of a lot of courage facing Lutcher. I wanted you to know that first, so you wouldn't lose that famous temper of yours before I was finished."

"Will you, for the love of heaven, get on with it?" She held up her hands. "All right, all right! I promise not to lose my temper."

Clint took a deep breath. "When Jeff bought my third interest, he was actually acting for Lutcher. It was Lutcher's money, and Lutcher actually owns the interest..."

"I knew it, I knew something was wrong!" Charlotte said explosively. "It didn't feel right at the time. Damn Jefferson, he hasn't changed. He's betrayed me again!"

Clint said, "Lotte, you promised."

"Yes, Charlotte." Ben touched her arm. "You did promise to listen without interrupting."

"All right." She threw up her hands again, and walked

over to the window. She stood with her back to them, staring out into the night, listening as Clint told them the rest of it.

When he was done, she faced around. "You mean Lutcher spent fifty thousand dollars just so he could tell Jefferson how to vote at our executive meetings?"

"Jeff thinks it was a little more than that. Lutcher calculated that if he could drive you into bankruptcy, he would then have a foot in the door, and could take over King Tobacco easily. That's the impression your brother has, anyway."

Ben said slowly, "So when Lutcher learned from Charlotte that Jeff wasn't voting the way he was supposed to, he blew up?"

"Jeff had yet to see him when we talked, but that's the logical conclusion."

"Then Jeff *is* showing a lot of courage in facing him alone."

Clint said, "I offered to go with him, for support, but Jeff would have none of it. I figured this was something he had to do to regain his self-respect. And that reminds me . . ." He took out his watch and looked at it. "I told him that if he wasn't back here within an hour, I'd come looking for him. It's past that deadline now."

Charlotte felt a surge of alarm, her brother's treachery forgotten. She realized that she had already forgiven him for this latest betrayal, and his facing up to Lutcher should be penance enough. If anything happened to him . . . !

She said, "We have to go see about him!"

Clint looked at her quizzically. "We? I'm going, in a minute, but not you, Lotte. There's no way of knowing what I'll run into over there."

"And there's no way I'm staying behind," she retorted. "Jefferson is my brother, and if Sload Lutcher has harmed him in any way, I want to know. I intend to see that he pays."

Both Clint and Ben started to speak at once, then stopped, exchanging knowing glances.

Clint said resignedly, "You're one stubborn lady, Lotte.

I know from past experience that about the only way to leave you behind is to tie and gag you."

"And I'd like to see you try and do that!"

Ben said, "We'll all go."

"No, Benbo, I don't think that's wise," Clint said thoughtfully. "I have an odd feeling. I think that Lutcher just might send his thugs over here to wreck the plant. I think you should stay behind. Better yet, go round up Jacob and his people and get them over here as quickly as possible, armed with clubs or whatever you can find."

"Not even Lutcher would be crazy enough to do something like that," Charlotte interjected.

"I have a bad feeling that he just *may* be that crazy. Certainly, he's far from normal. Anyone who would spend the time, money, and effort, Lotte, to get back at you simply because you defied him, has to be somewhat addled. Anyway, I can't see any harm in assuming the worst."

"You're right, Clint," Ben said. "I'll round up Jacob and the others. I only hope I can do it in time. If they're coming, they could be here any time. You two be careful over there, and take care of Charlotte, Clint."

"I'll do my damnedest," Clint said dryly, speaking to Ben's back as he was already hurrying out of the office.

"Let's go, Clint," Charlotte said impatiently.

"All right."

He took her arm and hurried with her downstairs. Ben had already disappeared into the night.

Just before they started out the door, Clint turned her toward him. "Lotte?"

Unexpectedly, he pulled her into his arms and kissed her. For a brief moment everything else was driven from Charlotte's mind at the thrilling touch of his mouth on hers, the remembered feel of the hard-muscled contours of his body. Just as her senses began to spin dangerously, he moved his mouth away to murmur, "My dear Lotte, I thought I would never again have a chance to kiss you."

She remembered Jeff and their purpose, and stepped back out of his embrace, suddenly furious. "Clint Devlin, you are absolutely impossible! At a time like this, you decide to kiss me."

"Methinks the lady protests too much, and too late."

"Clint," she said frantically, "have you forgotten about Jefferson?"

He gave a start. "You're right, Lotte. I'm sorry. Let's go."

Outside, he paused at his buggy to pluck a pistol from under the seat, and rammed it into his belt under his coat. Then, arm in arm, they hurried down the street, covering the short distance to Lutcher's building in just a few minutes. The front of the building was dark, showing not even a chink of light.

"I hope we're not too late," Charlotte said in a tense whisper. She was already trying the front door; it was locked.

"Jeff told me about a door around in the back, which was usually left unlocked for him to slip in and out," Clint said, also in a whisper.

They went quickly down the side of the building. There was just light enough for them to find the small door. Clint took hold of the knob. It turned in his hand. He eased the door open, and they slipped inside. There was a faint light coming from upstairs, enough to reveal the narrow staircase leading up to the second floor balcony. Clint put a finger to his lips, and they stood a moment, listening intently.

"I don't think there's anyone here," Charlotte said in a despairing whisper. "We're too late!"

"We'll soon see."

They went quickly but quietly up the stairs. At the top they saw that the light was coming from an open door. Charlotte placed her mouth close to Clint's ear. "That's Lutcher's office."

They went on tiptoe down the balcony. Just before they reached the open door, Clint touched Charlotte on the arm, motioned her behind him, then was inside the room in two strides.

Sload Lutcher sat behind his desk, as still as a statue.

The light from the lamp on the desk threw his face into shadow, giving the impression that his eyes were set into deep pits in his skull.

"Mr. Devlin," Lutcher said calmly. "Somehow I have been expecting you."

Charlotte stepped up beside Clint. "Where's Jefferson? Where's my brother?"

"Why should I know of his whereabouts, Miss King?" Lutcher said calmly. "He is no longer in my employ."

Clint advanced a few more steps into the room. In a harsh voice he said, "Jeff came here to see you, Lutcher. Now, where is he?"

Lutcher placed both his hands flat on the edge of the desk. His eyes glittered. "He may have told you he was coming here, but he never did." He sneered. "He is probably afraid to face me."

Charlotte's glance had dropped to the floor. "Clint, look!" She pointed to the floor directly in front of the desk. "That's blood!"

Clint's hand went under his coat, his finger curling around the pistol butt. "You're stalling, Lutcher..."

He broke off as Lutcher's hands dropped below the level of the desk. In one quick move Clint raised a foot, braced it against the front edge of the desk, then shoved hard. The desk skidded, striking Lutcher just below the chest. It toppled him over, and both Lutcher and the chair went down with a crash.

Clint was around the desk in a flash, the pistol out and pointing down at Lutcher sprawled on the floor. The gun that Lutcher had been reaching for lay beside him, and now his hand was grabbing for it.

With a kick Clint sent it skittering away. He cocked his pistol and aimed it between Lutcher's eyes. "Now, you rotten bastard, what did you do to Jeff?"

Lutcher's eyes blazed with madness. "You're too late, Devlin. That piece of cow dung is dead!"

A cry of anguish was wrung from Charlotte.

"Then where is his body, if he's dead?" Clint moved the gun barrel closer. "Tell me, or I'll put a bullet between your eyes. Don't think I won't; it would give me the greatest pleasure."

Lutcher's eyes flickered. Then he motioned with a jerk of his head. "In the room next to this one."

Clint said, "Lotte, pick up the lamp, and lead the way." He moved back two steps, motioning with the pistol. "On your feet, Lutcher."

His gaze never leaving Clint's face, the man got to his feet. Clint stepped around behind him, jamming the gun muzzle against Lutcher's neck. "Go ahead, Lotte, lead the way into the next room. If you make one wrong move, Lutcher, you're a dead man."

With Charlotte leading the way, they went out onto the balcony and to the room next door. Charlotte opened the door and then gasped, hurrying on into the room. Clint prodded Lutcher on into the room and turned them both sideways so he could see Charlotte.

She was kneeling beside Jeff's prone figure, the lamp beside her on the floor. Tears were streaming down her face. "Jefferson? Please, God, don't let him be dead! Jefferson?"

To Clint's astonishment and relief, Jeff stirred. He was lying on his back, and his head lolled toward Charlotte, his eyes fluttering open. "Charlotte, is that you?"

"Yes, Jefferson. Thank God, you're alive!"

"Is Clint . . . ?" His voice gained a little strength. "Is Clint with you?"

"I'm here, Jeff boy."

"The factory, Lutcher sent Jenks and a gang of his toughs to destroy the factory."

"We're ahead of you, Jeff. We figured that might happen. Jenks and his bullies will have a reception committee waiting for them." Lutcher grunted, his muscles bunching as if he was about to move. Clint pushed the gun barrel into the back of his neck, wringing another grunt from him. "That news upset you a wee bit, Mr. Lutcher?"

Clint glanced over at Charlotte. "Lotte, there's a doctor two blocks up, you know where he lives. Run and fetch him as quickly as you can. I'll wait here for you."

She turned a dazed face to him. "But the factory . . . ? You heard what Jefferson said!"

"I would say your brother's life is more important than the factory right now. Or don't you think so?"

She looked again at Jeff, reached down to touch his face fleetingly, then was up and running from the room with a whirl of skirts.

It took Cob Jenks thirty minutes beyond the promised hour to round up fifteen roughnecks, but he finally had them corralled and on the way. They were a motley, drunken crew, armed with axe handles and sledges. So far as he knew, Jenks was the only one carrying a sidearm.

He pulled it when they were within a block of King Tobacco and waved it at the boisterous bunch. "Now listen to me, you numbskulls! The way you fellows are carrying on, you'll wake up the whole of Durham, including the graveyard. They're not expecting us, but there's sure as hell a watchman or two, and they can hear you coming. So from now on, we go quiet as a pack of mice. One wrong peep out of any one of you, and I'll lay you out with my pistol butt alongside your skull! Once inside the place, make all the damned noise you want. Now, nice and quiet, hear? If just one of you mucks this up, nary a one gets paid."

The gang quieted immediately and moved ahead with Jenks in the lead.

They know who's buttering their bread, Jenks thought with satisfaction. This was going to be a nice piece of work, and Mr. Sload Bloody Lutcher was going to pay well for it. Jenks knew that he would get great satisfaction from giving Miss High-and-Mighty Charlotte King her come-uppance, but he also expected to be handsomely paid for his efforts. He had done Mr. Lutcher's dirty work for a long time, and although he had been adequately paid, for tonight's piece of work, Mr. Lutcher had promised a large bonus.

They arrived at the King Tobacco building. It was dark and quiet. Jenks nodded to himself, pleased.

"Just as I figured," he murmured to the man next to him. "Quiet as a church." He took hold of the doorknob, and was a little surprised to find it unlocked.

He turned to the man behind him. "Pass the word to the others," he said in a hoarse whisper. "I'll open the door and go in first, leaving the door wide. Then I'll step aside out of the way, and the rest of you pour in after me, making all the noise you like."

Jenks pushed the door open with the palm of his hand. The hinges squeaked slightly, and he held his breath. No cry of alarm sounded. He stepped inside quickly and to the side. One of his followers voiced a strident rebel yell, and they all charged in, bellowing at the top of their voices.

The moment the last man was in, three lanterns suddenly flared, spaced widely apart. Jenks blinked in astonishment, his gaze raking the room. At a fast count he made out just a half-dozen men altogether, armed with clubs. He recognized Ben Ascher, and realized that he had somehow gotten wind of what Mr. Lutcher had planned. His own men, startled by the unexpected opposition, began milling about, muttering, and Jenks saw a couple backing toward the open door.

"Hold fast!" he bellowed. "Can't you count? Hell, we outnumber 'em three to one! Wade in, drive 'em into the ground like railroad spikes!"

He tore the axe handle from the man next to him, and charged at the nearest King man—a burly, broad-shouldered fellow with an inch-long cigar stub in his mouth and a thick cudgel in his hands. Yelling, Jenks charged, the axe handle high above his head.

As he brought it slashing down, the burly man gripped his cudgel by the ends, and brought it up to counter Jenks' attack. It was too late for Jenks to change the direction of his aim. His axe handle smashed into the thick cudgel. The impact jarred Jenks to his toes. Before he had time to recover, the other man changed his grip, both hands locked around one end of his cudgel. He swung it in a low arc, connecting with the axe handle in Jenks' loosened grip, and it flew from his hand.

Then, almost contemptuously, the man with the cigar smacked Jenks across the side of the head with his giant hand. Jenks, already off-balance, flew several feet across the floor, landing on his rump. His head rang.

The man with the cigar, who Jenks now recognized as Jacob Lefkowitz, turned away and joined the general melee, which was raging back and forth across the big room. Jenks, still slightly stunned, was glad to see that his men had regrouped and were taking the fight to the defenders. The King people were so badly outnumbered that they could do little except give ground grudgingly but steadily.

Jenks, seeing that he was not needed at the moment, was happy to remain where he was. As soon as the attackers had beaten the King employees unconscious, then they could start in on the planned destruction. From the look of things that would not take long. Even as Jenks thought this, he saw two of the defenders go down, clubbed unconscious. And now another. The only ones who seemed to be holding their own were Ben Ascher and Jacob Lefkowitz, who stood his ground, bellowing like a madman, wielding his cudgel with telling effect.

Jenks got shakily to his feet. If Lefkowitz and Ascher were eliminated, the two remaining defenders could easily be disposed of. Jenks pulled the pistol from his belt, raised it, and waited until his own man was out of the way so he could get a clear shot at the Jew.

All of a sudden, a pistol shot rang out. Jenks blinked in bewilderment, for a moment thinking that he had fired without knowing it. Then he realized that the shot had come from behind him. He whirled, his mouth falling open at what he saw.

Sload Lutcher stood just inside the door, and behind him stood a man Jenks recognized as Devlin, who once had been a part of King Tobacco. Now Devlin fired a second shot into the air, then brought the gun muzzle down to press it against the back of Lutcher's neck.

The second shot succeeded in getting everyone's attention. Attackers and defenders alike stood frozen, staring at the two men in the doorway.

Devlin said, "Tell them to back off, Lutcher. Tell them to put down their weapons and leave, one by one." As Lutcher remained silent, Devlin twisted the gun barrel. "Tell them, damnit!"

"All right! You men, put down your weapons!" Lutcher shouted. "Do as he says. Put down your weapons and leave!"

Jenks, seeing his handsome bonus disappearing, was goaded into shouting, "No, Mr. Lutcher! We can't let them get away with it!" He raised his pistol. "Jump aside, Mr. Lutcher, and I'll kill the sonofabitch for you!"

"No, you fool, no!" Lutcher screamed. "Don't shoot, Jenks!"

The words failed to register on Jenks. "Jump aside, Mr. Lutcher, jump!" He took aim.

Clint was staring at Jenks in disbelief. He had to be out of his mind! At the last instant Clint sensed that Jenks was indeed going to fire, and he gave Lutcher a hard shove. He was not fast enough.

Jenks' pistol discharged, and Lutcher staggered, clutching at his chest, and slowly he began to fall. Belatedly recognizing his own danger, Clint threw himself to the side and down. Jenks fired a second time, and later Clint was willing to swear that the bullet fanned his hair, it passed so close.

He hit the floor with such force that his pistol was almost jarred loose. He managed to retain his grip, and levering himself up to a sitting position, he snapped off a shot at Jenks, and missed. He thumbed the hammer back, and fired again. This time his aim was accurate. The bullet struck Jenks over the heart, and the man stumbled backward, his gun flying from his hand.

Clint's ears rang from the repeated gunshots, and now an almost eerie quiet fell. His glance went from Jenks to Sload Lutcher, and he saw that both were limp and still.

As though taking the sudden quiet as a signal, Jenks' men broke for the door. Several of them reached the door at the same time, and they created a bottleneck, fighting each other to get out. Jacob, waving his cudgel, bellowed and ran at them.

Clint raised his voice. "Let them go, Jacob. It's all over."

Jacob skidded to a stop, and glanced around dazedly. Then he grinned broadly. "It is all over, eh, Mr. Devlin?"

Clint nodded tiredly, and got to his feet, as Ben hurried over. "Are you all right, Clint?"

"I seem to be, Benbo. How about the three I see on the floor?"

"They'll be all right, except for sore heads in the morning." Ben mopped sweat from his brow. "You saved the day for us, Clint. They were besting us. I hurried back here with Jacob and four men, with word sent on to the others. But I don't think they would have arrived in time."

Jacob had gone over to inspect Jenks and Lutcher. He turned about. "These two will never trouble you and the boss lady again, Ben. They are dead." He came toward them, taking the nubbin of a cigar from his mouth, and throwing it aside.

Clint fumbled in his inside coat pocket, and found two cigars—his last two. He held one out to Jacob. "Here, Jacob, smoke a decent cigar for once. You've earned it this night."

Jacob took the cigar, rolled it back and forth between his fingers, sniffed its rich aroma, then grinned slowly. "Thank you, Mr. Devlin."

Ben said, "How's Jeff, Clint?"

"Lutcher shot him, but how bad it is I don't know. At least he's still alive. Charlotte is seeing to him. Ben . . ." He motioned. "Why don't you send someone for the law, and let's get everything cleared up before Lotte returns?"

Two hours later, matters were more or less settled. The bodies of Lutcher and Jenks had been taken away. Jacob and his men had gone to their beds, and Ben, at Clint's urging, had done the same.

The downstairs had been cleaned up, and Clint lounged in Charlotte's office, booted feet up on her desk, enjoying his last cigar. He had left two lanterns burning downstairs, there was one on her desk, and the office door was open.

Finally, he heard sounds below, and knew that Charlotte had arrived. He did not move. He heard her footsteps moving back and forth, and then she called, "Clint? Ben? Are you here?"

He still did not respond.

Her footsteps had an angry sound on the stairs as she came up. Then she stepped through the door, and came to a sudden halt as she saw him. She struck a belligerent stance, arms akimbo. "So there you are!"

"Here I are," he said lazily.

"What happened here? Didn't Jenks and his men show up?"

"Oh, they showed up." He waved his cigar languidly. "Ben and I handled it. Jacob helped a bit."

"Downstairs, it looks like nothing ever happened."

"Quite a bit happened, Lotte. Both Lutcher and Jenks are dead. Jenks killed Lutcher, and I killed Jenks."

"Both dead?" Looking stunned, she wandered over to a chair and sat down. The moment she did, she seemed to sag with weariness.

"And your brother? How's Jeff, Lotte?"

"What?" She glanced up with a start, running her fingers through her already disarranged hair. "Oh, the doctor thinks Jefferson will recover, in time. The bullet hit nothing vital. But he will be a long time healing. Lucinda is with him now."

Clint heaved a sigh, and slumped even lower in the chair.

Charlotte straightened up, her eyes narrowing. "What are you doing in *my* office, in *my* chair, your feet on *my* desk?"

"Why not?" he said reasonably. "It was empty, and you weren't here."

"That's not the point," she said in outrage. "You are so blasted infuriating! You just stroll in here, and take charge like it's your office!"

"Lotte, please." He held up a hand. "Peace, all right?

At least for a few minutes. It has been a rugged night all around, and I'm really not in the mood for our usual light banter."

Charlotte was on her feet and striding back and forth, her energy renewed. "Sload Lutcher is dead then? From what I knew of the man, he had no living relatives, so we should be able to get that third interest back."

"If what you say is true, yes." He watched her with amusement. "His estate will revert to the state, and I'm sure they will be happy to let you and Ben have it back for a nominal sum."

Charlotte nodded. "But where does that leave you?"

He gazed at her serenely. "My dear Lotte, you need not concern yourself with my welfare. I made my bed, I'll sleep in it without complaint."

"The doctor says that Jefferson won't be able to return to work for months."

Slowly, Clint took his feet off the desk, and leaned forward. "Are you about to make me an offer?"

Her eyes rested on him in speculation. "Clint, do you love me?"

For the first time in his life Clint Devlin was speechless.

"If you do, that's one thing. If you don't, that's another. I realized something tonight . . ."

"Lotte . . ."

". . . when I was kneeling beside Jefferson, not knowing if he was dead or alive. I realized that there were some things in this life more important than King Tobacco . . ."

"Lotte, will you shut the hell up for one minute!"

She fell silent, staring down at the floor.

"Yes, I love you. Is that what you wanted to hear?"

She nodded without looking up.

"Do you love me?"

She nodded again.

"Damnit, will you look at me!" he roared.

Her eyes came up, huge and soft and awash with tears, and then he was around the desk, sweeping her into his arms.

Charlotte burrowed against him, rubbing her face against his shirt.

His chest heaved as he rumbled laughter. "Do you think a wedding of Devlin and King would work, given the way we're at loggerheads about eighty percent of the time?"

She leaned back just enough to gaze up into his face. "I don't know why not. We always make up, don't we?"

"Yes, my dear." His laughter grew. "In a manner of speaking."

## ABOUT THE AUTHOR

A few years ago Patricia Matthews was just another housewife and working mother. An office manager, she lived in a middle class home with her husband and two children. Like thousands of other women around the country she was writing in her spare time. However, unlike many other writers Patricia Matthews' own true life story has proven to have a Cinderella ending. Today she is "America's leading lady of historical romance" with eleven consecutive bestselling novels to her credit and millions of fans all over the world.

Along with her husband, Clayton, who is a very successful writer himself, Patricia travels over 20,000 miles a year researching her books. She likes to know each place she writes about, and her exotic locales have ranged from the Alaska wilds to southern plantations. She also co-authored the novel, MIDNIGHT WHISPERS, with her husband. The Matthews, who say they have a "paperback perfect" marriage, live in Los Angeles.

Dear Friends and Readers:

Matt—my husband, Clayton Matthews—and I have received so many nice letters concerning our last collaboration *Midnight Whispers*, and so many requests as to when we would do another book together, that we thought this would be a good opportunity to tell you about our most recent mutual effort, *Empire*, which Bantam will be bringing out in the fall of 1982. *Empire* is a family saga played out against the background of the Alaskan pipeline. It concerns the wealthy and powerful Cole family: Jeremiah, the crusty and still-in-control 99-year-old patriarch who founded Cole Enterprises after striking it rich in the Klondike; his son Joshua, a United States Senator who prefers politics to managing the Cole holdings; Joshua's son Will, who is finally corrupted by the trappings of power and by a beautiful woman; and Dwight, who has renounced his family in an effort to save the ecology of the state he loves. Finally, there is Joshua's daughter Kelly, whom Dwight describes as "the best of the lot," a strong, outspoken young woman who has managed to remain uncorrupted by the wealth and prestige of her family and who, with Chris O'Keefe, a handsome, young pipeliner who eventually controls Cole Enterprises, is at the heart of the story and the mystery which surrounds the family.

Both Matt and I are very excited about *Empire* and we hope that you will share that excitement.

For those of you who have been asking about my next historical novel, I have been busy on that too. It will take place in Tampa, Florida at the marvelous Tampa Bay Hotel during the Spanish-American War. This novel, as yet untitled, will be published by Bantam early in 1983.

Wishing you all good things,

Patricia Matthews